ANGELS PASSING

ANGELS PASSING

Graham Hurley

ORION

First published in Great Britain in 2002 by
Orion
An imprint of the Orion Publishing Group
Orion House, 5 Upper St Martin's Lane, London WC2H 9EA

A CIP catalogue record for this book
is available from the British Library

ISBN 075283 189 5

Typeset by Deltatype Ltd, Birkenhead, Wirral

Printed in Great Britain by
Clays Ltd, St Ives plc

Acknowledgements

My thanks to the following for their time and patience: John Ashworth, Colin Ayres, Alan Bell, Wayne Campbell, John Christie, Roly Dumont, Bob Elliott, Peter Gallagher, Ron Godden, Jason Goodwin, Andy Harrington, Keith Hebberd, Nick Huband, Jack Hurley, Steve Jackson, Margaret Kelly, Simon King, Bob Lamburne, June Leiper, Rhona Lucas, Andy Marker, Colin Michie, Sarah Milne, Laurie Mullen, Diane Munns, John Murray, Brian Partridge, Adrian Prangnell, Kitty Price, David Price, Nick Pugh, Brett Rennolds, John Roberts, Dave Sackman, Morag Scott, Peter Shand, Martin Shuker, Colin Smith, Ray Stead, Jenny Stevens, Karen Traviss, Larry Waller, Kevin Walton, Charlie Watts, Ian Watts, Steve Watts, and Richard Wharton. Simon Spanton, my editor, has been Joe Faraday's unflagging champion while Lin, my wife, remains the very best reason for putting pen to paper.

I believe and hold it as the fundamental article of Christianity, that I am a fallen creature; that I am myself capable of moral evil, but not of myself capable of moral good, and that Guilt is justly imputable to me prior to any given act, or assignable moment of time, in my Consciousness. I am born a child of Wrath.

SAMUEL TAYLOR COLERIDGE, *Notebooks* (1810)

Chapter one

FRIDAY, 9 FEBRUARY, *early morning*

For months afterwards, awake and asleep, Faraday dwelt on that final second and a half. He'd measured it by eye, standing on the pavement in the chilly dawn, trying to imagine something solid falling from the roof above. A rock, a parcel of some kind, flesh and blood, it made no difference. You got to the edge, you let go, and gravity did the rest. Was it true that your heart stopped the moment your plunge began? Did God have a way of sparing you the onrushing pavement below? He rather doubted it.

The impact had split the back of her skull wide open, spilling brain matter onto the wet paving slab, florets of thick grey jelly pinked with blood and matted with hair. More blood had trickled from her ears, pooling blackly amongst the tufts of grass growing between the slabs. She'd been wearing jeans and a green cotton sweatshirt, far too skimpy for the middle of winter, and her thin, outstretched wrist was circled with a silver bracelet hung with tiny charms. Her eyes, oddly, were still open in her unmarked face. Lovely eyes. Green. Ignore the wreckage at the back of her head and she might just have woken up.

While Scenes of Crime wrestled a heavy plastic screen into position around the body, Faraday took the lift to the twenty-third floor and then found the stairs that led up to the roof. The warden, a blonde woman in her fifties, was talking to the PC standing guard at the open door. Faraday stepped carefully past them and out onto the roof, ducking to avoid the lattice of washing lines that criss-crossed the drying area. The roof space was big and walled on all four sides: brickwork up to chest level and then a metal grille to let in the views. Above the grille there was another four feet or so of bricks but corners and crevices offered a purchase for hands and legs, and to a certain kind of youngster the challenge of the climb would have been irresistible.

The girl lay on the pavement towards the western corner of the building and Faraday began to haul himself up towards the parapet above her, curious to put the climb to the test. He wasn't good with heights, never had been, but there was something in the girl's face that obliged him to try, and he finally managed it, standing cautiously upright on top of the encircling wall before peering down.

The sheerness of the drop dizzied him. Even the undertaker's van, backing slowly towards the cluster of tiny figures at the kerbside, seemed too dinky to be real, and as his stomach churned he had to find something else to look at. Several floors below him, infinitely bigger, a pair of black-headed gulls were chasing a third. His eye followed them as they banked and soared on the chill February wind and he found himself wondering whether the girl, too, might have glimpsed some bird or other in the darkness as she gazed down. Had she met this terrible death on purpose, garnishing her final moments with a swallow dive? Had she spread her arms, taking one last lungful of air, standing there? To the alarm of the warden, Faraday tried it himself, arms out wide, chin up, ignoring the drop, recognising at once where the image led.

A bird on the wing, he thought. Or the figure on the cross, betrayed and crucified.

Even half asleep, DC Paul Winter knew he couldn't do it. The plane left Gatwick around noon. Cathy had arranged for some local woman to meet him at Faro and drive him to Albufeira or wherever her mate's place was. The snaps Catty had sent across in the internal mail showed the view from the balcony of the apartment block. There was a harbour, fishing boats, the chance to lie around in that gorgeous Portuguese sunshine. Even in February, the temperature could be way up in the sixties, and he knew that for sure because Cathy had phoned him last night and told him so. Pack your bathers, she'd said, and plenty of Factor 15. Yet he still couldn't do it. Not with two long weeks yawning in front of him and nothing to think about but the emptiness of the bed he slept in.

The kettle took forever to boil and Winter filled the silence with his usual hit of early morning news from the gloom merchants on Radio Four. A couple of minutes of this, he always thought, and the day could only get better. Eighty flood warnings across the south as yet another frontal system swept in from the Atlantic. Scientists warning of unexpected problems with GM food. Major car bomb in Jerusalem. And – if you were still around to enjoy them – designer babies within the next thirty years.

Winter ignored it all, gazing out at the bareness of the back garden, wondering quite how he would put it to Cathy. Her kindness had touched him, no question, and he'd almost believed her when she'd insisted he needed a decent break. It was true he was working all the overtime he could screw out of Faraday. And it was true, as well, that most nights he dog-legged home via a series of pubs. But who wouldn't in his position? What was so cosy about drawn curtains and a night in with *Peak Practice*?

He splashed hot water onto the single tea bag and left it to brew while he broke the news to Cathy. She'd very definitely be pissed off but he'd simply have to be upfront about it. He was too young for retirement and too old for make-believe. Whatever fantasies she might be having about holiday romances and getting away from it all were strictly for the birds. He was forty-seven, overweight, and far too particular about other people's company to leave anything to chance. End of story.

Lifting the handset in the lounge, he noticed a call waiting on his nearby mobile. He picked it up, keying the message as he did so. The call had come in at 02.37. It was a voice he didn't recognise – gruff, male, slightly slurred – and he knew at once that it belonged to a grass. Not one of his regular gang, not one of the registered informers he'd nursed so carefully through the traumas of the last year or so, but someone new, someone who'd been enterprising enough to get hold of his number and had decided that the time was ripe for a confidence or two.

The message was brief and Winter replayed it twice. 'Bastard's gonna do Brennan's tonight,' the voice said. 'Check it out. There's shitloads of gear there. He's just gonna help himself.'

Bastard? Brennan's? Winter peered at the line of digits on his mobile, feeling the warmth flooding his body. Later he'd make some enquiries but odds-on the call had come from a local BT box, somewhere discreet and untraceable. The bloke, whoever he was, had a grudge, wanted to get a poke or two in. Winter glanced at the clock on the mantelpiece and reached for his phone. Cathy normally left home at around half seven. By now, she'd be sitting in a jam on the M275. Perfect.

She answered his summons on the second ring.

'Cath? It's me.' Winter beamed at the mobile. 'Something's just come up.'

Faraday was debating whether to chase up one or two of the door-to-door enquiries when the Crime Scene Manager beckoned him in from the rain. He was standing in the entrance to the block of flats, a clipboard in one hand and a tape measure in the other. Uniforms had chocked the main door open as they came and went, spreading slowly upwards towards the twenty-third floor.

'Can't we do anything about the punters?' The CSM nodded at the growing crowd beyond the blue and white tape. In the swirling rain, at least half a dozen of the women were on the phone to friends, doubtless speculating on what lay within the plastic screen.

Faraday shrugged. There was always an unspoken tussle about crime scenes like these, about who should take responsibility, and this morning's CSM didn't make it any easier. Faraday, as the Detective Inspector on site, was Senior Investigating Officer, but the CSM was charged with the collection of evidence at the scene of crime and obviously believed in playing it by the book. He was young and ambitious, and rather too cautious for his own good. At this rate, they wouldn't be clear by lunchtime.

'The kids'll be coming to school next.' Faraday nodded towards the nearby comprehensive. 'Might be nice to move it along.'

'You want to give me that in writing?'

'No.'

Faraday's mobile began to ring. He stepped back into the rain, turning his back on the CSM.

'It's Cathy. I've had Winter on.'

Cathy Lamb was one of Faraday's DSs, back in the Southsea CID office. Paul Winter was a cross that everyone had to bear, but Cathy always seemed to carry the burden more lightly than others. Until now. She explained about the information on Brennan's. She sounded extremely angry.

'I thought Winter was off to Portugal?'

'He was. He just cancelled. Seems to think he's better off back in the office.'

'And Brennan's? Winter's sourced this information?'

'No. He says he's never heard the voice before. Guy called in the early morning, left a message.'

'And we believe it?'

'Believe it? Brennan's? That's hardly the point, sir, is it?'

Faraday permitted himself a weary smile. Cathy was right. Ray Brennan was a one-time builder and decorator who now ran a huge DIY cash-and-carry operation on an industrial estate in the north of the city. His generosity towards the police currently extended to a brand new Ford Escort carefully badged with the Brennan's logo, 'Helping Build a Better Tomorrow', plus smaller contributions towards a couple of public awareness events. In situations like these, that kind of support earned him the benefit of the doubt.

Cathy was asking about tonight. If they went for the full stake-out, how many bodies would be required? Faraday didn't answer. Brennan's was a big site if his memory served him right; there were access roads on three sides. Say ten men and an area car – a mix of CID and uniforms – and the overtime implications would be substantial. That would mean a head-to-head over the duty roster and a conversation with the Ops Superintendent, two good reasons for hoping to God that Winter had it right.

'I'll sort it when I get back,' Faraday said at last. 'Give me an hour.'

The Scenes of Crime photographer had emerged from the screened area around the body. He was a tall, thin civilian with deep-set eyes and a wardrobe of pink shirts. His job exposed him to the worst that human beings could do to each other and Faraday had often marvelled at the way he seemed to survive all those hideous images. On this occasion though he looked ashen, and when he caught Faraday's eye he offered a tiny shake of the head. Not just me, Faraday thought. Him too.

Cathy wanted to know about the girl. What had happened?

'Too early to tell. She obviously came off the roof. Might be a jumper. Might not.'

The girl's body had been found by the milkman around half five in the morning. The patrol Sergeant and a PC from Central had attended and the duty DC had been called out. He, in turn, had alerted Scenes of Crime and roused Faraday from his bed. By then it was nearly seven.

'The girl was stiff by the time I got here. It's ballpark but I think we're talking one, two in the morning.'

'You've got a name?'

'Not yet. There's no ID on the body and the duty DC checked overnight Mispers.'

Mispers was police-speak for Missing Persons. The current tally was running at nearly ten a day, mainly teenagers, but none of them answered to the broken body at the foot of Chuzzlewit House.

'CCTV?'

'Still checking. The set-up's run from a control room over the way. They cover five council blocks from a central point. There's a load of cameras on a matrix so it's going to take a while.'

'You want me to run with that?'

Faraday and Cathy discussed availability. A couple of DCs could come down right away. More later, if required.

'Who have we got?'

'Ellis and Yates.'

Faraday grunted assent. Dawn Ellis was perfect. Bev Yates too.

'These flats are full of old people,' Faraday said. 'No kids allowed.

Uniform's doing a trawl on the door-to-doors but my guess is we'll end up with a short list. That'll need patience, as well as time.'

He paused, looking up at the flats. The area was called Somerstown. It figured prominently in all the social indices that increasingly governed his working life – poverty, domestic violence, family breakdown – and the very look of the place seemed to mirror the brutality of life on the streets. Chuzzlewit House towered above him, one of a cluster of sixties blocks, a looming, malevolent presence curtained with rain. The yellow panels beneath each window might lift the spirits on a sunny day but just now they simply underscored the bleakness of the scene.

A girl had died here. She looked no more than fifteen. She might have been drunk or out of her head on some drug or other, or just desperate. The post-mortem would resolve the substance issue but as far as Faraday knew there was no known test for despair. Had she really been a jumper? Was it as simple – and complex – as that?

Earlier, the Crime Scene Manager had been talking about fall parameters, a phrase that had done nothing for Faraday's peace of mind. Bodies tipping face first off a roof begin to tumble, turned upside down by the weight of the head. The girl had hit the pavement on her back – hence the lack of damage to her face – and in the measured view of the young CSM it was probable that the girl had been facing outwards when she fell. That wasn't the point, though. The question wasn't how but why. Why do it? Why make this terrible pact with gravity?

Faraday wiped the rain from his eyes. He could see the body plunging towards him now, the flailing limbs, the outstretched hands, and when Cathy asked him for the second time whether to send Winter up to Brennan's for a recce and a chat, he found it difficult to frame a coherent answer.

'Why not?' he said in the end.

The last time Winter had been to Brennan's Superstore was a couple of years ago. He'd bought a flat-pack garden shed, an episode which ended with Joannie calling in a friend's son to dismantle Winter's handiwork, sort out the plot he'd neglected to level, and start all over again. So much for his talent for DIY.

Now, Winter parked his Subaru beside a rain-soaked collection of bird tables and set off on a private tour of the site, heartened by the huge yellow banners announcing unbeatable price cuts. The early spring sale was due to start tomorrow, an event which presumably sucked in mountains of extra stock. Winter's new friend had clearly done his homework.

Minutes later, the geography of the place clear in his mind, Winter went in search of the management. Ray Brennan ran the superstore from a chaotic suite of offices in two Portakabins on the other side of the car park. He was a big, broad, sandy-haired Irishman with a solid marriage, umpteen kids and extraordinarily few enemies. Winter had known Brennan since his early days as a jobbing builder and had always wondered what really lay behind the bone-crushing handshake and the big smile. No one could be that cheerful. Even with a business this successful to his credit.

Winter wanted to know about security. Brennan's had grown like topsy: first a builders' merchant, then a timber centre, and now a retail operation that jigsawed everything for the home and garden onto the three-acre site. What happened out of hours? Where were the cameras placed?

'Cameras?'

'You haven't got CCTV?'

Brennan looked briefly pained, then dismissed the thought with a wave of his huge hand. His brother, Vic, had been banging on about cameras for years, but himself, he'd never seen the point. Most of the stuff that got nicked went out of the yard in the backs of builders' vans and he had a trusted old boy on the gate to check every load against the paperwork. CCTV, on the other hand, was aggressive. People wanted to enjoy themselves when they shopped. What kind of welcome was a camera in your face?

For a moment Winter thought he was taking the piss but there were clues in this cluttered little office that suggested otherwise. One of them was a wall calender from the Church of Our Lady, a big Catholic pile up near the top of the city. Another was a colour photograph of Brennan presenting a cheque to the Lord Mayor. Clearly Ray's generosity extended well beyond the police force.

Winter changed tack. He wanted to know about tomorrow's sale. Did the discounts apply to the pricier stuff?

'Sure.'

'Like what?'

'Like the top-of-the-line goods you don't have to plug in. Like cordless drills and sanders. Like Workmates. Like brushes and paint. Like whatever you want. We're talking up to thirty per cent off here.'

'So how much? For a cordless drill?'

'£116 today. £89 tomorrow. Believe me, that's a steal.'

The word brought a smile to Winter's face. He was already convinced that tonight's visitors would be targeting high-value items with a ready market on the dodgier housing estates, and tomorrow's sale would offer the richest of pickings. Even if you lost a big whack when you fenced the stuff, a vanful of cordless drills would keep you in lagers for at least a week.

Winter leaned forward, explaining about the information received, about the likelihood of some kind of break-in, and about the traps he was planning to set. The site was a nightmare – he'd counted five potential exits – and doing the job properly would call for some serious manpower. Might he take a look at the retail stockroom?

Brennan, more thoughtful now, led the way back across the car park. The rain was lashing down and by the time they made it to the Retail Centre both men were soaked. Items for the weekend's bonanza were in the warehouse area at the back and the moment Winter saw the Black and Decker boxes piled high on trolleys he knew he'd called it exactly right. In Paulsgrove and Wecock Farm, estates up on the mainland, this lot would go in seconds. Easy, easy money.

'What's this?'

Winter was standing beside the biggest of the trolleys. Brennan followed his pointing finger.

'Security systems. It's self-fit. You take a screwdriver to the detector thing, and door contacts and one or two other bits and pieces, and then stick that big yellow box over the front door. An hour, max. Can't fail.'

'Price? Normal retail?'

'£99.99. But cheaper tomorrow.'

Winter was beaming. He knew dozens of criminals, Pompey's finest, who'd lift gear like this by the truckload. They'd hit cities along the coast – Chichester, Brighton, Bournemouth – and target people who didn't know better, old people especially. For a cut-price five hundred pounds or so they'd offer to install the security system of your dreams – total peace of mind – and the scam would be even sweeter if the gear was itself nicked. Winter could hear them screaming with laughter on the way home. Five hundred quid for an hour's work and every last penny theirs for the taking? No expenses? No guarantees? No comeback? Fucking re-sult.

Winter beckoned Brennan into a corner of the warehouse, away from the staff. Strictly speaking he should have the rest of this conversation back in the office but time was moving on.

'How many work in this section?'

'Couple of lads. Off the New Deal.'

'I'll need their names. Plus everyone else on the payroll.'

'Why?'

'Because someone's been speaking out of turn.' He nodded towards the towering piles of merchandise. 'I'll run the names through the computer just in case they've got previous. Beyond that we're talking

8

association. Tonight's the easy bit' – he patted Brennan on the arm – 'believe me.'

It was one of the uniforms, a WPC from Central, who alerted Faraday about a call from the school across the road. A teacher had taken a smashed mobile from one of the kids. He'd been doing a paper round at the flats, almost an hour after Scenes of Crime had arrived, and he'd come across the mobile on the other side of the block. It was lying in the road there, just asking to be nicked, and now she was bringing it over in case it was important.

Faraday intercepted the teacher as she rounded the corner of the flats. The Crime Scene Manager watched him from a distance, intensely curious, then walked over. The rain had stopped again but Faraday sensed it was only a truce.

The CSM produced a plastic evidence bag. He held it open beneath the mobile.

Faraday was looking at the teacher. It was by no means certain that the phone had any connection with the dead girl but he was grateful that she'd spared the time to bring it over.

'How many other kids touched this?'

'I've no idea. He's a popular lad. Half a dozen? That's a guess.'

The mobile was a neat little Nokia, purple with a glitter effect. The plastic case was shattered beyond repair but – intact – it was all too easy to imagine it pressed to the ear of the girl behind the screen.

The CSM still had the bag open and was visibly losing patience. This wasn't about evidence any more, it was about ownership. His crime scene. His shout.

'It's useless,' Faraday pointed out. 'Useless as a phone and useless forensically. I suggest we see what the sim card tells us.'

Without waiting for an answer, he shook the little wafer of silicon out of the Nokia and slipped it into his own mobile. The last call had gone to a local number and Faraday made a note before keying up the stored contacts list. There were dozens and dozens of names, ports of call in a busy, busy social life: Katie, Tazz, Anna, Jordan, Peaches, Billy, Azul. He scrolled slowly through them, looking for an obvious lead. Then he glanced up at the teacher, struck by the obvious thought. There were lots of secondary schools in the city but this one might be a good place to start.

'You keep a daily register?' he asked.

The teacher was looking at the screen around the body.

'Of course.'

'How many absentees this morning?'

'For my class? Four.'

'What kind of age?'

'Year Eleven. Fifteen to sixteen.'

'We're not talking flu here?' Faraday suggested drily. 'The weather we've been having?'

The teacher favoured him with a brief, cold smile.

'I doubt it.'

Her gaze returned to the screen. The heavy plastic was billowing in the wind and every now and again a gust lifted the bottom of the structure, permitting a moment's glimpse of wet denim. Finally, Faraday asked the inevitable question.

'It's a question of ID.' He nodded towards the body. 'If you'd prefer not, I'd quite understand.'

The teacher bit her lip, saying nothing. Then she nodded and Faraday took her by the arm, stepping carefully around the Crime Scene Manager. A flap at the back of the screen permitted a view of the body. The teacher stood motionless for a while, staring down at the dead girl's face. Finally, she looked up at Faraday.

'Do you know her?'

'No.'

'Would you know her?'

'That age? In school? Definitely.'

She glanced down again, one last look, then brushed away a tear. It was an abrupt gesture, anger as well as sadness, and she didn't say another word until Faraday had escorted her back to the corner of the building. Faraday had his mobile out again. There was an issue over whether circumstances warranted calling in a Home Office pathologist and he knew he owed his Detective Chief Inspector a call.

The teacher accepted his outstretched hand. She hoped the Nokia would be a help.

'I'd phone her mum if I were you,' she muttered. 'They normally store the number under "M".'

She ducked her head and then turned and hurried away. The DCI was engaged, so Faraday scrolled through to 'M' on the Nokia's contact list and found an eight-digit number under 'Ma'. He wrote the number down, then put a call through to the force control room at Netley. They kept a reverse phone book on computer and, within seconds, Faraday was scribbling in his pocketbook again. Mrs Jane Bassam. 27, Little Normandy. Old Portsmouth.

Old Portsmouth?

Faraday frowned, looking up at the roof. Old Portsmouth, while barely a mile distant, was a middle-class enclave for professional couples and wealthy retired folk, light years away from the violence and chaos that passed for life on this estate. Kids from Somerstown were into organised shoplifting before they left primary school. Kids from Old Portsmouth took piano lessons and sailed dinghies. If he was right about the mobile, if it really had belonged to the girl behind the screen, then what on earth was she doing here?

Chapter two

Jane Bassam occupied a modest post-war house in a quiet cul-de-sac near the Anglican cathedral. There was an S-registered Renault in the drive and one of her front windows featured a poster advertising a forthcoming performance of the Verdi Requiem. Dawn Ellis and Bev Yates exchanged glances. Neither of the two DCs had much taste for breaking bad news but year on year scenes like these seemed increasingly to go with the territory. In Ellis's view, it was odds-on that they were about to plunge this woman's world into chaos.

It was still pouring with rain. They got out of the car, pushed through the garden gate and sought shelter under the tiny porch. The door opened as soon as they rang the bell and Ellis found herself looking at a tall, thin, striking-looking woman in her late thirties. She had a long fall of auburn hair and the designer wire-rimmed glasses suited the gaunt boniness of her face. Barefoot in her jeans and V-neck red sweater, she stared blankly at the proffered warrant cards.

'Mrs Bassam?'

'That's right.' The woman glanced at Ellis. 'What do you want?'

Yates was peering beyond her, into the gloom of the tiny hall. Ellis suggested they might talk inside.

'Of course. Come in.'

Mrs Bassam led the way into the lounge. The curtains had been pulled back but it was still very dark. Mrs Bassam paused by the door and the moment the light went on Yates's attention was drawn to a big framed photograph on the wall above the mantelpiece. A girl in her early teens was leaning back against a set of railings. She had the kind of face that would turn any man's head, an innocence tainted by something deeply arousing. Even in death, sprawled across the wet pavement, that suggestion of mischief hadn't quite left her.

Ellis had seen the photograph, too.

'Is that your daughter, Mrs Bassam?'

'Yes, it is. Why do you ask?'

'Is there anyone else here? Your husband maybe?'

'No.'

'A neighbour then? A friend?'

'No.' She shook her head, alarmed now. 'Nobody.' She looked from one face to the other. 'Has something happened to Helen? Why don't you just tell me what's going on?'

Ellis explained about the body at the foot of the block of flats. There was a long silence. Nobody could say for certain that the dead girl was Helen Bassam, not until the body had been formally identified, but already the laws of probability suggested that it had to be true.

The colour had drained from Mrs Bassam's face. Ellis helped her into an armchair, then knelt beside her. The last thing she needed was more questions but it was best to be certain.

'When did you last see her? Helen?'

'Last night, early, around seven. We had supper together.'

'And then she left?'

'Yes. She was going to a friend's. She was going to sleep over.'

'What was she wearing? Can you remember?'

'Of course.' Mrs Bassam looked down at her hands, trying to concentrate, trying to fumble her way through this terrible news. 'Jeans. And a silly little top. Cotton.'

'Colour?'

'It was green.'

'No coat?'

'No. I told her to take a fleece but she wouldn't listen.'

'Any jewellery at all?'

'Yes.' She was staring at Ellis. 'She had a bracelet, a silver thing with charms on it. She wore it all the time, even in bed . . .' She shook her head, lost for words.

Ellis looked at her for a moment, then asked about the kitchen. Maybe a cup of tea might be a good idea.

'Through there.' Mrs Bassam gestured vaguely towards the open door.

Ellis left the room. Yates settled himself in the other armchair and produced his pocketbook. From the moment he'd seen the photo on the wall, he'd had absolutely no doubts that this woman had just lost her daughter, and everything she'd just said – the clothes, the bracelet – made it all the more certain.

Jane Bassam seemed to know it too. Her eyes were closed and something odd seemed to have happened to her breathing. She was taking little shallow breaths, as if she was surfacing from a deep, deep dive and didn't quite trust her lungs any more. At length she visibly stiffened, taking hold of herself, back in command.

'You mentioned a block of flats,' she said.

'Chuzzlewit House. Somerstown.'

'And you say she fell?'

'Yes.'

'Are they big flats? Tall?'

'Yes.'

'Quick, then.' She nodded to herself. 'A quick death.'

There was a long silence. From the kitchen came the bubbling of an electric kettle as Ellis made a pot of tea. Yates asked again whether Mrs Bassam wanted to phone her husband. This was a difficult moment for anyone. The body might or might not belong to Helen but in Yates's experience the burden of something like this was best shared.

'There's no point,' Mrs Bassam said stonily. 'My husband and I are divorcing.'

'But even so . . .' Yates explained about the mortuary and the ID procedures. Might it be better for Helen's father to attend?

Mrs Bassam shook her head.

'He can't. He's a lawyer. He's on a case in London all this week.' Her eyes strayed to the photo on the wall. 'You really think it's her, don't you?'

'I can't say, Mrs Bassam, not for sure.'

'But that's what you think, isn't it?'

Yates looked at her without saying anything. Something in this woman's face – weariness, resignation, grief – told him that the news hadn't come as a surprise. Ellis reappeared with a tray of tea. Mrs Bassam watched her filling the three mugs.

'There were cups in the corner cupboard,' she muttered.

Her voice trailed off and, as Ellis asked how many sugars she took, Yates found himself looking round the lounge: the chairs and sofa pushed to the very edges of the room, the over-neat rack of magazines beside the television, the carefully arranged spray of dried flowers in a cut glass vase on the bookcase. Compared to the intimacy and clutter of his own domestic arrangements, the room had a chill that central heating would never touch. This woman lived in a show house. It smelled of air-freshener and furniture polish. No wonder the girl was out all hours.

Yates returned to his pocketbook.

'Do you mind if I take some details, Mrs Bassam? It may save time later.'

'Of course.'

Yates started on his list of questions. Helen Christine Bassam. DOB

14

17.10.86. For the last three years, she'd been attending St Peter's Comprehensive, Southsea. Until this morning.

Yates glanced up.

'Has she been upset at all?'

'Upset enough to throw herself off a block of flats, you mean?'

'I didn't say that, Mrs Bassam. I'm just asking whether she'd been . . . unhappy at all.'

Mrs Bassam thought about the question. She had both hands round her mug of tea.

'I'm not sure,' she said at last. 'Sometimes I think she was born unhappy.'

'What do you mean?'

'Well . . .' she shrugged hopelessly '. . . she hasn't been the easiest person to have around, not recently anyway.'

'You're telling me she might have been depressed?'

'I don't know. Depression sounds so grown-up. Do girls of fourteen really get depressed?'

Ellis had settled herself on the sofa. Now she leaned forward.

'Where did she go after you had supper?'

'To Trudy's. Trudy's her friend, her special friend.' The phrase had a bitter edge to it, a flag raised in a strong wind.

'Trudy . . .?'

'Gallagher.' Mrs Bassam nodded towards the telephone. 'Maybe you ought to talk to her yourself.'

Yates got to his feet and retrieved a battered address book from a drawer beneath the telephone. Mrs Bassam watched him leaf through for the number and transfer it to his pocketbook. Her hand had found the small gold cross on the chain around her neck and she was fingering it absently, the way you might worry a spot or a scab.

Ellis wanted to know about the relationship between the two girls. Was it especially close?

'Very. Trudy knew my daughter better than I did. In fact she's been practically living there these last few weeks. One less worry, I suppose.'

'How do you mean?'

'At least I knew where to find her. Some nights I hadn't a clue where she'd end up. I'm not saying she'd come to any harm; I think she was perfectly able to look after herself. But she was just . . .' she frowned '. . . wild.'

'Wild?'

'Yes, wild like an animal. And rude too. Hostile. Aggressive. She could be horrible sometimes, believe me.' She nodded. 'Hard to imagine, isn't it? Your own flesh and blood . . .' For a moment she gazed sightlessly into the middle distance, and then she began to cry.

The tears coursed down her face but she made absolutely no sound. It was like watching a silent movie, and this sudden grief was all the more affecting for the way she'd fought so hard to restrain it.

Ellis got up and tried to comfort her, kneeling beside the armchair again and putting her arms around Mrs Bassam's shoulders, but she shook her head.

'Would you mind?' She gestured hopelessly towards the kitchen. She wanted privacy. She wanted to be left alone.

Yates closed his pocketbook.

'Do you mind if we take a look at Helen's bedroom, Mrs Bassam?'

'It's upstairs. Help yourself.'

Ellis followed Yates towards the door, then paused. There was something infinitely pathetic about this woman, hunched in her chair in this cold, cold room. So much for the comforts of religion, she thought. In some ways, Mrs Bassam looked more broken than her daughter.

'Are you sure there's no one we can phone for you?'

'Please . . .' Mrs Bassam nodded towards the stairs '. . . just go on up.'

Ellis was first into the bedroom, recognising the scene at once. At twenty-nine, you kidded yourself that you were beyond all this but in your heart you knew it wasn't true: the unmade bed, the floor strewn with discarded bits of clothing, the ripped-out fashion pics Blu-tacked to the wall, the tiny dressing table littered with pots of hair gel and lip gloss. The contrast with downstairs couldn't have been starker, and Ellis began to suspect that the gaunt, brittle figure in the armchair had simply given up.

There'd have been confrontation after confrontation about this room of Helen's; it happened in every household. But there were certain kids who blocked the path to a nice simple life. When the shouting began, they shouted louder. Appeal to their better nature, they'd laugh in your face. Threaten them with punishment, even physical violence, and they'd probably get their revenge in first. She knew this for certain because she'd been that way herself, a total nightmare, and it was only the long years of living alone that had taught her how to be human again. The inside of Ellis's head had once looked like this room and, even now, she could still taste the intoxicating turmoil of those teenage years. Adolescence could take you to the very edge. The trick was to go no further.

Yates had found a pocket diary under the girl's pillow. It had a picture of Nelson Mandela on the front and he flicked quickly through it, page after page of doodles, squirly spiral shapes that occupied most of January. On the 13th, a Saturday, he found a line of exclamation marks, and a couple of weeks later – the 26th – a big fat question mark. At no point had the girl made any kind of written entries, except for a number at the very front of the diary.

1337? Yates turned to find Ellis.

Ellis was going through the drawer in the dressing table. So far, she'd found a Walkman, CDs by Destiny's Child and Lauren Hill, a Boots receipt for £8.95, two sticks of chewing gum, a pocket French/English dictionary, seven National Lottery tickets, a broken watch, a lighter, two more bracelets, a 27p token from a packet of crisps and a building society bank book. The account offered instant access and the name in the front was Helen Bassam's. Ellis paged slowly through it. Someone was putting £160 a month into the girl's name, the whole of it withdrawn in ten and twenty-pound hits through a cash card. At fourteen, money was clearly the least of her problems.

'Forty quid a week,' Ellis murmured. 'Can you believe that?'

'Easy. It's conscience money, from Dad.'

'You think so?'

'Put my life on it. He's gone off with some bird or other and he wants to make it right with his little girl. It's shagging money. It makes him feel better about himself.'

'But forty quid? A *week*?'

'It's small change, love. The guy's a lawyer. The money just walks in through the door.'

Yates had started on a row of books on a shelf beside the wardrobe. A leather-bound copy of the New Testament looked unread but next to it was a much-thumbed paperback collection of poems. Yates opened it. The poems were in French.

'Here . . .'

He passed the book to Ellis. As he did so, a photograph fluttered to the floor. Ellis picked it up. The photo was black and white and showed a man in his early twenties sitting at a café table. He had a strong face – curly black hair, dark complexion – and a lovely smile, at once mischievous and wistful. The open copy of *Le Monde* and the glimpse of a busy concourse behind suggested one of the big Paris railway stations. She turned the photo over, peering at the inscription. It was handwritten in red ink, difficult to follow, but at last she made it out. *La première entreprise fût, dans le sentier déjà empli de frais et blêmes éclats, une fleur qui me dit son nom.*

She turned to Yates.

'How's your French?'

'Crap.'

'Me too.' Her eyes returned to the photograph. 'What do you think?'

'Seize it. Faraday does French, doesn't he?'

Ellis wasn't convinced. This wasn't a scene of crime. Nothing bad had happened here, not in the eyes of the law. No, their interest lay in developing a picture of the girl – of the life she'd led, of her friends, her interests, her ambitions, her dreams. Bits and pieces of this jigsaw might help explain her death but with a photograph like this it was all too easy to jump to conclusions. He might be someone she'd met abroad on some school trip or other. God knows, it might even be a photo she'd lifted from someone else, a hook on which to hang a whole winter of fantasies. Girlies could be like that. As Ellis knew.

There was a movement behind them, a stirring of the air. Mrs Bassam was standing at the open door, staring at the photo. She'd found a cardigan from somewhere, a heavy piece of cable-stitching that made her look ten years older.

'Do you know this person?' It was Yates.

She nodded, tight-lipped. 'Take him with you.' She turned away. 'I don't want him in the house.'

Paul Winter was back at Southsea nick by just gone ten. He found Cathy Lamb juggling two phones in the big first-floor CID office that looked out onto Highland Road. Fourteen detectives worked from here, more than half the city's total strength, and Winter – more used to the cosier set-up at Fratton – had taken a while to settle in. Now, though, he'd managed to establish squatter's rights over a desk by the far window, a position that gave him a perfect view of everyone else in the room. In offices like these, as in life, it paid to be the watcher, not the watched.

With Cathy giving both phones a hard time, Winter made himself a cup of coffee. The modest catering arrangements lay beside a display of custody mugshots pinned to a big wall board, a local rogues' gallery of domestic burglars, con men, shoplifters and hard-eyed thirty-some-things who'd turned Saturday night violence into an art form.

Winter knew these faces by heart. He knew their wives, their ex-wives, their mates, and the funny little kinks that occasionally gave him a chance for a quiet chat. Turning informer in this city wasn't something you'd do lightly, not if you were ever hoping to make retirement, but there were a million reasons why a man might suddenly decide to offer a titbit or two, and Winter was fluent in the language of betrayal.

Waiting for the kettle to boil, he let his eye drift from face to face. In a minute or two Cathy was going to have another go at him, he knew she was, but the truth was that he was at his happiest in this shadowy no man's land between the good guys and the bad, between law enforcement and the help-yourself chaos that now passed for society.

He knew the geography. He understood the rules. He relished the short cuts. Better Pompey, he thought, than some half-arsed flat in Albufeira.

Cathy at last came off the phone. She had a solid frame and she'd put a bit of the weight back on since Pete had returned home, and under stress she'd developed a habit of letting her left hand stray up to the tiny fold of flesh beneath her chin. There was nothing there really, nothing to warrant the increasingly manic visits to the gym, but just now she was clearly close to bursting. Asking her why would be pointless. The list would go on forever.

Winter drew up a chair, carefully balancing his coffee on his knee.

'I checked Brennan's out.' He announced cheerfully. 'A dozen bodies should do it.'

'Are you kidding?' Cathy was scowling at the phone. 'I'm trying to get five uniforms out of Bannister and all he can talk about is bloody money. Are we going to fork out for the rest days? And can he have it in writing?'

Bannister was one of the uniformed Inspectors up at Kingston Crescent. Policing the Southsea nightclubs on a Friday night was becoming a major peacekeeping exercise, and manpower was stretched to the limit. Winter's mystery caller couldn't have made life more difficult.

'What about our lot?' Winter was eyeing the duty roster.

'That's a pain as well. We've got five abstractions already and Rick Stapleton's gone down with flu. The guys on leave aren't back until Monday and I've got a stack of jobs as long as your arm.'

The mention of leave tempted Winter to point out that he was back on the strength, an unforseen bonus, but under the circumstances he left it alone. Better to let Cathy rant for a while. Get it off her chest.

'This bloody job needs a magician, not a copper like me. Something like this comes up and they expect you to conjure bodies out of thin air. Money will solve it, of course, because it always does, but that's not my conversation.'

Winter took a sip of coffee. He knew exactly what Cathy was saying. It was Faraday's job to take the bid to the Ops Superintendent and screw him for the overtime. Seven months as an acting DI had given her an intimate knowledge of that kind of grief and she was buggered if she was going to let him off the hook. In any case, she and Faraday had had a serious run-in over Pete Lamb's moonlighting, and relationships had never been quite the same since. Far from it.

'Where is he?'

'Christ knows, you tell me.' Cathy rolled her eyes. 'They called him out on the jumper this morning, young kid in Somerstown. No one's seen him since.'

'Leading from the front. Like the book says.'

'Oh really? Which book's that?'

Winter let the question hang in the air. He loved Cathy in these moods – reckless, angry – not least because it confirmed a conclusion he'd come to himself.

'He's losing it, isn't he?' He was leaning back in his chair, a big smile on his face.

'Who?'

'Faraday. Something's got to him. God knows what, but you can see it in his face. He's not at home any more. The place is up for sale.'

'Really? That makes you the lucky one. I hardly see him at all.'

'That bad?'

'Yeah, if you really want to know.' Cathy glanced round. There were other detectives in the room but not many. She frowned. She knew there were conversations she shouldn't have, and this was very definitely one of them, but in truth she was way past caring. Faraday should be back in his office by now, shackled to the duty roster and the overtime budget, trying to corner enough resources to spring tonight's little trap and scoop up some worthwhile villains. Instead, he'd simply disappeared. Again. 'I put it down to his sex life,' she muttered. 'I think he's shagging a married woman. In fact I know he is.'

'Really?' Winter looked delighted. 'And is that a problem?'

Cathy gazed at him a moment, then offered a tired smile.

'Yeah,' she said, 'but only if you're Faraday.'

It was the warden at the flats who told Faraday about the resident on the top floor. She'd mentioned the name earlier to one of the PCs, and he'd made a note, but the resident had somehow been forgotten in all the commotion. The woman Faraday needed to talk to was Grace Randall. She lived in 131. Kids popped up to see her from time to time and she'd certainly know all about the dead girl.

'How come?'

'Because she was always nipping up to Grace's.'

'But I thought kids weren't allowed here?'

'They're not, unless they've got good reason. That's why you should have a chat. Mrs Randall's old, mind, but you might be lucky.'

Lucky?

There were 136 flats in the block and the door-to-doors had so far only reached as far as the seventeenth floor, concentrating first on residents living directly above the point of impact. It was highly likely that the girl had come off the roof but it was just possible to squeeze through the windows within the flats themselves. So far, to no one's surprise, enquiries had drawn a blank, but it was still important to eliminate some prank or other that might have gone horribly wrong.

Faraday rode alone in the lift to the very top of the building, watching the numbers climb in the digital readout above the sliding doors. He'd managed to secure a POLSA search team, four specially trained PCs from Central, in addition to a couple of extra DCs from Fratton. He'd set up a temporary incident room in the day centre on the ground floor, and the POLSA team had conducted a fingertip search on the roof. The latter had produced nothing except wet knees, and a similar search around all four corners of the block looked just as unpromising. The Crime Scene Manager, though, had finally released the body to the undertaker and alerted the senior technician at the mortuary. After a long phone conversation, his Detective Chief Inspector had decided against calling in one of the Home Office pathologists to do the post-mortem. There were no indications of foul play and a Death by Misadventure verdict at the Coroner's inquest wouldn't justify the added expense.

The lift juddered to a halt on the twenty-third floor. There were flowers on occasional tables along the corridor and the place had just had a fresh coat of paint. Faraday paused to get his bearings, then retraced his path to the double flight of concrete steps that led to the roof. Access was normally barred by a locked door but first thing this morning, to the warden's bewilderment, the door had been wide open. Thanks to the Nokia, and the efforts of Yates and Ellis in Old Portsmouth, they at last had a name. In all probability, subject to formal ID, Helen Christine Bassam had been up these steps only hours ago. But why?

It took a while for Grace Randall to get to her front door. She peered out at Faraday, a thin figure bent over a Zimmer frame. She was wearing an embroidered white nightdress and a pair of pink slippers with tiny bells on the toes. A twist of ribbon, also pink, hung from her snow-white hair.

Faraday showed her his warrant card and stepped inside. The flat had a strangely sweet smell, almonds tainted with bleach, and he could hear familiar music from an open door at the end of the tiny hall.

'Puccini?' he queried.

The old woman was locking the door behind him. She moved very slowly and when she spoke Faraday could hear a deep bubbling in her lungs.

'*La Bohème*,' she whispered. 'Would you care for a sherry?'

Faraday flattened himself against the wall as the bells shuffled past. The room at the end was the lounge. After the gloom of the hall, it was flooded with light.

While Grace bent to a glass-fronted cabinet in the corner, Faraday stood in the window, staring out. The weather was beginning to clear at last, livid shafts of sunlight spearing through the tumble of clouds over the distant swell of the Isle of Wight. The view was extraordinary and Faraday could see the city mapped beneath him, 150,000 souls jigsawed into acre after acre of terraced streets. To the west lay the forest of grey cranes in the naval dockyard and the muddle of buildings around the cathedral in Old Portsmouth; to the south the long sweep of Southsea seafront with the Solent beyond; while out to the east he could see a chilly gleam of light on the gunmetal waters of Langstone Harbour. He stood there for a moment longer, remembering the view from his bedroom window only hours earlier: at seven o'clock, dawn had been no more than a promise in the rain-lashed darkness and the puddles were inch-deep on the track outside his garage.

He shook his head, trying to pick out the contours of his harbourside house. He'd lived and worked in this city for more than two decades and it never ceased to take him by surprise. There were always new perspectives, sudden changes of view, and this was undoubtedly one of them.

He turned to find a brimming glass of sherry at his elbow. The old woman's hand was shaking and he rescued the glass before any more spilled.

Grace licked the sherry from her fingers.

'I have binoculars,' she wheezed. 'You can see Osborne House on the better days.'

Osborne House was on the Isle of Wight, way out beyond the navy's parade ground at Spithead. Faraday had been there once with J-J, depressed by the relentless gloom of the Gothic interiors.

Grace sank into an armchair by the window. Biscuit crumbs and the odd crisp lapped at the semicircle of stained carpet at her feet. She gestured Faraday towards the cluttered sofa and then reached for the rubber mask on the low table beside her chair. The mask was connected to a tall metal cylinder and she sucked at the oxygen while Faraday finally tore himself away from the view. The sofa, like Grace Randall herself, had seen better days.

Faraday made a space for himself amongst a week's worth of *Daily Telegraphs*, wondering quite where to start. Listening to Grace Randall fighting for breath, he recognised the symptoms. His grandfather, a lifelong smoker, had also suffered from emphysema. This could be one of the longer conversations.

'There's been a fatality,' he began. 'A young girl.'

He outlined what had happened overnight. He understood that no children were allowed to live in the block but the warden seemed to think that Mrs Randall might have kids as visitors from time to time, one young girl in particular. True?

The old woman offered an emphatic nod. The oxygen had pinked her face. She stared at Faraday for a while as if weighing her next move.

'Describe this girl.' It was no more than a whisper.

Faraday mentioned jeans and a green top. Sprawled on the paving stones, it was hard to be precise about height but five five, five six would be a reasonable guess.

'Hair?'

'Dark. Curly.'

'And here?' She touched her wrist.

'A bracelet. Silver, with charms.'

Grace nodded and turned her gaze towards the window. There was a long silence. Fat drops of rain were splashing against the glass again.

'I used to be a singer on the boats,' she managed at last, 'before the war. Funny life.'

She lifted one thin arm and Faraday realised she was pointing towards the Solent. The big transatlantic liners used to come this way, outward bound for New York.

'This girl, Mrs Randall,' he prompted. 'You may be able to help us.'

'I can, Mr Faraday.' She took another gulp of air. 'I can.'

She wanted him to see her photographs this time. They were on the drinks cabinet, in a big album. She waited for Faraday to fetch them. Standing at the cabinet, he heard the quiet hiss of gas. More oxygen.

'She was here last night. She's often here,' she said at last.

Faraday was back on the sofa, the album open at a section of sepia portraits, professionally posed and artfully lit. Age and cigarettes may have wrecked Grace Randall's lungs but her profile had survived the years. The same proud tilt of the chin. The same fine-boned, hawk-like face.

'She loves those pictures.'

Faraday put the album to one side. Grace Randall's use of tenses was beginning to worry him. He had to be sure that she understood what he'd been saying. The girl was dead. She'd fallen from a great height. Had Grace managed to follow this? Or had old age and too many sherries blurred the world around her?

He went through the likely sequence of events again. Finally, he asked the girl's name.

'Helen,' Grace wheezed. 'My Helen.'

My Helen?

Gradually, with infinite patience. Faraday managed to tease out her story. Grace had a great-granddaughter, Trudy. Trudy was a frequent visitor. She ran little errands. She fetched bits and pieces of shopping. Helen was her friend and one day she'd come up too. After that, she came often. Grace would tell her about the old days on the Cunard boats, about the songs she sang in the first-class lounge, about the time she'd fallen in love with one of the musicians in the band, and Helen had opened her heart in return. How sad that little girl's life had been. How much music she'd have in her if she could only listen to herself.

'She used to paint my nails . . .' Grace extended her long, trembling fingers '. . . black.'

Helen had been here last night, she repeated. She was very upset. She had a boyfriend but something had happened, something she wouldn't talk about. Grace had taken her tablets and gone to bed past midnight but Helen didn't want to leave. She'd said she'd sleep on the sofa again. She loved that sofa.

'She often spent the night here?'

'Oh, yes.' Grace nodded.

Faraday pressed her further, wanting to know more about the girl's state of mind, whether she'd got over being upset, whether or not Grace had heard her leave, but the old woman didn't seem to be listening. There was something else she wanted to say, another fragment of the evening that had come back to her. Helen had answered the door, late. She had a friend, a little boy, a scrap of a thing. She'd seen him in the hall through her open bedroom door. He had a strange laugh, high-pitched, almost a shriek, and an even stranger name.

Faraday waited and waited, knowing there was no point trying to hurry the conversation along. At length, Grace gave a little nod, pleased with herself.

'Doodie,' she whispered. 'She called him Doodie.'

Chapter three

FRIDAY, 9 FEBRUARY, *late morning*

Faraday read the quote a second time, testing the phrases on his lips. Dawn Ellis and Bev Yates had returned to the ground-floor day room at Chuzzlewit House, answering Faraday's summons for a meet and an update. A WPC, meanwhile, was stopping with Mrs Bassam until word came from the mortuary that Helen's body was ready for the formal ID.

'"The first venture, on a path already filled with cool pale radiance . . ."' Faraday paused, checking the final phrase '". . . was a flower who told me her name."'

Yates and Ellis exchanged glances. Yates had never had much time for poetry. Flowers with the gift of speech didn't figure much in the pages of *Jet-Ski Monthly*.

Faraday turned the photo over and studied the face again.

'You say the mother gave you a number?'

'It's a mobile, boss.' It was Ellis. 'Turned off last time we tried. His name's Niamat according to her. He's Afghan. She thinks he's got a bedsit or something in St Ronan's Road.'

'She's met him?'

'Yes. The last time was around Christmas. Apparently he turned up at the house with some flowers he wanted to give her but she sent him packing.'

'She doesn't like flowers?'

'She doesn't like him. She accused him of hanging round her daughter and apparently he had a bit of a go.'

'Speaks English, then?'

'Must do.'

Faraday was still studying the photo. Mrs Bassam had doubtless been shielding her daughter from predatory males but there might be worse options in this city than a multilingual Afghan with a taste for

French poetry. Most kids of Helen Bassam's age could barely speak English, let alone muster the energy to tackle a foreign language.

'And the daughter was involved? Is that the story?'

'Dotty about him. Besotted. Mum did her best to get between them but anything she said just made it worse. Lately, she said she's been tearing her hair out. The girl was just too young. At fourteen, you make all the obvious mistakes.'

Faraday looked to Yates for confirmation. In his early forties, the DC had recently married the twenty-two-year-old daughter of a wealthy family in the Meon Valley. Bev Yates had never looked his age, and he and the lovely Melanie made a handsome couple, but if anyone knew about the generation gap it should be him.

Yates reached for the photo. He seldom missed an opportunity to state the obvious.

'He's shagging for Kabul,' he said briefly. 'Best place for him.'

'You think he's an illegal?'

'No idea, boss. I'll let you know when we find him.'

Faraday retrieved the photo and added a note to the pad at his elbow. Lover boy would doubtless be holed up in one of the many near-derelict houses that had been bought for a song and toshed for the small army of asylum seekers which had recently descended on the city. At £500 per month, straight from Social Services, it was easy money for the landlords who preyed on the refugees, but that was another story.

'The girl spent part of last night here, a flat on the top floor,' Faraday said. 'Every tenant has a key to the roof area but the old girl who owns the flat can't find hers. That explains how the girl got on the roof. Did the mum mention the flats at all?'

'No. We asked her, but the answer's no. When the girl stayed away at night, she assumed she was kipping at her mate's.'

'*Assumed?*' This girl was fourteen. Old Portsmouth was a God-fearing, respectable area.

'Mum and her didn't get on. I think our family welfare friends would call it breakdown.'

'That bad?'

'So she says. The father's off with a new partner. She doesn't strike me as a woman with friends. Maybe the FLO . . .'

Faraday nodded, making another note. In situations like these, he'd be requesting a Family Liaison Officer, schooled in coping with the aftermath of sudden death. In Mrs Bassam's case, it would at least put a human face on all the questions they might need to ask.

'There's a kid called Doodie . . .' Faraday began. 'Young. A boy. The old girl puts him in the flat around midnight.'

'How old?'

'She thinks around ten.'

'*Ten?*' Yates exchanged a look with Ellis. Ten-year-olds belonged in a different script. Surely.

Faraday paused for a moment, wondering whether to describe his exchange with Grace Randall, but decided he'd never do justice to the woman's strangely lucid dottiness. At ninety, she was living proof that you ended up entombed in your memories, a life no less rich for being almost over.

'She's up for company,' he said instead, 'and I think the girl probably was as well. Old folk like people dropping in, especially ones who keep coming back.'

'But what was this Doodie kid doing in some old biddie's flat at midnight?'

'She doesn't know. She says she'd never seen him before. Ask Mrs Bassam. Ask her whether Helen ever mentioned Doodie. Put it on the list.'

Yates produced a pad.

'And you think he might have the key to the roof?'

'I think he might be a witness. I've checked on the overnight Mispers again but no Doodie. I've put a couple of calls into the CPU but they haven't come back yet. Plus no one else seems to have heard of him.'

The CPU was the Child Protection Unit, working from an office at force training headquarters at Netley. Their database drew on inputs from Social Services, Educational Welfare Officers and the city's Persistent Young Offender team. If anyone had a lead on Doodie, it would be the CPU.

Yates was gazing at his pad. 'But how did the girl get into the flats in the first place? There's a swipe system on the doors. You need a special key.'

'Mrs Randall had a code number she'd give to carers. You tap it in at the main entrance door downstairs.'

'And she gave it to Helen?'

Faraday nodded.

'Either that, or her friend did. The old lady's got a great-granddaughter, Trudy. She was mates with Helen.'

'Trudy Gallagher?'

'That's right.'

Yates shot Ellis a look. He'd already rung the number they'd got from Mrs Bassam and found himself talking to the girl's mother.

'And?'

'Trudy's at home.'

'Not at school?'

'No. She had a couple of wisdom teeth out earlier this week and apparently she's not feeling too clever. I checked it out with the school and it seems to be kosher.'

'So what about last night?'

'At home. Like I say.'

'Did Helen Bassam come round?'

'The mother says definitely not. Hasn't seen her all week.'

'So when Helen told her mum . . .?'

'Exactly.' Yates nodded. 'The girl was talking bollocks. Whoever she saw it couldn't have been Trudy.'

Faraday glanced at his watch. He'd lose the uniforms at lunchtime. From that point on, the enquiry was effectively in the hands of Yates and Ellis. For the time being, Faraday himself would remain in charge as Senior Investigating Officer, though that too might change. As soon as possible, he wanted Yates to check the CCTV tapes for the period around midnight. The kid Doodie had to be on the entry cameras and presumably one of the two lift cameras as well. They needed to establish when he got in and when he left and Faraday wanted a printout of the best of the mugshots.

He paused.

'And if he stops the lift on any other floor, check out the residents. OK?'

Faraday got to his feet. Scenes of Crime had finished outside and he'd shortly be returning the day room to the warden. He'd get the G28, the form for reporting a sudden death, to the Coroner's Office but he wanted Dawn Ellis to accompany Mrs Bassam for the formal ID on the girl's body. Ellis pulled a face.

'Can't the WPC run Mrs Bassam up there?'

'No, I'd prefer you to do it. The girl's got to be her daughter. Maybe she'll tell you more once she's seen her for real.'

Ellis shrugged, resigned to another difficult scene. 'A shoulder to cry on,' she said softly. 'Never fails, does it?'

Winter was on the phone, waiting for his call to answer, when Faraday got back to Southsea nick. Winter watched him put his head round the corner of the CID office, summoning Cathy with a nod, and found himself wondering again about the DI's love life.

He'd long had Faraday down as a loser when it came to women. Twenty years bringing up a deaf son had obviously cramped his social style, and office gossip suggested that a brief affair with the widow of a local art dealer had quickly hit the buffers, but with the boy at last off his hands he seemed to be making up for lost time.

In one sense, Winter wished him nothing but good luck. In his own experience, affairs with married women offered the perfect fusion of theft plus brilliant sex. Once you'd blagged it off a woman who was dying for the odd variation or two you knew there was nothing better. But the thought of Faraday at it with someone else's wife sat oddly with everything else he knew about the man. When it came to the job, Faraday could be a nightmare. He'd never met anyone else who was so straight.

At last, Winter bent to the phone. He'd lost count of the number of calls he'd made this morning, trying to pin down the job at Brennan's. The informers he rated were plugged in right across the city but so far all he'd drawn was a big fat blank. No one had heard as much as a whisper. Brennan's was known as a dodgy place to screw. Word was the bloke kept Alsatians on site at night and never fed the bastards. Who'd trade their arse for a vanful of fucking cordless drills?

The voice at the other end hadn't a clue. After yet another dispiriting football conversation about Pompey's last home performance, Winter hung up. Soon Cathy Lamb would be after him for hard intelligence on tonight's little expedition. She'd have chivvied Faraday into negotiating the overtime, but this kind of extra resource would only come at a price. No one parted with fifty hours' overtime unless they were guaranteed a result. That's the way the job worked these days. That's why fewer and fewer of the troops were prepared to take a punt. Stick your neck out, wave a flag for a bit of that nice pre-emptive policing, and God help you if you got it wrong. Winter thought about it for a moment or two longer, then pushed back his chair and headed for the door. In situations like these, there were certain calls you couldn't risk from the office. Not if the word 'pension' meant anything at all.

Mrs Bassam wasn't at home when Dawn Ellis returned to Old Portsmouth. She'd already tried her mobile with no result and now she understood why. According to the WPC parked outside, Jane Bassam had taken herself off to the cathedral for a while.

The cathedral was a couple of minutes' walk down the High Street, a pleasant modest building that had once served as the township's parish church. Ellis hesitated at the door, wondering quite where CID procedure ended and privacy began. Anyone in this situation deserved an hour or so of quiet contemplation, she thought. Lose your only child and there'd be knots that only silence could untie.

Inside, she thought at first that the cathedral was empty. Rows of seats extended across the nave towards the organ loft. Beyond were the choir stalls and finally the altar. She paused, telling herself that Jane Bassam was already on her way home or on the nearby seafront, but then her eyes adjusted to the big, shadowed spaces and she recognised the tall, erect figure in a distant pew, bent in prayer.

Ellis found a chair at the back of the nave and settled down to wait. It was rare to make a space like this for yourself in the working day and almost at once she was drawn back to the sprawled, broken figure on the wet pavement beneath the flats. Whether or not this girl's death deserved a full-scale CID inquiry wasn't the issue. People like herself and Bev Yates were there to investigate breaches of the law but in this case the only law that really mattered was the law of gravity. Something had tipped Helen Bassam over the edge and the truly frightening thing was how many other Helen Bassams – kids, for Christ's sake – had taken that final step.

Only months before, she'd been called to another jumper, a young lad of seventeen who'd chosen the top of the city centre's multi-storey car park to launch himself into oblivion. The brief CID inquiry had run out of steam after a couple of days but its findings had been both uncomfortable and depressing.

The boy had done wonders at GCSE. His predicted A levels were outstanding and he was a dead cert for a business studies degree at one of the better universities. Under these circumstances, no one had him down as a manic depressive or a suicide, least of all his parents. Yet there he was, on another metal tray in the mortuary fridge, leaving behind a note that was all the more chilling for its rationality. He'd looked hard at life. He'd played by the rules. He'd done his very best. And he'd decided, in the end, that it was all crap.

Ellis leaned back, resting her head against the pillar behind the chair. How do you answer a challenge like that? How do you persuade a kid with everything to live for that he'd got it wrong? The note had run to a couple of pages, a charge sheet against a society he'd come to regard as obscene. The relentless materialism. The political cowardice. The pollution. The greed. The hypocrisy. Everyone got it in the neck, from Rupert Murdoch to Tony Blair, but the real sadness wasn't the hole he left behind, or even the waste of a young life, but the fact that in so many instances the lad had been right.

A copy of the note had done the rounds in the CID office, and different hands had added extra charges to the indictment. They ranged from gripes about political correctness to the strange sentencing habits of certain magistrates and they formed a characteristically acid footnote to a document that was terrifying in the bluntness of its truth. The fact was that the lad had been spot-on and the trick nowadays, Ellis had concluded, was finding a way to survive all the crap. If you were lucky, and thick-skinned, you got by. Otherwise, if you were young enough and had the guts, you might start thinking seriously about fall parameters.

Ellis heard the squeak of a chair as Mrs Bassam got to her feet. She made her away towards the aisle, genuflected, hesitated for a moment, and then walked towards the back of the nave. Ellis intercepted her at the door, knowing at once that she was the last person this woman wanted to see.

'This won't take very long,' Ellis heard herself saying, 'I promise.'

All morning, Faraday had known that there'd be no alternative to a head-to-head with Hartigan about the Brennan's job. From the moment Cathy had briefed him on the intelligence that had come Winter's way, he'd anticipated the path that led to the Ops Superintendent's door. Everything in the world now boiled down to money. And as far as volume crime was concerned, Hartigan held the purse strings.

The Superintendent's office was at Fratton police station. Hartigan was a small, intense, obsessively neat little man who'd acquired a well-earned reputation for management prowess. He'd sniffed the winds of change that had blown through the upper corridors of police forces all over the country and knew that serious ambition was best served by falling in step with their new political masters.

If fighting crime required a mastery of New Labour-speak, then so be it. If Best Value Performance Indicators and European Foundation Quality Management flagged the path to ACPO rank, then Hartigan was the first in the queue to volunteer for the endless seminars, translating the lessons he'd learned into a blizzard of must-read memos that fluttered slowly down to the shop floor. Some of these memos had become collectors' items, but strip away the fancy language and what you were left with was the simplest of messages: think money. The politicians were demanding more and more for less and less, an unsquareable circle that led to confrontations like these.

Hartigan was on his feet behind his desk, supervising his management assistant as she cleared away the remnants of the last meeting. As Superintendent in charge of operations city-wide, he'd done well from recent upheavals in the organisation of Portsmouth's policing and, judging by the number of coffee cups, he'd soon be needing a bigger conference table.

'You're a busy man, Joe.' Hartigan waved Faraday into a chair. 'This won't take long.'

He summarised his brief conversation with Cathy Lamb. Winter had produced untested intelligence with regard to the Brennan's site. While Ray Brennan was undoubtedly a pillar of the community, one couldn't be seen to confer special favours. In short, he needed more than a nod and a wink from the likes of Paul Winter to authorise a substantial overtime spend. With two months to go to the end of the financial year, he was already five per cent over budget and an operation like this – especially on a Friday night – would only make the deficit worse.

Faraday, who'd anticipated every word of this little speech, enquired what alternatives Hartigan had in mind. As he understood it, Ray Brennan was already aware of the impending raid because DC Winter had told him. As a ratepayer, if nothing else, he'd expect a little protection. Might he not have a point?

'Of course he would. Which is why I'm prepared to make a patrol car available, all night if necessary, two up.'

'Visible?'

'Of course. That's why the guys are there. Even our criminal friends won't be able to miss them. Assuming they turn up, of course.'

'Meaning?'

'Meaning that we don't always get it right, Joe. Did I ever tell you about the missing gynaecologist who was allegedly buried under a block of flats? Found him in Jersey, didn't we? After you wanted to dig up half of Gunwharf.'

Faraday ignored the jibe. Last year's hunt for the high-profile Misper had indeed led to Gunwharf, but at the time the intelligence and deductions had seemed solid enough. Winter again, and a definite result at the end of it all.

'You agree, Joe? About Brennan's?' Hartigan was looking at his watch.

'I see the logic, yes.'

'But?'

'But I just thought we might do better than that.'

'How can we?'

Faraday gazed at him a moment, then allowed himself a smile.

'Arrests would be nice,' he said mildly.

A tiny muscle fluttered under Hartigan's left eye. He leaned forward, his carefully buffed nails spread across the desk. His patience, like his time, was clearly limited.

'Let me spell it out, Joe. Staking out Brennan's will cost me a fortune. So far we've got nothing to go on but Winter's word.'

'Are you telling me he's lying?'

'Of course not. But can he put a name to this source? Have we provenanced it? Is he properly registered? Is there any other intelligence to back it up?'

Faraday, for a moment, was robbed of an answer. Instead, he found himself gazing at a line of family photographs arranged in a neat semi-circle on one of Hartigan's filing cabinets: the bemedalled Superintendent and his wife at a Buckingham Palace garden party, his oldest son graduating from Cambridge, his daughter beside the font at her new baby's christening. Hartigan lived in a world where appearances mattered a great deal. No wonder he'd fallen in love with New Labour.

'Warning these guys off just moves the problem sideways,' Faraday said at last.

'I agree. *If* we're taking this threat seriously.'

'You really think we shouldn't?'

'I have my doubts.' He nodded at the phone. 'So do the CIMU.'

The Crime and Incident Management Unit worked from a nearby suite of offices, twenty-seven clerks and police officers charged with keeping their ears to the ground. Like everyone else, they knew the way that Hartigan liked to provide himself with scapegoats ahead of any operation, and they'd be less than keen to put their heads above the parapet. In circumstances like these, if you were truly cautious, hard intelligence would amount to names and addresses, supplied well in advance.

'But we're coppers,' Faraday pointed out. 'Most days we're working in the dark so sometimes we have to take a punt or two.'

'Wrong, Joe. That's playing catch-up. Those days are over. It's all about hard intelligence now. It's all about knowing how and why and when and being there when it happens. That's what the community expects and that's what I'm determined to deliver. Get me evidence that Brennan's is definitely on and I'll look at it again. Otherwise, the answer is no.' He stood up, offering Faraday a tight smile. 'Happy?'

Faraday got to his feet. On certain days he was beginning to hate the job, and this was one of them. It was bad enough attending to the remains of a fourteen-year-old jumper, bad enough trying to work out why on earth she'd done it, but these were mysteries that lay deep inside the girl's head. Brennan's was something else entirely. Brennan's was where the bad guys surfaced for an hour or so and set themselves up for a little surprise. Yet here he was, the poor fool detective, listening to a lecture on resource management from a boss who didn't have the first clue about CID work.

In these situations, with prats like Hartigan, it didn't pay to give up. Not if you valued your sanity.

'I'll have a word with the CIMU guys,' Faraday grunted. 'And see how Winter's getting on.'

'Of course.' Hartigan's smile had vanished. 'And you might knock on Mr Willard's door as well. I gather he wants a word.'

Dawn Ellis was still a mile from St Mary's Hospital, stuck in traffic, when she mentioned Doodie. Jane Bassam said she'd never heard the name.

'*Ten*, you say?'

33

'That's right.'

'But why would Helen have known him?'

'I've no idea, Mrs Bassam. We believe they were together last night.'

'You mean . . . on the roof?'

'Possibly.'

Mrs Bassam nooded, staring out at the roadworks puddled with rain, and Ellis knew she was still fighting to understand this terrible event that had turned her life upside down. In front of them was the back of a garbage truck. The dustmen had wedged a lone teddy bear beneath one of the retaining bars. The stuffing was spilling out round his middle and his head wobbled comically every time the truck inched forward.

Ellis wondered about putting the radio on but decided against it.

'I've been trying to work out how you must be feeling,' she said instead. 'But to be honest I don't know where to start.'

Mrs Bassam managed a small, cold smile.

'Neither do I,' she muttered. 'The last couple of months, it's been like living with a stranger.'

At the hospital, Ellis parked round the corner from the mortuary. A side entrance led to a waiting room. Jake, the senior technician, was in a jacket and tie, as sombre as the undertaker's men.

'Your daughter's in the Chapel of Rest.' He nodded at the connecting door. 'Just say when you're ready.'

Ellis asked Mrs Bassam whether she wanted to do this alone. All Ellis needed was confirmation that it really was her daughter. There was a chair beside the body and her time was her own.

Mrs Bassam said she understood. She'd be grateful if Ellis could come in with her. Jake led the way into the tiny chapel, standing carefully to one side as the two women approached the body.

The trolley on which the girl lay had been softened with a draped white sheet. Her body was covered with a funeral pall and her head lay on a pillow. Cotton wool in her ears had stemmed the trickle of fluids from the wreckage of her brain and her eyes were closed.

Mrs Bassam stepped slowly towards the body, then stopped. She was staring down at the girl's unmarked face and for a second or two Ellis wondered whether they had, after all, got it right.

'It's her,' Mrs Bassam said at last. 'She looks different but it's her.'

'Different?'

'Yes. Here and here.' Mrs Bassam touched her own temples, her own cheekbones. 'She looks slightly Chinese, flatter faced.'

Jake murmured something technical about the force of the impact. It could have a compressive effect on the shape of the skull. He used the word accident.

Mrs Bassam was still gazing down at her daughter. 'It wasn't an accident; it could never have been.' She shook her head. 'Helen didn't take those kinds of risks.'

There was a long pause. Then Ellis cleared her throat.

'On purpose, then? Suicide?'

'Never.' Mrs Bassam reached out and touched her daughter's cheek. 'She was far too selfish for that.'

Chapter four

Bev Yates started sorting through the CCTV pictures from Chuzzlewit House shortly before lunch. Fifty-seven cameras from five massive blocks on the estate fed real-time coverage to a central control room in Palmerston House, and the pictures were captured on a matrix on two recording machines. The footage was watched twenty-four hours a day by the concierge staff but feeds from the various cameras were rotated automatically through the seven monitor screens and it was pure chance whether the Chuzzlewit cameras were displaying at moments critical to the inquiry. None of the staff remembered seeing a ten-year-old on the monitors after midnight, so Yates tucked himself away in an alcove behind the control room to go through the recorded Chuzzlewit pictures, camera by camera.

He first spotted the tiny figure on an exterior camera bolted high on a corner of the flats and remotely controlled from Palmerston House. According to the digital readout, it had been 23.58 on 8.2.01. The boy's jeans looked several sizes too big and he was wearing a baggy grey top with the hood pulled low over his face. At the entrance to the building he kept his face shielded from the camera, reaching up on tiptoe to punch numbers into the automatic security device. For a ten-year-old, he seemed to know a great deal about video surveillance.

Yates made a note of the time and spooled through the pictures on the other cameras to pick up his passage into the building. In the ground floor hallway, as aware as ever, the boy kept his back to the camera, jiggling up and down as he waited for the lift. When it arrived, he crabbed in sideways, the hood still pulled down. The camera inside was up high, tucked into a corner, and throughout the ascent to the twenty-third floor he remained facing the door. But the jiggle was still there, one foot to another, a kid who just couldn't keep still, and the moment the lift doors opened he was gone. Scamp.

There were no cameras on the landing, or any on the stairs up to the roof area. What Yates now needed to establish was the time of Doodie's departure. For the next hour and a half, beginning with the cameras in the two lifts, he spooled through the video coverage, condensing the entire night into a blur. No one came or went. Both lifts remained empty. Only at 05.35, once the milkman had found the body and raised the alarm, did anyone appear.

Had this savvy little kid stayed up in the flat while Faraday's old lady was asleep? Had he kipped on the floor and slipped out once things got hectic? Yates rather doubted it, returning to the pictures from the exterior camera. At, 12.43, though the operator in Palmerston House had panned it away to a different view after reports of a disturbance in the shrubs behind the block, and it stayed that way for the rest of the night – one reason why no video pictures of the girl's body existed.

The only remaining exterior camera was built into the security control panel at the main entrance to Chuzzlewit House, and Yates bent to the monitor, his finger on fast forward, watching for movement. For hours nothing happened. Once again the milkman arrived, his face bagged with shadows under the harsh overhead light. Only when Yates was winding back, the tape speed slower, did he spot a blur of movement at a door beyond the main entrance. There was another exit, had to be, and this was the one that Doodie had used. He ran the pictures frame by frame, watching the door slowly open then a small grey hooded figure emerge, bolting away into the darkness beyond the street lamps.

02.57. 9.2.01.

Had the girl come off the roof by now? Was she lying dead on the pavement under the rain? If so, why had this scrawny little kid avoided using the lifts? Why had he run down twenty-three flights of emergency stairs and done his best to stay invisible? Was he frightened? Traumatised? If so, why hadn't he looked for help?

Yates inched the sequence backwards, then selected a frame that offered just a hint of a face, a smudge of white against the enveloping greys. Evidentially, for ID purposes, the picture was useless. He'd make arrangements to take a hard copy of the image because the time was as important as the possibility of a positive ID, but he knew he was no closer to giving this scrap of a child a name or an address. He could be any of dozens of similar kids. The estates and the shopping centres were awash with them, maybe not quite so young but certainly as streetwise.

As the image juddered on the monitor screen, Yates found himself wondering about his own child, Freya. In a couple of months' time, he and Melanie would be celebrating her first birthday. For the time being they were still living in a rented cottage up the Meon Valley, Melanie's home patch, but as soon as they could manage it, he planned a move back to the Southsea area, somewhere with a bit of a buzz. After the collapse of his first marriage, Yates had spent thirteen happy years in a tiny terraced house near the seafront and the city had got into his blood.

Looking at this ghost-like presence on the screen, though, Yates felt the first stirrings of doubt. The sight of the girl's body sprawled on the pavement had been bad enough. You wouldn't be human if a jumper that young and that pretty didn't get to you. But she was part of something bigger, and so was the kid Doodie.

Lately, Pompey kids like these seemed to be everywhere. Something had happened, someone had let them off the leash, and he wondered if he was really prepared to expose his own flesh and blood, his precious Freya, on these same streets. Wind on ten years or so and it might be her face on the video cameras, her name in the CPU files. Maybe Melanie's mother had it right about the charms of country living. Maybe clean air and decent neighbours really did give you a better chance in life.

He frowned, knowing in his heart that there was more to Pompey than kids like Doodie. One way or another, they'd find him. God knows, he might even have a story of his own.

He reached for his mobile. When Cathy Lamb answered, he got to his feet.

'Faraday back yet?'

It was Willard's idea to talk over a snatched lunch. The Detective Superintendent ran the Major Crimes operation from a secured suite of offices at Fratton police station, and the social club was only a couple of floors above. Cheese salad baguettes and instant coffee was hardly haute cuisine but Faraday seldom bothered with food at midday, even if he could find the time to eat it.

Detective Superintendent Geoff Willard was a detective's detective, a bulky man with a mop of greying curls and a taste for nicely cut suits. He had no patience with gossip or office politics and set a keen pace for the ever-changing army of DCs he roped in for major investigations. As the senior CID officer for the county's Eastern Area, his fiefdom covered a huge swathe of territory from the Isle of Wight in the south to Aldershot and Farnborough in the north. The heart of this empire was Portsmouth. The city had a combustible social mix – lots of young people, lots of drugs, lots of booze, lots of single men – and Willard's core team in the Major Crimes suite were seldom short of trade. They dealt in the currency of murder, serious assaults and stranger rape, and under Willard's watchful eye they'd developed a no-nonsense, nuts-and-bolts style of detective work as effective as it was unglamorous.

Willard, in his gruff way, never tired of preaching the virtues of patience, thoroughness and rat-like cunning. On serious crime, in his view, you had to make certain assumptions about the human condition. Expect the worst, and then some. Never be fooled by a smile. Faraday respected him a great deal.

'What's the strength on Brennan's?'

Faraday went through the latest developments. He'd talked to some of the guys in the CIMU and they were sending an officer to run his eye over the Brennan's premises and plot the parameters up. This was nothing that Winter hadn't done hours earlier, but if the system insisted on a second opinion, so be it. The intelligence was still there, and they'd be mad to ignore it.

'Don't get in a pissing match with Hartigan,' Willard warned. 'You'll lose.'

There were turf implications here but Willard seldom made anything of them. Faraday's CID strength answered to Hartigan. He was the Operational Superintendent, one of the city's top uniforms, and regarded the likes of Faraday as a resource at his command, foot soldiers to dam the tidal waves of volume crime. But Faraday also had a separate CID boss in the shape of Willard, a division of loyalty that could occasionally be tricky. Whatever Willard thought of Hartigan, he largely kept to himself.

'He needs collateral,' Willard concluded. 'Another source.'

'He's got one.'

'Really?'

'Crimestoppers put a call through to the CIMU. They had a guy on about an hour ago. Exactly the same whisper.'

Willard nodded. Crimestoppers offered a direct route into the intelligence system and it was open to any member of the public to make a call on the advertised number. Willard, like most detectives, regarded it as a worthy civic initiative but largely useless. The best intelligence still came from the coalface, from the dwindling numbers of paid informants who ghosted around in the underworld

'It's down in writing, though,' Faraday pointed out. 'And no one knows that better than Hartigan.'

'Sure.'

'So maybe it'll concentrate his mind. He wouldn't want to be caught napping with that in the log.'

'Yeah?'

Willard demolished the last of his baguette and changed the subject. He'd heard about the girl coming off the flats last night and he wanted to know what Faraday was doing about it. There might, in the end, be an outside chance of declaring it a Major Crime and the last thing he wanted was surprises.

Faraday laid out the sequence of events. If Willard took over the investigation, his own involvement would cease. He had enough shoplifters, house burglaries and vehicle thefts to fill any working day but Helen Bassam's death offered a different kind of challenge and there were threads in the girl's story that he wanted to tease out for himself. Better, therefore, to keep the incident low profile and hang onto the role of SIO. Not that Willard was easily snowed.

'You're sure she came off the roof? Not some flat or other?'

'Ninety-nine per cent.'

'Any witnesses? Anyone with her?'

'It's possible. There's a kid we're trying to TIE.'

Trace, Implicate or Eliminate. Willard wanted to know more.

'He's young.'

'How young?'

'We think around ten.'

'*Ten?*' Willard whistled. 'What's wrong with this city?'

It was a good question; Faraday didn't volunteer an answer. Instead he mapped the routes the inquiry was taking. There was nothing to help them on the Misper list. The CPU at Netley had yet to send anything through. The post-mortem wouldn't happen until Monday.

'You think she jumped?'

'It's a possibility.'

'But why would she do that?'

Faraday explained about the Afghan boyfriend. According to the mother, she was wild about him and something seemed to have gone wrong.

'Wild enough to kill herself?'

'Wild enough to do something crazy.'

'How old's this guy?'

Faraday hesitated, thinking of the face in the photograph. It was a question he'd asked himself, but according to Yates the mother hadn't been sure.

'Mid-twenties? Older? We don't know.'

'And the girl?'

'Under age. Fourteen.'

Willard shot Faraday a look then bent forward. There was a low table between them and he moved his plate to one side, an almost unconscious gesture that suggested the conversation was about to move on. For the first time it occurred to Faraday that there was another

40

reason for this casual invitation to pop upstairs. Not just an update after all.

'There's a job coming up,' Willard began, 'and it might be worth you having a think about it.'

Bev Yates finally raised Niamat Tabibi, the Afghan, on his mobile. The man's English, though heavily accented, was near perfect. In particular, he seemed to have mastered the art of evasion. He was very busy just now. It would be very hard for him to find the time for a chat. No, he had no idea where the police station might be in Highland Road. And, no, his place was in no state to entertain visitors.

Yates sensed an opening. Asylum seekers needed work permits for paid employment.

'Busy doing what exactly?'

'Teaching. I teach.'

'Teach what?'

'French. And mathematics.'

'For the love of it?'

'Of course. I have a great deal of time. I spend it on other people. Is that a crime?'

'Depends.' Yates had the photograph at his elbow. Even on the phone you could sense this man's charm. He was quick-witted and plausible. No wonder the girl had been suckered.

'I'm making enquiries in connection with someone you may know,' Yates began. 'Helen Christine Bassam.'

'Helen?' His manner changed at once.

'You know her?'

'Of course.'

'Then I really think we ought to talk.'

To Yates's surprise, he said yes. There was a café he sometimes used. It was in Milton, a little place on the main road. It was called Kate's Kitchen. The woman did cheap vegetarian breakfasts.

'Round the corner from the police station?' Yates enquired drily.

'That's it.'

It took Yates and Ellis a couple of minutes to walk the quarter mile to the café but the Afghan was already there, sitting at the table in the window. He'd lost a little weight since he'd had the photograph taken and if anything it underscored the hint of wistfulness in his smile. That at least was Ellis's view. 'Hunk,' she muttered as Yates pushed the door open.

Niamat got to his feet at once. He was wearing black jeans and a scruffy leather jacket with an old Manchester United shirt beneath. A copy of the *Guardian* lay open in front of him and there was a plastic bag full of potatoes beside his chair. Strictly speaking this was Yates's party but Ellis headed him off before the going got difficult. Despite his slightly Italian good looks, Bev had a definite problem with foreigners.

'There's something you ought to know about Helen,' Ellis said at once, 'unless someone's told you already.'

The news that the girl was dead visibly shook the Afghan. That she'd fallen to her death from a block of flats seemed to make the news even worse. He sat down very slowly. Under different circumstances, Ellis would have offered him a stiff brandy.

'You didn't know?'

'Of course not.'

'Of course not?' It was Yates this time. 'You're telling me you're surprised?'

Niamat didn't seem to understand the question. He was looking at Ellis with an expression close to panic. Help me, he seemed to be saying. Give me a moment or two to get to grips with this thing.

Yates again, leaning forward across the table. Already this could have been the interview room.

'We understand you were close.'

'We were friends, yes.'

'You and a fourteen-year-old girl?'

'Of course.'

'Why of course?'

'Because I taught her.'

'At school?'

'No, at home.'

'Whose home?'

'Hers.'

'You went round to her own house to teach her?' Yates was losing his bearings. 'Did her mother know?'

'It was her mother's idea, her mother's invitation. That's how we met. She was doing so badly at school that her mother wanted extra teaching. I have a card in the window of her local shop. French and mathematics. I'm very cheap. She rang me.'

Yates exchanged glances with Ellis. No wonder Mrs Bassam had been so bitter about her daughter's infatuation. Not only had Helen Bassam lost her heart to this man but her mother – with the best of intentions – had been responsible for bringing them together in the first place.

Ellis asked Yates to organise some teas. While he was at the counter, she pressed the Afghan further. How often did he and Helen meet? When had he last seen her?

42

Niamat was still trying to remember when Yates returned with the teas. He put Ellis's question a little more bluntly: 'What were you doing last night?'

'I was with friends.'

'We'll need their names. We'll want to talk to them.'

'Of course.'

'Where did you go?'

'Nowhere. We have no money. We stayed at home.'

'And watched television?'

'The television was on, yes.'

'So what did you watch?'

The shock and the helplessness had gone now, replaced by something much closer to anger. Yates, with his usual tact, had sparked this man, and nothing gave him greater pleasure than listing the previous night's programmes one after the other.

'You think I'm lying? You want to know what they were about? I'll tell you.'

He began to lay out the plot of last night's ITV drama, and Ellis sensed the gift he so obviously had for one-to-one contact. He used his hands a lot, explaining a particularly crass narrative twist, and after a while Ellis started to wonder whether even a drama as crap as *At Home with the Braithwaites* might have some merit.

Yates seemed to have lost interest. He reached for the sugar bowl, stony-faced, and it fell to Ellis to produce the photograph. She turned it over, showing Niamat the inscription on the back.

'Is this your writing?'

Niamat barely looked at it.

'Yes, I wrote it for my wife.'

'*Wife?*' Yates was back in the loop. 'You're telling me you're married?'

Niamat nodded. Seconds later, Ellis was looking at another photograph he'd produced, colour this time. The shot had been taken indoors. His wife, unveiled, was raven-haired with full lips and a melting smile. Her name, he said, was Elif. One day, should Allah will it, she'd be able to join him here in England.

'You're seeking asylum?'

'Yes.' He nodded. 'My father was in the army. He never liked the Taliban and in the end they shot him. After that, they came looking for me.'

There was something so simple and matter-of-fact in the way Niamat put this that Ellis knew at once it must be true. He'd fled with three others. His mother had sold the family's land and $9000 had bought Niamat's passage to London. He'd come through Iran and Turkey, avoiding soldiers and wolves on the border. A sand dredger had taken him from Istanbul to an Italian beach near Bari and from there he'd ridden north on a series of lorries. The last one, thanks to Eurotunnel, had landed him in Dover. It was night-time and it had been raining. The security man, to his surprise, hadn't touched him.

'This stuff about the flowers.' Yates was examining the back of the photo. 'What was Helen supposed to make of that?'

'I've no idea. It comes from a Rimbaud poem, *"Aube"*. It's a beautiful poem. It's about dawn. It's about the beginning of the world. I told you, the quotation was for my wife.'

'It's a love poem then?'

'Of course, if you read it that way.'

'So why give it to Helen?'

'I didn't,' he said stonily. 'She stole it.'

Back at Southsea nick, half an hour later, Yates and Ellis found Faraday working through a mass of emails in his office. He'd started a Policy Book on Helen Bassam's death, a running log listing every new decision on the inquiry together with a brief rationale, and it lay open on the desk beside the computer. Half an hour earlier, according to Faraday's scrawl, Scenes of Crime had phoned to confirm that the blood patterning on the pavement around the dead girl's body was consistent with a fall from height.

'Rocket science,' Faraday murmured, aware of Yates's interest. 'What about our Afghan friend?'

Yates described the conversation in the café. In his view, Niamat Tabibi was talking a load of bollocks. Odds-on he was shagging the girl though he appeared to have a solid alibi for last night. Ellis said nothing. The open email on the screen had come from the Superintendent in charge of Community Safety at force headquarters in Winchester. He wanted Faraday's thoughts on a rumoured sighting of a pied billed grebe in the bird reserve at Farlington Marshes, and so far Faraday's reply had stretched to three paragraphs.

'I've had the headmaster on from St Peter's,' Faraday was saying. 'The girl was at school there. Her grades have been going from bad to worse and lately she hasn't been turning up at all. They're setting up a case conference with the welfare but there's obviously no point any more. The head's got a stack of pupils wanting to attend the funeral. It seems she had lots of friends.'

Ellis turned away. This morning's developments were now public knowledge. Helen's name had been released to the media, featuring in news reports on local radio. Whether Helen Bassam was popular or not was beside the point. Nothing caught the adolescent imagination more than the prospect of a good funeral, preferably in the rain.

'I don't see it the way Bev does,' she said quietly. 'I think the Afghan guy's kosher.'

'Meaning?'

'Meaning they were just friends. That wasn't what she wanted but that's all she got. The rest was fantasy. She made him up.'

'Wasn't the mother convinced they were screwing?' Yates enquired. 'Or am I imagining things?'

'The mother's loonier than her daughter. The husband's gone, that's the clue. Break a marriage like that and you're left with a bloody great hole. Niamat filled it, don't ask me how, but he did. That's not breaking the law, not so far anyway.'

Faraday smiled and turned back to his computer, putting the finishing touches to his email. It turned out he'd seen the grebe himself, only a couple of days ago. The bird had blown in from America, an orphan borne east on the ever-deepening frontal troughs.

Yates read the email over Faraday's shoulder, rolling his eyes when he realised what it was about. He'd never understood Faraday's passion for birdwatching, least of all when the jobs were piling up like this. Finally, he took Dawn Ellis's elbow and steered her towards the open door. Only when they were in the corridor outside did Faraday call after them.

'There's an overtime job on tonight,' he said, 'Brennan's.'

Winter had the details in the CID office. Hartigan was authorising a scaled-down stake-out at the DIY superstore, five uniforms and three CID. Cathy Lamb was working out the details and the briefing would be over at Fratton at six sharp. Winter's money was on a bust around midnight. Allow a couple of hours afterwards for the paperwork and they'd all be in bed by three at the latest.

He sat back in his chair, hands clasped behind his neck, beaming up at Bev Yates. Dawn Ellis, who was mates with Cathy Lamb, wanted to know what had swung it with Hartigan. According to Cathy, the Ops Supt wouldn't go beyond a dare-you squad car, the cheapo option. Now he was spending serious money. How come?

All eyes turned to Winter. Part of his legendary reputation for getting results rested on the fact that no one in the office really knew him. He was loud and boastful, and gloried in a congratulatory lager or two when his latest punt came good, but he rarely shared his trade secrets, preferring to hide behind the word 'hunch'. The fact that there were no forms for hunches never bothered him in the least. On the contrary, he revelled in his contempt for paperwork, believing that a good detective spent as little time at the keyboard as possible.

'Well?' It was Ellis again.

Winter glanced at his watch then shrugged.

'Some bloke belled Crimestoppers,' he murmured. 'Never fails.'

Chapter five

Faraday was still at his desk when the file arrived from the Child Protection Unit. They were currently fielding twenty referrals a day from every corner of the county and this morning's request hadn't been actioned until after lunch. More to the point, the keyword 'Doodie' had found no echoes in the database, and only a PC with a good memory had recognised the nickname from inputting additional details a month or two back.

The fax stretched to two pages, a digest of information from every agency in the city touched by Doodie's young life. His real name was Gavin Prentice and his date of birth put him at ten years old. He'd first appeared on the police radar screen nearly nine months earlier after an incident in Somerstown. A neighbour had watched him setting fire to a wheelie bin, something at which Doodie evidently excelled, and she'd called the police. In the dry, spare prose of the local beat man, Gavin Prentice had a history of nuisance, and a number of other householders had confirmed similar incidents. Several days later, his mother was invited to attend Central police station where her son was given an informal warning by the duty Inspector.

Faraday reached for a pen. Doodie's mother went by the name of Denise Prentice and lived in one of the busier Somerstown blocks, five minutes' walk from Chuzzlewit House. There was a mobile number entered beside her name but a later note suggested the phone was no longer operational.

After this first brush with the law, Doodie's young life went rapidly out of control. Entries from the Educational Welfare Officer established that he was no longer attending school. Automatic notifications to Social Services and the Youth Offending Team had followed the visit to Central, but letters to Mum from both organisations had gone unacknowledged. Two months later, Doodie had been detained again, this time in Woolies where he'd been caught nicking Pokémon cards. A second informal warning had followed but Doodie plainly hadn't been listening because – within three weeks – he was back in front of the Inspector after breaking into an empty property in Southsea and – once again – getting busy with the matches. There'd been no element of gain in this escapade but the Inspector had nevertheless issued a Final Warning.

Doodie was still a child, of course, but the age of ten marks the start of legal responsibility, and when he started taking a hammer to parked cars, reaching through the shattered glass to lift whatever he could, he found himself before the magistrates in the Juvenile Court. On 17 November last year, he'd been given a two-year Supervision Order. That meant reporting for regular sessions with a supervising officer at the Youth Offending Team, a woman called Betsy, but she'd quickly recognised that parts of Doodie lay way beyond her reach, and he'd been referred on to the city's Persistent Young Offender project. In a parting shot, Betsy had described her brief relationship with young Gavin as 'particularly challenging', a form of words which clearly did Doodie scant justice. The kid was a nightmare.

Faraday quickly scanned the rest of the fax. He had regular dealings with the PYO project and admired the woman who ran it, a combative fifty-three-year-old, Anghared Davies. Dealing with tearaways as young as Doodie required a great deal of patience as well as a preparedness to take substantial risks, and he scribbled himself a reminder to give their office a ring first thing Monday. Doodie would have been assigned an individual support worker, maybe even two, and in theory they'd been seeing him on a near-daily basis. In the meantime it was important to get hold of the kid, and the best place to start was his home address.

He reached for the phone. The CPU fax had been right about Denise Prentice's mobile: the number was no longer available. Faraday checked his watch. Half past five. Dawn Ellis, to his certain knowledge, was out on another inquiry, while Bev Yates would be driving over to Fratton for the Brennan's briefing. Tonight, he was due to meet Marta for a drink before going on to a concert in the Guildhall. That still gave him an hour or so to pay a visit to Doodie's mum.

Denise Prentice lived on the seventh floor of Raglan House, another gaunt sixties block which always reminded Faraday of the wastelands of Eastern Europe. Sodden chip wraps and pizza boxes clogged the gutters in the street outside while an upended supermarket trolley lay in the pool of light outside the main entrance. Bucharest, maybe. Or East Berlin before the Wall came down.

Doodie's mum lived in 703. Faraday rang the buzzer on the speaker phone but got no reply. He buzzed again and this time a voice answered. It was a woman's voice, husky with fags. Faraday announced himself. He was a policeman. He wanted a word in connection with Gavin. The speaker phone went dead. Nothing else happened.

At length Faraday took advantage of a returning resident to get inside the building, standing beside the guy as the lift creaked slowly upwards. These people could smell the Filth. He knew it. At the seventh floor he got out of the lift without a backward glance, making his way around three sides of the block until he found 703. The nearest of the overhead lights was out but even in the gloom he could see that the door lock, a Yale, had recently been replaced.

He knocked twice. He could hear kids inside and the blare of a television. The television was really loud, a cartoon of some kind, and it took four more knocks, ever harder, before the door opened. Faraday found himself looking down at a tiny girl. She was wearing a grubby, food-stained vest and not much else. How she'd ever managed the door was beyond him.

'Is your mum there?'

A woman appeared, shooing the girl away. She was thin and blonde with a sharp face and stained teeth. Her Gap T-shirt was cut low enough around the neck to show a fading love bite and there was a dark blue tattoo in the shape of a flower beneath her left ear. She looked exhausted.

Faraday held up his warrant card while she struggled to push the door closed against the weight of his body. Finally, she shrugged and gave up.

The flat was cold and bare, and smelled of dogs and old chip fat. Through an open door Faraday could see three kids, all young, sitting on the lino in front of the television. Even the little girl who'd opened the door had ceased to take any interest in the new visitor.

'You're Mrs Prentice?'

'That's right.'

'I've come about Gavin. Is he here?'

The woman gave him a long hard look. A bit of make-up, Faraday thought, and a decent meal and she'd be halfway attractive.

'No,' she said at last, 'he ain't.'

'You're sure?'

'Of course I fucking am.'

'Mind if I take a look?'

'Help yourself. Everyone else does.'

She leaned back against the wall and folded her arms while Faraday

49

looked quickly round the flat. The bottom had fallen out of the single armchair in the TV room while the kitchen seemed to house little more than a microwave, a packet of Coco Pops and an empty carton of milk. There were the remains of a Chinese in a dog bowl on the floor while rubbish was spilling out of the black plastic sack in the corner. The open window above did little for the smell. Mrs Prentice had lit a cigarette. Faraday stepped carefully round her. Down the tiny hallway were two bedrooms. One contained an unmade bed with a smaller mattress beside it. The other door was locked.

'What's in here?'

'The dog.'

'Is that the kid's bedroom?'

'Yeah.'

'You've got a key?'

The look again, garnished with a smile that Faraday didn't altogether trust.

'Good with dogs, are yer?' She produced a key from her jeans pocket and tossed it towards Faraday.

The moment he inched open the door, the dog lunged towards him. He wasn't a big dog, a Jack Russell maybe, or a mongrel, and Faraday managed to hold him off for long enough to confirm that the room was empty. Three beds side by side. What looked like sleeping bags. Plus a Pompey poster on the wall. The dog was yapping fit to bust. Faraday shut the door.

'You want it locked again?'

'Of course I fucking do. They'll have him out otherwise.'

Faraday locked the door and returned the key. The woman stared him out. She'd been pretty once. Definitely.

'Where's Gavin then?'

'Haven't a clue.'

'When does he normally come in?'

'Pass.' She sucked in a lungful of smoke, tipping her head back to expel it again. 'Pub quiz, is it? Only I'm really busy.'

Faraday persevered. What really pissed these people off was staying calm. Lose your rag, and they'd walk all over you.

'Gavin's ten,' he pointed out. 'I expect he'll be home for tea soon.'

'I doubt it. He's off somewhere.'

'Any idea where?'

'Not the slightest.'

'What about last night? What was he up to last night?'

'Haven't got a clue.'

'You didn't see him last night?'

'Nope. Nor the night before. Nor the night before that. He comes home when it suits him. Like most men.'

'He's ten,' Faraday reminded her. 'And he's your son.'

'So?'

She stepped into the kitchen, grinding out the remains of the cigarette in the sink. Faraday wondered how quickly you'd get used to the stench.

'You'll have a photo,' he suggested.

'Of Gav?' The woman was grinning now, taking the piss. 'You from the telly or something? Gonna make him famous?'

For a moment Faraday toyed with explaining about this morning, about what they'd found outside Chuzzlewit House, but decided against it. Mrs Prentice was way beyond caring, least of all about a nice middle-class girl from Old Portsmouth lying dead in the rain. Looking at her, Faraday could hear the phrases already. Shit happens. Big deal.

'The name Doodie,' he began. 'Does everyone call him that?'

'Who?'

'Your Gavin.'

'Doodie?' She mugged a big, stagey frown. 'Never heard of it. His name's Gavin. I calls him Gavin. The kids calls him Gavin. Everyone calls him Gavin. OK?'

'So where does he sleep at night?'

'Loadsa places. His nan's. Friends. Loadsa places.'

'But you don't know? You don't check?'

'No point. He'd only get in a strop and then I'd never see him at all, would I? Thing about Gav, he'll always come back. Maybe tomorrow. Maybe next week. But he's like the dog, can't do without us. Know what I mean?'

'Food?'

'He gets by, looks after himself. Never hungry, not my Gav.'

'And school?'

'Hates it. Can't be doing with it. Hits the teachers, even women teachers. He's wicked that way, really naughty. Like I tell them, they're better off without him.' She laughed – a short, mirthless bark of laughter – then nodded towards the front door. 'That it then?'

'What about his dad?'

'What about him?'

'Does he live here?'

'With us, you mean? Are you out of your mind?'

'You've got a name? A contact number?'

She was back against the wall, arms crossed again. She offered Faraday a slow shake of her head. No, she didn't have a name. She'd long got the tosser out of her life and there was no way he'd ever get back in. Woman's right. Woman's privilege. Now fuck off and leave us alone.

Faraday nodded, thanking her for her time. He'd doubtless be back and he wanted her to know that.

'Do you have a mobile?'

'Binned it.' She nodded back towards the kitchen.

'Any other way I can get hold of you?'

'Yeah. Write me one of those nice letters with a big fat cheque inside. Know what I mean?'

She pushed herself off the wall and pulled the front door open. From the kids' bedroom came the sound of barking again. Then the little girl was back in the hall, clutching at the bottom of her vest. She gazed up at Faraday, big brown eyes, then reached for her mother's hand.

'Where Doodie?' she whispered.

The Brennan's briefing over, Winter settled himself in the corner of the bar at Fratton nick. Bev Yates, who had a wife to pacify, had disappeared home for a couple of hours but Cathy Lamb had stayed on, determined to screw a couple of drinks out of Winter in return for her efforts to get him to Portugal. Winter, recognising a peace opportunity when he saw one, was only too delighted to oblige, extending the compensation to the offer of a curry afterwards. The stake-out was due to kick off at ten o'clock. Plenty of time for a vindaloo.

Cathy shook her head. A pint of Stella would be nice but she had a couple of things to attend to before they settled in at Brennan's.

'But I thought you told me Pete was away?'

'He is. You think I'd be sitting here with you if he wasn't?'

Winter grinned. One of things you liked about Cathy Lamb was the way she always took life head-on. When she'd caught Pete shagging a young probationer from Fareham nick, she'd first thrown him out and then done her best to give the girl a real hiding. Now, with Pete at last back in harness, she couldn't get enough of him.

'When's he back, then?'

'Next week. He's on a job in Germany.'

Out of the force now, Pete Lamb was working for a big Pompey-based insurance company, investigating dodgy claims. The work took him away a good deal, doing absolutely nothing for Cathy Lamb's blood pressure.

'You need a holiday, skip.' Winter reached for his Pils. 'I know just the place.'

'Wouldn't have the tickets as well, would you?'

Winter tipped his glass in salute.

'I mean it. The place sounded perfect.'

'So why didn't you bloody go?'

'I meant for you, Cath, you and Pete. If you're really lucky it might even rain. Then you wouldn't have to get up at all.'

Cathy ignored him. Several members of Willard's Major Crimes team had appeared at the bar and one – to Winter's amusement – had given her a little wave. Now he came over and whispered something in Cathy's ear. Cathy stared up at him, astonished, and he nodded in confirmation before returning to the bar.

Winter didn't even bother asking. There were certain categories of gossip that Cathy Lamb could never keep to herself and he sensed that this might be one of them. She sat motionless for a moment or two then leaned forward.

'Guess who's favourite for the next DI job.' She gestured back towards the knot of watching detectives. 'On Major Crimes.'

The café-bar was already busy by the time Faraday arrived. Le Dome, with its big horseshoe bar and warm conversational buzz, had become a regular rendezvous before the Friday night Guildhall concerts. The place was often full of foreign students huddled together over cups of cappuccino, and Marta said she felt at home there.

Faraday found a quiet table near the back. He'd bought a paper from the newsagent across the road and he studied the weather report, wondering about prospects for the weekend. It seemed to have been raining non-stop since Christmas, and tonight's chart showed yet another frontal system out in the Atlantic, preparing to dump a couple more inches on the swamp that had once been Faraday's front garden. Weather like this could seriously get to you, yet another reason why Marta had become so important. Five minutes in her company, and the sun came out.

As ever, she caught him by surprise, approaching from behind and kissing him softly on the cheek. She was wearing a beautifully cut cashmere coat, filmed with rain, and a richly striped silk scarf wound turban-style around her head. Faraday had watched her knotting that scarf dozens of times and her deftness never ceased to amaze him. She smelt wonderful too, a subtle, slightly musky scent that always reminded Faraday of their first nights together. This was a world away from Raglan House, thank Christ, and Faraday got to his feet, pulling out the adjoining chair.

Marta had driven straight in from the big IBM complex at the top of the city. She had a huge job there, something to do with marketing, but it was one clue to this strange relationship of theirs that he'd never quite fathomed what she actually did. Face to face or even on the phone he was sure she could sell anything. He'd never met anyone so self-confident, so vividly themselves. But whenever he'd pressed her for details on her role or her responsibilities, she'd always change the subject. His was the job they should be talking about, she'd say. Something real for a change.

She loosened her coat and asked for a glass of white wine. Faraday had already talked to her on the phone, a snatched conversation between afternoon meetings, and now she wanted to know about Willard's offer.

'It wasn't an offer,' Faraday said hastily.

He did his best to explain the way Willard had put it. There were three DIs on the core Major Crimes team. They all reported to the Detective Superintendent, and Willard described them as the hinge on his door. They were the ones who'd act as his deputy on the really complex inquiries that couldn't be handled on division. They were the ones he'd trust to run the well-oiled investigative machine that, in the end, had to deliver a result. Getting the right people was never easy. And with a vacancy looming, Willard had decided that Faraday was the ideal candidate.

Marta's eyes were bright with excitement. A single glance would tell you she was Spanish: the dark eyes, the perfect make-up, the sheer animation in her face. Mediterranean women, Faraday had concluded, were seldom frightened of showing their emotions. Unlike the glum, blank, clouded faces he saw all around him, they challenged you with a smile.

'Brilliant,' she was saying. *'Perfecto.'*

Faraday grinned, warmed by the recklessness of her enthusiasm. No ifs or buts. No agonising about the downside. Just do it.

'It's not that simple. It's a different set-up. At the moment I'm my own boss. On Major Crimes, you report to Willard. He sets the pace. We do the running.'

'You run already, my darling. All the time.'

It was true. Faraday couldn't remember a day when his desk had been empty, when he'd finally caught up with the backlog of so-called volume crime. Nicking domestic burglars and serial shoplifters might be the dream of every politician but the facts argued otherwise. In the real world, you'd never put all the bad guys away.

'It's a pain,' Faraday admitted.

'Then listen to this man. Let him help you.'

'Help me?' The thought brought another smile to Faraday's face. Benevolence had never been part of CID management style. If Willard wanted him on board then there was something in it for Willard. But what?

'You think I should do it?'

'Definitely. Big, juicy murders? *Claro*.' She bent towards him, her head close to his, and kissed him on the lips. 'You smell terrible,' she whispered. 'Where have you been?'

The concert was built around a performance of Berlioz's *Symphonie Fantastique*. Faraday and Marta sat through a Beethoven overture and a piece from Vaughan Williams, waiting for the evening's highlight. Faraday had recently developed a passion for Berlioz, and Marta had given him a big two-volume biography for Christmas.

The young Berlioz had written the symphony in just six weeks, breaking most of the accepted rules of orchestration in the process. He'd based its development quite shamelessly on episodes in his own life and Faraday warmed to the notion of an overpowering, obsessional passion for the woman of his dreams. A year at French evening classes had offered Faraday a working knowledge of the language, and the phrase *idée fixe* stirred definite echoes. It was these same evening classes, after all, that had given him Marta.

The first movement began and Faraday settled back, letting the suddenness of the rhythmic changes envelop him. The real pleasure of music like this was the depth of the moat it dug between himself and the increasingly brutal demands of his working day. Berlioz was no stranger to the kind of inner turmoil that could take you to the very edge but he'd managed to conjure something magical and lasting from the experience. Unlike Helen Bassam.

Faraday thought about the girl as the music swirled on. On Monday there'd be a post-mortem. Maybe the pathologist might throw up a lead or two. On Monday, as well, he'd have to organise a serious bid to pin down the kid, Doodie. At first he'd been tempted to dismiss the mother's version of events out of hand. The thought that a child of ten was on the loose somewhere, living from hand to mouth, was absurd. He'd already put the boy's name on the official Mispers list, a heads-up for every beat man and squad car in the city, but he still clung to the assumption that Denise Prentice had been lying. This was 2001. The city of Dickens, of vagrant kids fending for themselves, had long gone. Or had it? Maybe life at 703 Raglan House really was as desperate and threadbare as appearances suggested. Would anyone in his right mind want to live in circumstances like that? Would Doodie?

The first movement came to an end and Faraday felt Marta's hand in his lap. She was looking at him, a hint of concern in those deep, brown eyes.

'OK?'

He smiled and gave her hand a squeeze, glad to forget at last about

Misper kids and teenage corpses. She'd made every difference, this woman. She was funny and sexy and immensely stylish, and she'd brought light and laughter to parts of him that had been shadowed for decades. For a working detective, it was worrying that he'd taken so long to discover that she was married but even this realisation hadn't made him any less needful. They'd been seeing each other now for more than a year, and each new stolen evening convinced him they were a perfect fit.

Back in September, she'd somehow managed to steal a whole week away from work and family. Faraday had booked a last-minute package to Corsica, and they'd flown out from Gatwick. The holiday had been a dream – empty beaches, tiny bays, fabulous snorkelling – and towards the end of the week they'd taken a train inland, finding a back-street hotel in Corte and walking the mountain paths deep into the Restonica Valley. There'd been warblers darting in and out of the *maquis* and the distant silhouette of buzzards riding thermals in the hot afternoons. At night, from their hotel bedroom, he could hear the call of a scops owl, clear as a bell, and he'd whispered the name to Marta in the warm darkness.

The magic of those days had made him unusually bold. They had an unspoken pact that banned discussion of life back home but the last evening in Corte they'd gone shopping for presents and Marta had emerged from a toy shop with an armful of goodies for her kids. The sight of a Star Wars Landspeeder and a bright yellow teddy bear had been too much for Faraday and over supper that night he'd demanded to know where this relationship of theirs was going. Her husband's name was Francis. He was a civil servant of some kind. David was eleven, Maria just five. Where, exactly, did Faraday fit in this tight little ménage?

Marta had put her finger to his lips. They were on holiday. They were enjoying each other. Why ruin it? Faraday, having seen off the first bottle of Patrimonio, was in no mood for compromise. This refusal of Marta's to discuss either her family or her work had always sat oddly with her openness in every other respect. When she told him she loved him, he didn't doubt her for a moment. When she gaily found time to see him on a couple of weekday evenings, or even a whole Saturday, he'd almost come to take her warmth and passion for granted. Yet when they finished making love, up in Faraday's big, book-lined bedroom, there'd always come the moment when she'd reach for her watch and clip it to her wrist, and then suddenly – after the briefest shower – she'd have gone.

Faraday, alone in the darkness, had come to hate that watch. To him it seemed that it ran his love life the way his own Omega ran his working day. Occasionally, far less often than he'd have liked, he'd try and talk to her about it but she always changed the subject. Relax, she'd say. Relax and enjoy it.

That night in Corte, over the remains of wild boar and *loup de mer*, he'd been determined to get some answers. What did she really want from him? Where would this relationship take them? Once again, she'd simply shaken her head, filling her own glass with mineral water, and in the end Faraday had lost his temper, accusing her of bolting him onto this other life of hers, of using him to fulfill the bits of Marta that weren't quite satisfied with two kids and a husband, and the weekly trek to Safeways. She'd listened to him, attentive at last, and when he'd got it off his chest she'd leaned forward over the table and looked him in the eye, and told him there was always an alternative. If he wanted her that badly, really needed her, then she'd leave her husband, abandon her kids, and come to him. There was no middle way, no negotiation. It was an offer that was wholly typical of the way she conducted every other transaction in her life. All or nothing.

Faraday, even drunk, finally realised he was lost. He knew about single parenthood. He understood what it was like to bring up a child alone. And most of all, he had twenty years' experience of trying to fill in for a wife who'd died. There was no way he could wreak that kind of havoc, not wittingly, no way he could rob two kids of their natural mother and still look himself in the eye when he shaved every morning. Marta was the cross he'd made for himself, and if he occasionally sagged under the weight of the relationship, then so be it.

As the quarrel blew itself out and they walked back to the hotel, Marta herself volunteered a phrase for it. *Llevamos nuestro merecido*, she whispered. They'd earned their just desserts.

Was it really as simple – and final – as that? As the orchestra surged into the fourth movement, The Walk to the Scaffold, Faraday found his feet tapping, keeping pace with the music. Joe-Junior, his own son, had fled the nest nearly a couple of years back. He was living in Caen now, with a French social worker called Valerie. The fact that he'd always been deaf made telephone conversations a non-starter but father and son still communicated by email, increasingly brief conversations that simply confirmed – at the age of twenty-three – that J-J had acquired a life of his own.

Faraday, in his private moments, was proud of the childhood and adolescence they'd shared, of the way they'd built a life together, but the boy's abrupt exit for France had left a huge hole and only Marta's flamboyant arrival had filled it. But where next? And how? Or was Faraday sentenced forever to a series of doomed relationships? First a deaf son who'd fled the nest. And now a married woman about whom, like Berlioz, he was crazy.

The symphony came to an end with a flourish from the conductor. He turned to face the audience, acknowledging the applause, then brought the orchestra to its feet. Faraday was beginning to wonder about supper, a Chinese down in Southsea perhaps or one of the new places on Gunwharf Quays. He glanced across to Marta to see which she preferred. That bloody watch again.

'I have to go.' She leaned across, kissed him, then tapped the handbag where she kept her mobile. 'Be good, darling. Ring you tomorrow.'

Faraday was parked on the seafront. The haddock and chips had been limp and greasy, and he wound down the window to get rid of the smell. At 11.15, it was far too early to check on events at Brennan's and he settled instead for late-night jazz from one of the FM channels. Beyond the blackness of the Solent, he could see the lights of Ryde on the Isle of Wight. From somewhere much closer came laughter and the sound of someone throwing up. She should be here now, Faraday thought. She should be giving me a good ticking off for the haddock and chips, for settling for rubbish. They should be tucked into the corner of some restaurant, putting the world to rights. That's what friends did, as well as lovers. *N'est-ce pas?*

Long minutes later, thoroughly depressed, he gunned the engine and headed east along the seafront. Home was the Bargemaster's House beside the water on Langstone Shore, the modest little timber and brick cottage that represented more than two decades of his life. It was a solace as well as a home, and just the thought of the curlews calling across the mudflats gave him comfort. He was duty DI for the weekend, on call should anything major come up, but he'd still treat himself to a whisky or two and maybe play a bit more Berlioz. There were worse things in life than solitude.

The Bargemaster's House lay towards the end of a quiet cul-de-sac. He pulled in towards the garage, surprised to see the lights on. Only Marta had a key. Was this another game of hers? Had she prepared another of those little surprises?

He opened the front door, knowing at once that it wasn't Marta. She always put music on, or the radio. She hated silence.

'Hello?'

Nothing. Wary now, Faraday dropped his briefcase by the door. The kitchen lay beyond the big living room. He stepped towards the open door, recognising the familiar clang of the grill pan, then stopped in his tracks. The hair was shorter and he'd lost a bit of weight, but no one else in the world buttered toast that way.

Faraday reached out, touching his son lightly on the shoulder.

'J-J,' he signed. 'What's going on?'

Chapter six

By half four in the morning, Bev Yates was beginning to have serious doubts about any kind of result on the Brennan's job. He and Paul Winter had spent the last six hours in the warehouse area behind the Retail Centre, eyeing hundreds of boxes of cordless drills, self-fit alarm systems and other DIY goodies in the confident expectation that someone would arrive to nick them.

Outside, in a series of hastily surveyed Observation Points, the rest of the team were deployed – five uniforms and one CID. Cathy Lamb, coordinating the ambush, had insisted on strict radio silence in case the opposition were using scanners, and so the night had passed in a chilly silence occasionally broken by whispered conversation. The temperature had plunged after the rain and Yates and Brennan were as frozen as the guys outside. Winter had done his best to persuade Ray Brennan to keep the heating on in the warehouse but the store boss had made some excuse or other about the timer settings. No wonder he made so much money.

Yates eased himself upright beside the pillar he'd been using as a backrest, and did another set of stretches to get some warmth back inside his body. Winter sat beside him, huddled in a big old car coat. He'd flattened some empty cardboard boxes and used them as insulation against the cold of the concrete floor, and for the second time that night Yates wondered whether he'd gone to sleep.

He reached down and gave him a shake.

'All right?'

Winter grunted something Yates didn't catch and a match flared briefly in the darkness. Winter's third cheroot of the night. Bad sign.

Yates set off for another circuit of the space around him. His eyes had long got used to the darkness and he padded silently from pallet to pallet, wondering yet again whether Winter had got this thing right.

The man had balls, he'd never doubted it, and recently he'd pulled a couple of major strokes for which Faraday – in particular – had been extremely grateful. Last year's Gunwharf job, when Winter had broken a bizarre scam to bury a body under umpteen million quids' worth of harbourside apartments, had spared the force a great deal of embarrassment, and Yates had seen a couple of the memos that had gone Winter's way. Winter being Winter, he'd probably papered half his house with photocopies, but that didn't alter the fact that the guy was an oddball, a relic, the kind of exhibit you'd put in a museum dedicated to the bad old days.

Yates himself was very nearly Winter's age. At forty-three, he'd lived through the culture changes that had dragged the CID out of the Stone Age. Not for a moment did he believe that hours at the computer and near-abstention from alcohol had made them better detectives. On the contrary, the bloody job was harder than ever and he wasn't alone in wondering whether it was even possible to make a difference any more.

But that wasn't the point. Winter, with his bent little ways, actively refused to bend the knee to the squeaky clean code of professional conduct that had become the CID bible. It was lunacy, he said, to have to spend half a day at the computer simply to register a new informer. Just like it was crazy to have to fill in a million forms to put some nutter under surveillance. The fact that a lot of this grief came from legislation – politicians rather than the management – made not the slightest bit of difference. Winter had always got results by trusting his own MO. And likewise, the fact that he broke every rule in the process didn't matter. He put the guys away quite a lot of the time, and compared to most of the blokes around him that was a very definite result.

A lot of Winter's front was bluster, of course, but that hadn't occurred to Yates until recently when he'd taken a hard look at the way the guy really operated and realised that Winter would always do the bare minimum to cover his arse. These days, you had to keep up with the form-filling because the defence brief would rip you to pieces in court if you didn't. Winter knew that, and sorted out the necessary paperwork well in advance, but he always made it very plain – and very public – that he resented every second he wasn't out there making life difficult for the scrotes who kidded themselves they were immune to law and order. These were the guys CID ought to be seizing by the throat. Otherwise, he said, they might as well call it a day and become public librarians, filing all those nice books away and worrying about the backlog of unpaid fines.

Outside, miles away, Yates heard the clatter of an early morning train. Every minute that passed made it more unlikely they'd see any action. In his experience, villains were just like everyone else. Get the job sorted as soon as possible and fuck off back to bed.

He paused by the big steel doors, peering back into the darkness. He could just make out the glow of Winter's cheroot and he wondered again about the intelligence he'd produced to stand this job up. He didn't claim to understand, or even like, Winter. The guy, most days, was a total head case. But what did deserve a bit of sympathy was what had happened to his private life. You had to feel sorry for a bloke who'd lost his wife like that, blown away by cancer after all those years of marriage. Winter had been no angel when it came to helping himself to passing crumpet, far from it, but he'd seen him and his missus together on a couple of social occasions and you could sense how much he relied on her.

Yates made his way back towards Winter, cursing as he stumbled into a forklift truck. There comes a moment in every stake-out when you cut your losses and run, and minutes later it was no surprise to hear Cathy Lamb at last breaking radio silence. It was gone five in the morning. Pretty soon, people would be going to work. No point hanging around any longer.

Winter struggled to his feet, farting noisily in the darkness. Come Monday, Yates knew there'd be the mother and father of a post-mortem. With all that overtime to pay, Hartigan would be looking for blood. Yet Winter, typically, seemed untroubled. If it wasn't tonight, it would be tomorrow, or the night after. Shame they couldn't have fun like this more often.

The radio crackled again, and Cathy came on. This time it was a message for Winter.

'I was right in the first place,' she said briefly.

'Come again?'

'You should have stuck to bloody Albufeira.'

Faraday awoke from deep sleep to the trilling of his bedside phone. His head hurt and it was still dark. He turned the light on and fumbled for his watch. Nearly seven. Cathy Lamb, he thought, with news from Brennan's.

'Sir?'

It was a male voice, the overnight duty DC. He was up at Hilsea Lines and he was looking at a body hanging from a tree. Scenes of Crime were on their way and some uniforms were already on site. As duty DI, maybe Mr Faraday should drive up.

Faraday fumbled his way to the bathroom, swallowed two ibuprofens, and did his best to ignore the wreckage in the kitchen. At God knows what hour, he'd thrown together a meal for himself and his son, and the evidence was everywhere. Why so many saucepans for spaghetti Bolognese? And how come *three* empty bottles of red?

He backed his Mondeo into the road, uncomfortably aware that he was probably still pissed. At this hour the roads should be empty but he never underestimated the vindictiveness of the guys on traffic. Most of them would give a week's salary to pull CID on a drink/drive, and a DI at the wheel would make it even sweeter.

He headed north, through the interminable miles of takeaways and charity shops, aware of the first cold fingers of dawn above the rooftops away to his right. On mornings like this, muddle-headed and slightly nauseous, Faraday would have given anything for a couple of vigorous hours' birding in the New Forest, combing Boldrewood for bramblings. The last thing he needed was another suicide.

Hilsea Lines straddled the very top of the island, a couple of miles of fortified ramparts designed to keep the French at bay. They'd gone up in the mid-nineteenth century, overlooking Portscreek, the thin, muddy strip of water that cut the city off from the mainland and served as Pompey's moat. Faraday had always rather liked the area. Overgrown and thickly wooded, it offered a home for a satisfying range of winter birds as well as the small army of predatory gay men that had turned the area into – in Cathy Lamb's phrase – a top bogging spot.

Access to Hilsea Lines took Faraday past a newish housing estate. First right, and he was in the cul-de-sac that ended in a big patch of rough ground that served as a turning circle. The road was already taped off, and Faraday pulled to a halt behind one of the SOCO vans from Cosham. On his left, in the thin grey light, were the brick bastions at the rear of the ramparts; on his right, behind a tall steel fence, a small industrial development.

A bulky figure in a white zip-up suit emerged from behind the van. To Faraday's relief, it was DS Jerry Proctor, the most senior of the Scenes of Crime team. Unlike the young Crime Scene Manager who'd made yesterday morning such a pain, Proctor had turned years of experience into a blunt, no-nonsense working style that managed to preserve every particle of forensic evidence while keeping everyone onside. He was a huge, bear-like man with a dry wit and a heavy-duty handshake, the kind of painstaking, nuts-and-bolts copper who compelled instant respect. Faraday had worked with him on countless jobs and trusted him implicitly.

It was a cold, raw morning and everything felt wet underfoot. Proctor nodded up towards the frieze of trees on top of the ramparts. The body was a young, white male. Proctor judged him to be in his early twenties. He'd been discovered by one of the locals, a guy out with his dog around half five in the morning.

'Why so early?'

'He's saying he runs a football team, bunch of young lads, decent league side. They're playing on the Isle of Wight today, eleven o'clock kick-off. Hence the early start. Moffat is checking it out.'

Moffat was the overnight duty DC. The dog-walker had phoned 999, and a uniformed patrol had hauled in Moffat.

Faraday was looking up at the top of the earth rampart. He caught glimpses of white through the trees as Proctor's team went about their business but he knew there was no point asking for a look. Already the SOCO had established an inner and outer cordon, lengths of blue and white tape dancing in the chilly wind, and no one would be allowed near the body until Proctor was happy that he'd combed every last square foot of ground within the taped area.

'So what's the strength?'

They were at the back of the van. Proctor was hunting for a clipboard and tape measure. In cases like these, it was important to establish some kind of chain of events. Men suspended themselves from ropes for all sorts of reasons. Some did it for thrills, heightening the pleasure of masturbation before loosening the knot. Others were distressed enough to do it for real and end it all.

'He's practically naked, for a start.' Proctor had found the tape measure. 'Just a thong, a woman's thong, around his crotch.'

'What about his clothes?'

'In a pile, nearby. Jeans, trainers, socks, boxers, but no top.'

Faraday nodded. Last night, while not as cold as this morning, had been pretty unpleasant – certainly chilly enough to warrant a shirt of some kind. But why the thong?

'Haven't a clue. Might be a wanker or a suicide, of course, but I'd say neither.'

'Why's that?'

'Someone had a go at him first.'

'You're sure?'

'Pretty certain. There's bruising down here . . .' He touched his own ribs on the right-hand side. 'And his face is a mess. Cuts and abrasions around the eyes. You don't get that from a rope.'

'Hands?'

'Not much. No knuckle damage that I can see. He may have been tied up.'

Faraday raised an eyebrow. No one in the SOCO's position, least of all someone as experienced as Proctor, jumped to easy conclusions. The fact that he'd pretty much excluded suicide already was immensely significant.

'Have we got a name?'

'Nothing. Nothing in his pockets, no mobile, no keys, no money even. And by the look of his Reeboks, he was dragged up the bank there. Mud all over the toes. He might have been unconscious. He might even have been dead already. Too early to tell.'

'Vehicle?'

'Has to be. But the guy with the dog walked right along this road before going up on top and says he saw bugger all first thing. The place was empty.'

'What was he doing up top? In pitch darkness?'

'He said the dog did a runner. In fact it was the dog who found the body. Barked like a bastard, he says.'

'Tyre marks?' Faraday nodded down the road towards the end.

'Everywhere, multiple patterns. This is a great shagging spot, famous for it.'

Faraday produced his mobile, realising with some relief that his headache had gone. Then he paused, looking across at Proctor.

'He'd need to jump off something . . .' he frowned '. . . wouldn't he?'

'Yeah.'

'And?'

'There's an old Schweppes crate up there, the kind you put empties in. If you upended the thing to give yourself the height, and you'd got the rope good and tight . . .' He shrugged. 'The crate's up there beneath the body, so I suppose it's possible.'

Faraday was trying to envisage the way you'd do it, with a plastic crate and a length of rope, half naked in the pouring rain. A moment's thought and it seemed even more unlikely.

'You're thinking other people?'

Proctor shot him a look. There was a protocol here, an unspoken ban on leading questions, and Faraday had just ignored it.

'Yeah,' he said at length, 'I am. And something else, too. Whoever strung him up, if he was strung up, was sending a message. Bloke looks pathetic in that thong. Just like he's meant to. Hang a notice round his neck and you couldn't make it plainer.'

Proctor gave Faraday a parting nod and excused himself. There was a ton of stuff to get through and he'd leave Faraday to have a think about calling in the Home Office pathologist. His tone of voice left no doubts about his own opinion in the matter but strictly speaking the decision belonged at headquarters level, the request routed through Willard. Either way, as both men well knew, the Detective Superintendent would expect to be in on the action from the start.

Another vehicle had just turned up. There came the slam of a car door and Faraday turned to find himself face to face with the Scenes of

Crime photographer who'd attended Helen Bassam. Two bodies in two days. He gave Faraday a brisk nod as he began to unpack his gear.

'Can't keep meeting like this, sir,' he muttered, screwing a wide-angle lens onto the body of his Canon.

Faraday walked away, following the tape as it looped in towards the rampart. At a scene like this, he knew that Proctor would be spoiled for evidence. He had the rope for a start, especially the knot. The rope might offer DNA, as well as the chance of establishing ownership, and there were now experts who could interpret all kinds of information from the way a knot was tied. The bough over which the rope had been thrown would be sawn off and the groove marks anaylsed to shed light on the exact sequence of events. Then there was the crate and the clothes to be examined for DNA traces, plus a fingertip search around the site. Proctor's team would be looking for anything that may have been dropped, as well as significant footprints. Soil and leaf samples would be invaluable if other people later came into the frame, as would bark scrapings from the tree.

Later, with more bodies at his disposal, Proctor would organise a POLSA search across a wider area while the body itself would be declared a separate scene of crime. At post-mortem, in the hands of a Home Office pathologist, detailed examination would be able to test Proctor's theory about an earlier assault while various bodily fluids would offer chemical clues to this nameless stranger's last twenty-four hours. Scenes of Crime procedures were meat and drink to detectives like Faraday and Proctor. Violent death was seldom pretty but the cool, increasingly scientific language of detection – talk of nasal flushings and low copy number, of pollen analysis and spore counts – offered some small consolation.

Faraday was halfway up the rampart, a couple of hundred metres west of the scene of crime, when he finally got through to Willard. It was still only ten past eight. The Detective Superintendent seemed to be on the loo.

'Morning, sir.'

At first Willard assumed the call was about Helen Bassam, an update on enquiries, but Faraday said there'd been nothing really solid and then explained what had happened up at Hilsea Lines. He needed a decision on calling in the Home Office pathologist and a steer on the direction the inquiry might take. Just now, by virtue of his presence on site, Faraday was Senior Investigating Officer, but he couldn't see that situation surviving very much longer. Already, from the conversation with Jerry Proctor, this would-be suicide had the makings of a major crime. Willard's team had been set up to deal with exactly these kinds of incidents and Faraday knew how Willard relished the challenges of ambuiguity. The guy might or might not have gone for the ultimate wank and got it wrong. He might or might not have topped himself. If not, then who killed him? And why did they go to such lengths to dress it up as something else?

'A thong, you say?'

'Yes, sir.'

'And no idea who he might be?'

'None at all.'

'Excellent.' Faraday could hear the cistern emptying. 'Give me half an hour.'

It was Cathy Lamb who roused Winter. By half nine, he'd been asleep just over three hours. Was sleep deprivation part of the job now? Weren't there Health and Safety rules about this kind of thing?

'You're lucky to get any kip at all. The Custody Officer at Central was on at half seven.'

'Why's that?'

'Hartigan had just phoned him about the Brennan's job. Wanted to know how many bodies we'd locked up.'

'And?'

'The Custody Officer told him none. Hartigan wasn't best pleased, as you might imagine. Apparently he thinks you've been taking the piss.'

Winter struggled upright in bed. This conversation was beginning to upset him.

'What the fuck does he expect?' he grunted. 'When he goes fishing, does he ask the bloody trout for a schedule?'

'Hartigan doesn't go fishing. He goes to the supermarket like anyone else would. It's means and ends, Paul. He put in the means and we came up with fuck all.'

'That's because they chose not to turn up.'

'Brilliant. It's going to be a short conversation then.'

'What do you mean?'

'When he holds the post-mortem.' She began to laugh. 'Don't you wish you were in Portugal?'

At Willard's insistence, he and Faraday returned to the top of the ramparts, careful to stay outside Proctor's jealously guarded inner cordon. On Faraday's advice, Willard had turned up with a pair of wellington boots. They were blue, with yellow tops, and they sat oddly with his sleek grey pinstriped three-piece suit.

A muddy path ran along the top of the ramparts, much used by walkers and kids on mountain bikes, and Willard and Faraday had a good view of the crime scene from a distance of perhaps twenty metres. The tree, a gnarled old oak, lay in a bowl immediately below the path. The bowl was full of sodden leaf mould and the near-naked body hung on a tatty old length of what looked like nylon rope, strung from an overhanging bough.

The photographer had finished with his first set of pictures and was checking the digital images while Jerry Proctor taped plastic bags over the hands, feet and head of the corpse. From a distance, this pitiful figure could have been even younger than early twenties and Faraday saw at once what Proctor had meant by 'humiliation'. He was thin to the point of emaciation. Blood had pooled in the lower half of his body, giving it a reddish tinge, while his face, a bluish purple, was twisted at an angle to his torso as if he was still trying to slip the noose. His long, thin arms hung stiff with rigor mortis and even from twenty metres the bruising around his ribs was plainly visible. The thong was scarlet, fringed with lace around the top, and barely covered his groin.

Willard studied him for a long moment as Proctor, with the help of two colleagues, prepared to cut the rope above his head. Lowered to the ground, he would be photographed again before the waiting plastic sheet was wrapped around his body. Parcelled with gaffer tape at both ends, the corpse would then be shipped to the morgue at St Mary's Hospital to await the afternoon's post-mortem. Willard, after the briefest call to the Head of CID at headquarters, had OK'd a Home Office pathologist. Proctor had made the necessary arrangements and expected the PM to start around three.

'Mispers?' Willard muttered.

Faraday was watching the line of uniformed PCs combing the road below them. They advanced in a line, step by careful step, like slow-motion guardsmen on parade.

'Nothing that fits.'

Willard was looking beyond the cluster of figures beneath the tree. The ramparts fell away steeply towards the road.

'It wouldn't have been easy, dragging matey up here.' He paused. 'If that's what happened.'

'No, sir.'

'Any ideas on time?'

Faraday shook his head. Rigor set in four hours or so after death. The body had been discovered at half five and Scenes of Crime had confirmed rigor at around seven. That put the time of death at three at the latest. Willard was already busy figuring out various scenarios. Friday nights, for one thing, were indivisible from violence.

'Bunch of guys on the piss? Things get out of hand?' He glanced across at Faraday. 'Would you buy that?'

'What about the thong?'

'Practical joke? Some kind of celebration that goes pear-shaped?'

'Unlikely.'

'I agree. What else then?'

Faraday didn't answer. Speculation at this point was, in his view, a waste of time. The stiff little parcel inside the double-wrapped plastic could have come from anywhere. It didn't have to be Portsmouth. It could be Southampton, Brighton, London even. The shortest cut to any kind of lead would be a firm ID and, until that happened, all bets were off. Rule one in situations like these was very simple: investigate every death as if it was a murder until you can prove otherwise.

'We've started the house-to-house, sir.' He nodded towards the nearby housing estate. 'It was pissing down last night and this is a respectable area so I shouldn't hold your breath but you never know, someone might have seen a vehicle.'

'Go to bed early, do they?'

'So the beat man says.'

Willard was watching the men from the undertaker's standing in a huddle beyond the tape, waiting for the body to be delivered by the SOCO team. Their van was parked beside them, the rear doors open, and Faraday let the image settle in his brain. Not paradise, he thought, or even hell. But the back of an S-reg Transit, smelling faintly of bleach.

'It was a no-no last night,' Faraday said.

'Where?'

'At Brennan's. We had eight bodies there, booted and spurred, but no one turned up.'

'And Hartigan?'

'Gone ballistic, according to Cathy. He's holding a post-mortem first thing Monday. Major grief for Mr Winter.'

Mention of Winter's name brought a glint of interest to Willard's eyes. Like anyone with a stake in the CID's reputation, he had definite views on Winter's more reckless adventures, but reputation wasn't necessarily the same as performance and he had a softish spot for certain aspects of old-style detection. The problem with people like Winter was reining them in. Off the leash, they could do you serious damage.

'Someone told me he had leave booked.'

'He did. He was going to Portugal. He called it off.'

'Why?'

'God knows. Cathy Lamb thinks he can't do without the job.'

'Really?'

Willard let the question hang in the air, taking Faraday by the elbow and walking him away from the activity below. He was declaring the investigation a major inquiry. He'd be running it personally from the Major Crimes suite at Fratton and hoped to have a squad together by nightfall. He'd be getting onto Operational Support at headquarters and pushing for at least ten bodies, DCs abstracted from CID offices across the Eastern Area. It was very early days but the inquiry already had the feeling of something more complex than usual, and if the right kind of progress warranted it, you could bet your life he'd be back on the phone, banging the drum for more resources.

Faraday permitted himself the faintest smile. Willard had arrived from the Met with a reputation for impatience as well as painstaking detective work. At his level ambition came with the grade, something you'd take for granted, but it had never ceased to amuse Faraday the way that youngish guys on the move like Willard always associated career advancement with resources. Lay hands on a decent-sized squad, extend your reach into every pocket of the city, and you'd already made the kind of statement that would find its way into every CID office across the county. That's the way reputations were made. By fielding a bigger army than the next guy.

They'd paused in a clearing with a view north through the trees. Away to the west Faraday could see clouds of gulls over the landfill site beside the motorway, while there were a couple of brownish specks pecking at the mud beside the nearby creek. Dunlin, Faraday thought, or maybe redshanks. Beyond the creek, on the mainland, more fortifications topped the fold of chalk that was Portsdown Hill. If you were looking for evidence that Portsmouth was an island within an island, a little bubble of its own suspended in place and time, then here it was. Geography and the long saga of imperial conquest had created this extraordinary place and Faraday had long come to the conclusion that there was nowhere else remotely like it. Did Willard understand that? With his Met background and his canny, painstaking, impatient ways? Did anyone?

Willard was checking his watch. Time was marching on. He had a million things to attend to. Together the two men scrambled down from the ramparts and Faraday realised that this was the moment of handover, the moment when leadership of the inquiry passed to Willard. Willard, who could read a face better than most, was watching a couple of white-suited Scenes of Crime officers carrying the body away on a stretcher. Sensibly, they'd decided to use a longer route that led along the top of the ramparts rather than risk the slope.

As the impromptu cortège disappeared behind a line of trees, Faraday felt Willard's hand on his arm. He was smiling, an expression he reserved for special occasions.

'I'll be SIO but one of my DIs will be at the sharp end.' He gave

Faraday's arm a little squeeze. 'Could be you in a couple of months, eh, Joe?'

Chapter seven

The sun was out by the time Faraday got back home from Hilsea Lines. He stepped into the garden and circled the house, feeling the sodden turf squish-squishing beneath his feet, and then stood by the rusting iron gate beyond the front lawn that opened onto the path beside the harbour. The low winter light lanced off the water, throwing the little flotilla of moored boats into dramatic silhouette, and he watched a turnstone for a moment or two, entranced by the way it was relentlessly drawn to shreds of bladderwrack or a cluster of pebbles. He must have seen this little drama a thousand times, often from this very same spot, but this bright, cold, suddenly glorious morning seemed to gift-wrap everything, offering the possibility of an early spring. There was even a little warmth in the sun, and Faraday tilted his face and closed his eyes, wondering vaguely about breakfast.

Inside the house, J-J was still in bed, his long body humped under the duvet. The duvet was on the small side and Faraday gazed at his son's huge feet poking out of the bottom. He'd offered few clues last night about the reason for this sudden visit but already Faraday had the feeling that he might be staying a while. His enormous rucksack had been stuffed to bursting point and there was a big cardboard box as well, secured with string.

Back downstairs, Faraday took a kitchen knife to the box, cutting the string. He'd been in these situations before, playing mum, and it was no surprise to find the box full of dirty laundry: socks, shirts, underwear, towels. J-J must have left in a hurry because the stuff was just thrown in but then, at the bottom, he found an envelope with his son's name on it. The envelope was blue and there was a little seagull shape on one corner. Faraday lifted the envelope to his nose. It smelled of perfume, a hint of lemons that took him straight back to last summer when J-J had arrived to celebrate Faraday's birthday, with Valerie in tow. He could see her now, perched in a stool in the kitchen, nursing a glass of pastis. He propped the envelope on the mantelpiece and gathered up the laundry before heading for the washing machine. She must have packed the box herself, he thought, wondering why J-J had to cart his laundry across the Channel to get it washed.

J-J descended about an hour later, appearing at the kitchen door in jeans and an old T-shirt. He looked terrible – unshaven, red-eyed – and stumbled around trying to find the kettle, sparing Faraday barely a glance. In the end it was Faraday who made the tea, settling his son in a chair at the long table and getting no response when he signed a query about breakfast. He might have been blind as well as deaf, Faraday thought, glancing at his watch. As duty DI, he had to be available for call-out all weekend. Bad news normally went in threes and he'd begun to wonder who'd be next for the heavy-duty plastic and the roll of gaffer tape.

Over breakfast he tried to get some sense out of J-J. In the literal meaning of the word, the boy had always been quiet. He used his hands rather than his voice to communicate. But he had tremendous energy as well as a burning curiosity, and in most moods he could fill any room with wild flurries of sign. It had always fascinated Faraday to watch how quickly non-signers could grasp the essence of what J-J had to say but this morning that vivid, bright-eyed determination to get his message across seemed to have deserted him. Faraday enquired about life in Caen, about Valerie, even about his plans for the coming day, but all J-J could muster in reply was a shrug. Normally ravenous, he picked at his scrambled eggs and curls of bacon before pushing the plate away and leaving the kitchen without a backward glance. Already, it was like sharing the house with a stranger.

Faraday was in the garden, pegging out J-J's washing, when Marta arrived. He recognised the growl of her Alfa and turned to find her at the back gate. Lace-up boots, a long woollen skirt and a cashmere scarf draped over an exquisite brown leather jacket normally signalled an out-of-town expedition, Chichester perhaps or even Brighton. They'd have lunch together and spend the afternoon drifting from shop to shop. Quite how she managed to make the time without upsetting her domestic routine baffled Faraday but he'd long given up asking. Marta, he'd decided, was the rarest of creatures – quite beyond classification – and the last thing he wanted to do was frighten her off.

He led her inside, reminding her about call-out. Much as he fancied a day away from Pompey, he was bound hand and foot by his mobile. Plus, of course, there was J-J.

The boy was sprawled on the long sofa that faced the big floor-to-ceiling double glass doors in the lounge. Marta pounced on him at once, giving him big wet kisses on both cheeks. Back last June, they'd made friends in seconds and, days later, drunk at the ferry port, J-J had told his dad just what a brilliant mate he'd found. She was funny and kind. She laughed a lot and made Faraday laugh with her. How many other people had ever done that?

Now, though, even Marta seemed unable to drag J-J out of his misery. She did her best to chivvy him along, using Faraday as the go-between when she suggested that J-J accompany her to Arundel in his father's place, but the boy could barely manage a smile in reply. Faraday blamed it on last night – he'd found a fourth empty bottle in the waste bin under the sink – and assured Marta he'd be back to normal by the afternoon, but already he'd begun to wonder whether his optimism was misplaced. There was a darkness about J-J that he'd never seen before, a brooding, introspective gloom as uncharacteristic as his reluctance to get to his feet when Marta announced her departure.

Out in the sunshine again, she toyed with her car keys beside the gleaming Alfa.

'Something's happened,' she said. 'Poor boy.'

Faraday agreed. He was on call-out all weekend but she was welcome to come over tomorrow and take a chance on Sunday lunch. She looked at him a moment, weighing the invitation, then shook her head. He should spend some time with his son, try and get to the bottom of whatever was wrong. She'd give him a ring next week to see how things were going.

'No chance of a meet?'

She put a gloved hand on his arm.

'I'm really busy, darling. Take care of your boy.'

The hand found his face and she kissed him on the cheek. Seconds later, she was smiling up at him through the car window before starting the engine and selecting reverse. Faraday stood by his garage, watching her accelerate away towards the main road. For once, she didn't look back or even wave.

The sofa was empty when Faraday returned to the lounge and it took him a moment or two to realise that the blue envelope on the mantelpiece had also gone. The kitchen was empty. He stood in the open doorway, wondering whether or not to go upstairs, decided against it, then changed his mind.

J-J's bedroom door was closed. The door beside it led to Faraday's study. Faraday opened it and slipped inside. Bookshelves lined three walls, rows and rows of birding magazines, maps, travel books and a complete nine-volume set of *Birds of the Western Palearctic*. A leather-bound swivel chair sat in the big picture window and there were a pair of 20 × 60 coastguard binoculars mounted on a pedestal screwed to the wooden floor.

The binos were a recent acquisition, a present from Marta to mark a particularly lovely weekend they'd managed to steal in Lyme Regis. She'd bought them on impulse from a specialist outdoor pursuits shop in Bridport, fired by the expression on Faraday's face when he spotted them through the window, and Faraday could never use them without thinking of how incredibly spontaneous she could be, parting with the best part of a thousand quid on the evidence of a big, big grin. He reached for them now, sinking into the leather chair. Way out in the harbour, a small raft of black-necked grebes. Closer in, his wings outspread in the wind, a lone cormorant perched on a buoy. Faraday sharpened the focus, marvelling again at the purity of the optics, waiting for the moment the cormorant folded those prehistoric wings, gave himself a little shake, and took flight. But the moment never came because the door opened behind him, the door that led directly into J-J's bedroom, and he looked up to find himself face to face with his son.

The outstretched hand was holding a letter. Same colour paper. Blue. Faraday took it, aware of J-J returning to his bedroom. He pulled the door closed behind him and Faraday heard the sigh of bed springs followed by silence.

The letter was in French and covered both sides of the paper. Valerie wanted to say that she was sorry. She'd never meant J-J to find out the way he did. She was going to tell him but she couldn't find the words. They'd had a great time together. In lots of ways she still loved him. She wanted him to know this, to understand it. But there was no way forward now, not when something like this had happened. Maybe they could still be friends. Maybe, next time she came to England, they could meet for a drink and a chat. He might feel better about things then, less angry. For now, though, she could only say sorry and hope and pray that he believed her. She'd never wanted it to end like this. Not in a million years.

Faraday read the letter again and then stared out at the harbour. The bright expanse of water was shadowed with cloud and when he checked on the buoy, the cormorant had gone. At length, he got to his feet and went to J-J's door. He paused for a second before knocking and then pushed it open. His son was lying face down on the bed. After a while he rolled over, staring up at his father.

Faraday still had the letter.

'What happened?' he signed.

J-J looked away for a moment, then wiped his nose on the back of his hand.

'She was doing it with someone else. In our bed.'

'How do you know?'

'I walked in. And saw them.'

Winter was at home, contemplating his line of first defence, when the phone rang. He'd have to sort out some proper checks on the names he'd got from Ray Brennan. He'd have to give his tree a bit of a shake and see what fell out. That would take a couple of days at least, enough time to stall Hartigan before he banished Winter to lost property and traffic cones.

He finally got to the phone. It was a DI he knew called Sammy Rollins, one of the blokes on Willard's Major Crimes outfit.

'There's a job on. We're putting together a squad.'

Briefly he explained about the body at Hilsea Lines. Boss had declared a Major Crimes inquiry and Winter's name was on the first list of abstractions. He understood Winter had pulled out of planned leave.

'Correct.'

'So that's a yes? You're available?'

Winter was examining his nails. There were ways to play these scenes. Never make it simple. Never reveal anything, least of all enthusiasm.

'There's going to be a problem on Monday,' he began, 'with my guvnor.'

'Hartigan?'

'That's right.'

'Sorted. Boss wants you down here PDQ. Squad briefing at 14.20. OK?'

Winter shifted his gaze to the TV. National Hunt racing from Uttoxeter. He couldn't believe his luck.

'14.20 sounds sweet to me.' He chuckled. 'Lots of overtime, I hope.'

Despite Faraday's best efforts, J-J didn't want sympathy. Instead, he pulled on an old sweater, wrapped a scarf round his neck and headed for the door. What hurt him most, he'd told Faraday, was the deceit and the betrayal. They'd been together for more than a year. He'd trusted her completely. They'd even discussed having a baby together. And yet there she was, screwing a mutual friend called Henri, right in front of his nose. Not just then. Not just when he happened to come back early and wander into the bedroom. But for weeks, maybe even months, before. How could people do that? How could people behave that way? Two-timing their partners?

J-J had left him with the challenge, savagely delivered, hands spread wide, before disappearing down the harbourside path towards the distant smudge of the Farlington bird reserve. Good question, Faraday had thought, watching him go.

Now, early afternoon, the phone was ringing. Faraday answered the call, expecting another summons. Given the last half-hour, a third session with the Scenes of Crime lads would be a positive relief.

'Mr Faraday?' It was a male voice he didn't recognise, middle class, well spoken, sure of itself. 'My name's Bassam, Derek Bassam. I had a daughter called Helen. Do you have a moment?'

Faraday stared at the phone. He was ex-directory. He wanted to know how Bassam had got his number.

'I'm a lawyer, Mr Faraday. I have contacts.'

'Police contacts?'

'Of course. But I apologise for the intrusion. Under any other circumstances, I wouldn't have dreamed of calling you like this.' He paused, then wondered whether Faraday had time for a meeting. There were one or two issues that might need clarifying. He'd be truly grateful for the chance to do so. 'And as I understand it you are on call-out, after all.'

Faraday felt the first stirrings of anger. There were rules here, tacitly accepted, things you should and shouldn't do, but this man had simply ignored them. Just who had Bassam been talking to?

'I'm busy just now,' Faraday said briskly. 'You can go to any police station if it's urgent or call me at Southsea on Monday.'

'Monday's awkward, I'm afraid. I'm back in London. If you could spare me the time now, I'd be more than grateful. It needn't take long. I'm parked outside.'

'*Outside?*'

Faraday resisted the urge to check through the window. Having his phone number passed on to a stranger was one thing; confiding an officer's address was a hanging offence.

'Who told you where I live?'

Bassam wouldn't say. Fifteen minutes tops. Then he'd be away again. Faraday checked his watch. Just gone two.

'Meet me at Southsea police station at three,' he said. 'We'll discuss this further.'

Winter arrived with seconds to spare for the briefing at Fratton. The Major Crimes suite occupied an entire floor at the back of the police station, two rows of offices with a central corridor between. The largest office lay at one end and served as the Major Incident Room. The MIR was equipped with enough desks and computers to handle the ever-changing demands of a complex inquiry. Other offices further up the corridor were being readied for the intelligence and forensic teams.

Like most detectives, Winter loved the feeling of specialness that came with a posting like this. For once in your life you were free to concentrate on decent crime. No more bimbling around after scrotes nicking bicycles. No more fruitless hours nailing down some twelve-year-old vandal with a taste for keying new motors. No, this was the real thing. Get the chemistry right – the right faces, the right crack – stir in a helping of murder or rape, and you'd be pushed to find a happier way of filling your time. Add the fact that it could be incredibly lucrative – dozens of hours of overtime – and you were in piggy heaven.

Willard launched the briefing with an account of events on Hilsea Lines. The bloke who'd discovered the body had now been eliminated from enquiries – his story checked out – but the house-to-house enquiries were still ongoing. No one, to date, had seen anything suspicious or unusual in the way of vehicles below the ramparts, but then it was a piss-awful night and anyone with any sense was tucked up indoors. The SOC team was still combing the area around the body but Jerry Proctor anticipated releasing the scene by nightfall. The POLSA search was complete and all waste bins in the area had been emptied and sieved. Once again, nothing. Not even a name.

There was a stir around the room. To detectives with serious experience, this was looking very promising indeed. To find a body without a shred of ID on it was itself an indication of foul play.

Willard was introducing his core staff. One of the regular DSs on Major Crimes would be in charge of outside enquiries, tasking the two-man teams of DCs. These individual 'actions' would be sourced from the other DS, who would serve as Statement Reader as well as Receiver, combing incoming testimony for the beginnings of a pattern that might flag pathways forward. This constant, self-renewing circle of seek-and-find would generate huge amounts of data, inputted into the HOLMES computer program by a couple of keyboard operators. In theory, the system had fine-tuned years of investigative experience nationwide but Winter, for one, knew run quickly it could run out of control. HOLMES was a monster. The more you fed it, the hungrier it became.

Willard, of course, had known this from the off. So far, headquarters had coughed up ten DCs but he left his little squad in no doubt that he'd be banging on Operational Support's door for extra resources if circumstances demanded more bodies. These were early days, he kept saying, and priority number one was a solid ID. The Misper list was a non-starter but detectives all over the city were working their informers for rumours about some major ruck. Had anyone gone missing? Might

78

the death at Hilsea be drugs related? In the meantime, a separate line of enquiry was examining the log recording Friday night's stop-checks. Had the traffic cars pulled anyone suspicious? Filed a report that might link with our friend up there on the ramparts, dangling in the rain?

Within days if not hours, Willard said he was confident of establishing a positive ID. The post-mortem was due to start any time now and with luck they'd get a result from fingerprints if the guy had a criminal record. Failing that, if they were really pushed, there'd be dental records or a tip from some punter following a media appeal through TV, radio and the local paper. One way or another, they'd come up with a name and then the serious work would begin.

He looked round at the watching faces. Most of these guys he'd met before, detectives who'd passed through the MIR on previous jobs, and he wanted them to know they had his confidence. He expected them to work bloody hard, to think on their feet and to understand that nothing mattered more than a solid result. There was nothing certain yet. It might even turn out to be some bizarre twist on suicide. But there were already indications that they were dealing with murder, and if that was the case then everything, but *everything*, had to be nailed down in black and white. Think evidence, he said. Think court.

There was a pause while he glanced towards his deputy, Sammy Rollins, the DI who'd phoned Winter earlier.

'What are we calling this, sir?'

Every operation had a codename, the label that would attach itself to a thousand computer files. They were drawn from a list held at headquarters.

'*Bisley*,' Willard grunted. 'Operation *Bisley*.'

Minutes later, Winter bumped into the DC he'd been paired with for initial enquiries. He was a tall lad in his early twenties. His name was Gary Sullivan and he'd just driven down from Petersfield. He had bitten nails, an uncertain smile, a mop of curly red hair and a tie with a fuzzy pattern that Winter put down to bad taste.

They were standing in the cubbyhole at the end of the corridor that served as a kitchen. Winter spooned Nescafé into two mugs and asked how long he'd been out of uniform.

'Three months,' he said, 'next Monday.'

Winter's spoon wavered a moment, before plunging into the sugar bowl.

'Excellent,' he murmured.

Faraday was forty minutes late for his meeting with Derek Bassam at

Southsea police station. He parked his Mondeo in the yard at the back and checked with the desk clerk that Bassam was still there.

'He's out the front, sir. Been through *Frontline* twice.'

Frontline was the force newspaper, free to the public at every police station, a digest of cheerful faces, award ceremonies and upbeat articles on high-tech policing. Read *Frontline*, as Bassam had obviously done, and you'd start believing that the police had it cracked.

Faraday pushed through the double doors to the waiting area by the front entrance. Derek Bassam was a large, solid-looking man in his late forties. He was wearing an open-necked shirt under a battered leather jacket. His greying hair was cropped fashionably short and he had the kind of tan that can only come from an expensive mid-winter break. Dressed like this, Faraday would have put him down as a successful car dealer or full-time yachtie, not a lawyer at all.

He got to his feet. Faraday ignored the proffered handshake, holding the door open and directing Bassam down the corridor to the right. The interview room was a bleak, oblong space that had once served as a stationery store. There was a single desk, four chairs and a 'Be Aware' poster on the wall. The poster urged householders to secure their doors and windows against casual intruders and Faraday wondered whether to point it out to Bassam. Instead, he asked him to take a seat.

'So who gave you my details?'

Bassam began to bluster about mutual friends.

'We have no mutual friends, Mr Bassam. And I'd be grateful if you could answer the question.'

Bassam stared at him. Good living was beginning to cushion his chin, and his face, close to, was mapped with tiny broken blood vessels.

'I've come here to talk about my daughter—' He began.

'Nothing happens until you give me a name, Mr Bassam. Then we can talk about whatever you like.'

'OK.' He shrugged. 'You know Pete Lamb?'

'Yes.'

Bassam held his gaze, unprepared to go any further, and Faraday found himself wondering why he wasn't surprised that this breach of faith should be down to Lamb. When push came to shove, Cathy's errant husband was reckless enough to trade anything for a favour, and life as a private investigator obviously relied on getting professional men like Bassam onside. Later, at a time of his own choosing, Faraday would sort the matter out, but the last thing he intended to do now was give Bassam the satisfaction of taking this part of the conversation any further.

'So how can I help you, Mr Bassam?' Faraday slipped into the chair opposite.

Bassam leaned forward, confidential, man to man.

'It's about Helen. As you might imagine, it hasn't been the easiest twenty-four hours but there are one or two points of detail that it might be worth discussing.' He paused. 'You'll know that her mother and I are divorcing?'

'Yes.'

'Well . . .'

He eased the chair back from the table and then propped his elbows on his knees. With his body bent and his head bowed, it was an almost supplicatory pose. He wanted to be frank about one or two things. He wanted Faraday to understand.

'Understand what, Mr Bassam?'

'That my wife, my ex-wife, hasn't taken any of this well. In fact she's had a kind of breakdown. The marriage going wrong, me leaving, she simply hasn't been able to cope.' He looked up at last, seeking eye contact. 'I'm not blaming her, Mr Faraday. It's nothing like that. I'm simply trying to explain why Helen went off the rails. In some ways, I suspect it was inevitable.'

Faraday heard the first faint trill from the alarm system hard-wired into his head. Off the rails? Helen? It was his turn to lean forward.

'What are you telling me, Mr Bassam?'

'You won't know about the shoplifting but I'm starting to think it doesn't end there.'

'Your daughter was shoplifting?'

'I'm afraid so. This was recently, just a couple of weeks ago. It was one of those boutique places in Southsea. Helen had the sense to get a phone call through to me before the store owner called you lot and I managed to talk her out of pressing charges. Nice woman. Blonde.'

Faraday began to relax. He'd checked the automatic crime recording system for any entries on the girl but it wasn't unknown for data to go astray. The fact that Jane Bassam hadn't volunteered any of this wasn't her fault. Under the circumstances, she'd probably been too shocked to even remember it.

'You mentioned other stuff . . .'

'I did. Helen had obviously been shoplifting before. She as good as admitted it to me afterwards. Clothes, of course, but make-up as well, stuff from Boots. Apparently all the kids do it. To be frank, I don't think they understand about money any more.'

'But you were giving her an allowance, weren't you? A generous allowance.'

'That's just it. I was. £160, first Monday of every month.'

'So where did all that go?'

'Good question. She wouldn't tell me. I pressed her, believe me I pressed her, but she hasn't been easy to handle recently.' He studied his hands for a moment. 'You'd have ideas, wouldn't you, getting through money like that?'

He glanced up, challenging Faraday with the ghost of a smile, but Faraday stared him out. This was a fishing expedition, he told himself. This man, as slippery as any experienced lawyer, wanted to find out exactly how much Faraday – as SIO – really knew about his precious daughter. That way he might be able to limit the damage. And that way, more to the point, he might be able to address his own guilt. Girls especially needed their dads. A house without a father was a standing invitation, in Bassam's own phrase, to go off the rails.

'You think she was using drugs?'

'I'm afraid it's more than possible.'

'What kind of drugs?'

'I don't know. My poison comes in a bottle. What do kids use these days? Ecstasy? Cocaine? Heroin? I haven't a clue.'

'Did you see her regularly?'

'Not as regularly as I should.'

'Was there some kind of arrangement?'

'To begin with, yes. But my partner and Helen . . .' He shrugged, making it plain where his real loyalties lay. The girl would have seen this, Faraday thought. She'd have seen her dad's awkwardness, his reluctance to risk this new relationship of his, and she'd have drawn her own conclusions about where to head next. Why that journey should have ended on top of a block of flats in Somerstown was anybody's guess but there were parts of Helen Bassam's story that were at last beginning to slip into focus.

'Tell me . . .' Faraday began. 'Did she ever mention a lad called Doodie?'

Bassam thought hard about the name, then shook his head.

'Not to me. She was out and about with some pretty strange people, that was another worry, but I can't recall—'

'What kind of strange people?'

'Kids mainly, kids her own age, but losers, you know? The kind of kids who bunk off school. The kind of kids who hang around Commercial Road all evening, just looking for trouble. There were a couple of lads she used to talk about, and then there was a girl called Trudy. I don't think Trudy had been to school for months.'

'Neither had Helen. Not regularly.'

'No.' He nodded, sombre. 'So I understand. Have you talked to Trudy at all? About Helen?'

'No, Mr Bassam, we haven't.'

'I see.'

There was a long silence. Then Faraday enquired about the Afghan. Had Helen ever mentioned a man called Niamat Tabibi?

'No, but her mother did. I gather there was some kind of private tutor deal to begin with but she became almost manic about him. Believe me, he got it in the neck for everything.'

'And you never mentioned any of this to Helen?'

'Of course I did, but she just refused to talk about him so I never formed a judgement either way. He may have been important to her, he may not. She'd just clam up. She was good at that, Helen. In fact she was world class.'

Faraday produced a pocketbook and scribbled himself a note, remembering Dawn Ellis's take on this strange relationship. In her view, the Afghan had become a kind of substitute father. No wonder Helen Bassam hadn't tainted him with exposure to the real thing.

Bassam was talking about his daughter again, about the many ways he'd let her down, about the amends it was too late to make. If he'd known then what he knew now, he'd have made some very different decisions in his life. He'd have stayed in his marriage. He'd have made it work.

Faraday let the little speech wash over him. He'd disliked this man from the moment he'd answered the phone. He resented the way Bassam had tracked him down, and he resented most of all having to listen to all this confessional drivel. If Derek Bassam had a real problem dealing with his own guilt then there was professional help available. He was a wealthy man. He could could buy himself a session or two of counselling. God knows, he could even try the church. Detectives were there to solve crimes, not offer forgiveness.

'Is there anything else you want to tell me about Helen?'

'No, that's pretty much it really. I just thought, you know . . .' He looked at his hands again and then shrugged helplessly. 'This isn't something you'd wish on anyone.'

'I'm sure it isn't, Mr Bassam. The post-mortem's on Monday. It may well be that we'll have more information after that. If so, I'll give you a ring.'

Faraday got to his feet, pocketing his pen. Bassam had produced a card: *Gillespie, Bassam and Cooper. 91 Hampshire Terrace.* He gave it to Faraday.

'Do you have any children, Mr Faraday?'

Faraday studied him a moment. Strictly speaking, it was none of

Bassam's business but for once he was prepared to give him the benefit of the doubt.

'I have, Mr Bassam. A son. Twenty-three.'

'No problems?'

'None at all.' He offered Bassam a chilly smile. 'Lovely boy.'

Chapter eight

By seven o'clock, they had a name for the occupant of drawer 17 in the bank of tall fridges at the St Mary's Hospital mortuary. The Home Office pathologist had taken prints from all ten fingers. The prints had gone straight to the force fingerprint department at Netley for checks against the newly installed NAAFIS system, software programmed with prints from every individual with a criminal record, and within hours they were looking at a result.

Winter got the name on his mobile from a clerk in the incident room. To his intense disappointment, he'd never heard of him.

'Bradley Finch?' he said blankly.

'Yeah. DOB 11.3.80. He's got previous for burglary and possession with intent to supply. LKA Leigh Park.'

Winter scribbled down Finch's last known address. Leigh Park was a huge post-war housing development on the other side of Portsdown Hill. He and Sullivan were already on the edges of the estate, trying to tap up an old contact, so the redeployment came as no surprise.

The call had been transferred. Winter recognised the flat Essex vowels of Dave Michaels, the DS acting as Receiver and Statement Reader in the Major Incident Room. His job was to get inside Willard's head, sieving every incoming document as the mountain of intelligence got higher and higher.

Now he was talking about Bradley Finch: 'It's the family address, as far as we know, his mum and dad's place. We got it off prison records. The ID's kosher so take it easy, eh? A recent picture would help, if they've got one.'

The phone went dead. 'Easy' meant that Winter and Sullivan were charged with breaking the bad news. A Family Liaison Officer would doubtless be along later but just now the priority was Bradley Finch.

What kind of son was he? Who did he run with? Where had he been these last few days?

Winter could hear the football results from a very loud television in the front room when he rapped on the door. The house was brick-built, with a sagging porch and paving slabs where the front garden should be. There was an ancient caravan parked outside but both tyres were flat and someone had taken a screwdriver to the big window at the back.

'Yeah?'

The figure at the door was in his fifties, thin and stooped with lank, greying hair. Winter offered his warrant card. He wanted a word or two about a lad called Bradley Finch.

'What's he done now?'

Winter ignored the question. He was looking down the narrow little hall. The television was even louder with the door open and he could see a fat woman in a voluminous tracksuit bent over the sink in the kitchen. Watford 2 Portsmouth 2. Some small crumb of comfort before the news got abruptly worse.

With some reluctance, the man at the door stepped aside and Winter heard Sullivan establishing his name. Terry Naylor. Bradley's stepdad.

'In here, Mr Naylor?'

Without waiting for an answer, Winter pushed into the front room. The gas fire was on full blast and the sharp bite of roll-ups was overwhelming. Even the ceiling looked yellow.

The woman from the kitchen joined them. She was drying her hands on a tea towel and she stood by the door, weary, apprehensive. More trouble.

'Mrs Naylor?'

She nodded. Winter was looking pointedly at the TV but nothing happened. At length, he turned it off himself.

'I'm afraid I've got some bad news . . .' he began '. . . about your boy.'

Winter told them about Bradley, sparing them one or two of the more intimate details. He was brief, factual and offered them his sympathies. These were violent times and it was terrible that stuff like this had to happen, but life could be tough sometimes and it was his job to try and get to the bottom of it all. When Sullivan began to make a little speech of his own, confirming how sorry they were, Winter shut him up with a single glance.

Mrs Naylor had collapsed in the armchair by the door. Her husband remained rooted to the square of coconut matting beside the TV. The space between them spoke volumes.

Winter wanted to know whether young Bradley had been depressed lately. Naylor stirred.

'You're telling me he topped himself?'

'We don't know, Mr Naylor.'

'Never. He'd never do that. Would he, Marge?'

The dumpy figure spilling out of the armchair didn't venture an opinion, just sat there staring into space. Sullivan couldn't take his eyes off her. This was terrible, he thought. The heat. The smell. The oppressive silence.

'When did you last see him, Mr Naylor?' It was Winter again.

'Dunno. Before Christmas? Must have been.'

'Doesn't pop round at all?'

'Brad? Never. He's just not like that, never has been. All over the place, Brad. Real gypsy. Eh, Marge? Go on, tell 'em.'

Winter began to sense the picture here. Bradley was Marge's boy. By the look of the rosary beads draped over the framed Sacred Heart picture over the mantelpiece, there was probably a small tribe of them. Then Naylor had stepped into her life and now he wanted nothing to do with the baggage she trailed behind her. He'd probably been banging on about the boy Bradley for years.

'Mrs Naylor?' Winter could charm for England when he felt the need.

'Yeah?' She was looking up at him, eyes shiny with tears.

'Tell me a bit about him. What kind of nipper was he?'

She thought about the question, then sniffed and wiped her nose on the tea towel. He was a good boy really, just never got it together. He'd met the wrong people, too. He was soft in the head that way, easily led.

'What kind of people?'

'Horrible people. People in all kinds of trouble. People who didn't care. People who'd . . . you know . . . lead him on.'

'Is this as a kid?'

'Yeah, then too. He always chose the wrong friends. That's why he did so bad at school. Couldn't handle it. Couldn't handle anything.'

'He's been away, hasn't he?'

'What do you mean?'

'Inside. Prison.'

'Yeah.' She nodded. 'He has.'

'Why's that, then?'

'Drugs. He got involved with drugs. I always told him. I knew. You could tell, but he never listened.'

'What sort of drugs?'

'Them tablets. Don't ask me.'

'But he was selling, too, wasn't he?'

She nodded, bending before this wind that had blown so suddenly into her life.

'Yeah, he was.'

'Recently. Only a couple of years ago. Before we locked him up.'

'Yeah.'

'So he must have had a car, musn't he? Getting out and about? Keeping his customers happy?'

Mrs Naylor looked across at her husband, pleading for help, but Naylor was busy with another roll-up. At length, she nodded. Winter was right about the car. He'd had an old banger, a wreck of a thing.

'What sort?'

'I don't know. I can't remember.' She frowned, wanting an end to these incessant questions. 'I think he once said it was Italian.'

'Fiat?'

'Might be.'

'Colour?'

'White.'

'Big car? Small?'

She stared up at Winter, panic-stricken,

'I dunno. Medium. I dunno.' She swallowed hard, twisting the tea towel in her lap. 'He was terrible with money, Bradley, always has been. He just spent it all the time – spend, spend, spend. Lend him a fiver and it was gone, just like that. It was like an illness. He hadn't got a clue.' She looked up again. 'Was he hurt at all?'

'He was dead, Mrs Naylor.'

'I know, but—' She buried her face in her hands. Winter stood beside the chair, a hand on her shoulder. Sullivan stirred uneasily behind him.

'These mates of his you mentioned. You wouldn't have any names by any chance?'

She buried her head in her hands. Winter gave her a moment or two and then put the question again. Mates. Blokes he hung around with. People who might be able to help on a terrible, terrible day like this.

At last her head came up. In the space of a minute, she seemed to have aged years.

'No.' She shook her head, emphatic, then plucked at the baggy tracksuit. 'Head like a sieve, me.'

Winter got slowly to his feet, thinking about the scene on Hilsea Lines. Back at the briefing in the incident room, Willard had made a big point of the scarlet thong. It was the first thing he'd noticed, he'd said.

'What about girlfriends?'

Winter stood beside the chair, waiting for an answer, but Mrs Naylor had had enough. Then there came the scrape of a match and a rattly cough as smoke from the roll-up hit Naylor's lungs.

'He never went short.' He coughed again, then swallowed hard. 'Had a mouth on him, Bradley. Talk any woman into bed.'

'He had lots of girlfriends?'

'Yeah. Never kept them, but yeah.'

'Anyone in particular? Anyone recent?'

'Haven't got a clue, mate. Like I say, it wasn't like we saw him every day.'

Winter nodded, then gestured casually back towards the stairs in the hall.

'What about stuff of his? Clothes? Bits and pieces? Mind if I take a look?'

The expression on Naylor's face – first surprise, then panic – brought a smile to Winter's lips. He turned and headed for the stairs. Naylor came after him but quickly had second thoughts. There were four doors off the landing at the top. Winter tried them one after the other. Third time he was lucky, switching on the light for a better look.

There were piles of boxes stacked beside the MFI wardrobe, the kind of gear a good burglar could screw in a couple of minutes. Most of it was stuff for the kitchen: food mixers, coffee machines, good quality saucepans, stuff you could shift to housewives on the estate. Winter took a closer look, searching for evidence of a particular outlet, but the goods must have been nicked from stock before they got anywhere near a shelf. There might be serial numbers, though, and if so it should be child's play getting a match on recently reported break-ins.

He quickly checked the wardrobe and the battered chest of drawers, then backed out of the room and gave Sullivan a yell. When he got to the top of the stairs, he nodded towards the open door and told him to get on the mobile. He wanted a photographer and a van. Quickly.

Naylor was waiting at the bottom of the stairs.

'Well?' The grin was back on Winter's face. 'What's the story?'

'I was kidding about Brad,' Naylor mumbled. 'He's been here all the time.'

'You mean living here?'

'Yeah.'

'In that room?'

'Yeah.'

'So why's the wardrobe empty? Doesn't he have a change of clothes?' Naylor took a little half-step backwards, trying to avoid the traps. 'When I say living here—'

Mrs Naylor appeared in the open doorway behind him. Her face was scarlet with anger.

'That's all garbage. It's true what he said before. We haven't seen Bradley for months.'

'Sure.' Winter beamed at her, ever helpful. 'And the fairies left the stuff upstairs.' He turned back to Naylor. 'You've got a problem here, my old mate, but there are ways and means we can help you. Assuming, of course, you want to keep your missus out of it.'

'Marge?' Naylor looked blank.

'Yeah. Conspiracy to handling.' Winter shook his head regretfully. 'In the Crown Court she could be looking at fourteen years. Some juries can be bloody unreasonable.'

The colour had drained from Mrs Naylor's face. For a moment, Sullivan thought she was going to collapse completely.

Winter was still looking at her husband.

'So why don't we go through the story again,' Winter suggested, 'starting with those mates of Bradley's?'

Back home from Southsea police station, Faraday settled down to wait for J-J's return but the longer he thought about it, the more he realised that he wasn't up for a lengthy post-mortem on the boy's love life, not now, not yet. Their life together had revolved around the spillage left over from childhood and adolescence – shared memories of birding trips, days on the beach, occasional expeditions to London – and this new J-J, this refugee from the grown-up world of shipwrecked relationships, was an altogether different proposition. After the best part of a day waiting for the lad to return, he realised that the last thing he wanted was a lengthy conversation about commitment and betrayal.

He thought he'd put the printout from Helen Bassam's mobile in his briefcase, and he was right. They were all there, all the numbers she'd so carefully stored, and Trudy Gallagher's even included her nickname. Carrot.

Faraday picked up the phone and dialled the number. On call-out days, he told himself, it was OK to quietly volunteer for extra duty. He glanced at his watch. 18.50.

'Who's that?'

She had a Pompey accent, sandpapered by too many cigarettes. It didn't sound like a young voice at all.

'Trudy Gallagher?'

'No chance. Who wants her?'

Faraday gave his name. He could hear music and bar laughter in the background.

'Old Bill, you say?' There was more laughter, much closer. This woman had an audience.

Faraday persevered. He was CID. He was investigating a serious incident. He needed to have a word or two with Trudy Gallagher. Was he talking to someone who knew where she was?

'I'm her mother. I'm the last person who'd bloody know.'

'I thought this was her mobile?'

'You're right. It was until I nicked it off of her. Bills that massive, what else could I do?' There was another cackle of laughter. 'She in trouble then?'

It occurred to Faraday that Trudy's mother might be a shorter cut to the boy Doodie than Trudy herself. Talking to kids, even on an informal non-interview basis, could be tricky. Make one slip and the defence lawyers would be all over you.

'Maybe you could help,' he suggested.

There was a moment's pause. In the background, muted voices. Then the woman was back again.

'We're at the Café Blanc,' she said. 'Help yourself.'

The Café Blanc was in Southsea: sleek black and white decor, chrome and leather seats, gleaming maplewood floor and lots of smoked glass. It had only been open a couple of months and already it had become the happening place for estate agents, car dealers and young professional folk prepared to pay £3.50 for a bottle of Mexican lager. Word on the street suggested that it was a launderette for washing cocaine money and Faraday was in a position to suspect that the rumour was true.

He parked on a single yellow line opposite and looked across. The big picture windows went with the clientele. Weekends, places like this filled early and already most tables were occupied. These were people who enjoyed being on show.

He played a game with himself for a minute or two, trying to guess who had been on the other end of the phone, then gave up and dialled the number again. It was a woman sitting at a table in the window who dived for her bag, and the moment she produced her mobile, Faraday rang off.

She was drinking with two friends. They were getting towards the bottom of a bottle of white wine, and there was another upside down in an ice bucket beside the table. She was tall and striking, with a torrent of jet-black hair that tumbled over her shoulders. She had her legs up on a spare chair, angling herself sideways across the window as if she owned the place. She was wearing tight jeans, red heels and a see-through blouse with a dark blue bra underneath. Her face looked a good deal older than her body.

Faraday watched her peering at the readout on the mobile to try and identify the call. Three glasses down, he thought; she'd have forgotten his number. He studied the group for another minute or two, trying to work out who was bossing the conversation, and finally concluded that they were all too pissed to care. At length he got out of the car and walked across. Trudy's mum spotted him before he'd even got the door open.

'Mr Detective!'

She was on her feet, pushing the spare chair towards him. The buzz of conversation stilled as eyes turned towards Faraday. In this harshly lit goldfish bowl he'd seldom felt so obvious, so exposed.

'Mrs Gallagher?'

'Call me Misty.'

The name cracked up her two pals. They were all the same age, late thirties, and eyed Faraday up and down, the frankest of appraisals.

'Do you have time for a chat?'

'Definitely.'

'Is there somewhere we can go?'

'You name it.'

More laughter. Faraday nodded towards the door.

'I've got a car across the road. This needn't take long.'

Misty Gallagher retrieved her bag and headed for the door. Faraday held it open for her, refusing to give her friends the satisfaction of a backward glance. Inside the car she settled herself into the passenger seat. The four-year-old Mondeo was clearly a disappointment.

'Is this yours, then?'

'Yes.'

Faraday had started the engine. The seafront, quiet at this time in the evening, was a minute away. As they passed Southsea Castle, he glanced across.

'Why Misty?' he enquired.

'You wouldn't want to know, love.'

This was a new tone of voice – businesslike, wary. Without an audience she was a very different woman. Faraday pulled into a car park beside the Leisure Centre and turned off the engine. There was a silence while she produced a cigarette and lit it.

Faraday wound down the window. Misty let her head fall back, expelling a long plume of smoke.

'What's she done then? Trude?'

'Nothing that I know of. Nothing criminal, that is.' Faraday paused. 'How is she?'

'Better.' She drew on the cigarette again, not bothering to explain further.

'Back to school next week, then?'

'Maybe, if it suits her.' Misty shifted her weight in the seat, bringing herself round to face Faraday. The spill of light from the security floods fell across her blouse, though her face was still in shadow, and Faraday found himself wondering how many times a week she popped along to the gym.

'She's got a life of her own, you know, my Trude.'

'What does that mean?'

'It means she does what she does.'

'She still lives with you, then?'

'Some nights, yeah.'

'And other nights?'

'She doesn't.'

'At her boyfriend's?'

'Might be.' She folded her arms across her chest. 'What is this anyway?'

Faraday explained about Helen Bassam and the flats. She'd fallen to her death at some point on Thursday night. Grace Randall lived on the top floor, Trudy's greatgrandma. Correct?

'My nan, yeah.'

'Helen used to go up there, according to Mrs Randall. Trudy must have done the introductions.'

'So what?'

'Were they still mates, Trudy and Helen?'

'Up to Thursday night, you mean? Yeah, they were.'

There was another silence, longer this time.

'You don't seem too upset,' Faraday said at last, 'about Helen.'

'That's because I knew already. It's been on the radio. The whole fucking world knows.'

'And Trudy?'

'Upset. Really upset. What do you fucking think?'

Faraday accepted the point with a nod. He wanted to know more about Trudy's boyfriend. A name would be useful, and a contact number.

'That's down to Trudy.'

'How old is he, as a matter of interest?'

'Thirty-four? Thirty-five? Looks older sometimes but then he works hard, bless him.'

'And that's where she is? Nights she's not with you?'

'Yeah. Takes care of her nice, he does. Nice place. Nice car. Loads of money. Really special bloke. Shows Trude a good time. Always.' There was the flash of a smile as she stirred in the half-darkness. She was utterly shameless, proud even.

'So what does he do that's so special, the boyfriend?'

'Dunno. We don't have those conversations.'

'I meant for a living.'

'I know you did.'

Faraday looked across at her, recognising where this exchange was going. Half a bottle of Californian Chardonnay hadn't touched the parts of this woman that really mattered. Despite the vaudeville back at the Café Blanc, she was in total charge.

'There's a kid called Doodie . . .' Faraday began. 'He's ten years old and we need to find him. Trudy might be able to help us.'

'Why's that then?'

'Because Trudy knew Helen, and Helen seemed to be mates with the kid Doodie.'

Faraday paused, beginning to lose his temper. Spelling it out like this made him feel like some teacher in front of a class of retards, precisely the effect the woman was after. She was watching him carefully now. She'd moved again, and the lower half of her face was chalk-white in the glare of the security lights. Full lips. Perfect teeth.

'How well do you know this city, Mr Detective?'

Faraday turned away. He wasn't up for these kinds of games and he was beginning to regret this little spell of extra duty. He could have been at home with J-J, analysing why every relationship in the world seemed to be falling apart. Not sitting in the freezing darkness, getting wound up by a woman who hadn't the slightest intention of trying to help him.

'You haven't answered the question,' she reminded him.

'That's because it's meaningless.'

'Who says? A girl jumps off a block of flats. My Trude's shacked up with a bloke twice her age. You're looking for some kid of ten. The world's gone crazy, Mr Detective, and maybe that's where you ought to start.' She flashed him another smile, wider this time, and then ground out the cigarette in the ashtray on the dashboard. Faraday heard the soft clunk as she opened the door, then she was back again, leaning across the car, much closer this time. 'You know something?' she murmured. 'You'd look great in glasses.'

She let the thought hang between them, then touched him lightly on the cheek with the back of her hand the way you'd comfort a child, before pushing the door open and getting out. Faraday watched her walking back towards the main road, mystified.

Glasses?

They were halfway back to Fratton nick before Sullivan got it off his chest. Winter was at the wheel, trying to shift a dawdling Metro with bursts of full beam.

'That was totally out of order,' Sullivan muttered.

'What was?'

'Back there. The way you handled it.'

94

'Is that right?' Winter glanced across. If anything, he looked amused.

He'd sat Naylor down and explained the facts of life to him. They'd be seizing the property upstairs, pending checks on recent break-ins. There'd be plenty of people keen to find out exactly what all this bent gear was doing in Naylor's spare room but in the meantime Winter would be grateful for a little help with these names that kept cropping up. Bradley's mates. The ones that kept leading him astray.

Naylor, even without his wife giving him the evil eye, had been extremely reluctant to even hazard a guess on who they might have been but Winter had left him in no doubt about the consequences of clamming up. If he valued his liberty, and his marriage, then now was the time to give that dodgy memory of his a bit of a shake. There were ways that Winter might be able to help them both. But only if Naylor came up with some names.

In the end, convinced that Winter meant it, Naylor rummaged around for a piece of paper and scribbled a couple of names for Winter to take away. By staying mute, by not permitting these names to pass his lips, he seemed to cling to the belief that he hadn't parted with anything important, but Winter knew otherwise. One of these two blokes, Colin McGuire, was a serious head case and the back of a Littlewoods envelope was now proof positive that Naylor had grassed him up. That was what always amazed him about these people: they were so, so thick.

Sullivan was still having a go about the way Winter had tackled the Naylors. It seemed his CID training hadn't prepared him for anything like this. What about PACE requirements? What about the need for a warrant if you started poking round other people's houses? Didn't any of that matter any more? Or had Winter just chucked the book of rules away?

They were driving up the northern slope of Portsdown Hill. At the top, where the ground fell away, the windscreen was suddenly filled with the city below, mapped with line after line of orange lights stretching out towards the blackness of the Solent. The main road dropped to the right here, down towards the suburb of Cosham, but Winter pulled the Escort abruptly left. Another road ran along the crest of the hill. Within half a mile, there was a car park. Winter coasted to a halt and killed the engine.

'OK, son. So what's your real problem?'

Sullivan was ready for this. He turned on Winter, word perfect on the charge sheet. The way they'd just burst in. The way he'd played the wife off against the husband. The traps he'd set. The leading questions. The implicit threats. There were procedures here, strokes you shouldn't pull, and as far as he could see there wasn't a single rule he hadn't broken. They depended on public trust, on people's respect. A couple more gigs like that and no one in his right mind would ever talk to CID again.

Winter, his eyes shut, might have been asleep. At length he yawned.

'You really believe all that drivel?'

'It's not drivel. And if you were halfway decent, you'd understand that.'

'You're telling me Naylor would have come across if I'd played Mr Nice?'

'I've no idea. You never tried.'

'Too fucking right, I never tried. And do you know why? Because these people are shit, total arseholes. The only language they understand is force. We can't smack them around any more but next best is just as effective. You turn them against themselves, son. You find out where the weaknesses are and you go in and sort them out. I don't know what they taught you at Netley but in my book that's the way you get the job done. We're not talking textbooks here, we're talking real life.'

Sullivan wasn't having it.

'Shit's a good word,' he said hotly. 'That's exactly what you made me feel back there. You were an embarrassment, the way you treated them. I felt like something I'd brought in on my shoe. Is that why I put my hand up for this job?'

Winter permitted himself a long sigh, more regret than anger. The job had changed. Everyone said so. But what kind of planet did this sanctimonious little bastard come from? Did he really believe in all this civil liberties crap? All these endless mission statements about the need for transparency? Did he really think that tea and sympathy would charm a result from the likes of Naylor?

'They're animals,' he repeated wearily, 'and you give animals a good kicking.'

'So why didn't we statement them?'

'Because I want to let him think about it a bit. The longer he thinks, the more stuff we'll have on young Bradley. Jesus, Naylor might know the whole fucking story but the only way we'll ever find out is by him believing he's got a bit of latitude, a bit of room for manoeuvre. If he thinks we'll hold off on the gear then it's odds-on he'll start talking.'

'OK, so then what?'

'I don't follow you.'

'What happens if he gives us everything? Everything he knows?'

Winter frowned for a moment, making sure he'd understood the question. 'Afterwards, you mean? After he's come across with some decent names?'

'Yeah.'

Winter shook his head in disbelief. 'We nick him, of course. Handling at the very least.'

Sullivan nodded, his point made. Before they'd left the house, he'd asked Mrs Naylor for a recent photo of her dead son and she'd gone through a couple of drawers in the kitchen before laying her hands on a colour shot that had evidently been taken a while back. The photo was propped on the dashboard in front of him. The boy was in a pub somewhere, his arm round the barmaid.

Sullivan reached out for the photo and switched on the interior light. Alive, behind the drunken grin, Bradley Finch looked thin-faced and haunted, someone for whom life held nothing but bad news.

'You know what really gutted me?' Sullivan tapped the photo. 'This guy's their son. I don't care what kind of arsehole he is, the lad's dead. He's been dead less than a day. We were there to tell them. We gave them about a second and a half to sort that out, to come to terms with it, and then you were all over them like some fucking rash.' He looked across at Winter, disgusted. 'Have you any idea what it means to lose someone that close?'

Winter was staring straight ahead, his face quite blank, his fingers tapping lightly on the steering wheel – some half-buried rhythm, dee-dum-dee-dum-dee-dum. Below them, the city twinkled against a curtain of black.

'You just blew it, son,' Winter murmured after a while. 'You just blew it big time. You ever say that to me again, ever, and I'll give you the smacking of your life. Depend on it, OK?'

He looked across at Sullivan, underlining the threat with a slow nod, then reached for the ignition key.

'And another thing.'

'What's that?'

'Don't ever think I'm interested in an apology.'

Chapter nine

Last thing Saturday night, Faraday had checked the tide times and sunrise. According to the *News*, high water springs were at 07.43, an hour after dawn. Perfect.

· The alarm woke him at five. He stole into the bathroom, doused his face with water, and then returned to the bedroom to get dressed. Outside in the darkness, the wind was beginning to pick up and he could hear the familiar 'slap-slap' of halyards against metal masts in the nearby dinghy compound. Most Sundays the sailing club organised Laser races around a triangular buoyed course out in the harbour.

Not so long ago, J-J would have been out on the sea wall with his binos, eyes peeled for rule infringements, and Faraday wondered whether any of this cheerful, artless, harbourside childhood had stuck. Nothing would please him more than to return to find his son raging about some cheat who'd grazed a buoy and neglected to put in the regulatory 360-degree turn.

The empty Thermos was waiting for him in the kitchen. Faraday boiled a saucepan of water and poured it into the Thermos. Into his rucksack with the Thermos went a sachet of powdered French onion soup, a small jar of fresh milk and instant coffee in a twist of paper. Umpteen early starts up on the marshes at Farlington had taught him the importance of having something hot to put in his stomach. Winter or summer, dawn could be chilly.

The walk north along the towpath took him the best part of an hour. He had a torch in his daysack but he preferred to trust his night vision to avoid the potholes and knotty little stands of marram grass that could tip him over the sea wall and onto the foreshore below. The city was off to his left, the nearest road half a mile away, but the distant sodium lights still cast a loom over the scrub and bushes of Milton Common, and it never ceased to amaze him how much detail he could make out. In twenty years beside the water, he'd never known it truly dark.

Half an hour's brisk walk brought him level with the island's waist. There was a proper stone quay here, still used by the dredgers which tied up to disgorge hundreds of tons of dripping shingle, and he paused for a moment or two, alerted by a splashing in the shallows. Teal, he thought. Or maybe blackwits washing and preening after a hard night on the mudflats.

He stood on the little promontory that nosed into the harbour, looking south, back towards his house. Recently, he'd got to know a local, a man in his mid-fifties, who'd been born a stone's throw from his back garden. Where Milton Common now lay, there had existed a long tongue of water, Velder Creek, and over the course of a couple of evenings at a local pub Faraday had been entranced by the memories of this man's childhood. He'd been born on a houseboat, a converted MTB, and his first conscious memory was his dad ringing a big brass bell he'd fixed up just forward of the stubby little bridge

There'd been dozens of similar houseboats, beached relics from the war, and they'd sustained a tight little community of kids and grownups who had savoured life on the mudflats. It was all too easy to imagine this Bohemian post-war idyll – no running water, no electricity – so rich in its simplicity. There'd been discharged naval officers living there, survivors from the Russian convoys with no interest in rejoining the rat race, and men who fed entire families by weaving lobster pots from flotsam salvaged from the highest tides.

Often, on hot summer afternoons, parties of inmates from the big psychiatric hospital on Locksway Road would wander down to gaze out across the harbour. Amongst them was an artist, Edward King, who had won an international reputation for his vivid, beautifully captured landscapes. The Blitz had robbed him of the last of his sanity and the canvases he'd painted amongst the ruins of the city had done ample justice to the wider madness of war. One of his pictures, a garish study of the bombed wastelands around the cathedral, still hung above the staircase at Highland Road police station, and Faraday often paused to admire it. Fifty years of peace had covered the city's scars, but every new working day suggested – to Faraday at least – that the madness lived on.

He pushed north again, chilled by the stiffening wind. Normally, at low tide, the exposed mud would be thick with bird life, and when he finally made it to the big sea wall that circled Farlington Marshes, he knew that his luck was in. A short-eared owl flew within yards of him, then settled on a fence post, yellow-eyed, unblinking, staring him out.

A good night amongst the voles, Faraday thought, waiting for the owl to bring this perfect moment to an end.

Dawn had come and gone by now, and a thin, grey wash had spread across the harbour, light the colour of brushed steel. The wind was from the south, bringing with it the taste of rain, and as the tide began to creep back in the birds retreated with it. Soon they'd be packed on the scattered little islands that dotted the upper harbour, shuffling around and bickering amongst themselves for the best positions. One way or another, thought Faraday, Portsmouth was a city which had always dealt in the currency of aggression.

But what of J-J? He'd returned last night at just gone ten. At some point during the day he'd visited a barber's shop, acquiring a Pompey grade one crop, a down payment, Faraday realised, on a lengthy stay. With the near baldness, he'd camouflaged himself for the months to come, and afterwards – maybe after catching sight of himself in a shop window – he'd gone to some pub or other and got very drunk.

He'd been staggering by the time he got home, offering a flurry of sign that signalled a gleeful, incoherent return to the city of his adolescence. He was glad to be back, he told his father. Glad to be shot of Valerie and all those French friends he'd been stupid enough to trust. From now on he'd know how to play it. Look out for number one. Take nothing at face value. When Faraday had pressed him on exactly where he'd been, and who he'd been with, it turned out it wasn't a pub at all. J-J had dropped into Threshers with what was left on his debit card, and sunk six cans of Kronenburg in a cemetery opposite St Mary's Hospital.

Why, in God's name, a graveyard? The boy had looked at him uncomprehending, then signalled a weary goodnight and reeled off to bed. Watching him weaving up the stairs, Faraday had felt an immense heaviness in his own heart. This was exactly the moment when it might have been nice to lift the phone and share a thought or two with Marta. But that, alas, was out of the question. Birds, in a phrase he understood only too well, occasionally come home to roost. He lifted his binos again, sweeping the foreshore way down the harbour and glimpsing the first signs of activity in the dinghy park beyond his house. The Laser boys were early this morning and Faraday glanced at his watch, wondering whether J-J would be even conscious by the time he got home.

Sullivan had been at the MIR at Fratton for nearly half an hour, haunting the little kitchen at the end of the main corridor, by the time Winter arrived. It was nearly nine'o'clock and Winter waved the offer of a coffee aside.

'Had one already,' he said briskly.

DS Dave Michaels was in his office next to the incident room. He was a squat, cheerful forty-year-old with a lifelong passion for football. His years turning out for the CID team had given him a taste for keeping goal, and his reputation as a safe pair of hands had stuck. Like Winter, he knew most of Pompey's major villains on first-name terms and if he got out less often than before, then maybe that was a perk of this new role of his. There were worse things in life than despatching Willard's troops to the four corners of the city. He'd been in since six.

'So how did you get on last night?'

Winter was examining a photo scissored from a recent edition of the *News*. Pinned to the wall board next to the duty roster, it showed a team of eleven-year-olds staring grimly at the camera. AFC Anchorage were heading one of the junior Sunday leagues and Dave's boy, according to the names beneath, was captain.

'Fine.'

Winter outlined the visit to Naylor's place and dropped the photo on the desk. Michaels studied it with interest. Prints from the SOCO photographer were in an envelope on his desk and he told Winter to help himself. Winter shook out the photos and leafed quickly through them. A length of nylon rope and a night out in the rain had done nothing for Finch's complexion but it was definitely the same face. The lolling head and bloated purple features reminded Winter of shots he'd once seen on an exchange visit to Polish colleagues in Lodz. The atrocity museum at Auschwitz was full of images like these.

'What about the post-mortem? They get a result?'

'Definitely. Two rib fractures here, down the right side, and a compound fracture up here.' He indicated his cheekbone, just beneath his right eye. 'Plus multiple abrasions and bruising. Someone had been whacking him, definitely. There were a couple of other rib fractures, too, but they were a while back.'

'Anything else?'

'Cause of death was asphyxiation due to hanging but they got some interesting marks off his wrists. He'd been tied up before he died. Oh yeah, and a couple of other things. He was well pissed, nearly four hundred micrograms, and his arse was a mess. You know the score, damage to the rectal tissues consistent with the introduction of a foreign object. Plus a puncture wound.'

'In his arse?'

'Left foot.'

'*Foot*?'

'Yeah. Deep penetration, fairly recent. Might have been a knife, skewer, anything. We're checking it out with A and E in case he booked in.'

Winter was still studying the photos. Finch had certainly taken a beating, and then some, but even without the tally of injuries ID'd at the post-mortem, he still cut a sorry figure. There wasn't an ounce of spare flesh on his thin body, and Winter couldn't help thinking of his mother, spilling out of the armchair, a monument to a lifetime of crisps and Mighty White.

'The parents were fuck-all use,' he grunted. 'Except for a couple of names off the stepfather. He's been fencing stolen gear, by the way. I got it photographed and booked in last night.'

'Did you pull him?'

'Not yet.'

'Statement him?'

'No point. He'll come across with more once he's had a bit of a think. Colin McGuire? Tony Barrett? That's all he's managed so far.'

Michaels scribbled himself a note.

'McGuire's inside,' he said. 'ABH and the Alliance and Leicester job. What was the strength on Barrett?'

'Naylor says he's been tipping up sometimes. Looking for Finch.'

'Recently?'

'Week before last, he says.'

'They mates, or what?'

'Naylor thinks yes. Apparently Barrett has a couple of greyhounds. Naylor hates dogs.'

Michaels had turned to his computer. As far as he knew, Barrett had a place in Southsea. He'd been a half-decent central defender once, team of heavies in the Dockyard League, but the drink had got to him and he now scraped a living by shoplifting to order and flogging happy pills to students. Michaels named the pub where he did most of his deals. He was a lazy bastard and his pad would be close by.

'Yeah, here it is.'

Winter peered at the screen. Barrett lived in Shaftesbury Road, a street of tall, once-handsome Victorian houses that had since been subdivided for the vagrant army of students and single men that washed through this corner of the city. Winter made a note of the address and checked his watch. Sunday morning, it was odds-on that Barrett would still be asleep.

'Thanks for the vehicle, by the way.'

Winter had phoned in about the Fiat last night. Pressed for details, Naylor had come up with a roof rack, a towbar and a lot of rust. It seemed his stepson had been running the old banger for at least a couple of years and had parked it outside the house while he was doing his bird. Naylor had never done anything as sensible as writing the registration down but it was definitely a Uno, and he thought it might have been a K plate with an A and a couple of 7s in the number. Overnight, these details had been flashed to every traffic car in the county, and this morning Michaels would be extending the search further.

'Finch was disqual. D and D. Did he mention that?'

Winter shook his head. This was shaping up nicely. Personally, he'd never heard of Bradley Finch until yesterday but there were dozens of little scrotes in the city who could have ended up in the SOC photo envelope, petty criminals at the very bottom of the food chain. The fact that he'd lost his driving licence for some drink/drive offence went with the territory. If they weren't driving round with a bellyful of Stella, they were out of their heads on all kinds of other garbage.

Michaels wanted to get moving on the Fiat. Yesterday he'd called for CCTV tapes from cameras across the city. The nearest camera to Hilsea Lines was nearly half a mile away and the tape would be analysed this morning. Hard intelligence on the Fiat offered a solid lead, something to go on, and he could now set about organising a street-by-street search. Tomorrow, once the city got back to business, he'd sort out checks on scrapyards in case the car had been dumped. Then there'd be the spreadsheet from the CIMU guys recording every vehicle stop-check over the past month or so, plus a general circulation to neighbouring forces along the coast. If necessary, he'd even bid for the services of Boxer One, call sign of the force spotter plane, a brand new turboprop Islander garaged at the old Fleet Air Arm base at Lee-on-Solent.

Michaels scribbled himself another note then stood up for a stretch. Most of the murders he dealt with were three-day events, domestic killings so obvious there was rarely any point in firing up the HOLMES system and calling for the cavalry. It was normally the husband or the boyfriend and some row that got out of hand, and in most of these cases a simple confession saved a great deal of paperwork. But this one, '*Bisley*', had the feel of a definite runner, an opportunity to get in amongst the city's low life and see who they could sort out in the way of suspects. Like Winter, he found the prospect of the next few days deeply pleasurable, and the two men were debating who else might be in the frame when a figure appeared at the door. It was Sullivan.

'All right, son?' Michaels gestured towards Winter. 'Breaking you in, is he?'

Sullivan and Winter were in Shaftesbury Road by half nine. Saturday night had left a trail of polystyrene cartons, kebab sticks and broken glass down the middle of the road and someone had carpet-bombed the pavement outside number 17 with the half-digested remains of a Chinese. Winter stepped carefully around the crusting splat and pushed at the broken gate. The big bay windows on the ground floor were hung with blankets and there was a faded Creamfields poster in the flat upstairs.

Barrett lived at the top of the building on the third floor. It was dark on the staircase and the lino was sticky underfoot. A couple were at it as they passed a door on the way up and Winter could hear water pouring from an overflow outside.

There were two black plastic sacks on the landing outside Barrett's flat. Winter gave the nearest one a kick, hearing the rattle of cans inside. He shot Sullivan a look then rapped at the door. A dog began to yelp, then another, but nothing else happened. Finally, at the umpteenth knock, the door opened. The tottering figure on the threshold was wearing nothing but a grimy towel. He was tall and flabby with spindly legs and a scarlet face. He hadn't shaved for a couple of days and he looked wrecked.

'Tony Barrett?'

'Yeah?'

He peered at them in the gloom. Winter pocketed his warrant card and pushed past him into the flat, leaving Sullivan to close the door. The dogs were in the main room that looked out over the street, two skinny greyhounds, both tied to a table leg. One of them had recently crapped on an open copy of the *Sun*, spread beneath the table. A stench like this was something you were supposed to get used to but Winter wasn't at all sure. The quicker they were out of here, the happier he'd be.

'Bradley Sean Finch,' he grunted. 'Know him, do you?'

Still dazed, Barrett found trouble mustering an answer. Finally he nodded. 'What of it?'

'He's dead.'

'Yeah?' He blinked and ran a hand over his face. He seemed genuinely surprised. 'Since when?'

'Yesterday morning.'

'Shit.'

'Exactly.'

Sullivan had backed away a little, putting space between himself and Barrett. His face was chalk-white and he'd loosened his tie. Any minute now, Winter thought, he'll be out on the pavement, doing his own bit for Shaftesbury Road.

'Knew him well, did you? Bradley?'

'I knew him, yeah.'

'Business? Pleasure?' Winter paused, waiting for an answer. When nothing happened, he took a step closer. 'Who feeds these dogs, then?'

'I do.'

'That's bollocks. Look at them. You could play a tune on those ribs.'

'They're fucking greyhounds. They're meant to be thin.'

'Yeah? And what about that one? All that mange?' He nodded at the smaller of the two dogs. 'We're pals with the RSPCA, Tony. Not a lot of people know that.'

He let the thought sink in, then returned to Bradley Finch. He wanted to know when he'd last seen him. He wanted times and dates.

Barrett couldn't take his eyes off the dogs.

'Last week,' he said at last.

'Where?'

'Up Fratton.' He named a pub.

'Why's that then? Why did you meet him?'

'You don't wanna know.'

'I do, my friend, I do.'

'We did a bit of business. He wanted to unload some stuff on me.'

'What kind of stuff?'

''Es mainly. Some speed too. I didn't need it.'

'That piss him off, did it?'

'Yeah. He copped, big time. But that was a laugh, wasn't it? Skinny little cunt. My kid sister could sort Bradley out and she's fucking thinner than those dogs. Know what I mean?'

'But it's the little guys you have to watch, isn't it? The little guys with that funny look in their eyes?'

'You're joking. Brad couldn't fight his way out of a paper bag. He was all mouth. That's why he got slapped around so much.'

'Yeah?'

'Yeah. Famous for it. Sometimes you'd think he must have enjoyed it, got off on it, know what I mean? There are some people in this city you shouldn't fuck with. Everyone knows that. It's respect, ain't it? Respect and having something up here.' He tapped his head. 'But that was Brad's problem. He never fucking stopped to think. The first thing that came out of his mouth, someone would cop. Some of these guys, like I say, you'd cross the fucking street to avoid. That's if you had any sense.'

'And Brad?'

'Not a fucking ounce of sense in him. Not two brain cells to rub together. He just walked straight into it, every time. Never failed.' He smacked his fist into an open palm. 'Bam.'

Winter nodded, thoughtful, then produced his pocketbook. Under the table, the bigger dog was taking another crap, its hind legs spread wide, its whole body shivering with the effort. Winter watched it for a moment, then motioned for Barrett to sit down.

'Names?' he enquired softly.

Faraday was still en route home, eyes glued to a distant skein of Brent geese, when he got the call on his mobile.

'Joe?'

It took him a step or two to place the voice. Then he had it. 'Devlin?'

'Yep. Listen, I'm really sorry to phone you on a Sunday but something's come up. You've got a moment?'

Faraday told her to carry on. He'd known Merry Devlin for years. She'd been a reporter on the local rag, the *News*, but had tired of the poacher's life and turned gamekeeper instead, joining the press relations team on the city council. She'd been there ever since, a wise old head amongst the eager young media graduates, and Faraday had always enjoyed her company. They had a relationship that overlapped their respective jobs and one of the reasons Faraday liked her was the fact that she respected his privacy. She seldom bothered him after hours. Phoning on a Sunday was unheard of.

'What's the problem?'

'It's complicated, Joe. It needs a conversation.'

Faraday was watching the geese. He was ashamed to admit it, but this call might just be the answer to his prayers.

'You want to have a spot of lunch and talk about it?'

'I'm booked for lunch but coffee would be nice.' She hesitated. 'Only first you ought to know who this is about.'

'Go on then.'

There was another silence. Then she was back again. 'Jane Bassam,' she said. 'I gather you've had some dealings.'

Winter didn't bother returning to Fratton before paying another call. In a halting formal statement, reluctantly signed and dated, Tony Barrett had sought safety in numbers, naming practically every serious villain in the city as Finch's tormentors. Evidentially, Winter judged this to be practically worthless. What was far more interesting was another lead he offered, the woman who might well turn out to be Bradley Finch's current girlfriend.

From the car, he finally managed to get through to Dave Michaels. 'She works at a caff in Queen Street,' Winter said. 'But he hasn't got her name.'

'What about the caff? Tried there?'

'We're outside now. It's closed all day.'

Winter heard Dave talking to someone else in the office. The Happy

Skate Café was wedged between a naval tailor and a second-hand book shop. Finally Dave came back.

'We'll find the keyholder.' He said. 'Give us five.'

Winter grunted an OK and returned the mobile to his pocket. Sullivan sat behind the wheel. He'd scarcely said a word all morning.

'Bit quiet, old son? Not grumpy, I hope?'

Sullivan shot him a look but still said nothing. He'd cut himself shaving and botched it with a twist of cotton wool. Tiny white wisps still adorned the scab beneath his nose and Winter began to muse aloud about his domestic arrangements. They were partners, after all. This might go on for weeks. They owed each other the odd confidence.

'Married, are you?'

'*Married?*' Winter might have accused him of child molesting.

'Shacked up then? Someone nice? Huge tits? Brilliant cook?'

'I've got a girlfriend, yeah.'

'Does she have a name at all?'

'Mel.'

Winter reached across and patted him on the arm. Listen, he wanted to say, I do this for a living, chiselling information out of people. Why make it so hard for yourself?

Winter's mobile rang. It was Dave again, back with a telephone number.

'Guy called Eddie Galea,' he said. 'If he employs this bint he's bound to know where to find her.'

Winter rang the number. After a while, a man answered. Winter introduced himself. He was one of a team engaged on a major inquiry. He needed some information about a woman alleged to be working at the Happy Skate. He'd gladly call round to confirm his ID but time was moving on.

'What's this about then?'

'I'm afraid I can't say.'

'It's serious?'

'Very.' Winter smothered a yawn. 'Trust me.'

There was a moment's silence, then the voice was back. The girl's name was Lou Abeka. She was Nigerian, been working for him for a couple of months now. Single-handedly, she'd put fifty quid on his weekly takings. At least.

'You're telling me she's a looker?'

'Yeah, but a nice girl with it, know what I mean?'

Winter could read the hidden message here. Go easy on her. No more grief than strictly necessary.

'She have a boyfriend at all? Anyone special?'

The man laughed. 'How much time have you got?'

'That special?'

'Too right. But listen, it's not the way you might be thinking. It's not her fault the way she looks. So gentle, my friend, eh?'

'Sure.' Winter was enjoying this. 'So where does she live?' He wedged the phone to his ear, scribbling down the address, then brought the conversation to a close.

'Somerstown.' He looked across at Sullivan and nodded at the ignition key. '107 Margate Road.'

Chapter ten

Merry Devlin insisted on buying the coffees. She was a small, neat, open-faced divorcee who kept herself in shape with regular visits to the squash court. She often played at lunch times with one of the civilian indexers in the CIMU and Faraday wasn't the least surprised to learn that she had amazing stamina and hated to lose.

They were sitting in a café-bar in the middle of Southsea. Apart from a hung-over couple picking at plates of scrambled egg, they had the place to themselves.

Faraday refused the offer of sugar and began to sip his cappuccino. Already, he was glad she'd spared the time to phone.

'You're sure about the *News*?'

'As sure as I can be. John doesn't pass on idle gossip. You know what he's like.'

Faraday nodded. Merry's current partner was a senior journalist on the city's daily paper – an older, slightly bookish man with a surprising talent for turning the small print of Pompey lives into thoughtful, page-long features that often nested awkwardly amongst the usual fusillade of bad-news stories.

'So what are they after exactly?'

'It's a project they've been nursing about youth and education and drugs . . . you know, the whole nine yards. They're planning a series of major articles over a week and they want to kick off with something really topical.'

'You mean controversial.'

'I mean eye-catching. John says they've been waiting for the right story to come up. Now they think they've found it.'

'Helen Bassam?'

'Exactly.'

Faraday took another mouthful of coffee. There were things that didn't add up here. How, for starters, did Merry Devlin know for sure that Faraday was involved with the Bassam girl's death? And who, more importantly, had made the link between the body outside Chuzzlewit House and some form of drug abuse?

'The post-mortem's not until tomorrow,' he pointed out. 'No one knows what the girl had been doing to herself.'

'That's what John says. That's why he was worried.'

'So who's talking drugs?'

'The editor, Harry Thompson.'

'On what evidence?'

'Apparently he's got a friend. One of your lot.'

'You've got a name?'

'Yes.' She nodded. 'Hartigan. Harry admits it openly. In fact he even boasts about it. Top cop. Comes through on his private line.'

Faraday permitted himself a smile. It was Hartigan's style to cultivate key contacts across the city – councillors, media people – and the editor of the *News* would be way up his Christmas card list. People like Hartigan believed that networking was the shortest cut to promotion and there wasn't a conversation he ever had that wasn't conducted with one eye to his own advancement. Faraday himself had absolutely no interest in political games like these and if he felt anything at all about Hartigan's passion for public profile, then it was quiet amusement. Until now.

'So what's he actually told Harry? Does John know?'

'I think it's a heads-up. Harry knows the girl's only fourteen. He knows she's middle class. And you don't have to be ace-bright to see the front-page potential in that. I also gather that your Mr Hartigan had been approached by the girl's father. Prior to his conversation with Harry.'

Faraday tried not to register his surprise, though he realised at once that he should have anticipated something like this. Professional people always started at the top when it came to other people's organisations. Hence Bassam going to the Superintendent first.

'So if the girl's death does turn out to be drug-connected . . .?'

'Then Harry will have someone round to Jane Bassam's sharpish.' She paused, leaning forward. 'I'm afraid it doesn't end there, either. Have you met this woman yourself?'

'No, a couple of my DCs have been dealing with her.'

'Did they tell you she used to be a teacher?'

'No. Should they have done?'

Merry glanced round, then beckoned Faraday closer. Jane Bassam had been teaching history at an all-girl comprehensive near the top of the city. According to the head, she was excellent at her job but was having big problems with discipline.

'Par for the course?'

'Absolutely, but she just wasn't handling it. There were a couple of kids in particular; there always are. These happened to be girls and I think they must have known they'd got her on the run.'

'And?'

'It came to a head over something or other and she threw one of the girls out. Happens all the time. They normally go to the loo for a spot of mirror therapy and then come back for the next lesson. This time she never made it to the loo.'

'Why not?' Faraday was engrossed.

'God knows. Any rate, the girl walked straight back in and thumped her.'

'Thumped Jane Bassam?'

'That's right. Punched her a couple of times and then tried to kick her. There was a huge fuss – you can imagine – but the head managed to contain most of it. Jane was offered an ambulance but settled for a taxi home.'

'So what happened to the girl?'

'That was the point. You'd normally exclude for something like that but these days you try and avoid exclusions. The girl blamed it on period pains, not feeling herself, and the head settled for a written apology. Jane never came back.'

Faraday nodded, listening while Merry finished the story off. These days, threats from parents and siblings were routine for most teachers. So were obscene text messages and vandalism if they were silly enough to leave their cars at school. But what Jane Bassam had been through had upped the tariff and the fact that the girl had walked away, scot-free, had been the last straw.

'She's still on full pay,' she added. 'But I know she's going to jack it in.'

'And the *News*?'

'They've been sitting on the story for a while. They've talked to the head and a couple of parents, but what they really want is Jane Bassam's side of it. So far, she's refused to talk to them. The drugs thing, if there is a drugs thing, might change all that.'

'Because?'

'Because she's vulnerable. The poor bloody woman loses her job? Loses her marriage? Loses her daughter? And then finds out the girl was some kind of junkie? Can you imagine where that would take you? You'd be angry, wouldn't you, as well as shattered? Journalists thrive on stuff like that. Anger makes brilliant copy. Manna from heaven.'

Faraday was running the implications through his head. Derek Bassam, the lawyer, had talked about his ex-wife having some kind of breakdown. Maybe Merry was right. Maybe this kind of pressure would push anyone to the brink.

'So what's your interest?' He gestured at the cups. 'Why phone me?'

'You want the truth?'

'Yes, please.'

'Number one, I feel sorry for the poor bloody woman. And number two, we hold a media relations brief for the Education Authority. The schools in this city get a bad enough press as it is. If the *News* went to town on Jane Bassam, it wouldn't make things any easier.'

Faraday began to understand. A couple of years ago responsibility for managing education had returned from the county to the city. Which put Merry Devlin and her colleagues in Media Relations in the firing line.

'So what do you want from me?' He said at last.

'An opinion. A best guess.'

'About the drugs?'

'Yes. In our game, forewarned is forearmed.'

'I can't give you that, Merry. Nobody can. Not even Hartigan. Not until we get the tox results back from the post-mortem.'

'You don't have a gut feeling?'

'No, and if I did, I wouldn't be sharing it with anybody else.'

'You wouldn't? Even after me buying the coffees?' Merry was grinning at him. Nice try.

Faraday glanced at his watch. Something was still nagging at him.

'Did you phone on the off chance?' He asked. 'Thinking I might just know about this girl?'

Merry looked at him a moment, then shook her head. 'Of course not.'

'So who told you?' Faraday frowned. 'Changing-room talk, was it? That squash partner of yours?'

There was a long silence, then Merry stood up and retrieved her coat from the back of the chair.

'That's a blind guess, Joe.' She wound her scarf around her neck. 'But I'd keep an eye on Mr Hartigan if I were you.'

Winter and Sullivan had been waiting outside the house in Margate Road for the best part of an hour before the girl returned. The student who opened the door had said she'd gone to church up the road and would be back any time but it was nearly one o'clock before she rounded the corner.

She was tall and erect and walked the way they teach you at model school. She wore a battered-looking pair of leather boots and a bulky black puffa jacket zipped up over a woollen dress, the kind of gear which would have turned most women into a parcel, but Winter saw at once what the café owner had been suggesting on the phone. Certain people were born to compel attention and this was very definitely one of them.

Winter was first out of the car and onto the pavement. The girl examined the warrant card with some surprise. She had a wide, flat face and eyes the colour of amber.

'Louise Abeka?'

They paused at the front door while she fumbled for a key. Winter had already noticed slight damage to the woodwork around the lock.

'What's that then?'

The girl looked at him, startled. Then she shrugged.

'I don't know. It happened last week. But the lock still works. Look.'

She turned the key and they all went into the house. The place had been recently subdivided and she had a room upstairs with access to shared cooking facilities and a communal bathroom. Her room was bare but spotless: single bed, knackered square of carpet, flat-pack chest of drawers, and a second-hand dressing table with photos Blu-tacked around the mirror. There was a big grey suitcase under the bed and a poster of Lagos on the wall.

Winter was looking at the photos round the mirror: kids on a beach with a blue, blue sea behind.

'These your family?'

'My little brothers, yes.' She hadn't unzipped the anorak. She wanted to know why they were here.

'It's in connection with a sudden death.' He asked her whether she'd like to sit down.

'What death?'

Winter gestured towards the bed again. The girl didn't move.

'His name was Bradley Finch.' He paused. 'Bradley Finch?' The girl nodded.

'I know Bradley. Is that why you're here?'

'Yes. Did you know him . . .' Winter offered her a smile '. . . well?'

'Yes, quite well.'

'Did you . . . have a relationship?'

'We were friends, yes.'

She looked between them for a moment, then from one to the other, then sank onto the bed. She said she couldn't believe it. How come he was dead?

'I'm afraid we don't know. That's what we're trying to find out.'

'But . . .' she frowned '. . . was it violent? Was he in trouble?'

'Why do you ask?'

She shook her head and studied her hands, clearly wanting this conversation to end.

Winter sat down beside her, making himself comfortable.

'Why don't you tell me about him?' he suggested.

There was a long silence. The girl looked up at Sullivan, trying to make a friend of the younger man, but Sullivan didn't return her smile. Instead, he nodded at Winter.

'He asked you a question. The quicker you answer it, the quicker we're gone.'

Louise looked down again, then began to talk. She'd first met Bradley Finch back last summer. He used to come into the café for breakfast.

Sullivan cocked an eye.

'What was he up to? Did he ever say?'

'No.'

'Did you ever ask him?'

'No.'

After a while, he'd invited her out for a drink. She didn't like alcohol or pubs, so in the end she'd settled for a walk on the seafront.

They'd only gone out that once. Whole weeks went by and she'd never see him in the café. Then he turned up with a couple of tickets for a reggae band. He wanted to take her and she said yes.

'When was this?'

'In the autumn time. It was great. I loved it.' She smiled at the memory and at last unzipped the jacket. She had a thick patterned sweater underneath, red cable stitch zigzags on white, and for one brief second Winter was convinced that Joannie must have run it up. Her kind of pattern. Her colours.

'So when did you last see him?' He asked. 'Bradley?'

'I don't know. I can't remember.' She was looking at the window, evasive again. 'Last week sometime?'

'How was he?'

'Just the same as usual. Hungry. Not much money.'

'Did he seem nervous at all? Depressed?'

She thought about the question for a while, picking at the hem of the nylon bedspread.

'He was always nervous,' she said at last. 'He was always running around, always on the move. I think that's why he was so . . . you know . . .'

'What?'

'So thin.'

'Did he ever offer you drugs?'

'No.' She sounded shocked.

'Did he ever talk about drugs?'

'Never.'

'What did you talk about then?'

'All kinds of things. I'd talk about Africa. My family. The places I'd been. What I want to do when I've finished my course here.' She was studying English at the university. Once she'd got her degree, she planned to go back to Nigeria and teach.

Winter took the conversation back to Bradley. How much did he tell her about his own life?

'Not much. I don't think he was very happy, not in himself, not inside. I don't think he had many friends, not people he could trust.'

'No one at all?'

'No. Except his nan, his mother's mum. He said he used to stay there sometimes. When he had nowhere else to go.'

'So where was he living otherwise?'

'I don't know.'

'You don't know? And you never asked him?'

'No, I did ask him. But he never told me.'

'Never told you much, did he?'

'No.'

'But you still liked him.'

'Yes.'

Winter nodded. She was lying – he knew it – and he didn't need anyone to tell him what charm and patience could do. Toerags like Bradley Finch could pull a real number on someone as tasty and naive as this girl appeared to be. Look soulful enough and in the end she'd insist you screwed her.

'This nan of his where he used to stay. Where did she live?'

'I don't know.'

Winter made a note to phone Mrs Naylor, then glanced at Sullivan and nodded towards the girl. Your turn.

'Did you ever talk on the phone?'

'Not really. Maybe once or twice.'

'He had a mobile?'

She nodded but when he asked for the number she said she couldn't remember it.

'Was it pay-as-you-go or was he on a plan of some kind?'

She shrugged. Again, she didn't know.

'Where did you write it down?'

'I can't remember. Somewhere. I don't know.'

There was a long silence. Winter was leaning against the chest of drawers watching the exchange, the faintest smile of approval on his face. At length Sullivan nodded at the handbag at her feet.

'Do you mind?'

Without waiting for an answer, he picked it up. Her address book was in a zipped-up compartment inside. He thumbed through it. Bradley Finch was under 'B', three numbers, all of them crossed out. He transferred the numbers into his own pocketbook, taking his time while the girl sat on the bed looking down at her hands.

'You've got a mobile too?'

'No.' She shook her head.

'You *haven't*? How did you phone him, then?' Sullivan tapped the list of numbers. 'Call boxes, was it?'

Louise shut her eyes a moment, then swallowed hard.

'I lost it,' she said at last.

'When?'

'Yesterday.'

'How convenient.'

Sullivan held her gaze. When she heard the scrape of wood from the chest of drawers across the room, she flinched. Winter was peering down at the contents of the top drawer.

'Are these yours?'

He held up a handful of thongs, most of them red.

'Yes,' she said.

Dawn Ellis was in the CID office at Southsea nick when the tall, lost-looking young man wandered in. For a moment, she thought it must be someone off the street who'd somehow bluffed their way past the secured entries. Then it occurred to her that he might be in the job.

He was standing by the door, looking round. He had a scary suit on, the kind her parents had once bought her kid brother for his first interview, and the tie had a definitely Caribbean feel to it, but he had a nice face under the mop of ginger curls and plainly needed help.

Sundays, the big office was nearly deserted. There were only two duty DCs in, and the other guy had gone out for a paper.

'Who are you after?'

Ellis was sitting at the far end of the office. He strolled down towards her.

'DC Winter's desk?' He gestured round.

'Who wants to know?'

He stopped and extended a hand. His name was Gary Sullivan. He was down from Petersfield on the Hilsea Lines job, working from the MIR. He was paired with Winter and he'd come down to pick up a contacts book. Second drawer down. Right-hand side.

'Bloody nerve.' Ellis was amused. 'Are you doing his laundry, too?'

Sullivan muttered something she didn't catch. Then he explained that

Winter was banged up with the management team, Willard and his deputy, over at the MIR. They'd scored this morning with a potential witness and Winter was determined to bottom the thing out. Hence the need for the contacts book.

He paused, eyeing the rows of desks.

'He does work here, doesn't he?'

'Yeah.'

'How well do you know him?'

'Paul? Pretty well.'

She watched Sullivan as he perched himself on the edge of the adjoining desk, trying to work out how old he was. Twenty-one? Twenty-two? At that kind of age, he wouldn't have a prayer with Winter. Especially if he'd taken all the stuff they'd told him at training school at face value.

'How are you getting on, then?'

'I just told you; we got a definite result.'

'I meant with Paul.'

'Ah, right . . .' He nodded. 'Yeah . . . interesting.'

'What does that mean?'

'Nothing,' he said hastily. 'It's just . . . he's a bit different, that's all.'

'You mean difficult?'

'Yeah, sometimes he can be difficult. Actually, it's not that, it's just the way . . .' he frowned '. . . he goes about things. Know what I mean?' He paused, looking at her, trying to weigh how truthful he could afford to be. 'Tell you the truth, the man's an embarrassment,' he muttered at last.

'Really?' Ellis was enjoying this conversation. There were a million ways you could describe Paul Winter's MO but this wasn't one of them. Bent maybe, and certainly unorthodox, but never embarrassing.

'Personally, you mean?'

'No. More socially.'

'*Socially?* Are you partying together? Does he take you to pubs a lot? I thought Major Crimes was all graft and car chases?'

Sullivan coloured slightly, then began to describe the encounter with the dead lad's parents, up in Leigh Park. The way Winter had handled them was out of order. It didn't matter that the bloke had a load of stolen gear. Fact was the woman had just lost her son and deserved a bit of respect. He ought to have known that. He ought to have known what something like that must feel like.

Dawn Ellis was gazing up at him, knowing exactly the way it must be between these two very different men. Not just a generation gap, not just a culture clash, but a cosmic black hole squillions of miles wide.

Winter and Sullivan were on separate planets and she wondered what on earth might ever bring them together.

Sullivan was still banging on about the Naylors. The problem with Winter was obvious: he had no sympathy. He just couldn't imagine what it was like to be someone else.

Ellis shook her head. 'You're wrong, Gary. That's exactly where he's brilliant. He gets inside their heads all the time. I've seen him do it. That's his skill. And there's something else, too, you ought to know.'

'Yeah?' Sullivan had visibly stiffened. 'What's that then?'

'He lost his missus to cancer last year, just like that.' She snapped her fingers. 'So he probably knows a lot more about death than you might think.'

Willard made Winter go through it in detail. They were sitting at the conference table in Willard's office. Sammy Rollins, the Deputy SIO, and Dave Michaels were there too, each of them making occasional notes.

'Number one, she's obviously lying,' Winter began. 'She lied about the mobe numbers, and it's odds-on she lied about the relationship. She's obviously been tucked up with Finch for months.'

'Can you evidence that?'

'No, not yet I can't, but you get billing on those numbers and I bet she was yakking to Finch most of the time. Plus the thongs we seized look like a match for the one he was wearing. Right down to the lacy bits.'

'What about other witnesses? These people she shares the house with?'

'Students,' Winter grunted. 'There are three of them but we've only seen one so far. He recognised Finch from the mugshot. Said the bloke was round a lot, all hours.'

'Boyfriend? Relationship?'

'Couldn't say.'

'What about the girl on Friday night? What was she up to?'

'Friday?' Winter glanced at his notes. 'Friday night she says she was working late at the café. When I asked how late she said nine, ten o'clock, until the place closed, but then I mentioned chummy who owns the place and said we'd obviously be checking all this out and suddenly, bang, she changes the story completely. Made a mistake. Got the wrong night. Wasn't working at the caff at all. No. Friday night, Plan B, she leaves at half five and goes for a walk. For three hours. In the pouring fucking rain.'

He leaned back, his hands spread wide, his case made. Even Willard was trying to suppress a smile.

'Did she see Finch at all on Friday night?'

'She says not.'

'And you think?'

'I think she's got another problem with that memory of hers.'

'But why would she be lying?'

'I dunno, boss. For starters, she's frightened. In fact she's shit-scared. You can see it in her face.'

Dave Michaels was sucking his pencil. 'Maybe she's got a visa problem. Maybe she's not legit. Happens all the time.'

Willard nodded, looking at Winter.

'Yeah, maybe, but it's more than that. When I invited her down the station, she came like a lamb. She was glad to be out of there, you could tell. Plus she'd just been to church, first time in ages.'

'We can't crime her for that.' Dave Michaels again.

Everyone laughed except Willard. He wanted to know how Winter could be so sure about this girl's sudden decision to go to church.

'Because I asked her, boss. Don't get me wrong; she's a nice girl. Deep down, I think she's honest too. In fact she must be, to lie as badly as she does.'

'So why isn't she coming across?'

'Good question.'

Winter sat back in his chair while Willard brooded. Finding the woman who might well turn out to Bradley Finch's girlfriend was the first major break in the inquiry. There was still no joy with the Fiat, and last night's trawl of the area around Hilsea Lines had netted nothing more than a handful of cottaging gays, none of whom had any light to shed on Friday night's events. Intelligence was beginning to dribble in about Finch but none of it was very surprising: small-time thief, drug dealer and general waste of space. Laying hands on someone really close to him, someone who might have a handle on the last twenty-four hours of his life, would be a significant step forward.

Willard was looking at the pad at his elbow. 'Anything else?'

'Someone had been having a go at the front door lock. Nothing heavy but the damage looked new.'

Willard nodded. Like everyone else around the table, he was thinking Friday night. Might Finch have been in the girl's room? Might there have been some kind of confrontation? Him and the girl? Someone else with a grudge? He frowned, bending to his pad again, checking each of the trophies that Winter had brought back from Margate Road.

Twenty years in the job had enabled Willard to turn scepticism into a fine art. He had little taste for wild theorising and absolutely no time for hunches. Nothing was real until he could stand it up in court. This painstaking determination to test every link in the evidential chain had served him well but younger men sometimes found his lack of visible enthusiasm deeply dispiriting. Not that they were ever silly enough to confuse wariness with indecision.

'OK.' He looked up. 'Here's what we do.'

Faraday was back home in the kitchen, wondering what to sort out for lunch, when J-J finally appeared. He was wearing an old khaki sweater he must have picked up in an army surplus store and a pair of Asterix boxer shorts. His toes curled up on the cold tiles and he was hugging himself for warmth.

'Hungry?' Faraday signed.

He shook his head and disappeared again. Half a minute later he was back with a bag of shag tobacco and a packet of Rizlas. Faraday watched while he rolled himself a cigarette. He'd obviously been doing this for some time.

'You smoke a lot?'

'Sometimes.'

Faraday nodded and turned away, determined not to be provoked into a row. J-J was doing this on purpose, he knew he was. He was staking out turf, testing his father's limits. I'm my own person now, he was saying. And I'll do what I bloody well like.

The harsh, acrid tang of the roll-up pursued Faraday around the house. He prowled from room to room, trying to tell himself that the boy deserved a bit of space, a bit of freedom. It was his house as well as Faraday's. That had been the deal from the very start, from the morning all those years ago when Faraday had opened the airmail letter from Seattle to find a cheque for $200,000 from Janna's parents.

Judy and Frank had come across for the funeral, staying long enough to realise that Faraday would never be able to cope alone with his infant son, not if he wanted to stay in the police. A probationer's pay might stretch to a deposit on a mortgage but it sure as hell wouldn't buy the kind of childcare he'd need if he was to hang onto the job. And so, with their money, Faraday had bought the house by the harbour, using the rest to secure a nanny for J-J, and in the regular correspondence he'd maintained with his in-laws ever since, he'd always made a point of joint ownership. Our house. Our view. Our good fortune.

Now, though, for reasons Faraday didn't fully understand, it felt very different. Between them, he and J-J had weathered a childhood that could have been disastrous. They'd built a relationship baggy enough to hold them both. They'd been friends, good buddies, as well as father and son. Faraday had never bothered to find himself another partner because – in the shape of J-J – he already had one. Then, as he should, J-J had moved away and led a life of his own. At the time it had left a big, big hole in Faraday's life and for a while he hadn't known quite what to do with himself. But then Ruth had come along, and now Marta, and Faraday had made the necessary adjustments. Indeed, in modest and quite surprising ways, he'd been extremely happy. Now this.

Downstairs, J-J had switched on the television. He seemed to have hit the wrong button on the remote because the volume was way up, a fact that would be lost on him because he was deaf. Unless, of course, he'd done it on purpose. Faraday did his best to fight this suspicion. It was unworthy. It was needless. It was winding him up. Then his patience snapped and he went downstairs again. The big lounge, with its huge views of the harbour, already smelt like a prison cell. J-J was sprawled on the sofa, tapping ash into a mug. Of all the programmes he might have chosen, he'd settled for a game show.

Faraday retrieved the remote and killed the sound. J-J didn't move.

'Something to eat?' Faraday queried again.

This time, J-J didn't even bother to reply. Faraday manoeuvred himself in front of the set, staring down at him. The least he was entitled to was a little respect. Was it his fault Valerie had found herself another lover? Was it his role to end up as punchbag for J-J's raging anger? In truth, he didn't know the answer to either question but there was a major problem here and he'd spent half the night wondering what to do about it. In his saner moments Faraday was a big believer in communication. Even if you were deaf, there were ways of talking this thing through.

'The computer's on upstairs. Why don't you email her?'

'Who?'

'Valerie.'

J-J frowned, then buried the remains of the roll-up in the mug.

'Why would I want to do that?' he signed.

Upstairs again, Faraday sat at his desk in the study debating what to do next. An eternity of Sundays stretched ahead of him. More roll-ups. More gloom. More crap television. He'd lived by himself for too long now to welcome this sudden invasion and he realised for the first time how precious his privacy had become. Maybe that's why it worked so well with Marta, he thought. Because she came with a guarantee that the house – with its stillness and its peace – would always, in the end, be his. He permitted himself a rueful grin at the irony of it all: missing her one minute, missing solitude the next. Then he checked his watch and reached for the phone.

Dawn Ellis answered on the second ring. Faraday wanted to check the status of the G28 on Helen Bassam. Had the sudden death form gone to the Coroner's Office yet?

'No, boss. You told me to hold off.'

'What time's the post-mortem tomorrow?'

'First thing. Nine o'clock.'

Faraday was peering out of the window at the last of the returning Lasers. Post-mortems involving individuals with previous for drug or alcohol abuse routinely tested for toxicological substances. In Helen's case, this wouldn't have been deemed necessary but the conversations with her father and Merry Devlin had now put a rather different interpretation on events.

'I want you there tomorrow,' Faraday said. 'Make sure the pathologist takes blood for tox.'

Chapter eleven

Winter noticed the change in Sullivan almost at once. The boy was more talkative, more relaxed, respectful even. Returning from a visit to the corner shop across the road, he'd even bought a packet of Werther's Originals, Winter's favourites.

'Who've you been talking to, then?'

'No one.' He offered the bag across. 'Just liked the look of them.'

They were parked in a side street in Portsea, beneath the shadow of the dockyard wall. The owner of the Happy Skate Café lived in a looming block of flats over to the right, and according to a phone conversation they'd had an hour or so ago, he'd be back from his mum's any time now. Eddie Galea was second generation Maltese and family was still important. Who'd stand their mum up on a Sunday and live to tell the tale?

Winter was already on his second Werther's.

'What d'you think then? About our little jungle bunny?'

Sullivan ignored the remark. Willard had wanted them both to re-interview Louise Abeka and take a full statement, concentrating on her movements on Friday. Her attendance at Central police station was entirely voluntary. She wasn't under caution and she knew she could leave any time. The last thing he wanted them to do was frighten her.

Between them, Winter and Sullivan had done his bidding in the stuffy little interview room, courteous to a fault, letting the girl take them step by step through her day. How she'd gone to work as usual, arriving around eight to help Eddie open up. How she'd grabbed half an hour before the lunch-time rush, taking a bus down to the city centre to bank her week's wages. How she'd left the café at around half five, regretting the fact that she'd never invested in a proper mac. She had some things to think about. She didn't mind the rain. She walked for hours, way out along the seafront, all the way to the Hayling ferry and then all the way back again. She'd gone home to change and because there was nothing worth watching on the TV, she'd caught a bus to North End and gone to the cinema. The film was *Castaway*. It was OK but nothing special. Back home by half past ten, she'd done some work for an exam she was about to sit and gone to bed around midnight.

When Winter had asked her about Finch again, and the strength of their relationship, she'd repeated that they were just friends. They met from time to time. She hadn't seen him for a while. He'd always been nice to her. She liked talking to him. Winter had finished the interview with an enquiry about the stuff Finch normally wore. His body had been naked except for an ear stud and a scarlet thong. Did he have a watch? Rings on his fingers? Some kind of wallet? Louise had thought about it, then nodded. He had a couple of rings on the first and second fingers of his right hand. One was big and quite distinctive. Winter passed her his pad and asked her to sketch the design. Then there'd been a watch, a big chunky thing. She thought it was black. As for a wallet, she'd never seen one, which wasn't really a surprise because he never had anything to put in it.

'Skint, was he?'

'I'm sorry?' The girl hadn't understood.

'No money?'

'No. Never.'

Sullivan, at Winter's request, had made notes throughout this account, carefully writing it up as a statement, but at no point had either of them challenged her. What was more important was establishing exactly the way she wanted to play it; no arguments on their part, no second thoughts on hers. Indeed, when it came to her visit to the Odeon, North End, they didn't even ask about Tom Hanks or the movie's plot.

Afterwards, the interview over, Winter had explained a little more about the guys in the white zip-up suits who'd descended on the house in Margate Road. They were there to take a look around. They'd probably be at it for the rest of the day and Winter made a point of saying how grateful he was for the loan of her key. As detectives they were responsible for finding out exactly how Bradley Finch had died, and the kind of help they were getting from Louise was absolutely invaluable. Was there somewhere she might go until, say, early evening? Did she have friends in the city?

She'd said yes to both questions and left the police station around four in the afternoon, totally unaware of the two-man surveillance team that DI Sammy Rollins had hastily organised. With a bit more notice, these jobs normally went to the Hampshire Surveillance Unit, but the HSU was often booked weeks in advance and Rollins scarcely had time to fill in the fast-track RIPA forms and find two bodies to do the job. It was Willard's belief that Louise Abeka would be in touch with other associates of Bradley Finch, either voluntarily or because they'd go looking for her. If Winter had it right about some kind of confrontation at the house in Margate Road, then the girl might represent unfinished business.

To Sullivan, it was the forensic search that was truly impressive. Willard had declared the house a potential Scene of Crime and Jerry Proctor's SOC boys were already busy covering all the usual bases. They'd be taking fingerprint lifts and tapings from Louise's room, the corridor outside and the shared facilities. They'd be lifting floorboards and exploring drain traps. The filter from the communal washing machine would be seized and the garden searched for evidence of buried clothing or weapons. After all that, Louise could return home.

Sullivan was musing on what might happen next. It was too early to speculate about fingerprints but any promising swabs would go up to Lambeth for DNA analysis, together with a sample from Bradley Finch's post-mortem. Willard was demanding the premium twenty-four-hour service. At £2300 for the minimum two samples that had to indicate more than a passing interest.

'She's in it up to here.' Winter drew a line across his forehead then looked across at Sullivan. 'You believe all that shit about walking to Hayling Island and back? It's fucking dark on the seafront for one thing. I know she's black but that doesn't make her invisible and there are some ugly bastards out there. No, she's not a bad girl but she's definitely implicated.'

'And Willard?'

'He knows that. He never shows it but it's there. Fuck knows what he does when he's happy.'

Winter nodded, musing contentedly about the characters he'd known who'd made it to Willard's level: high-flying university graduates with Ph.D.s in form-filling but clueless when it came to human nature. Over-promoted plodders without two ideas to rub together. And a legend called Tankie who, according to Winter, was the best detective he'd ever met.

'Took the hump one day, and just walked out,' he said. 'Saw the way it was going and voted with his feet. Lovely bloke. Completely his own man. And look what happened.'

Sullivan was watching a small figure in a heavy overcoat hurrying towards the main entrance of the flats. He was carrying a newspaper in one hand and a heavy-looking Lidl bag in the other. It was nearly dark now, the streets empty except for the occasional passing car.

'That's him.' Sullivan was already halfway out of the car.

He was right. Up in a small, cosy flat on the fifth floor, Eddie Galea put the kettle on and insisted they try his mum's Madeira cake. He sold it in the Happy Skate, eighteen slices per cake, and the whole lot always went by mid-afternoon.

'You know what would make me a rich man?' He licked the crumbs off his fingertips. 'The day I buy my mum a bigger oven.'

Sullivan wanted to know about Louise Abeka and Winter was happy to let him make the running. Buying the Werther's had been a clever move. The boy was brighter than he'd thought.

'Lou?' Eddie frowned. 'What can I say? You've seen her, talked to her. Lovely, lovely girl. If my kids were little babies again, I'd trust her with them, no question. If my son wasn't such a dickhead, she could make him the luckiest man in the world. The girl's an angel, I swear it.'

'You mentioned boyfriends.'

'Sure.' He nodded.

'Anyone in particular?'

'Two or three. Very popular girl.'

'Do you have any names at all? Does she talk about them?'

Eddie shook his head, a gesture of immense regret. He'd taken this conversation as far as he was prepared to go. There were things you didn't do in Portsea, and one of them was name names.

Sullivan produced the photo he'd picked up at the Naylors'. Eddie gave it a single glance. The smile had gone.

'Ah,' he murmured. 'Finch.'

He'd been coming in for years, off and on. He seemed to have business in the area but Eddie had never pried too deeply. Then Louise had arrived and after that Bradley Finch hadn't missed a day.

'Mad for her,' he said. 'Just crazy.'

'And Louise?'

'Puts up with him. Like we all have to. I told you; she's a good girl – kind. If you're looking for a relationship, I'd say she mothers him more than anything else.'

'*Mothers* him?'

'That's right. Blokes like Bradley Finch, they're all over the place. Give him a couple of years, you'll find him kipping out in some shop doorway with a can of Special Brew and one of them dogs. Give the girl credit, she does her best with him, but that's because it runs in the blood. People like us, family still matters. You're taught to care . . . know what I mean?'

Winter was contemplating another slice of Madeira. Cake like that, no wonder you stuck with your mum.

'Did he ever mention staying at his nan's place at all – Finch?'

'Not that I know of.'

'Any idea where he was living, then?'

'None. Like I said, the bloke was halfway a vagrant already. Dunno where he kipped. Girlfriends, I expect. And mates, if he had any.'

'Got any names, have you?'

''Fraid not. Conversation was something we never got into.' Sullivan wanted to know when Finch had last been in the café. 'Friday. I'll tell you exactly: Friday after lunch. Say two, two-thirty. Lou was doing the tables.'

'You remember what he was wearing?'

'Black. He always dressed in black. Black T-shirt, black jeans, manky old leather jacket. That wasn't the point though, see. He was limping, limping quite bad.'

'You know why?'

'No. He has a bit of a session with Lou, heads together like, then he's out the door again.'

'Could you see any damage?' Winter this time, touching his own face.

'No. They were over by the window, but no. He looked the same old dosser to me. Never shaved. Never discovered soap and water. Can you imagine that? Girl like Lou wasting her time with a bloke like Finch?'

'And you didn't see him again? He didn't come back?'

'No.' Galea shook his head. 'We packed up Friday around half five, six. Why don't you hang on till tomorrow? You can talk to him yourself then. He's bound to be in.'

Sullivan glanced across at Winter. Winter shrugged, and reached for the second slice.

'I'm afraid he's dead, Mr Galea,' Sullivan said.

Eddie frowned and then got to his feet and went to the window. He gazed down at the street for a moment or two.

'Dead how?'

'We think someone may have killed him.'

'And that's why you're here?'

'Yes.'

There was a soft swish as Eddie pulled the curtains. Then he was back with them, settling into the sofa with an expression of mild regret.

'You don't seem surprised,' Winter grunted.

'About Finch?' He looked at them both, then reached for his teacup. 'You're right. I'm not the least bit surprised. Bloke like that was put on earth to make trouble for himself. I don't suppose too many people will miss him either. Except Lou.'

*

Back at Fratton nick, Winter found Dave Michaels in his office next door to the incident room. People were coming and going all the time, swiping their cards through the electronic lock on the secured door that accessed the entire floor. So many bodies on a Sunday evening meant a sizeable overtime bill. Most murders were either solved within the first forty-eight hours or dragged on for months. Willard had obviously put his foot on the throttle.

Michaels was intrigued by Winter's news. This was the first definite sighting of Finch on the Friday of his death, and would anchor the time line Willard needed to establish. Only by plotting his movements hour by hour would they be able to implicate others.

'You telling me someone had a pop at him before he got into the caff?'

'I'm telling you the guy was hurt. I got a statement off this bloke Eddie. Finch had definitely been in the wars.'

'But the girl didn't say anything?'

'No.'

'Did Eddie ask her?'

'He says he did. She wouldn't talk about it.'

'So where did Finch go next?'

'Fuck knows. Back out in the rain.'

'Did he have the motor with him?'

'Eddie doesn't know, but the motor's interesting. Finch had got himself booked for a double yellow, right outside the caff.'

'When?'

'Last week. Apparently he'd been pissing off the local warden and the bloke was just waiting for his chance.'

'Excellent.' Michaels was already reaching for the phone. Information on parking offences was held at the civic offices. With the date and location, they could come up with a registration for the car from the database. The office was probably unmanned on Sundays but it was certainly worth trying.

Waiting for the call to answer, Michaels eyed Winter.

'Anything else?'

'Yeah. Finch was obviously in deep with all kinds of villains. This guy Eddie isn't into names and addresses but he didn't have to spell it out. Bloke was a right little scrote. Whatever he touched turned to shit.'

Michaels bent to the phone. One of the traffic wardens had finally answered his call. The office staff with access to the database didn't work on Sundays but given the urgency a call to the manager would get someone in to fire up the system. Michaels scribbled a number and then put the phone down. Winter was still standing by the open door. Michaels told him to close it.

'Willard's chuffed,' Michaels said. 'He'll never tell you but that was good, finding the girl. He thinks we can get a bit of leverage there. You know how many bodies he's asking for now? Starting tomorrow? Another dozen.'

'You're kidding.' Even Winter was impressed. A squad that big and there wouldn't be anyone left for the other thousand crimes awaiting investigation.

The phone rang and while Michaels answered it Winter mused on the direction this inquiry was taking. The thought that the entire city could be virtually stripped of cover for a scrotey little tosspot like Bradley Finch was deeply ironic. Alive, he'd already attracted more than his fair share of CID time. But that wasn't the point and Winter knew it. The skinny little corpse on Hilsea Lines had been a declaration. There'd been a perfunctory attempt to dress murder up to look like suicide but the evidence that Finch had taken his own life went no further than a noose and a kicked-over crate with the word Schweppes on the side. The rest – the broken ribs, the swollen face, the thong – sent a very different message. Take one look at Bradley Finch dangling in the rain, and you'd have a very pressing reason not to mess with whoever had done it.

To Willard, of course, that was unacceptable. In his own dry phrase, it was a question of appropriate behaviour. There were certain things you simply didn't do, not in a city for which Willard was responsible, and killing other people was one of them. There was a line to be drawn here. And Willard was only too willing to oblige.

Michaels had finished his phone conversation. He'd been talking to Jerry Proctor at Margate Road.

'What have they got?'

'They found blood in the bathroom. Spots on the splashback.'

'Enough for a swab?'

'Easy. They got some good lifts from the girl's room too. Jerry's sent them over to Netley.'

The fingerprint department at Netley would photograph the prints and then grid them for analysis on the NAAFIS computer. They'd have a result by tomorrow.

'What else?'

'They went through her rubbish. They found an interesting receipt.'

'What for?'

'Three bottles of champagne from Thresher's – Moët. And a bottle of Harvey's Bristol Cream.'

'When?'

'Friday night. 18.56.'

Winter was doing his best to make sense of this news. 'But the girl doesn't drink.'

'Exactly. That's what you said earlier. And there's more. They found three corks in the rubbish, all champagne, but only two bottles. No sign of the sherry either. So what happened to the third bottle of Moët?'

Winter was up to speed now. *Tearing of the rectal tissues consistent with the introduction of a foreign object.* He was gazing at Dave Michaels. Someone with an empty champagne bottle and a warped sense of humour? Someone who'd come to the house to add their own little contribution to the party?

'That's an assumption,' Michaels said. 'We've got nothing that puts him there, nothing solid.'

'Yeah, but . . .' Winter was frowning. There were three other guys in the house, all students. This morning he and Sullivan had seen one of them. What about the other two?

'We've seen them both. Friday night all three were out. The house was empty. Until the girl came back.'

'With chummy.'

'Maybe.'

Winter was trying to imagine the way it might have been: Bradley Finch confronted by someone determined to teach him a lesson. The evidence was there at the post-mortem, totally beyond debate.

'At least he was pissed,' he murmured.

He got to his feet and went to the window, thinking of Louise and wondering whether there was anything they could trust in the statement she'd signed earlier. According to Eddie, she'd lied about not seeing Finch recently. According to the student he and Sullivan had met at Margate Road, she'd lied about Finch never turning up there. And now, with the receipt, she'd lied about her movements on Friday. How could you be halfway to the Hayling ferry and buying champagne, all at the same time?

Behind him, Michaels was heading for the door.

'She's barmy, that girl,' Winter pointed out. 'She must have known the statement would fall apart.'

Dave Michaels laughed. 'You haven't heard the rest of it. I had one of the surveillance guys on just before you came in. Guess where she's been all afternoon?'

'Pass.'

'The bloody Odeon, up at North End. No one goes to see *Castaway* twice.' He frowned. 'Do they?'

It was supper time before Faraday and his son got round to their first real conversation. J-J had been asleep all afternoon, still sprawled on the sofa, and by the time he woke up he seemed to have shaken off the worst of the previous night's drinking. Quite what pleasure you'd get from sinking three litres of strong French lager alone in a cemetery was beyond Faraday but five hours of checking on his slumbering giant had made him conclude a pact with himself. He would, at all costs, avoid a confrontation. For both their sakes, they had – somehow – to work this thing out.

Rested and starving, J-J gladly signed up to roast chicken with all the trimmings, signalling to his dad not to forget the Yorkshire puddings. When he was happy, J-J sometimes had a habit of humming. Deaf, he'd been denied music and so humming some favourite tune was out of the question, but there'd been moments years back when Faraday had been astonished at how J-J occasionally stumbled across a sequence of notes that was recognisably musical. He was doing it now. Faraday picked up the tune and – without pushing too hard – arrived at a spirited version of the final movement of Beethoven's last symphony. A couple of stiff malts had put him in the mood for something stirring. 'Ode to Joy', he thought. Good sign.

Oblivious of his dad's musical efforts, J-J was reading a brochure on Corsica he'd found in the lounge. He picked it up and showed Faraday a page that featured the ancient citadel at Calvi.

'You've been there?' he signed.

'Yep.'

'When?'

With a surge of guilt, Faraday realised he'd never mentioned the holiday to J-J. No postcard. No lengthy email afterwards describing the afternoon he'd seen no less than three red kites riding the thermals high above the Restonica Valley.

'September,' he signed. 'Just a couple of days.'

'Who with?'

'No one. I went by myself.'

J-J lifted an eyebrow, plainly surprised, and Faraday knew at once that he'd made a big mistake. The Macallan might do wonders for his peace of mind but it blew his judgement completely. J-J knew Marta and liked her. If he was here to stay for a while he'd doubtless meet her again. What happened when he discovered that his dad had been lying about Corsica? And why, more importantly, had he bothered with the deceit in the first place? Was he that guilty about screwing someone else's wife?

'You enjoyed it?' J-J wanted to know more.

'Hot.' Faraday wiped his brow, then mimed eating and gave J-J the thumbs-up.

'Good food?'

'Excellent.'

'Fish?'

'On the coast, lots and lots. More stewy things and wild boar inland.'

'Wild *boar*?'

'Yes. Delicious taste.'

'But not as good as the seafood?'

'Nothing's ever as good as the seafood.'

'You had scallops?'

'Scallops this big.' Faraday shaped the air with his hands. 'I had them so often I nearly got sick of them.'

He ducked his head and looked away, aware of just how deep a hole these needless lies were digging. J-J seemed to have sensed it, too. Things didn't quite add up.

'*How* many days were you there?'

'Two. Maybe three. Two and a half.'

'You must have been eating all the time.'

'I was.'

'Really?' J-J cocked an eyebrow.

In any other context, this would have been comic, the all-knowing detective snared by his own carelessness, but at the bottom of this daft lie lay a deeply uncomfortable truth: Faraday was ashamed of what he was up to with Marta, and even more appalled about the possibility of his son finding out.

Life may have robbed J-J of a mother at a very early age but Faraday had devoted the next twenty years to making the very best of what they had left. In this, ironically, he'd been all too successful and he was now beginning to realise the price that J-J was paying. He'd gone to France with Valerie in the belief that relationships were forever. Now he was back knowing that they weren't. Not only that, but here was his father of all people busy wrecking someone else's marriage.

Faraday started on the batter for the Yorkshire puddings, wondering what he'd feel in J-J's place. Maybe he should simply own up. Maybe he should set the record straight about Corsica, and Marta, and her loved ones down the road. Maybe it was time to let J-J in on the secret: that life, married or otherwise, had become a gigantic free-for-all. That nothing, sadly, was forever.

He turned to find the travel brochure discarded for a colour supplement article on the best of this year's crop of RADA graduates. J-J was totally engrossed and it was only later, with the wreckage of the dinner strewn across the table, that he shared his big idea with Faraday. In Caen he'd been working with some of the local kids. He'd got himself involved in drama and mime. He'd liked the work. Maybe he could do something similar here. No?

Faraday warmed at once to the idea. He'd spent most of the day trying to figure out what to do with the boy. J-J's previous flirtation with paid employment hadn't been a success. He wasn't the least bit work-shy, or timid when it came to making friends, but people had sniggered behind his back and played the odd trick, and one day it had gone too far and he'd walked out, vowing never to return.

Voluntary work, however, might be less hazardous. God knows, there were some tough kids in the city, but Faraday had the feeling that kids who were truly on the edge often felt a kinship with rare birds like J-J. Was it fanciful, this notion? Or might this strange, eager, sullen, newly shorn twenty-three-year-old of his find a perch that truly suited him? Faraday didn't know but there was no alternative to finding out.

'Great idea,' he signed back. 'I'll make some enquiries.'

It fell to Winter and Sullivan to drive down to the Thresher's branch in Clarendon Road and check out the receipt from Margate Road. Business was slow for a Sunday night and they were in luck with one of the two assistants behind the counter. Yes, she'd been on duty on Friday evening. And yes, three bottles of Moët rang a bell.

Winter produced the receipt. It was grease-smeared from Louise Abeka's waste sack and the woman flattened it on the counter before peering at the date and time.

'18.56,' she confirmed. 'That sounds about right.'

She'd been busy that night. Fridays were always hectic but it was rare to sell Moët in threes.

'You remember the customer?'

'Very well.'

'You can describe her?'

'Her?' She was frowning. 'It was a bloke. Scruffy guy, thin. Leather jacket, black T-shirt. Real mumbler, too. I remember saying to Debs, bet he's on drugs.'

Winter took her through it again, making absolutely sure she was certain of the facts, then stepped into a tiny storeroom at the back to write out a formal statement.

Returning to the incident room half an hour later, it was Sullivan who voiced the obvious question. Finch, according to more or less everybody, was skint. So how come he can suddenly afford fifty quids' worth of Moët plus a bottle of Bristol Cream?

Dave Michaels, feet up in his office, had the answer.

'He's a tea leaf,' he pointed out. 'Guy nicks stuff. Sells stuff. Tabs.

Weed. Property. Whatever. It's the end of his working week. He's celebrating. Just like everyone else.'

Winter wasn't convinced. The way he heard it, Finch was disaster on legs. Put him in the movies, he'd be Frank Spencer. He couldn't do anything right. Ask him to cross a street and he'd be under a bus in seconds.

'The bloke was inadequate,' he said. 'Fifty quid would be a fortune.'

'So where did he get it?'

'Good question.'

Michaels eased his legs off the desk. Willard had appeared at the door. He'd been going through the informant reports again and he wanted a word. Winter began to back out of the office but Willard told him to stay.

'Shut the door,' he said.

Willard had the reports in a folder. He tossed them onto the desk. There was bugger all in there but that, in itself, was significant.

'You're right, boss.' Michaels had opened the file. 'No one's talking.'

'Yeah, and you know why? Because the word's obviously out. Everyone seems to know Bradley Finch, everyone seems to know what a little shit he was, but Friday night's suddenly a no-no. Everyone's blanking it. No one laid eyes on him. Not in a pub. Not at some party or other. He just disappeared. Any other night of the week you could find me half a dozen grasses who'd know exactly what he was up to, but all of a sudden everyone's really shy. So what does that suggest?'

'It means the message got through, boss,' Winter said thoughtfully, 'just like the man intended.'

Chapter twelve

The mortuary at St Mary's Hospital was a gloomy, Victorian red-brick building that always reminded Dawn Ellis of a Unitarian chapel she'd once been obliged to attend as a kid. It was battered, depressing and constantly featured in the facilities listed for demolition by the hospital trust management team.

Ellis found Jake, the senior technician, bent over a collection of pot plants in the post-mortem theatre. He'd already prepared the body of Helen Bassam for the pathologist, and she lay naked on one of the stainless steel tables. Her head was propped on a stained wooden block and the hose he'd used to wash her down lay dripping in a nearby sink. Beside the sink, neatly laid out, were a set of surgical instruments. The scalpel, in particular, looked enormous.

Jake was apologising for the late start. The pathologist was stuck in traffic after an accident on the motorway and the technician was taking the opportunity to give his plants a good seeing-to with Baby Bio. Health and Safety regulations required seventeen changes of air an hour in the theatre and in his view the plants thrived on it. He put them in here at the start of every weekend and he was certain they knew when Friday was coming round.

Ellis was looking at the body of the girl. She was still beautiful – long legs, lovely little breasts – and despite her injuries, Ellis could see the woman that she might one day have become. As it was though, she was waxy and lifeless, a doll that had suffered damage in transit and was now being returned to the makers. The back of her skull was caved in, a tangle of hair thickly matted with blood and bone chips, and there was an odd look to her torso, a dip as if someone had pushed too hard on her chest. Her arms lay beside her body, palms turned outwards, but Ellis could see a jagged splinter of bone, fiercely white, protruding through the flesh at her elbow, and more evidence of multiple fractures in both legs. Jake had done his best to tidy her up but gravity and God knows what else had scrawled a terrible message on her young body. Anyone who ever contemplated jumping off a twenty-three storey building should be in this chill, white room, thought Ellis. One look at Helen Bassam and you'd be back in the lift within seconds.

Jake had finished with the Baby Bio. He wanted to show her something on the body. Ellis stood beside him while he eased the girl's wrecked legs open. On the inside of each thigh, way up towards the top, was a message handwritten in blue ink. According to Jake, the ink was indelible.

Ellis bent to make sure she'd got the message right, one word on each thigh.

'*Pour vous?*' she queried.

Jake had been talking to someone who spoke French.

'It means "For you,"' he said, 'but apparently she got it wrong. Situation like that. . .' he nodded at her open thighs '. . . you'd use *toi*.' He looked at Ellis. '*Toi?*'

Ellis nodded. She could see the open drawer in Helen's bedroom, the little French dictionary amongst the jumble of make-up and CDs. She must have done this for her private tutor, Ellis thought. She must have picked up the two words, *pour vous*, and got busy with the indelible felt-tip. The phrase was an invitation, maybe even a command. More mutilation.

'You're staying for the PM?'

Ellis shook her head. She wanted the legs closed again. She wanted to be anywhere but here. She nodded down at the body on the table.

'We need full tox,' she said.

'No problem.'

Jake returned to his plants and scribbled himself a note for the pathologist. Tests for drugs and alcohol normally took between four and eight weeks to come back. Was Ellis asking for fast-track?

Ellis was still beside the girl. With her lids back, she had the loveliest green eyes.

'Definitely,' she murmured. 'Quick as you can.'

Faraday was a couple of minutes late for the meeting with Willard. The Detective Superintendent had phoned first thing, wanting him to drive over to the Major Crimes suite for nine o'clock, but they'd been having problems with a serial flasher targeting young women in ground-floor flats, and the guy had chosen last night to tap on more lit windows before dropping his pants. Already short-staffed, Faraday had struggled to find two DCs with the time to start sorting it out, and he was still wondering how they'd cope with last week's backlog when he stepped into Willard's office.

Willard was at his computer, authorising applications from the Intelligence Cell for access to billing on yet another mobile phone. These forms he then emailed to the Telephone Intelligence Unit at headquarters. Standing there watching, Faraday was amazed that a Detective Superintendent should be saddled with all this clerical work. The man was on £57K a year. Didn't that kind of rank buy you the services of a clerk down the corridor?

'You have to be joking.' Willard had just blacked half the form by mistake. 'You know how many unallocated actions I'm looking at this morning? Seventy-one. And you know how many blokes I've got on the sharp end? Ten. This is one job we can't afford to get wrong and we're already playing catch-up. Makes you wonder, doesn't it?'

He typed a final line of text, clicked on the mouse and shot a murderous look at the printer. Moments later, the form began to emerge.

'So . . .' he finally spun the chair round towards Faraday '. . . tell me about the girl.'

'Girl?'

'Off the flats. That little squad you've put together. Pressing, is it? Or something that might wait?'

Faraday understood at once where this conversation was leading. Willard was on the scrounge. Doubtless he'd already been on to Operational Support, begging for extra bodies, and now he wanted hard intelligence for the moment headquarters came back and told him the cupboard was bare. Nonsense, he'd say. Take Faraday's lot, for instance.

'We've put a lot of work in,' Faraday began, 'and thank Christ we did.'

He told Willard about the girl going off the rails, and about the company she'd begun to keep. Her father had come forward, voluntarily, with worries about drug abuse. He'd been giving his daughter a generous allowance and he'd started to wonder where it had all gone.

'Are we talking Class "A" stuff?'

'It's possible. I've asked for tox on the body.'

'When's the PM?'

'This morning.'

Faraday paused, and then began to tell him about Doodie. The kid, he said, was just ten. At least one witness put him in the flats around the time the girl went off the roof.

'And what does the boy say?'

'I don't know. We still can't find him.'

'You're telling me he hasn't turned up? Where have you looked?'

Faraday listed the lines of enquiry. The boy's mother hadn't been in touch since Faraday's visit to her flat but that wasn't a surprise. He had a call in to the woman who ran the Persistent Young Offenders project and if she couldn't help then he'd organise a ring round the other agencies. One way or another, they'd lay hands on the child.

Willard was interested now.

'You don't think something's happened to him?'

'I don't know.'

'What about mates? Every kid's got mates.'

Faraday mentioned his exchange with Trudy Gallagher's mother. Trudy had been big mates with Helen Bassam. Helen seemed to know Doodie. Odds-on, therefore, that the mother might have remembered the name.

'But no joy,' Faraday concluded. 'Name didn't ring a bell.'

Willard was leaning forward now. 'This is Misty Gallagher?'

'Yes.'

'You know who she's screwing?'

Faraday shook his head, alarmed at the weight of Willard's sudden interest. Stealing bodies from Faraday's divisional team was one thing but this was quite another. Show Willard a decent job, something really intriguing, and he'd nick it for Major Crimes.

'Who's that then?' he said stonily.

'Bazza McKenzie. She's been sorting him out for months. He's just bought her a place in Gunwharf, little love nest with one of those nice harbour views.'

Willard's phone began to ring and he pounced on it. Barry McKenzie was a major drugs dealer who was trying to stitch up the entire city. One of his many legit enterprises was the Café Blanc, which explained a great deal about Misty Gallagher sprawled across the window on Saturday night, just like she owned the place. Given the association with Bazza, she probably did.

Willard barked down the phone and then hung up. He scribbled something on a pad and spun round again. Faraday had never seen him so cheerful.

'Scenes of Crime.' He was beaming, 'We put a POLSA team back onto Hilsea Lines at first light. I wanted them to extend the search north. You know where I mean? Over the top and down towards the creek?'

Faraday nodded. He could picture it now. Flocks of dunlin pecking around on the mudflats.

'And?'

'They just found it. Exactly where I thought.'

Willard explained about the missing bottle of Moët from Margate Road. A PC on the POLSA team had retrieved it from the undergrowth at the foot of the ramparts. If Willard had got it right, they were looking at a forensic bonanza: DNA from Finch's arse plus prints.

He stood up. He had a ton of calls to make. On his way out, Faraday should put his head round Brian Imber's door. Brian was running the Intelligence Cell. He'd been putting together all kinds of stuff on McKenzie and some of it might be useful for locating Doodie.

'And hey, what did I tell you?' Willard's gesture took in every corner of his empire. 'Good fun, eh?'

Brian Imber was a DS from the Crime Squad up at Havant. Faraday had known him for years and liked him a great deal. He was a squat, combative, fit-looking fifty-three-year-old who lived on the seafront at Hayling Island and still ran three fast miles twice a week. He'd come to the job late after eight years in the merchant marine and had quickly developed an obsessive interest in the link between drug abuse and the ever-soaring crime rate.

That was back in the late eighties. Imber had gone into print, producing paper after paper to support his conviction that everything – street offences, robbery, fraud – linked back in some way or other to drugs. It was unusual for a working detective to go to lengths like these and in a stroke of organisational genius, headquarters had given him his head. The past couple of years, Brian Imber had headed the Intelligence Cell in the Havant-based Crime Squad, a hand-picked team of detectives charged with tackling cross-divisional villainy.

Just now, he was sharing the office next to Dave Michaels with two of his DCs from Havant. As intelligence began to flood in on the Bradley Finch inquiry, it was their job to sieve it for those little tiny nuggets that would establish time lines and a firm list of what Willard liked to term 'persons of interest'.

Seeing Faraday at the door, Imber got to his feet and pumped his outstretched hand. He'd heard the rumour that Faraday was joining Willard's little army. How was he getting on?

Faraday put him straight at once. He was still divisional DI down at Highland Road. Just like always. Willard was snatching bodies as fast as he could and it was Faraday's job to fight him off. Just like always.

'So how's it going?' Faraday asked.

'Slow. But then these things always are, aren't they? Once we get some serious billing, we can ping a few mobe sites and see what these buggers have been up to.'

Faraday was looking at a stack of the forms that Imber had been passing through to Willard for submission to the TIU. No one knew better than Imber that mobile telephony had transformed crime investigation. For a hefty fee, the phone companies could trace the geographical source for specific calls from mobile phones. In cities like Portsmouth, with lots of cell sites, they could sometimes be accurate to a hundred metres. As a device for breaking alibis, the new technology was invaluable.

Imber was talking about the first of the provisional suspect lists. Problem with a scrote like Bradley Finch was the sheer range of his social contacts. There wasn't anyone bent in the city that he hadn't pissed off in one way or another.

'Was he dealing?'

'Low level, yes, but he was pond life. He'd pick up tabs here, speed there, knock on a few doors, cash them in. Fifty years ago, he'd have been a tramp or a rag-and-bone man. Might have saved his life.'

'So who wanted him dead?'

'Good question, my friend. People we're talking to at the moment don't understand it. OK, he was a pain in the arse, but you don't knock someone off for that, do you? Establish a motive and we're halfway there.'

Faraday was thinking about the champagne bottle. Pain in the arse was about right, though it was news to Imber that the bottle had been found.

'That's a bonus,' he agreed. 'Definite gold star. What's with you, then?'

Faraday explained about Helen Bassam. There was a whisper that she'd been doing drugs.

'But that makes her normal, doesn't it?' Imber's dry laugh signalled anything but mirth. His implacable determination to get the upper hand in the drugs war was rooted in an incident that had affected one of his own kids, though no one was quite sure about the details.

Faraday mentioned Doodie. His real name was Gavin Prentice. He'd been on to the Child Protection Unit, read the file, but all that intelligence hadn't taken him an inch closer to finding the kid. Even the local beat officers, who'd only known him by his real name, hadn't a clue where he'd gone.

'So how can he just disappear?'

'Easily, Joe. OK, ten's young, but kids these days are on a different planet. And that's because they want to be. They've lost interest in the real world. We've explained the rules and they've had a bit of a think and then buggered off.'

'And drugs?'

'Definitely. Uppers. Downers. Anything they can get down their tiny throats. Heavy gear, too, if they've got the money. There are kids of twelve doing smack and cocaine. And men twice their age, blokes who should know better, selling it. Sort that lot out and we'd all be sitting on some big fucking beach, getting pissed all day.'

Faraday smiled. Imber, who had a legendary thirst, was one of the few serving policemen who'd dared to call for the legalisation of drugs. Not just cannabis, but all drugs. It wasn't the chemicals that upset him; it was the low life who made a fortune flogging the stuff.

'Tell me about Misty Gallagher,' Faraday said slowly. 'The girl who died was best mates with her daughter.'

'Trudy?'

'Yes.'

This was news to Imber – Faraday could see it in his eyes – and he wondered which piece of the jigsaw he'd handed him now.

'She fucks Bazza McKenzie,' Imber said carefully. 'I don't know what she does for him but it's bought her a big fat part of what he's putting together and, believe me, they don't come more ambitious than Bazza.'

Faraday could see one of the DCs nodding in the background. Bazza McKenzie had taken over where another major dealer called Marty Harrison had left off. Shot in the chest during an early morning arrest by Cathy's husband, Pete Lamb, Marty had beaten a sensible retreat with most of his extended family to Marbella, leaving the local drugs market wide open. Faraday was a bit woolly about the fine print but he was certainly aware that McKenzie had cranked the notion of indiscriminate violence up a notch or two, leaving a trail of appalling beatings behind him.

'Would Misty be in a position to keep Trudy supplied with drugs?'

'Certainly. Anything she fancied.'

'So the girl Helen Bassam . . .'

'Of course.' Imber was smiling. 'You've met Misty? Ever had the pleasure?'

'Saturday night.'

'And you know how she got the name?'

Faraday shook his head, aware of the same detective at the desk behind rolling his eyes in anticipation of a story he'd obviously heard a million times before.

Imber didn't care.

'She's a looker, isn't she, Misty? She's getting on now but younger, you can just imagine, and the thing is she had the best knockers you've ever seen. Just amazing they were, just . . .' he cupped both hands '. . . amazing. Well, here's the scam. She had a little game she used to play at parties. Everyone would have a few drinks and after a while she'd start looking round. It was always blokes with glasses she was after. Otherwise, she wasn't interested. OK, so she'd find some bloke she fancied and then she'd sit on his lap and after a bit she'd just lean forward and blow on his glasses . . .' he mimed it '. . . like that. Well, the glasses go all misty and by the time he's wiped them clean she's stripped off her top and he's looking at these incredible knockers. Never failed.'

The detective at the desk was nodding at Imber's back. Faraday took the hint.

'You saw this for yourself?'

'Better than that, my friend.'

'She did it to you?'

'Dead right, she did.'

'But you don't wear glasses.'

'No, I don't, but in my game you ask around a bit first.' He grinned at Faraday and then nodded. 'Borrowed some off a mate of mine. Worked a treat.'

Paul Winter, three minutes late to the management meeting down the corridor, incurred Willard's wrath.

'We're running a murder investigation here. It's my time you just wasted.'

'Sorry, boss.'

Winter settled into the spare chair at the corner of the long conference table. He wasn't part of the management group, far from it, but Willard wanted his input on the girl, Louise Abeka, and he was only too happy to oblige.

Willard called for a summary of the latest developments from Sammy Rollins. The Deputy SIO had been up half the night with the latest addition to his family and looked knackered. Best news had come from the parking office at the civic centre. The staff who looked after the database had come up with a registration on the white Fiat. The plate had been flashed to all traffic cars in the county and circulated on an all-forces bulletin beyond. At Willard's insistence, every street in Portsmouth was to be revisited in case the car had crept back into the city, and he'd made arrangements with Media Services at headquarters to have the details highlighted on TV and radio news bulletins. From the Force Identification Bureau at HQ, meanwhile, had come news that the car had been stop-checked only ten days ago in Cosham. The driver had given his name as Kenny Foster, with a Southsea address, and had failed to produce his licence and insurance details afterwards. FIB were currently tracing the traffic crew who'd filed the report and would be back in touch later in the day.

Willard was scribbling on his pad.

'Kenny Foster, anyone?'

Heads shook around the table. Willard called for Brian Imber, filling in more details while they waited. The Prison Department at the Home Office were sending down a wad of stuff on Finch's two spells inside. He might have made enemies and, if so, Willard wanted these people traced and eliminated. On Willard's prompting, Media Services had already been talking to the *Crime Watch* producers, and if the inquiry had made no headway by next month there was a definite prospect of a slot in the March edition. The first submission of forensic items had been despatched and he was expecting the results back by Wednesday latest.

Imber appeared at the door. Willard told him to pull up a chair.

'Kenny Foster ring any bells?'

Imber nodded.

'Hardest man in Portsmouth,' he said at once. 'Undisputed champion.'

'Mate of Finch's?'

'I doubt it.'

Foster, he said, repaired cars in a couple of lock-ups on a patch of wasteland behind the football stadium at Fratton Park. He'd only been at it a couple of years but he had plenty of customers from the rougher end of the motor trade. Word on the street suggested he wasn't fussy about ringing stolen cars and performing other bits of cosmetic surgery but no one had ever pinned him down, not least because of his reputation in another field.

'Like what?'

'Like bare-knuckle fighting. The man's an animal. Just lives for it. There's a kind of knockout competition on at the moment. Literally. Two blokes square up and knock the shit out of each other.'

'Wagers?'

'Nothing massive. It's about respect, not money.' This was plainly news to Willard.

'Where's all this happen then?'

'Private houses mostly. It's not a spectator thing, not like the old days. It all works on word of mouth. And Foster's never been beaten.'

'So what does winning mean?'

The other guy either jacks it in or he's unconscious. Normally the latter. Last one I heard about, the other bloke was on soup for a month while they mended his jaw.'

Willard nodded, looking at Sammy Rollins.

'So why was Foster driving Finch's car?'

Rollins shrugged and it was Winter who offered a possible answer.

'Maybe he wasn't,' he said. 'Blokes like Foster, Finch's just not in his league. There's no way.'

'You mean someone else gave his name?'

'Yeah.' Winter nodded. 'And you'd need to be seriously stupid to do that.'

Dave Michaels was sitting two down from Willard. Willard caught his eye.

'We need to TIE this Foster, Dave. ASAP.' He went back to Rollins. 'Anyone pay him a visit after the no-show with the licence?'

'No idea.'

'OK.' Willard nodded. 'Then let's get it done.'

He turned back to Winter. He wanted to talk about Louise Abeka. So far, she was their most promising line of enquiry. They'd banked her statement, most of which was nonsense, and in the end they'd have to pull her in for a formal interview under caution, but his inclination right now was to let her run. Purchase of the three champagne bottles put Finch at her place in Margate Road on the night he was killed. One of those champagne bottles might have been used to assault him. The blood in the bathroom might throw up a DNA match with Finch. According to the café owner, she'd already seen him earlier in the day. And her story about spending Friday night at the North End Odeon now looked highly unlikely. Given this tissue of lies, what, in Winter's view, was the likely nature of the girl's involvement in Finch's death?

Winter, who was no stranger to the art of speculation, chose his words with some care.

'Number one, I think she was in much deeper with Finch than she's admitted. Why, I dunno. She's real class. The last thing she'd need was a loser like him.'

'You think she'd feel sorry for him?'

'More than possible. She's a Christian. She might not have gone to church every Sunday but the fact that she toddled along yesterday tells me she knew she was in the shit. That's what you do, isn't it? When the chips are down, the big man takes care of it.'

There was an exchange of glances around the table. Everyone in this room knew about Winter losing his wife to cancer and one or two were wondering whether he too had called on the Lord.

Willard had another possibility. Might the girl have done it herself?

'Alone?'

'Yes.'

'No way. She says she doesn't drive, for a start. Plus it's all business, isn't it? Serious smacking, broken ribs, bottle of bubbly up your arse, rope round your neck. That says Pompey to me.'

'Then maybe she was part of it. Not all of it.'

'But why? And who with? The guy she works for, he'd tell me if she was in deep with the wrong guys. I might not get a name but he'd mark my card, I know he would. And those students she lived with, the one we talked to, the only bloke he'd ever seen come round for her was Finch. I just don't think it stands up.'

Willard was making more notes. When the billings came in on her mobile phone, he'd be better placed to make a judgement on her social life.

'So what are you telling me?' He was looking at Winter again.

'I'm telling you she knows a lot more than she's saying, and I'm telling you she's shit-scared. You had surveillance on her place last night?'

'That's right.'

'Just as well, because there has to be a reason she's so frightened.'

'Yeah, except no one turned up.'

'Sure. Maybe they phoned. Maybe they sent a pigeon. I dunno. All I'm saying is she's number one witness. So far.'

Willard sat back, throwing the meeting open with a flip of his hand. He wanted people to debate this, to put Winter's assumptions to the test. That's the way you did it on Major Crime. That's what teased sense out of chaos.

There was a brief silence. Then Imber cleared his throat.

'I think Paul's in the ballpark,' he said. 'We've been asking ourselves who's showing for it and we've obviously got a list. Problem is, it's a long list. But my money's on a biggish name, someone with a reputation, and that's where the problems start because none of those guys would bother with the likes of Finch.'

'Exactly.' Willard tipped his head back and sucked in a lungful of air. 'So tell me, Mr Winter, how come you're so sure about Louise Abeka?'

Winter took his time. Later, upstairs in the bar, people recalled the tiny smile on his face as he pulled the polythene evidence bag from his pocket. That very definitely wasn't the way you played it. Not with Willard at the head of the table.

'This was waiting at the café first thing this morning.' He held up the bag. 'Eddie Galea gave me a bell and told me about it.'

He passed the bag along the table. Inside was a white envelope with Louise Abeka's name on it. The writing was in capitals, two 'K's in the surname.

Willard stared at the bag.

'What's inside?'

'Finch's ring. The one she drew for us.' Winter folded his arms. 'And she's really, really upset.'

Chapter thirteen

Back at Southsea police station by ten o'clock, Faraday met Cathy Lamb on the stairs. One look at her face told him that the working week was already a nightmare. On top of the serial flasher had come word of three overnight break-ins along the same Southsea street. In one case, the householder had been kipping at his girlfriend's place and had returned to find only marks in the dust where everything valuable had once been. In another, the couple had gone to bed pissed, been robbed, and had only woken an hour ago. While the third house was occupied by a deaf eighty-three-year-old, puzzled by the damage to her kitchen door and the sudden absence of the telly.

Cathy tallied each of the break-ins. Her own calculations suggested that Bill the Burglar would have made, at most, a couple of hundred quid from his night's work, but that wasn't the point. The similar MO argued for a break-in thief prepared to risk being disturbed by the occupants. A situation like that could easily lead to serious violence. So how, exactly, was she supposed to magic yet more bodies to plug this latest hole in the Pompey dyke?

Faraday was looking at the Edward King painting that dominated the wall behind Cathy's left shoulder. The artist had added a garish tangerine lustre to the bombed-out ruins around the cathedral, a touch that Faraday had at first put down to insanity. Now, though, he wasn't so sure. Maybe disaster really was the colour of scorched brick.

'Well, sir?'

The 'sir' was an especially bad sign. Sooner rather than later, Faraday was going to ask a question or two about Pete Lamb passing on Faraday's address but this definitely wasn't the time. Cathy was clearly stretched to breaking point.

'You're telling me there's no one left?'

'No one who's not committed.'

'Anything else come in?'

'Only a couple of calls for you.'

'And?'

Cathy mentioned the warden at Chuzzlewit House. It seemed that a tenant on the twenty-third floor, a neighbour of a Mrs Randall, had just returned from Spain. Apparently he had some information about some kid or other.

Faraday nodded, still engrossed in the picture. What would this artist make of today's city? Unbombed but madder than ever?

Cathy was explaining about the other call. The duty pathologist had rung from the morgue at St Mary's and would appreciate a word or two. She paused, expecting some kind of decision from Faraday about the break-ins, then stared in disbelief as he threw her a brief smile and headed up towards his office.

He found the pathologist's number on his desk. It rang for an age before anyone answered. It was Jake. The pathologist had gone but Jake knew what he'd wanted to say. It was about the young girl, Helen Bassam.

'You took blood for tox?'

'Yeah. It'll go to Southampton this afternoon. Should get a result by the end of the week.'

Faraday glanced up at the calender above his desk.

'You're telling me Friday?'

'Yeah, but there's something else.'

'What's that then?'

'The girl was pregnant. Pathologist reckons a couple of months max.' Faraday heard Jake stifle a yawn. 'Just thought you ought to know.'

With the door shut and the big office empty, Willard left Paul Winter in absolutely no doubt that he'd just made a very silly mistake.

'There are some things that you never fucking do. And one of them is make me look a prat.'

His voice was very soft. Winter was still sitting at the long conference table. Willard was standing over him, his jacket off, his physical bulk blocking the light through the window.

'We understand each other? You get information like that, like you tabled just now, and you give it to me first, or Sammy Rollins, or Dave Michaels. There's a routine here, a way we do things. This isn't some game we made up for your benefit. You're not here to make a big impression. You're part of a team, no more, no less, and you either play by the fucking rules or I'll have you back in uniform checking tax discs on Cosham High Street. OK? You get that? Same wavelength, are we?'

Winter nodded. Situations like these, body language was all-important. He bowed his head, suitably contrite, wondering how quickly he could get the conversation round to Kenny Foster. Someone would have to go and talk to the man. And he knew exactly who it should be.

'Sorry, boss,' he murmured.

'You'd better be.'

'Won't happen again.'

'You're right.'

'So, ah . . .' he looked up '. . . about Foster.'

'Absolutely no chance.' Willard nodded towards the door. 'In a minute or two you're going to walk down that corridor and talk to Dave Michaels. And when you get there, he'll have a couple of jobs for you. If you're lucky, it might be going through the rest of those CCTV traffic tapes. Otherwise, it might be something really boring. You get my drift?'

In the heart of Old Portsmouth, Faraday parked his Mondeo across from the cathedral and walked north along the High Street. In three days, he'd built himself a mental picture of Jane Bassam. She'd have been distraught already about her daughter's behaviour, about her divorce, about her job. There'd been nothing in her life that hadn't gone catastrophically wrong. And then, on top of it all, came the moment when she had to confront the biggest crisis of all. Faraday knew about losing people. Once death robbed you of someone special, you'd give anything for another second or two in their company. Were daughters as irreplaceable as wives? He simply didn't know.

His footsteps faltered as he turned into the cul-de-sac. Jane Bassam's house was two from the end and he stayed on the pavement for a moment or two, thinking of the freezing bungalow at Freshwater and the long days before Janna's funeral when life without her was beyond his comprehension.

The door opened to Faraday's second knock and he found himself looking at a thin, tall woman dressed entirely in black. She had a gaunt, bony face shadowed with exhaustion but there was something about the eyes behind the rimless glasses that told Faraday he'd got it wrong. She had green eyes, like her daughter, and they shone with resolve. For whatever reason, this woman appeared to have found a kind of peace.

'Mrs Bassam?'

She invited him in. The living room was chill and spotless. There were cards of condolence in a perfect line along the mantelpiece, and a single red rose in a fluted vase on the table beneath the window.

Talking about post-mortems in situations like these was never easy and Faraday was still trying to soften the news when Mrs Bassam interrupted.

'So what did they find?'

Wrong-footed, Faraday gazed at her.

'Your daughter was pregnant, Mrs Bassam.'

She nodded, utterly calm.

'And should I be surprised?'

'I don't know. That was going to be my question, or one of them.'

'What else?'

'It's too early to say. We'll be doing blood tests but the results won't be back for a day or two.' He paused. 'Did Helen use drugs at all? That you'd know about?'

This time, Faraday thought he detected a flicker of pain, or perhaps anger.

'Why do you ask?'

'Because her father has expressed some worries on that score. She seemed to be spending a lot of money.'

'You've talked to Derek?'

'Of course.'

'And you believe him?'

'I believe he was worried, yes. And it's a matter of record that she was getting through that allowance of hers.'

'Worried?' She'd seized on the word, suddenly vehement, her icy composure gone. 'You really believe he was worried? A man who walks out on his wife and daughter? A man who wouldn't, for a second, dream of putting his own flesh and blood before that woman of his? May I let you into a family secret, Mr Faraday? Girls need their fathers and Helen needed hers more than most. Don't ask me why because he didn't deserve her but she did everything to get him back. I'd give you chapter and verse but frankly it's all a bit late in the day. At Christmas, do you know what he did? He sent her a postcard and a cheque. From Antigua. And do you know what else there was in the envelope? A photograph.'

Without another word, she left the room. Faraday heard the brisk clump-clump of her footsteps on the stairs, then movement overhead. Seconds later, she was back. The photo showed Derek Bassam squatting on a beach. He was wearing a pair of shorts and a new-looking Nike T-shirt. Nestling beside him was a younger woman, early thirties, in a blue bikini. Both of them were beaming at the camera, their hands gesturing at a message scrawled on the wet sand. 'Happy Christmas, darling,' it read. 'We love you.'

Mrs Bassam was watching Faraday.

'Does that qualify as evidence, Mr Faraday? Do you take that into account when you think about what killed my daughter? She spent most of Christmas in tears. Then I didn't see her for three days.'

Faraday blinked, then did the sums. The pathologist had estimated the tiny foetus at eight weeks. Maximum.

'Where did she go?'

'Where do you think she went?'

'I'm afraid I'm asking you, Mrs Bassam.'

'She went to see *him*, of course. She went to see her nice Afghan friend. I expect she stayed with him in that ghastly slum of theirs. I expect she shared his bed. Because that's what you'd do, isn't it? Faced with something as crass as that.'

Faraday looked at the photo again. Under the circumstances, crass was a mild description. What on earth had Derek Bassam expected? Did he really think this grotesque little billet-doux would sort things out with his abandoned daughter?

'It must have been difficult,' he murmured.

'It was, Mr Faraday, and now you're telling me she was pregnant.'

'Did you know? As a matter of interest?'

'No, I didn't. Helen had difficulty telling me the time of day. That's how bad it got. You know something? You know what really hurts? It's not losing my husband, I can cope with that. In fact in many ways it was a blessing. No, what really hurts is losing my daughter. Not because she's dead. Not because of what happened on Friday night. But because of everything that happened before that. The day Derek left is the day I lost Helen. She became someone else, Mr Faraday, and she never came back.'

Faraday rocked back on the sofa. Listening to this woman was like trying to survive in a hurricane. The blast of her anger was almost physical, a bitterness all the more forceful for being so well expressed. Earlier, he'd wondered about sharing the secret of Helen's intimate tattoos but just now he wasn't sure that Mrs Bassam was ready for a debate about the difference between *toi* and *vous*.

She was on her feet now, looking down at him. Yet another man soiling this tormented world of hers.

'So what are you going to do, Mr Faraday?'

'Do?'

'About Niamat. I don't know much about the law but fourteen's young, isn't it? To be pregnant?'

Faraday nodded. Sixteen was the legal age of consent.

'We can't act on supposition,' he pointed out, 'not without proof.'

'You need proof of obsession? Isn't my word good enough? That she was crazy about him? That she'd do anything for him?' She reached down for the photograph of her husband. 'The only thing that surprises me is that it took this to get her pregnant.'

Faraday was trying to remember Dawn Ellis's description of the contents of Helen Bassam's drawers.

'Was she on the pill, your daughter?'

'I've no idea.'

'You never discussed it?'

'No. We discussed love, when we were still talking, but never sex.'

'And the drugs your ex-husband mentioned? Had you ever . . .' Faraday gestured round '. . . come across anything at all suspicious?'

'Never. Helen came late to all this, Mr Faraday. Until Derek left, she was a child. In less than a year she became something else. God knows, he might be right. It could have been drugs, alcohol, solvents. I've no idea. In my situation, you don't ask because you fear the consequences. One step out of line, one false move on my part, and she'd just blow up. Screaming fits, tantrums, foul language. On a couple of occasions, she even attacked me physically. Once with a glass. Here, in my face. I had to fight her off, Helen, my own daughter. We were down there on the carpet, wrestling. She was like an animal, completely out of control.' She took a tiny step backwards, then steadied herself. 'You're a policeman, Mr Faraday, a detective. I expect you deal with hard evidence – facts – and I don't suppose that any of this is of the slightest relevance, but let me tell you something. Helen and that little scrap inside her didn't simply die, they were murdered. Don't ask me who by because it's not that simple. And don't ask me why because I just don't know. But murder is the word we should be using. Her life was taken against her wishes. It was just blown out, like a candle. Because that's the kind of world we live in, God help us.'

Faraday stared up at her. Merry Devlin was right. Quotes like these would be irresistible in the hands of a certain kind of journalist.

'Has anyone been in contact from the *News*?'

She blinked at him, her eyes moist behind the glasses.

'Yes. And I told them to mind their own business.'

Faraday got to his feet. 'Very wise,' he said. 'But don't think they won't be back.'

Willard was as good as his word. By lunch time, Paul Winter was at the front desk at the city's civic offices, waiting for an escort to the CCTV control room.

He'd been here on a number of occasions, as had most working detectives. Key areas of the city were now under twenty-four-hour surveillance from a network of over a hundred cameras, monitored by two-man crews in the control room. These guys played guardian angels for long, twelve-hour shifts, keeping track of tens of thousands of locals as day blurred slowly into night. Their take on Portsmouth was unique and Winter wasn't the only veteran who looked ruefully back over decades of freezing his arse off in unmarked cars and wondered how surveillance could have become so warm, dry, and – above all – safe. No more abuse from passing drunks. No more giveaways from lippy street kids who could smell the Filth a mile off.

Minutes later, Winter was making himself comfortable in the control room. In the six weeks since his last visit, they'd acquired two more potted plants and a brand new catering-size tin of Gold Blend.

'Milk, one sugar?'

Winter nodded. He was gazing at the banks of colour monitors racked beyond the control desk. The system was brilliant, no question, but there was something slightly eerie about chopping up the city's life this way. Concentrate on one monitor, zoom the camera, and you were watching some student trying to get his leg over a giggling redhead in a bulky anorak on the beach by South Parade Pier. Pan another camera in the Commercial Road shopping precinct, wait for the focus to settle down, and you were with the rest of the guys at the control desk, trying to work out if the bloke bent over the brand new Muddy Fox was nicking it or not.

'Over here, mate.'

Winter turned to find himself looking at a pile of video cassettes on a smaller desk at the back of the room. Dave Michaels wanted him to check out coverage on half a dozen cameras over a twelve-hour period last Friday. The time frame straddled the approximate time of death established for Bradley Finch at the post-mortem and might – with a definite on the registration – yield a positive sighting or two of the white Fiat.

The desk was fitted with a monitor, plus video machines to play and record. Winter could toggle the tapes into fast forward and reverse but even so he knew – barring miracles – that he'd be a video slave for the rest of his working day. He looked quickly through the tape boxes, matching the label on each to a specific camera on the wall chart beside him. Most of the CCTV cameras covered hot spots in the south of the island – the nightclubs along South Parade by the pier, the Leisure Centre at the Pyramids by Southsea Castle, the pubs on Spice Island beside the Camber Dock. These locations became a battleground on Friday and Saturday nights but the further north you went, the fewer cameras had been installed. One day, he thought, the whole bloody city would be taped, every single street, every single house, but for now video coverage had crept no closer to Hilsea Lines than a couple of cameras on major roundabouts half a mile away. He sorted out the relevant tape, and slipped pictures from the Portsbridge interchange into the play machine. To save video tape, this coverage was restricted to single still frames captured every two seconds.

Winter sat back, gazing at the screen as cars hopscotched towards the camera. By six o'clock on Friday night it was already dark and under the orange loom of the big street lights it was by no means easy to suss a white Fiat. He toggled into fast forward and the traffic became a blur. What if the Fiat had had a maniac at the wheel? What if he'd been doing seventy and had shot past in the brief couple of seconds between still frames? He shook his head, toggling back on the picture speed, trying not to think about Kenny Foster. Willard, just to make his day, had told Dave Michaels to sort out another couple of blokes to pay a visit to Foster's garage. Not just that, but one of them – on Willard's specific instructions – was to be Gary Sullivan. Winter shook his head, appalled at how vindictive the man could be, reached for his coffee and toggled the video into fast forward again.

The Brook Centre lay in the heart of Somerstown, an unlovely flat-roofed brick building surrounded by tower blocks, with a fenced-in play area round the back. Years of comings and goings had left their mark on the green swing doors, and someone had recently taken a crack at one of the wired windows.

The Persistent Young Offender project had found a perch in a suite of rooms on the top floor. The entrance door was locked and Faraday had to knock to attract attention. He'd promised Anghared Davies eleven o'clock. It was already quarter past.

Anghared was a small, bustling, bespectacled woman with a reputation for getting her own way. At fifty-two she was old for a job as demanding as this but she had a certain mumsiness that some of the kids, before they knew better, mistook for an easy touch. Faraday had known her for years, way before she'd pioneered the PYO project, and had always admired the deftness with which she managed to carve her way through the tangle of local government-speak that went with any youth initiative. Anghared, as anyone who'd ever crossed her knew to their cost, took very few prisoners.

Just now she was sitting behind a desk, sorting quickly through a towering pile of assessments. From somewhere nearby came the thunder of drums. No rhythm, no shape, just raw noise.

'Doodie, is it?' She was nearly shouting.

'Prentice.'

'Who, dear?'

'Prentice, Gavin Prentice. That's his real name.'

One of the support workers appeared at the open doorway with a youth of about eleven in tow. She had a question about Health and Safety. Did the budget run to earplugs?

Anghared ignored her. She was getting towards the bottom of the pile now, and Faraday left her to it, his eyes following the youth as he drifted across the room towards a revolving typist's chair beneath the window. He detoured to kick aimlessly at a waste paper bin, then pulled the chair into the middle of the room and sat down, spinning himself first one way, then the other, his body slumped, his feet dragging listlessly across the battered carpet tiles. Faraday watched him for a full minute, aware of the boy's eyes beneath the baseball cap, the way they locked with his each time his head came round. His expression was quite blank. Even when Faraday nodded a greeting, the face gave nothing away.

Anghared got to her feet and bustled away down the corridor. Seconds later, the drumming stopped. Back at her desk, she pulled a file from a drawer. Doodie, it transpired, had been on her books for nearly six months. She turned to the youth on the chair and told him to sort out some crisps for himself from one of the support workers. The youth nodded and wandered away. Anghared shut the door after him.

Doodie, she said, had been their little Pimpernel, attending only when there was something on offer that really turned him on. One of those activities was drama. All too often he could be as vile and abusive as any of the other kids, but give him another role to play – let him pretend to be someone else for a while – and you'd sense the depth of potential in the child. It was the same in the graffiti workshops. Get the kid to concentrate for more than ten seconds and interesting things started to happen. As far as Anghared could see, Doodie had shown a real talent for colour and design, an opinion she'd been rash enough to share with the ten-year-old. The following afternoon he'd absconded with a bagful of spray cans, the contents of which had ended up on a brand new Jaguar parked overnight in Old Portsmouth. Detection, in this case, had been simplicity itself. Doodie had signed the biggest of his praying mantis designs with the unmistakable 'D' he liked to use to badge practically everything. Lucky it wasn't in pink, Anghared had told the WPC who'd arrived to track him down.

'Why's that, then?'

'Pink's his favourite colour.' Anghared had hooted with laughter. 'Doodie and good taste were never friends.'

Faraday nodded.

'So where is he now, young Doodie?'

'Haven't a clue. His mum's over in Raglan House but you needn't bother. Most days she's out of it, and when she isn't, she's even more of a nightmare.'

Faraday pulled a face. He could still smell the kitchen, with its spilling refuse sacks.

'Out of it on what?'

'Smack, mostly. The guy she lives with deals a bit but doesn't use. If her luck's in, she gets the sweepings. She used to be into vodka big time but the bloke she was living with then, not the smack dealer, tried to bottle her one night after some row or other and after that she wasn't so keen. Plus I think she's got a liver problem. Any more abuse and it'll explode.' Anghared looked up from the file. 'Doesn't help you though, does it?'

Faraday asked about other places he might look. Doodie, it seemed, had turned ducking and weaving into a way of life, moving constantly from address to address. Some nights, allegedly, he kipped with some relative or other but no one had ever come up with an address. Other nights, he depended on friends, or friends of friends, or people whom – to be frank – she'd prefer not to think about.

'The boy sleeps rough a lot, has done for a while. Get him to concentrate for a minute or so, and he even claims to like it.'

'What does "rough" mean?'

'Houses for letting. Empty garages. Shared squats. Little hidey-holes on the seafront and round the Common during the summer. There's a whole other city out there. One we never see.'

'But he's ten, Anghared.'

'I know, and there's not much to him, either.'

'So how does he get by?'

'Thieving, mostly. Last year he was shoplifting for gangs of older kids. They go in mob-handed, upset stuff, and Doodie nips behind the till while the staff are trying to sort everything out. It's a trick you can only pull once but there are lots of shops. Doodie was on a percentage. I think the kids screwed him down to bugger all but he was helping himself before they even saw the takings so it worked out OK in the end.'

'You've got names for these kids?'

'No, and there's no point either. Last time I asked, he'd fallen in with some bunch of asylum seekers – Kosovans maybe, or Albanians. The way I heard it, they thought he was wonderful. Lots of guts. Lots of initiative. Funny, isn't it, how it takes a foreigner to see the worth in a child? This must be the worst country in the world to be a kid in.'

This was vintage Anghared, kicking against the Establishment line, and Faraday thought again of the youth in the revolving chair – bored, aimless, spinning ever more slowly in circle after circle. At least Doodie wasn't like that. At least he was making some kind of life for himself.

'The incident I mentioned on the phone . . .' he began.

'The girl off the flats?'

'Yes.' Faraday nodded towards the empty chair. 'Have the kids been talking at all?'

'Not that I've heard. She came from Old Portsmouth, didn't she?'

'That's right. But she had lots of friends from round here. Including Doodie.'

Anghared peered at him over her half-moon spectacles, unconvinced. 'How does that work, then? Nice middle-class girl like that straying over the border?'

Faraday shrugged. He wanted to explain about the mother, banged up in a nightmare of her ex-husband's making, about the daughter's life spinning out of control, about the fights and violence, but the truth was that Anghared would have heard it all before. Not in Old Portsmouth perhaps, but certainly here in Somerstown.

The truth was that Pompey was an island, 150,000 people living cheek by jowl, one of the most densely populated cities in the country. There were still social divisions, of course there were. There were still enclaves of tree-lined streets with off-street parking and freshly painted front doors where the middle classes hung on for grim death, believing desperately in all the New Labour tosh about choice and citizenship. But the fact remained that whole areas of the city had become tribal reservations, carpet-bombed by poverty, family breakdown and schools so woebegone and under-funded that even the teachers had given up. The evidence of this was everywhere – street fights, domestic violence, gangs of kids running amok – and in his bleaker moments Faraday had begun to wonder whether the Luftwaffe hadn't been a blessing in disguise. At least, after the Blitz, you knew you were in trouble. How many people recognised a crisis when all the kids were wearing designer gear and no one would be seen dead in trainers under fifty quid?

Anghared was asking him whether he knew how Doodie had got his nickname. Faraday shook his head.

'It came from last summer,' she said. 'All the kids swim in the sea. It's free and it gives them a chance to get up lots of people's noses. Wherever there's a sign saying "No Diving", they'll all have a go.'

Faraday smiled. This had been going on for years and one of J-J's favourite summer pastimes had involved sitting on the pebbles by South Parade Pier, watching the braver kids take a header off the end. At high tide you were relatively safe. A couple of hours either side and you were on your way to hospital. One year, no less than three kids had been seriously injured – one paralysed – in this Pompey rite of passage.

'And Doodie?'

'Round Tower. The kids here say he was the youngest ever off the top. Serious respect, my love. Believe me.'

The Round Tower lay beside the harbour mouth, a Tudor relic that had grown over the centuries. Now it was a favourite tourist spot, with a marvellous view up the harbour, and Faraday himself often climbed the long flight of stone steps, dizzied by the drop, after a pint of two in one of the nearby pubs. There were rocks heaped against the foot of the tower and anyone jumping had to clear them by at least a couple of metres to survive.

'So how did he manage that, then?'

'He didn't. He had to be thrown.'

'Other kids threw him in?'

'Exactly. But the point is, it was his idea. One took his hands, one took his ankles, gave him a couple of swings, heigh-ho, and in he went. Made a big splash. Believe me.'

'You were there?'

'God, no, but I've listened to the kids. That's why he's called Doodie.' She grinned. 'One cool dude.'

Chapter fourteen

By the time the tray of stickies appeared, four in the afternoon, Winter knew he was never going to find CCTV traces of the white Fiat within the parameters Dave Michaels had laid down. Of course it made perfect sense to concentrate on the cameras closest to Hilsea Lines, but those cameras only covered the exits from the island onto the mainland. Drive north, and the Fiat would have turned up on one camera or the other. Head south, back into the city, and there was mile after mile of streets without any coverage at all. Thousands of front doors. Hundreds of garages. And any one of them could still be home to a rusting K-reg Uno.

Winter helped himself to a doughnut and a custard tart. He'd been through the twelve-hour period four times – twice on the mainland cameras and twice, for luck, on a couple of cameras monitoring the major north–south roads down the western side of the island. As the traffic thinned during the evening and then became a trickle after midnight, he'd forced himself to concentrate harder and harder, examining the shape and the colour of the vehicle behind every pair of headlights, but all he'd got for his troubles was a headache. How the guys behind the control desks put up with this every working day was beyond him. Given the choice, he'd have been back in an unmarked Escort, tucked up some darkened side road, working his way through an entire bag of Werther's Originals.

Recorded tapes were kept for a month before being wiped and recirculated. The boxed cassettes were stored in a locked cabinet inside the control room, accessed only by the staff, and he checked the big camera location map pinned to the wall before requesting specific recordings. The Southsea branch of Thresher's, where Bradley Finch had bought the champagne, was in Clarendon Road, barely twenty metres from Camera 20. He located the tape for Friday 9 February and slipped it into the play machine. Pictures from CCTV cameras were recorded in multiplex – a grid of four pictures to each tape – and Camera 20 occupied the top right-hand corner. The time-of-day readout was down on the bottom left of frame. Tapes were always changed at four in the afternoon and he began to spool through, watching as a wet, grey afternoon quickly darkened. According to the note in his pocketbook, the Thresher's receipt was timed at 18.56. Give Finch ten minutes to sort himself out, and the action should kick off around quarter to seven.

At 18.48, a white Fiat appeared at the bottom of the picture. The camera was pointing east, down the road towards Thresher's, and Winter watched as the car halted at a pedestrian crossing beside a big department store. A woman pushing a wheelchair gave the driver a little wave and then the Fiat was on the move again, not bothering to signal left before pulling abruptly into the kerb and stopping on double yellow lines opposite the off-licence. Old habits die hard, Winter thought, watching a thin, slightly stooped figure emerge from the driver's side and limp across the road.

Winter toggled the picture to a halt and peered at the screen. You were supposed to be cautious in these circumstances. You were supposed to perform a little private risk assessment, weighing all the various rogue factors that could conceivably make this someone else – a chance shopper, an impulse buyer, a stranger from way out of the city who just happened to drive a white Fiat and just happened to fancy three bottles of Moët – but Winter knew at once that this was Bradley Finch. The black leather jacket. The black jeans. The lank hair just brushing his collar. The fact – after his appearance in the café – that he was still limping. In six hours this skinny little runt will be having the shit kicked out of him, he thought. And half an hour after that, if he's lucky, he'll be dead.

He toggled forward, keeping an eye on the time readout, trying to imagine the scene inside the offie: the women behind the counter, the scruffy bloke in the leather jacket eyeing the display of champagnes, the detour to the counter to collect the Bristol Cream, and then the 'ker-chunk' of the cash till as he swopped £50.47 for a neatly printed receipt. Where had he laid hands on money like that? How come someone who was perpetually skint was suddenly so flush?

Winter was still pondering this mystery when the passenger door abruptly opened on the Fiat. He slowed the pictures back to normal speed, watching a tall, striking-looking woman in a dumpy black puffa jacket emerge from the car. Closing the door behind her, she walked back towards the camera and stood beside the corner window of the department store, gazing at a display of ethnic rugs. She was there for a good minute – one minute fourteen seconds to be precise – and she must have been yelled at because she only turned round when Bradley Finch was back beside the car, holding up a weighty Thresher's carrier bag.

Winter toggled the pictures into reverse, sending Finch back into the off-licence. As she gazed at the rugs in the store window, the camera offered a perfect quarter profile of the passenger in the Fiat. Louise Abeka hadn't been on the seafront at all. She was here, in full colour, with a man she claimed not to have seen in days.

Prompted by Finch, she ran back to the car. The lights came on, and Finch pulled the Fiat into a tight U-turn ahead of an oncoming bus. Ignoring a couple of pedestrians venturing onto the crossing, he accelerated away, leaving – as he'd arrived – at the bottom of the screen. Winter stopped the tape and made a note of the time readout. There were facilities for dubbing sequences like these onto a fresh tape he could remove from the control room but he'd leave that until later. For now, he wanted to know where Finch was headed. Camera 49 lay at the end of Osborne Road, the continuation of Clarendon Road in a westerly direction. Winter found the tape and spooled through. The Fiat had left camera 20 at 18.59. At 19.00, exactly on cue, it sped into Camera 49's frame. Winter grinned. This was fun, a video game for real. He watched as the car stopped at the T-junction. Turn right, and Finch would be on his way back to Margate Road, where the girl lived. Turn left, and he'd be driving east, beside the big expanse of Common which stretched towards the seafront. He turned right.

Winter sat back a moment, trying to calculate the driving time to Margate Road. Friday night, in light traffic like that, it would be a couple of minutes at the very most before he'd be parking outside Louise Abeka's house. He swung round to the map. Camera 26 policed the traffic junction which offered access to Somerstown, the most direct route. He found the tape and loaded it but, to his disappointment, the white Fiat didn't appear. Not at 19.02. Not at 19.05. And not, as a last resort, at 19.10. They must have gone somewhere else, he thought. Maybe a quick pint of two in a pub somewhere, just to get them in the mood for the Moët. On the point of abandoning Camera 26, Winter stiffened. There it was, the white Fiat, coming to an untidy halt in the very middle of the picture. Winter froze the picture, trying to explain the time lag. 19.12. Too brief a delay for a pint, but far too long if they'd simply driven the half mile.

Aware of a movement behind him, Winter looked round. The shift leader wanted to know whether he fancied another cuppa. Winter nodded. He needed a phone, too. There was a handset built into the main control desk. Consulting his pocketbook again, Winter dialled a local number. He'd tried twice already today but on both occasions there'd been no answer. This time he was in luck.

'Mr Naylor? DC Winter. We met on Saturday. About your lad, Bradley.'

There was a muffled noise at the other end and Winter thought for a moment that Naylor had hung up, but then he was back. He wanted to know what the state of play was. About the gear Winter had seized.

'We're still making enquiries, Mr Naylor, but listen . . .'

He explained he was keen to talk to Bradley's nan. He understood the two were close.

'He'd keep an eye on her, yeah.'

'Did he ever stay there?'

'I've no idea. Why don't you ask her?'

'I'm going to, Mr Naylor. I just need to know where she lives.'

'Yeah?' There was another pause and Winter heard a woman's voice in the background. Flat 2. 59 Flint Street. Southsea.

Winter didn't bother to say goodbye. Hanging up, he returned to the wall chart, confirming what he knew already. Flint Street was only a tiny detour from the route north to Camera 26. Bradley Finch, the night he died, had paid a visit to his nan.

Faraday was alerted to the email while he was still wrestling with his report for Hartigan. One of the Assistant Chief Constables at headquarters was busy developing Project Implementation Documents to support the Chief's new policing strategy. There were dozens of individual subjects to be addressed and every uniformed Superintendent in the force had been assigned at least one of the PIDs.

Hartigan had drawn 'Investigating Burglary' in this management lottery and like every other Superintendent he'd promptly passed the paperwork down the line until the project had landed on Faraday's desk. The last thing Hartigan needed just now was the head-banging challenge of trying to boil down two years' worth of B & Es onto a single sheet of A4 but he suspected that the resulting Best Practice booklet would get the widest distribution and he was determined to earn himself a gold star. Just as long as Faraday did the work.

Faraday put his notes to one side. The email had come from J-J, and wasted few words. 'You promised to talk to someone about me doing drama with kids,' it went. 'What happened?'

Faraday glanced at his watch. He'd meant to pursue this with Anghared Davies and forgotten. She'd still be at her desk in the Brook Club. He lifted the phone and dialled her number. When he explained the idea she said at once that Gordon would love it. Gordon Franks was the young thesp she was using on the drama side. He had an unusual background – a spell in the Royal Marines before drama college – and one of his specialities was fight sequences. The kids loved the way he could choreograph violence and one of the reasons Doodie had taken to the drama sessions so quickly was a little playlet Gordon had composed, calling for Doodie to sort out three older boys with the aid of a cricket stump and a length of electric flex. Doodie had been meticulous about rehearsals, missing no opportunity to perfect his throttling skills before the big performance.

'J-J, you say?'

'That's right. He's been doing lots of drama over in Caen. Mime, mostly. He seems to have a talent for it.'

'Well, he would, wouldn't he?'

Faraday could hear Anghared laughing. She knew J-J from way back, when she'd had a job with Educational Assessment, and she'd always regarded him as a tryer.

'I'll give Gordon a ring right now,' she said. 'It'll be right up his alley.'

Faraday wrote the name down and looked up to find Dawn Ellis at the door. She'd been talking to Cathy Lamb and wanted to know more about the bloke who'd phoned in from Chuzzlewit House.

'I don't know any more. Cathy's got the details.'

'You want me and Bev to check him out? Only now's the time.' She tapped her watch. Today had plainly been a bitch.

Faraday looked up at her and then shook his head. There were decisions he'd been deferring far too long about Helen Bassam and the sight of Ellis at the door was a reminder that he couldn't let the inquiry simply dribble on. He had to make up his mind what was and wasn't important.

'The girl was pregnant.' He nodded at the phone. 'I talked to the pathologist this morning.'

Ellis nodded. Like Jane Bassam, she didn't seem the least bit surprised.

'Are we talking a crime here?'

'We might be. If it was the Afghan guy you told me about.'

'You want me to see him again?'

'Yes. Ask him what he and the girl were up to around Christmas. And tell him we might be interested in a DNA sample.' He offered her a bleak smile. 'OK?'

Operation *Bisley* was beginning to make its mark on Dave Michaels by the time Winter made it back to the MIR at Fratton. The DS was sitting in his office, gazing numbly at the photo of his kid's football team on the wall. He'd been getting by on five hours' sleep a night since the investigation began and already Saturday seemed half a world away. The days of cheering on AFC Anchorage from the touchline were temporarily over.

Winter shut the door before helping himself to a chair. Despite his run-in with Willard, he still regarded hot news as precious currency, to be invested with care.

'Told you, skip.' He put the video cassette in Michaels's lap. 'The girl was definitely lying.'

He explained about the tapes, and the sequence of moves that had taken Finch from the off-licence to Somerstown. The missing twelve minutes had been spent at his nan's place in Flint Street. He'd bet his life on it.

'What about later? Round Hilsea Lines?'

'Nothing. Fuck all.'

'How hard did you look?'

'As hard as the last guy.'

Winter drove the point home with a nod. He'd found the entry in the log the CCTV guys kept in the control room. Someone else from the MIR had trawled the same tapes only twenty-four hours earlier.

'Great use of resources, skip.'

'Two pairs of eyes are better than one.' Michaels nodded up the corridor towards Willard's office. 'You know how we like to get things bottomed out.'

'How is he, then?'

'Like a pig in shit. He got another ten guys at lunch time, came over from the Force Crime Unit. Just to tide us over, mind. They go back on Wednesday, close of play. Still . . .' he gestured at the pile of statements on the desk beside his PC '. . . better than nothing.'

At Willard's insistence, two-man teams of DCs had been combing the flats around Eddie Galea's café, calling door-to-door in case anyone had caught the delivery of the envelope containing Finch's ring. So far, enquiries had produced absolutely nothing though many addresses had been empty and the call-back list now stretched to two A4 pages. The ring itself, meanwhile, had been added to the second batch of items for DNA analysis, and would be on the morning run to Lambeth for the Premium One service. The ring had obviously been handled by someone who knew a great deal about Finch's death and even sweaty fingertips could leave enough material for the latest Low Copy Number technology which could retrieve even minute traces of DNA.

Winter looked pleased. Regardless of the bollocking, Willard had thought enough of his little coup to spend another couple of grand.

'What else, then?'

'We got a preliminary from the knot blokes on the rope round chummy's neck. Jerry Proctor sent their fax over. Nothing special but it's odds-on that whoever tied the knot was left handed. Fuck all use now but later . . .' he shrugged '. . . who knows?'

'What about the girl? Louise?'

'She's back in the caff.'

'Have you still got obs on?'

'Yeah, but Willard's fretting about bodies again. The blokes on the night shift are using a van outside the place in Margate Road and they're making noises about Health and Safety. The book says six hours. You can't argue that.'

Winter smiled, thinking of the CCTV control room with its pot plants, air-conditioning and endless supply of Gold Blend. There were worse places to be when the alternative was a borrowed removals van and the company of a guy with a dodgy gut.

'And Kenny Foster?'

For the first time, Michaels smiled. He'd known Winter far longer than Willard and unlike the Detective Superintendent he allowed mavericks a certain amount of leeway. Sometimes, just sometimes, it paid off, and if Winter's grandstanding led to scenes like this morning's in Willard's office, then at least they'd all have something to talk about in the bar. But the sight of Winter getting his comeuppance was also undeniably sweet, a settling of accounts that some said was long overdue.

'Kenny Foster?' Michaels smothered a yawn. 'I'd talk to young Gary, if I were you. Promising lad, that.'

Winter found Sullivan in the big office at the other end of the corridor. Operation *Bisley*'s task force of DCs was camped out at the half-dozen desks, keeping up with the paperwork between calls. Sullivan was by himself in the corner, hammering away at a keyboard.

Winter stood behind him, looking at the screen. Kenny Foster, it seemed, had been less than helpful. Sullivan had been to see him in the garage, along with an older DC, but mention of Bradley Finch had taken them nowhere.

'Said he'd never heard of him? Are you joking?'

'He meant personally. He'd seen the stuff in the paper.'

'So he knew he was dead?'

'Obviously.'

'But nothing beyond that?'

'No.'

'What about Finch giving his name to the traffic guys?'

'He said a uniform had been round. Hadn't a clue what the bloke was on about. Never heard of the Fiat. Never touched anything Italian.'

'So he blanked you?'

'Totally.'

'What about Friday night?'

'He told us he'd been round a friend's place. She runs a gym or something, and you'd believe it, looking at the guy. Scary, yeah . . .' he nodded, squinting at the screen '. . . definitely scary.'

Winter was thinking hard. Michaels had given him the OK to check out Finch's nan's place but Kenny Foster still fascinated him. You don't give a traffic cop a name like that without a very good reason. Not unless you have some kind of death wish. Winter bent to Sullivan's ear. In a couple of minutes they'd be off to Flint Street but first he wanted to know a little bit more about this gym.

'Where is it?'

'Albert Road.'

Albert Road was in Southsea, a mile of pubs, curry houses, scruffy antique shops and New Age emporia.

'What's the name of this place?'

'Hang on.' Sullivan flipped back through his notes. 'Captain Beefy.' He looked up, puzzled by Winter's grin. 'What's the score, then?'

Faraday was putting the finishing touches to his thoughts on investigating burglary when he got the call from the front desk. Two people to see him. A Mr Niamat and a lady who said she was a solicitor. Faraday checked his watch. 18.17. Ellis and Yates had barely had a chance to make a call on the Afghan. What on earth were they doing here?

He got Yates's mobile number from Cathy Lamb. He and Ellis were en route to sort out a loose end on another job.

'Have you seen the Afghan bloke?'

'Yes, boss.'

'What happened?'

'He went ballistic.'

'Why?'

'You tell me. We did what you said. We asked him about Christmas, and the girl, and he admitted that she'd stayed there. Boxing Day it was, and the day after.'

'And?'

'And nothing. The moment we got down to the business, he just went for us.'

'Physically?'

'No . . .' Faraday could hear Yates muffling a laugh. 'The man's not stupid. No, he just gave us a mouthful.'

Faraday sat back at the desk. Bev Yates doing the business wasn't an experience you'd wish on gentler souls. Twenty years at the sharp end of CID work had bred a deep, deep cynicism and he gave no one the benefit of the doubt, least of all a cultured Afghan with a taste for French poetry. Shagging mixed-up fourteen-year-olds was totally out of order. As he'd doubtless explained.

'He's downstairs now,' Faraday murmured, 'with his brief.'

'Yeah?' Yates was laughing again. 'That's the problem with these people. Don't know how to take a joke.'

Niamat Tabibi and his solicitor were waiting in the interview room on the ground floor. The solicitor's name was Michelle, a plump, freckle-faced woman in her thirties who'd recently joined a biggish practice on Hampshire Terrace. She specialised in criminal defence work and, as a newcomer to Portsmouth, she was known to be gobsmacked by the sheer volume of cases that crossed her desk. Her home town in Devon had never prepared her for anything like this.

'Tea? Coffee?'

Faraday was looking at the Afghan, Niamat. Unlike his solicitor, he'd yet to sit down. He was wearing jeans and a leather bomber jacket and he hadn't bothered to shave for a day or two, but Faraday could sense the passion in the man. Ignoring the offer of a hot drink, he rocked back and forth on his heels, his hands plunged deep in the pockets of his jacket, never once taking his eyes off Faraday's face. Bev Yates had been right. He was very, very angry.

'Tea, please.' It was Michelle.

Faraday left the room. By the time he returned, Niamat had taken a seat beside his solicitor. She took charge at once, explaining that Niamat had been her client since his arrival in the city. He'd walked in off the street and asked for legal representation. As an asylum seeker, he'd complied with Home Office requirements by filling in a Statement of Evidence form and sending it – recorded delivery – to the processing centre at Croydon. When his application for asylum had been turned down for late arrival he'd naturally wanted to appeal. She'd helped him through this process, and they were currently awaiting a date for the hearing. Hence the importance of the business in hand. Niamat was worried that any hint of a misdemeanour might put him on the next plane to Kabul.

'My client tells me you have grounds for ... ah ... complaint.'

'That's right.'

'May I ask why?'

Faraday quickly summarised the case against Niamat. It was a matter of fact that he'd been hired to tutor Helen Bassam in French and maths. It was also a matter of fact that the young girl, as impressionable as any fourteen-year-old, had developed a crush on her new teacher. There'd been a domestic falling-out between Helen and her mother on Christmas Day. She'd fled the house and sought refuge with Niamat. By mid-February, according to the pathologist who'd performed the post-mortem, she was around seven weeks pregnant, and it was her mother's belief that Niamat was responsible. There was also the question of the tattoos.

'Tattoos?'

'Here and here,' Faraday touched the insides of his own thighs, '*pour* and *vous*.'

'And that's it?'

'Yes.'

'No other evidence?'

'None.'

Michelle glanced across at Niamat. He'd been listening intently to Faraday, following every word. Now he leaned forward, his forearms extended on the table, his hands shaping the space in between. Faraday braced himself for a shouting match but the voice, when it came, was low and patient. This was a teacher with a particularly difficult pupil and if it took time to get one or two things straight, then so be it.

'You're right about Helen. "Crush" is a good word. Of course she came to me at Christmas. And you know why? Because she had nowhere else to go. Don't you find that strange? A girl of fourteen? At home with her mother? All those presents? All that food? And she runs away?'

Sensing where this conversation might lead, Faraday shook his head. 'They didn't get on,' he said, 'And Christmas can be difficult.'

'That's what she said. That's exactly what she said. And you know something else? Her mother had told me, too. Told me that exact same thing when I started to teach her daughter. That she hated Christmas because of what it did to families. I'm a Muslim. We have no Christmas. But we do have families. And we know there's a difference between presents and love. Do you know about her father? The present he sent her?'

Faraday remembered the overweight solicitor kneeling in the sand, the smile stretched tight across his jowly face. *Happy Christmas, darling. We love you.*

'He sent her a cheque,' Faraday said.

'And you know how much? Two hundred pounds.' Niamat frowned, feeling for the phrase. '*To buy yourself a little something.* She showed me the card, what he'd written. Two hundred pounds. For a fourteen-year-old.'

There was a long silence. A bus ground past outside. Two hundred pounds would keep Niamat going for a month, the way the Home Office did their sums. Was that what he was here to say? Or was there another message?

'So . . .' Niamat leaned back '. . . you're thinking the girl comes to me, in the place where we all live. She's upset. She thinks she loves me. We go to bed. And hey' – he clicked his fingers – 'a baby. That's what you think. I know that's what you think. She's attractive. She's young. She's easy. She wants me to do it. No man would say no.' He paused, spreading his hands wide, asking the unvoiced question, then let his body tip slowly forward again. 'You suspect what you like, Mr Policeman, but let me tell you something else. Life is more complicated than you think. Go back to Mrs Bassam, and ask her about the man at the cathedral. His name is Phillimore. Ask her about him.'

There was a long pause. Faraday was looking as astonished as Michelle.

'Are you making an allegation? About this Mr Phillimore?'

'Just talk to her. And maybe him, too.'

'Why?'

Faraday gazed at him, waiting for an answer, but Niamat stared him out, refusing to take the exchange any further. Finally, Faraday made a note of the name and then turned to Michelle.

'You must make your client aware of the seriousness of what he's saying,' he began. 'You can't just raise names like this.'

She nodded and then ducked her head as Niamat began to whisper in her ear. At length she glanced at her watch and turned to Faraday.

'My client has a request,' she said. 'But first he wants to know whether you still have the baby.'

'You mean the foetus?'

'Yes.'

'The Coroner won't issue authority for release until we've finished our enquiries. That could be a while yet.'

'Excellent. Then my client requests that you take a blood sample from him now and send it to the labs.' She offered Faraday a smile. 'For DNA matching.'

Sullivan did his best to pump Paul Winter about the gym but Winter wasn't having it. They were driving down to Flint Street from the MIR at Fratton and all Winter would volunteer was the name of the woman who owned it. He'd had quite enough of Gary Sullivan stealing a march on him and saw no point in making life any sweeter for the boy. Life shouldn't be easy in this line of work. There was a pecking order here, and it was Winter's job to reassert it.

'Her name's Simone,' Sullivan grunted. 'Foster told us that already.'

'And what else did he tell you?'

'Nothing.'

'There you are then.' He tapped his nose. 'Local knowledge.'

'What does that mean?'

'It means we ought to pay her a visit. I'll fix it with Dave Michaels. Leave it to me.'

They turned into Flint Street and Winter left the car under a lamp post. It was only a gesture but this could sometimes be a rough area and the forms you had to fill in for vandal damage were as long as your arm.

Flat 2 was on the first floor of number 59, one of a sturdy brick-built block of council flats that looked as though they'd passed into private ownership. Winter rang the bell a couple of times, hearing the sudden blast from a television set as someone opened an interior door. With the main door open, the sound was even louder. *Home and Away*, he thought.

'Mrs . . .?'

A small, wispy-haired woman peered out at him. She was wearing a pink shawl around her shoulders and a threadbare blue dressing gown underneath. She hadn't heard the question and it took Winter nearly a minute to establish her name. Finally, he got it. Mrs Prendergast. She shuffled back down the hall with the two detectives in tow. By the time they were inside the tiny living room, she was convinced they were from the gas board.

'Police,' Winter repeated. 'We're detectives.'

He caught Sullivan's eye and nodded at the television. Sullivan turned the sound down.

'It's about Bradley, Mrs Prendergast.'

'Who?'

'Bradley. Your grandson.'

For a moment, it occurred to Winter that they were lumbered once again with breaking the bad news, but then she sorted the name out in her head and told Winter that he was dead. She said it with some regret, nodding to herself, as if it was an apology. All this way in the rain. And young Bradley gone.

'We're very sorry, Mrs Prendergast.'

'What?'

'Doesn't matter.'

He helped her into the chair pulled up by the television and turned the set off completely. She watched the little white dot disappear, more confused than ever, then favoured Sullivan with a slightly crazed smile.

'Would you like an apple, dear?'

Sullivan said no thanks. He had his pocketbook out and he was studying a couple of cheaply framed photos on the mantelpiece. The younger Bradley, still unmistakable, had the kind of winning, trustful smile that could get a young lad into big trouble with certain kinds of older men.

Winter wanted to know when Mrs Prendergast had last seen her grandson.

'Often.' She nodded towards the open door. 'He stayed here a lot. Gave him a key, see?'

'But when did you last see him?'

'Had his own room, like. I'll show you.'

She held out both hands and Sullivan helped her to her feet. The three of them went back into the hall. A door at the end opened into Bradley's bedroom. Mrs Prendergast fumbled with the light switch.

'Did Bradley do all this?' Winter gestured round.

'Yes, I told you, this was his.'

The walls were painted black, though there were bits in the corner and down near the skirting board where he hadn't bothered. The single bed was unmade and there were the remains of a Chinese in a foil carton on the floor. Posters for R & B gigs at the Wedgwood Rooms were Blu-tacked over the bed, and when Winter opened the drawer in the little bedside cupboard he found himself looking at a roll of passport photos, four colour shots featuring Bradley and Louise Abeka. Of the two faces, the girl seemed infinitely happier, a really bright smile. Winter removed the photos and poked around amongst the rest of the clutter. Beneath a sheaf of Rizla papers and a decent-sized lump of cannabis he found a brown envelope. Inside was a roll of ten-pound notes. He counted them. One hundred and thirty pounds.

'Did Bradley live here all the time?'

'What, dear?'

'Bradley? Was this his home?'

He turned round to see whether she'd at last understood but she was shuffling away down the hall. Sullivan began to go after her but Winter stayed him, nodding at the chest of drawers. They went through them from top to bottom. More T-shirts, more jeans, even a pullover or two, all black. In the bottom drawer, beneath a tangle of unwashed socks and underwear, a red silk basque. Winter held it up against Sullivan, trying it for size.

'Bet it looks better on her,' he muttered.

On the other wall, behind the door, was an MFI wardrobe in white melamine. One of the hinges had worked loose and Sullivan held on to the door while Winter rummaged around inside. Unlike the clothes in the chest of drawers, there seemed no theme to the jackets and overcoats hanging from the rail. They came in different sizes and different styles, mainly suede or leather, and a couple of longer coats in lambswool or cashmere, and it took Sullivan to voice the obvious conclusion: 'They're nicked,' he said. 'Look.'

Every garment still carried a price tag, proof to would-be buyers that the gear was indeed brand new.

'And here.'

Sullivan had pulled out a holdall from the bottom of the wardrobe. Inside, under a pair of tracksuit bottoms and a ribbed khaki sweater, was a wrecking bar, a jemmy, a selection of screwdrivers and a number of other items. When he tried the torch, it still worked.

Mrs Prendergast was back in the open doorway. She was carrying two little glasses, the kind you win at funfairs. There was amber liquid in both and she gave one to each of them. Winter sniffed his and grinned.

'Sherry,' he said. 'Ten quid says it's Bristol Cream.'

He offered Mrs Prendergast a toast, Queen and Country, and then led the old lady gently back towards the living room. Sullivan still had the envelope with the money in it. Only when they were all sitting down did he notice the scrawled notes under the flap.

'Paul?'

He showed Winter. One line of figures was definitely a local phone number. The other, 38593 84247K, was harder to decipher.

'Seize it.' Winter had caught sight of the bottle of Harvey's Bristol Cream. 'We'll sort it out later.'

He got to his feet and helped himself to more sherry. Mrs Prendergast's glass lay on the low table beside her chair. He topped it up, asking again about Bradley. When had she last seen him?

This time the question seemed to register. She gazed at the television, a fierce frown of concentration. Then she had it.

'Friday,' she announced triumphantly. 'It was just starting.'

'What was?'

'*Emmerdale Farm.*'

'So what time would that be?'

'Seven o'clock, dear. On the dot.'

'Was he by himself?'

'Yeah.' She nodded. 'Seven o'clock.'

'But did he have company?'

'Cheers.' She reached for her drink and swallowed nearly half of it. Then she was on her feet again, unaided this time, bending over the television. She poked at the controls for a moment or two, then shook her head.

'I don't know,' she said. 'I don't know how he did it.'

'Did what, Mrs Prendergast?'

'When he showed me those pictures. Funny, it was, seeing me.'

'You?'

'Yes, dear. On the telly.' She peered at the set again, as if the pictures were still inside. 'How would you do that?'

Winter and Sullivan exchanged glances. Bristol Cream did nothing for this woman's sanity.

'Clever, eh?' She'd retrieved the bottle. She wanted Winter to feel at home.

Sullivan caught his eye, and then nodded at the telephone in the corner. It looked brand new, a Panasonic unit with fax and digital answerphone. Winter got to his feet. Nicked, he thought. Like everything else in Bradley Finch's life.

He looked down at the phone. There was a message waiting that Mrs Prendergast had yet to pick up. Not that very much would penetrate her deafness.

'May I?'

Winter pressed the replay button for the waiting message. There was a moment of silence, then a male voice, youngish, frightened, close to tears. 'Nan,' went the voice, 'help me. For fuck's sake help me. Nan, get the—' The line went abruptly dead.

Across the room, Mrs Prendergast was still gazing at the television. Winter bent to the phone, replaying the message. He'd heard this voice before, only days before, but he had to hear it again to be sure. The message came through once again, as panic-stricken as ever, the flat, gruff Pompey vowels unmistakable this time. Winter gazed at Sullivan. The voice on his own mobile, he thought. The lad who'd phoned him in the middle of the night about Brennan's.

For a moment Winter just sat there. Then he checked his watch and nodded at the phone.

'We'll have that, too,' he said.

Chapter fifteen

MONDAY, 12 FEBRUARY, *early evening*

This time round, Winter was taking no chances. The moment he saw Willard's Saab backing out of his allotted garage in the car park at Kingston Crescent, he told Sullivan to stop. Getting out of the car, he bent to Willard's open window.

'Just been round to Finch's nan, boss,' he began. 'One or two things you ought to know about.'

Willard was eyeing the clock on the dash. He had a rare social engagement he was determined to keep. What was so important it couldn't wait until the morning?

'Finch phoned me the night before he died. Only it's taken me a while to suss the voice.'

Minutes later, upstairs in the MIR, Willard convened an impromptu meeting. Seated around the conference table were Sammy Rollins, Brian Imber and the DS in charge of outside enquiries, a sturdy Yorkshireman called Paul Ingham. Dave Michaels, en route home, had been summoned back on his mobile. For Willard, the time had come to light a fuse under his ever-growing team of investigators.

On the basis of Winter's report from Flint Street, immediate lines of enquiry were pressing and obvious. Ray Brennan was to be contacted at once. He still owed Winter an up-to-date list of staff, and every one of them was to be TIE'd. That meant personal interviews as well as PNC checks. One or more of them must have known Bradley Finch and Willard wanted names ASAP. That way, Brian Imber and his Intelligence Cell could start some serious development of their association chart, the web of underworld contacts in which Finch had got himself ensnared.

Secondly, Willard shared the common view that Kenny Foster deserved a great deal more attention. The lack of any previous simply showed that the man was lucky, as well as clever. Five minutes listening to Brian Imber on the subject would convince anyone with half a brain that Foster was into criminality big time. There'd obviously been friction of some kind between him and Bradley Finch, and Willard wanted to know why. The stop-check on the Fiat which had left the traffic crew with Foster's name and address was barely a week old, and although murder sounded a touch extreme as a reprimand for this bit of harmless fun, Finch's recklessness may well have set him up for a smacking.

Thirdly, Willard wanted forensic to have a good sniff at the envelope Winter and Sullivan had seized at Flint Street. The phone number on the back had turned out to be the main switchboard at the local Inland Revenue office. Out of hours, there was only a recorded message but that had been enough to decode the other line of scribble beneath. 38593 84247K was a tax reference number. Whoever owned the envelope in the first place must have been talking to the tax people. With luck, the reference would lead to a firm ID.

At this point, Sammy Rollins wondered whether the tax reference might not have belonged to Finch himself, a suggestion that earned a snort of derision from Brian Imber.

'Little scrote never paid a penny of tax in his life,' he said. 'Depend on it.'

This interjection simply darkened Willard's mood. He wanted the people round the table to be in absolutely no doubt where they were. This inquiry wasn't young any more. They'd been at it since Saturday morning and in three long days they'd achieved nothing of great significance. Every line of enquiry indicated that they were dealing with professional criminals – maybe not the Premiership, maybe not even the Nationwide League, but bent guys who very definitely deserved a lesson in civilised behaviour. What you didn't do in this city was take the piss. By stringing up some ne'er-do-well and making some half-hearted attempt to mask murder as suicide, they'd done exactly that. These animals needed sorting, fast, otherwise this kind of mayhem would only spread. He wasn't having it. Not on his watch. And that was that.

In the ensuing silence, Winter raised a cautious hand. What about surveillance on the girl, Louise Abeka? Hadn't anyone turned up to put the squeeze on her? Assuming she knew what had happened to Finch? Willard pushed his chair back from the table and stood up. With luck, he could still make his date.

'We lost her coming back from work this evening,' he said briefly. 'You want the details, ask Dave Michaels.'

Back home by seven, Faraday found a battered Skoda parked outside.

Peering in through the driver's window, he could just make out a pair of muddy-looking football boots and a towel on the passenger seat. Letting himself into the house, he heard the sound of laughter from the kitchen. J-J's laugh was immediately recognisable, a high-pitched cackle that still scored Faraday's sweetest dreams, but there was someone else in there with him, deeper voiced.

J-J was standing by the stove, stirring something in a saucepan, while the stranger was sitting at the table with his back to the door, nursing a can of Stella. He was wearing jeans and a hooded top. Evidently fluent in sign, he was telling J-J a story that involved skiing, and as Faraday watched he pushed his chair back from the table, keeping his knees together and swaying his body as he sped down some imaginary mountain. J-J, who'd spotted his father at the door, signed his new friend's name.

'Gordon Franks,' he explained.

The newcomer spun round. He was thickset and fit-looking, with a grade one haircut and a small dragon tattoo on the back of his right hand. His handshake was a bonecruncher and his smile revealed an enormous set of teeth. He said he was sorry to have invited himself along like this but Anghared Davies had said there'd be no problem. As for the Stella, that had been J-J's idea.

Faraday poured himself a large Scotch, delighted that his call to Anghared had been so productive. Better still, it was obvious that J-J and Anghared's thesp had struck an immediate spark. Taking people at face value had never been a problem for J-J – indeed, he'd always had a truly heroic faith in his fellow man – but it was rare to find that kind of enthusiasm so quickly returned. Maybe Marta was right when she said that spirit – *animo* – was the key that opened every door.

J-J, halfway through his third can of Stella, happily surrendered the cooking to Faraday. He turned J-J's soup into the beginnings of a stew, adding mushrooms, leeks, carrots and thick roundels of chorizo sausage, while J-J sat across from Gordon Franks, explaining what he'd been up to in Caen. The stew ready, Faraday ladled it straight onto plates for the table. He broached a decent bottle of Rioja to go with it and let J-J saw the remains of the weekend's loaf into inch-thick slices to mop up the juice. Already the evening felt like an echo from the distant past: gusts of laughter and a blur of hands as the conversation pinballed from topic to topic.

Gordon had spent five years in the Royal Marines. He'd loved the physical challenges and the camaraderie, and the world-conquering feelings inside that went with the green beret, but in the end he'd called it a day, partly because some of the stuff was getting repetitious and partly because of his younger brother.

Steve had been an afterthought. Fifteen years younger than Gordon, he'd been born into a different world. Their parents had moved from Exeter to Plymouth. They had no money, a crap house and few prospects. Dad had got himself injured at the abattoir where he scraped a living and was resigned to being on the sick for ever. Young Steve, far from thick, had gone off to primary school, got bored, and made lots of trouble. At home, with troubles of their own, his parents had virtually ignored him. Steve fell into bad company. Things got quickly worse and before anyone could slow him down the kid was off the piste and over the edge.

At twelve, he was doing serious drugs. By thirteen, he'd become an apprentice dealer, successful enough to warrant a savage beating from three seventeen-year-olds who robbed him of everything and left him unconscious in a bus shelter. After a fortnight in hospital and several brain scans, Steve had at last got some kind of grip on his young life – but not before he'd put the fear of God into his few friends and his hopelessly dysfunctional family. Including, at 4000 miles' distance, Gordon.

'I was in Belize,' he signed, 'and I knew it was time to jack it in.'

Now, six years later, he'd put himself through drama school, started an MA in social studies, and developed a passion for mounting cutting-edge theatre in the local Portsmouth arts centre. In every one of these endeavours, he'd found a champion in Anghared Davies, who'd somehow screwed funding for a part-time drama post with the Persistent Young Offenders scheme. Gordon's brief was to open minds and change lives, and if make-believe violence plus a helping or two of more orthodox drama could achieve that, then so much the better.

'And J-J?' Faraday nodded at his son.

'He'll be brilliant with them.'

'Why?'

'Because the kids are so far off the pace. That's part of the problem. Most of them don't bother trying because they don't see the point. Talk to them properly, get their attention, and they'll tell you they're the bottom of the heap. They've got nothing to offer. Everyone thinks they're shit. Think that long enough, get to believe it, and – hey presto – you *become* shit. It's all nonsense, of course, just excuses on their part. OK, some are seriously deprived. OK, some aren't the brightest. But none of us, *none* of us, really understands what's inside. Listen' – he signed for J-J to come closer, exactly the way you'd share a secret – 'we had a sergeant on the Mountain Leader course, and you know what he used to get us to do? We'd be yomping up in Scotland. We'd be carrying the full kit, bloody great sack on our backs. We'd start on the west coast and we'd walk right across the Highlands to just short of

Inverness. Most of the time it would be pissing with rain and blowing a gale. You'd do twelve hours straight, just ten-minute smokos every hour. It would get to be the middle of the night and you'd be totally knackered. Then you'd hit yet another crest line and down there, in the valley, would be a dam and a bloody great reservoir, at least another hour away. OK, so one or two of us would have a moan, make a bit of a fuss, and this sergeant would come up to us and say, "Come on lads, this is the big one, and you'd better be bloody up for it because once we get down there, we're all walking across, single file." It was his party piece, that dam. Two-hundred-foot drop one side. Water so cold you're dead in minutes on the other. And you know how wide the top of the dam was?' He measured the space with his hands. 'Under a metre.'

J-J was spellbound. Given half a chance, Faraday thought, and he'd be up to Scotland on the train, searching map after map for dams. No wonder Anghared had so much time for her precious thesp. This man could turn anything into a story.

He was talking about J-J now. With his deafness and his rubber hands, he'd be priceless for the kids. Why? Because here was someone who'd had a *real* problem, who couldn't hear a bus coming or a band playing, or the roar of a football crowd; someone who'd had to confront a solitude, an isolation, that no ordinary bloke could ever imagine. His kids would warm to that. They'd understand, however dimly, about solitude and isolation. And the knowledge that someone like J-J had built himself bridges to the real world would be the best possible evidence that they weren't alone, that effort and determination would have their rewards.

Faraday, listening, could only agree. In the shape of J-J, he could see a way these kids of Gordon's might glimpse a future for themselves. He toyed with the remains of his wine for a moment, swilling it around the glass, then told Gordon to finish the bottle. Try as he might, he couldn't get Scotland out of his mind.

'So what happened when you got to the dam?' he asked at last.

Gordon passed on the wine, filling J-J's glass instead.

'We lost a guy,' he said softly. 'Which is what happens if you take risks like that.'

Later, while J-J and Gordon were seeing to the washing-up, Faraday went through to the lounge. There were a couple of messages waiting for him on the answerphone, and he paused to listen. The first was from a birding friend, reporting a pectoral sandpiper on the mudflats at Thorney Island. The second was from Marta. She sounded unusually tense, almost angry. She wanted Faraday to ring her. Not on the mobile, but at home. She left him the number, repeating it twice.

Faraday made the call from the extension upstairs in his study. He'd never before called her on her home line. Already, he had the feeling something terrible had happened.

'It's my husband,' she said as soon as Faraday announced himself. 'He's left me.'

'Why?'

'He found a card, a silly thing. It was for you. I left it on the kitchen table by mistake.'

'What did it say?'

'It was just saying sorry for the weekend. And it said I loved you.'

Faraday nodded. The wind was getting up again and he could hear the 'slap-slap' of halyards in the nearby dinghy park. He'd never met Marta's husband, never set eyes on her kids. None of that was part of the woman he knew.

'What now?' he heard himself say.

'Can you come over? Please?'

Captain Beefy lay between a kebab bar and a launderette on a stretch of Albert Road notorious for student drunks. Winter stepped carefully round a puddle of cooling vomit and followed Sullivan to the front door. Eight in the evening was early to be throwing up but he supposed it all depended when you got that first pint in.

The gym looked empty. A tiny bar in the lobby was stocked with five kinds of chilled fruit juice and there were a couple of low wicker chairs to take the weight off your feet. Trophy colour photos around the walls offered terrible warnings about what sustained weight training could do to your physique. One of them featured a blonde woman locked in the classic Schwarzenegger pose. She had a cheeky smile and nice eyes but the rest of her body looked like a satellite photo of the Hindu Kush: deep valleys between peaks of glistening muscle.

'Gentlemen?'

Winter and Sullivan turned to find a woman standing in the open doorway beside the bar. She was edging into middle age but a regime of exercise and fruit juice nicely filled the spray-on top. Pink wasn't Winter's favourite colour but he didn't let that stand between him and a pretty woman.

'Simone?' He extended a hand. 'Never had the pleasure.'

Simone was studying the two men. She didn't need lapel badges to guess their occupation.

'Business, is it? Or are you guys off duty?'

She took them through to the gym itself. Mirrors lined three walls and it was a challenge for Winter to edge his bulk between the various exercise machines. He'd come here to discuss Kenny Foster but that kind of agenda seemed lost on Simone. She'd had the gym up and running for a year now. It was already paying its way and she was proud of the fact that the bank loan was shrinking. Obviously Pompey, she had a taunting, no-nonsense attitude that spoke volumes about a girl's potential in a man's world.

'So where is everyone?' Winter gestured round at the empty gym.

'They've gone. We close at eight. Our regulars know that.'

Upstairs, past the line of potted plants and small plaster busts of ancient Greek athletes, there were more machines. To Winter, they looked almost mediaeval, devices designed to inflict a great deal of needless pain, but Sullivan was all eyes. He did a bit of working out himself, he told Simone. He'd never bothered to join a gym because he never had time to get proper value out of the subscription but the weight routines and all the stuff about progressive resistance and aerobic stamina had always fascinated him. Was it true this gear could sort you out?

Simone was watching him with interest. Of course it was true, she said. Some places were no more than social centres – dating agencies with a couple of pec-decks attached – but her operation offered straight down the line no-bullshit fitness.

'I'm the boss here,' she said. 'You come to me and you get the full assessment. I do a shoulder-to-calf workout. I want to know how you stand. How you breathe. What you eat. How much you sleep at night. The whole nine yards. Then we get to work. Everything's personalised. And in a couple of months you'll think you're God.'

Sullivan was definitely impressed. A particular machine across the room had caught his eye. To Winter, it was the usual combination of wires, pulleys and thickly padded contact areas but Sullivan wanted to know more.

'Abductors,' she said briefly.

'Ab what?'

'Here.' She slapped her thigh. 'We work on specific muscle groups. Abductors are on the inside.'

'How does it work, then?' Sullivan nodded at the machine. Winter looked pointedly at his watch. Any more of this and he might as well get himself a glass of cranberry juice and wait downstairs.

'Give it to me.'

Simone had her hand out. She wanted Sullivan's jacket. Sullivan slipped it off and got onto the machine. With his bum low and his knees up, the outsides of his thighs nestled against the padded supports.

'OK, now spread your legs.'

Sullivan did it, straining against the weights. Then again. Then a third time. Watching his contorted face in the big wall mirror, Winter began to laugh.

'You ought to be selling tickets,' he told Simone. 'You'd make a fortune.'

Back downstairs, Winter asked her about Friday nights.

'We close at eight,' she said at once, 'like I told you.'

'And last Friday night?'

'Eight.'

'Then what?'

Simone had a long, stagey think.

'I was with a friend,' she said at last.

'And who might that be?'

'Kenny Foster.'

'By yourself?'

'Yes.'

'No witnesses?'

'No.' She shook her head. 'Definitely not.' Her eyes strayed towards Sullivan. Sullivan ducked his head.

'So where were you?'

'Here, as it happens.'

'In the *gym*?'

'That's right. Kenny likes working out by himself. Never gets a proper chance during the week so a couple of hours on Friday nights are perfect. I open up for him special.'

Winter acknowledged the phrase with the faintest smile.

'What sort of time are we talking here?'

'Late, around ten, ten-thirty. Kenny prefers that. Loosens him up before bedtime, know what I mean?'

'And you?'

'I watch. Help where I can, you know . . .'

'Just the two of you.'

'Yeah.'

Sullivan was transfixed. It was clear that Winter didn't believe a word of what she was saying and it was equally clear that Simone didn't care. This was cartoon dialogue cooked up by people who enjoyed these kinds of games.

Winter was explaining that he had a problem. Colleagues of his had talked to Kenny Foster and it was really very important that some third person vouch for his movements on Friday night. They weren't talking a parking offence here. It was a great deal more serious than that.

Simone was looking at Sullivan again.

'You were one of them, weren't you? Round Kenny's place?'

'That's right.'

'Didn't you believe him, then?'

'It's not that, it's just procedure.' He began to colour. 'It would just help, that's all.'

'Help who?'

'Kenny Foster.'

Simone studied her fingernails for a moment or two. Then looked Sullivan in the eye. As far as she was concerned, Winter no longer existed.

'You want evidence, don't you? Of where we was on Friday night?'

'That's right.'

'Can you keep a secret, then? Only some of this stuff's pretty personal.'

'What stuff?'

She smiled at him, then disappeared into a curtained alcove behind the bar. When she re-emerged, she was holding a cassette.

'We've got cameras upstairs,' she said. 'Have you got a moment?'

Sullivan followed her back into the alcove. The space was tiny and served as a makeshift office. On the desk beside a pile of invoices was a television and a video player. Simone slipped in the cassette and fingered the play button. Winter hadn't moved.

'OK?'

Sullivan nodded. Close like this, it was impossible not to be aware of Simone's body. 'Captain Beefy' didn't do her justice. She was seriously firm.

A picture flickered on the screen. It showed the downstairs section of the gym with half a dozen punters pumping away on the weights. A time and date readout established it was Friday 17.34. Then the sequence came to an abrupt end and Sullivan found himself looking at the room upstairs.

It was much later, 23.49, and the room was empty except for a lone figure on the pull-down weights in the corner. Back in his garage, wearing oil-stained jeans and a tight T-shirt, Kenny Foster had made a very definite physical impression on Sullivan. Medium height, he looked to be in his late thirties. He had a worn, bony face and eyes of the palest blue. The ponytail with its twist of red ribbon and the tiny gold peace symbol on a chain round his neck might have tagged him as a veteran from the early Glastonbury days, a chilled-out hippy with a library of Dylan CDs, but there was something in the shape of his body beneath the black T-shirt that suggested otherwise.

Now, seeing him clad only in a pair of red satin shorts, Sullivan knew he'd been right. The bull neck. The muscled spread of his shoulders. The tight ripple of muscles across his belly. Every time he did a repetition on the machine, pulling down the weights, the tattoos danced on his chest. This was a man you wouldn't want to mess with. Ever.

'Wait . . .' Sullivan felt Simone's hand on his arm. The claustrophobic little space smelt powerfully of shower gel.

Seconds later, she appeared on the screen. She was wearing a black dressing gown, open at the front, and she was naked underneath. She paused in front of Foster, kissed him on the lips, then sank to her knees. Easing down the satin shorts, she teased the beginnings of a huge erection, then took him in her mouth, hollow-cheeked, and began to suck. Foster didn't miss a beat. Pull, release, pull, release. At length Simone withdrew, ran her tongue up his body, shrugged off the dressing gown, and then planted herself on the abductor machine. Naked, she began to exercise, thighs open, thighs shut, her head back against the padded rest. Foster appeared not to notice. Pull, release, pull, release. Then, with a shrug, he abandoned the machine, stepped out of his shorts and joined Simone.

Simone reached forward, indicating the time readout on the screen before hitting the stop button. Sullivan, uncomfortably aware of his own muscle groups, shot her a look.

'That could be evidence,' he said. 'We could seize that.'

'Help yourself.' She took a tiny step backwards and poked her head round the curtain. Winter was reading a magazine. When he glanced up, she smiled at him. 'Second house?'

By the time Faraday found Marta's house, her kids had gone to bed. To his surprise, it was a bungalow in a maze of tree-lined streets in a suburb called Park Gate. This was commuter country, half an hour's drive from Faraday's place, serving the busy corridor between Portsmouth and Southampton. Looking out at the pulled curtains and carefully barbered hedges, Faraday couldn't think of a worse place to live.

Marta must have seen him arriving. She had the door open when he picked his way around her parked Alfa, and took his coat without a word. There was a bottle of wine, half empty, on the kitchen table and she'd made a plate of sandwiches. Marta neither drank much alcohol nor stooped to anything as mundane as corned beef sarnies and margarine. More surprises.

'What happened?'

Marta went through it. There hadn't been a row. There hadn't been anything. She'd come back to find the card propped against the teapot and a note from her husband.

'What did it say?'

Marta reached for her bag and handed Faraday a folded sheet of white paper.

Pepita. I'd no idea you were that desperate. We've been here before, haven't we? This time, I think it's best for me to clear off for a bit. There was always a better way, you know. You could always have told me.

There was a kiss at the end but no name. Faraday refused the proffered bottle. *Pepita?*

'Does he always type messages like this, your husband?'

'He does everything on a laptop.'

'Everything? Even stuff like this?'

Faraday read the note again, then looked around. The kitchen, while undoubtedly expensive, was bare and functional. No pictures, no little touches, no warmth, not the slightest evidence of the Marta he thought he'd known.

'*We've been here before?*' he queried. Marta nodded.

'Eight years ago. Before Maria came.'

'What happened? Do you want to tell me?'

'Not really. I got confused. But it was me who left on that occasion.'

'Confused about what?'

'Another man.'

'And now?'

'I told you. I love you.'

'And what about your husband?' He nodded at the note. 'Do you love him too?'

'He's my husband,' she said simply.

Faraday loosened his coat. Sitting in this awful kitchen, he had an acute feeling of trespass, of straying onto other people's turf, but it wasn't just that. It was his own life, too. Love was an easy word. He loved Marta, and he wanted her. But her kids? And the guilt that she'd bring with her? And all the rest of the baggage? Was this the decision she was suddenly asking him to make?

Marta sipped her wine, not saying anything, her eyes watching him over the rim of the glass, and he found himself thinking about the house by the harbour, the view from the window and the privileges of living alone. Was he seriously up for swopping all this for a wife and someone else's kids? Was he really prepared to pick up the tab for thirteen blissful months?

'What do you want to do?' he asked her.

'I don't know.'

'What about your kids?'

'I haven't told them.'

'But if you did?'

'They'd hate it. They love their dad.' She paused, and then replaced the glass very carefully on the table. 'He's phoned already. Twice.'

'And?'

'He wanted to know who you were. How long all this has been going on.'

'What did you say?'

'I told him the truth. I said I loved you.'

'And your husband? What's his line?'

'He said he'd come back. But only if all this' – she indicated the space between them – 'stopped.'

'For real, you mean.'

'Yes, for real.' She didn't go on.

Faraday thought about it for a moment then suggested they all ought to take a deep breath, give it a couple of days, see how they felt. But already he knew in his heart that the decision had been made. It was there in her face, there in his hesitations. They'd enjoyed a glorious fantasy, some wonderful moments, and now it was all over. Real life had stepped back in, as abruptly as ever, and now he was back where he belonged. Alone.

'So how do you feel?' She leaned forward and, for the first time, kissed him.

'Gutted. If you want the truth.'

'Why gutted?'

'Because it's been so brilliant.'

'Been?'

'Yes.' He nodded. 'You don't have to spell it out.'

He reached for his coat, kissed her on the forehead, and made his way to the door. When he looked back along the hall, she was still sitting at the kitchen table. How come it's so quick? he thought. How come you can lose someone like that in five brief minutes? He reached for the door latch. Marta lifted a hand in farewell and began to say something, then had second thoughts. Faraday smiled at her. Then he stepped outside, into the chilly darkness, pulling the door shut behind him.

The fourth pint was Winter's idea. He'd hauled Sullivan into a pub across the road from Captain Beefy in order to review the day's events, and a sensible chat about lines of enquiry had quickly developed into something a great deal more passionate. Later, looking back, Winter concluded that this exchange of views was more or less inevitable. It was a bit like redecorating. Before you did anything else, you cleared the room of furniture.

Sullivan, it turned out, hated the job. Not *Bisley*, not the painstaking search for whoever had dragged Bradley Finch to his death, but all the other bits and pieces that cluttered up his day on division. Petersfield was a small market town, moneyed, pretty, with a couple of good restaurants and house prices rapidly going through the roof. Yet even there, in the heart of the rural dream, you didn't have to dig very deep before you were back into the swamp. Kids kicking the shit out of anything new on the estates. Booze-fuelled violence. Zombie husbands off the late train back from London, knackered out of their heads. Families falling apart. Young Gary had joined the force to sort out criminals. Instead, for most of the time, he'd become some kind of half-arsed social worker.

'But you were the one who wanted to be nice to the Naylors.' Winter was enjoying this. 'You were the one giving me a hard time up there in Leigh Park.'

'That's different. That's about respect.'

'Respect for scum like that? You're wasting your time, son. One sniff of all that touchy-feely crap and they'll turn you over. I've seen it happen a million times.'

'They'd just lost their son.'

'Yeah, and good fucking riddance. They never saw him. He was never there. The only one who cared a light was his nan, and she's off the planet. What kind of family's that?'

Sullivan frowned. Stella slowed him down. He had a point to make here, an important point, but every time he crept up on it Winter appeared from the shadows and whisked it away.

'It's the system.' He was staring at his hands. 'The job's hard enough as it is but the system makes it impossible.'

'What system's that, then?'

'The way we do things, the way we have to do them. I know I'm young and all that but you listen to the older blokes and it's the same with them. Everyone's watching their backs now. Put a step wrong, get out of line with all that Best Practice garbage, and you're in deep shit. You're right about the scrotes. Up our way, I could give you a list of little twats we'd be better off slapping. They cause us endless grief. But you can't do it, can you? We've got bloody forms instead of justice. When I'm not a social worker, I'm a fucking clerk.'

Winter mimed applause. He was impressed.

'So what happens,' he asked, 'to that nice career of yours?'

'Fuck knows. My mates on the outside thought I was crazy in the first place and maybe they're right. Most people won't be seen dead with a copper. Even when we're out there doing it, trying to screw some kind of result, you just get blanked. The other day we were trying to sort out a young lad. That involved going to a school but they didn't want to know. Most organisations hate the bloody Filth, won't have us anywhere near them. That makes you think, doesn't it?'

'Never. Start thinking about it, you're dead in the water. The system's like everything else. It's there to be ignored. You get results in spite of the system. Play by the rules and you might as well jack it in.'

'So how does that work, then? Like tonight? The old slapper across the road?' Sullivan nodded at the door, aggressive now.

'Well, you start with the obvious. The old tart's winding us up.'

'Of course she is. Anyone can programme the date on a video. They were probably at it before we arrived. No wonder she'd just had a shower.'

'Can you prove that?'

'No, of course I can't. And that's the problem, isn't it? He says he was with her. She says they were screwing all night. And, surprise surprise, there's even a video to prove it. It's all bollocks. You know it and I know it and she bloody knows it too. But without evidence, we're fucked.'

'No, we're not. Not if we're smart.'

'Oh yeah? So how does that work?'

'Good question.' Winter beamed at him. 'One for the road?'

An hour and a half later, near midnight, Winter insisted on dropping Sullivan off at the town station. The last train was due any minute and he could get a taxi at the other end.

Sullivan was watching a couple of teenage girls trying to cadge a freebie from a cab driver. He'd eaten better curries but at least the world was back in focus. He glanced across at Winter.

'You're all right really, aren't you?'

'You're pissed, son.'

'No, really, you're a good bloke. You do your best to wind people up but underneath it all, you're OK.' He nodded. 'You know something? People warned me about you. Watch your back, they said. Still, it's down to me, isn't it?'

'What's down to you?'

'Fuck knows.' He burped softly in the darkness of the car. 'Listen, there's something else I've been meaning to say.'

'What's that then?'

'I'm really sorry about your missus. That was out of order.' He turned to Winter and extended a hand.

Winter studied him a moment, then accepted the handshake. Since

Joannie's death, he'd spent a long time sitting in empty rooms, cooking for one, shopping for one, saving all his laundry for a single load at the weekend, and the beauty of this job, *Bisley*, was the way it had put the smile back on his face, returning him to a world he loved.

He nodded towards the station entrance.

'You're going to miss the train.'

'No, really, I mean it.'

'I'm sure you do.' Winter leaned across and opened the door. 'But you want to be careful, son. All this touchy-feely crap.'

Chapter sixteen

The fact that Willard insisted on driving out to take a look for himself was viewed with some misgivings within the MIR. Normally, the Detective Superintendent took a great deal of pride in running his team from the cool seclusion of his office. He trusted his lieutenants implicitly and believed in delegating the necessary authority. There was nothing to gain by dirtying his own hands. But on this occasion, as soon as Dave Michaels took the call from the force controllers at Tango One, Willard was in his car and away. *Bisley* wasn't going entirely to plan. It was time to make his presence felt.

The burned-out remains of the vehicle lay in a chalk pit dug into the side of a hill seven miles inland. Willard stood on the lip of the pit, gazing down. From time to time, gusts of wind funnelled up from the floor of the pit, bringing with them the sharp, bitter tang of charred upholstery and melted plastics. The Fire Service investigator had already poked around the cooling body shell and pronounced the job well done. Some form of accelerant had been used, probably petrol, and the tank must have been at least a third full to have torched the car so effectively. A SOCO team from Cosham was also hard at work and the preliminary report from the DS confirmed that the vehicle had been stripped of plates and all other identification. Plus the numbers on the engine block and chassis had been cut away to the full depth of the metal. Definitely a professional job.

Willard scrambled down the path, zipping up his Berghaus against the bitter wind. Sammy Rollins, his deputy SIO, was waiting by the Fiat. There was a handful of farms and cottages within a couple of miles' radius of the chalk pit and uniforms had begun knocking on doors. The fire itself had been reported at one in the morning but so far nobody had seen any vehicles in the area immediately beforehand. Soon, the SOCO team would be turning their attention to the flint-strewn track that accessed the quarry. It had been raining before midnight and there was an outside chance of wheel marks in the chalky mud.

'What d'you think?'

Sammy Rollins was watching one of the SOCO officers at work on the blackened body shell.

'I'm no expert,' he said, 'but I suppose it could be ours.'

Willard nodded. He'd organised for a mechanic from the main Fiat dealership to come up and pronounce judgement. A formal statement would be enough to establish make and model, but his own mind was made up.

'At least we know they mean it,' he said tersely.

The tax reference on the envelope seized at Bradley Finch's nan's place took Winter and Sullivan to Fawcett Road. The reference belonged to a second-hand store called Oddz 'n' Sodz and it was gone half past nine before the 'Closed' sign came off the shop's front door. Winter and Sullivan had been parked opposite for nearly an hour, waiting for someone to turn up. Must be a rear entrance, Winter thought, buttoning his coat.

Fawcett Road straddled the no man's land between Portsmouth and Southsea, a busy rat run for taxis and delivery vehicles. Battered shops on both sides sold everything from second-hand books to cut-price German lager, and the thoroughfare had recently attracted the attention of a Customs and Excise task force interested in the whereabouts of millions of quids' worth of contraband fags.

Winter crossed the road and intercepted a tall, skinny youth as he emerged from the shop with a trolley piled high with bric-a-brac. Winter showed the youth his warrant card, introduced Sullivan, and suggested they step aside. The youth wanted to know why.

'One or two things to discuss,' Winter said, nudging him in through the door.

The interior of the shop smelt soiled and damp. In the gloom, Winter could make out a jumble of broken-backed chairs, leatherette sofas, 1930s wardrobes with their doors hanging off and standard lamps with the kind of electric flex that belonged in a museum. Half close your eyes and you could have been inspecting Blitz damage the morning after a major raid.

'Got an office or anything? Somewhere a bit cosier?'

The youth shook his head. He was wearing a collarless shirt and a pair of torn jeans. His trainers looked as old as the furniture and a savage grade one had reduced his hair to a blue shadow against the whiteness of his scalp.

'What is it then?'

Winter produced a photo of Bradley Finch. He wanted to know the youth's name.

'Troy,' the youth said.

'Troy what?'

'Troy guessing.'

The youth looked to Sullivan for a smile but picked the wrong bloke. Three ibuprofen and a gallon of black coffee had failed to soften the after-effects of last night and he'd felt murderous since dawn. Now he stepped very close to the youth and repeated Winter's question.

'Troy Smith.' The youth took a tiny step backwards. 'That do yer?'

Winter showed him the photo again. He was investigating a murder. The victim's name was Bradley Finch. He wanted to know whether Smith had had any dealings with Mr Finch.

The youth peered at the photo.

'I sees him in the paper,' he said. 'That exact same photo.'

'Answer the question.'

'I just did, mush. I says I knows who he is.'

'That's because I told you. I'm asking you something else. I'm asking you when you saw him last.'

'I never.'

'You're lying.'

'Who says?'

Winter ignored the question. A nod to Sullivan was enough to send him wading through the furniture towards a door at the back. The youth had produced a cigarette but abandoned it in some haste.

He caught up with Sullivan and tried to pull him back. Sullivan spun round. In this sort of mood, the situation was non-negotiable.

'Get your fucking hands off me,' he said, 'or you'll be looking at an assault charge.'

The youth started giving him a mouthful but stopped the moment he heard the clunk of the door being locked. Turning round, he was in time to see Winter restoring the 'Closed' sign.

'What the fuck's going on? Mind telling me, do yer?'

Sullivan had found the little kitchen at the back. There was a single tap over the sink and a new-looking Hewlett-Packard computer perched on the wooden draining board. A desk against the adjoining wall was covered with more electronic equipment: printers, scanners and what looked like a brand new copier, still cocooned in its protective bubble wrap. Sullivan felt the kettle. It was still warm.

'What's this lot then?'

'Gear.'

'I can see that. Where did it come from?'

'Bought it.'

'Got the paperwork, have you?'

'With my accountant.'

'Fat fucking chance.' It was Winter. He was watching Sullivan filling the kettle. 'Two, with milk, please.' He shot a look at Smith. 'Got any bickies?'

The youth ignored the question. He wanted to make a phone call. He had rights here. They weren't dealing with some tosspot off the streets.

Winter eyed him coldly.

'Phones are for grown-ups,' he said. 'Don't get ideas above your station, son.'

'You fuck off.'

'No, my friend. You fuck off. And while you're about it, do me a favour, eh?'

'What's that?'

'Have yourself a wash in the morning. You smell like a bloody sewer.'

He gave the youth a push and Sullivan stepped aside as he fell amongst a pile of cardboard boxes in the corner. Winter was down beside him in a flash, his mouth close to the youth's ear.

'In a moment, when we've had tea, my mate and I are going to go right through this place. We're going to clear everything out onto the pavement and then we're going to lift every floorboard, take out every panel, give the place a proper going-over. And when we've found it, don't even dream about bail.'

'Found what?'

'You think I'm stupid? Is that what you think?'

Winter got to his feet, washed his hands in the sink and then wiped them dry on the long black mohair coat hanging behind the door. In the pocket of the coat he found a cheque book and three credit cards, all in different names.

'Whose are these then? Found them, did you? Pick them up in the street?'

'Fuck off. What do you want?'

'That's better.'

Winter leaned back against the sink, waiting for the tea. He wanted to know about Bradley Finch. He wanted to know what Smith had bought off him, Friday last.

'I wasn't here.'

'You're lying. We know you were here.'

'Yeah? How come?'

'A little bird told us.'

'Well, it wouldn't be that fuck-wit Finch, would it? Because he's dead.'

'Absolutely right. So why don't you tell us what you fenced for him. Before this gets unpleasant.'

'I never fenced nothing. I bought it. Legit. Cash. Fifty quid over the top too, little cunt.'

'Lovely. So what was it?'

Sullivan was pouring hot water into a couple of mugs. The youth on the floor looked resigned.

'Video camera,' he said at last. 'Brand new digital thing. Top of the range, according to fuck-face.'

'Where did he get it?'

'Haven't a clue.'

'You didn't ask?'

'What do you think I am? Stupid?'

Winter let the comment pass. The tea tasted foul.

'Where is it now? This camera?'

'Sold it on.'

'Who to?'

'Can't remember.'

Oh, yeah?

Winter gazed at his tea for a second or two, then poured it down the sink. Sullivan did the same. Winter had his mobile out. He tapped in a number, waited for a moment or two, then smiled.

'Customs and Excise? Get me Harry, please, and tell him it's urgent.'

The youth had got to his feet. The expression on his face told Winter everything he wanted to know. He pocketed the mobile and turned to Sullivan.

'I think Mr Smith is with us at last,' he murmured. 'Shall we leave him a chit for the camera?'

Try as he might, Faraday found it impossible to concentrate. He sat at his desk, going through the duty rosters for the next three weeks, trying to coax some kind of order from the usual chaos. The managerial treadmill had become the essence of his job, he knew that, and most days he coped with it like any other hamster in any other cage, but this morning was different. He felt excited the way you feel when you wake up in a foreign country with no clear recollection of how you got there. And he felt, as well, a little bit lost.

He glanced at his watch. At ten, he and Cathy Lamb were going to take a preliminary look at the arrangements for CID cover over Easter. At eleven-thirty he was due for a meet with a couple of nightclub owners wanting to twist his arm over an inquiry he was running into the activities of local bouncers. After lunch Hartigan was demanding a face-to-face to discuss the progress Faraday was making on the 'Investigating Burglary' PID. After that, he could make a start on catching up with yesterday's tally of petty crime, the minor cuts and grazes that never seemed to scab.

He returned briefly to the duty roster. If he moved this name to here, or this name to there, would it really make any difference? If he threw the whole pack in the air, all the available bodies, would it really matter in which order they hit the floor? The lines that boxed the eight-hour shifts began to blur and he felt himself wandering off again. It was something the Afghan had said, Niamat Tabibi. *Life is more complicated than you think.* Deliberately or otherwise, the lad had hit the spot. *Life is more complicated than you think.* Exactly.

Faraday eyed the phone. Every inquiry trailed its quota of loose ends and Helen Bassam's death was no exception. He'd done the Afghan's bidding. Mouth swabs had gone off for DNA matching with foetal tissues from the mortuary. He still owed a duty of care to Mrs Bassam, if only to assure her that things were still happening, but that was something he should pass on down the line – to Dawn Ellis, or more appropriately to the Family Liaison Officer from Cosham who'd yesterday added Jane Bassam to her bursting caseload. That's the way the system worked. That was the sensible division of labour that kept Faraday shackled to his desk. Get yourself promoted to DI on a patch as busy as this one, and your days on the sharp end were over.

Faraday at last picked up the phone. Cathy Lamb didn't even have the chance to argue.

'I'm out for a bit. We'll pick up on the Easter stuff later.' He paused. 'And remind me to have a word about that bloody husband of yours.'

Winter was back at the MIR before he had a chance to take a proper look at the video camera. It was a Sony TRV 15E, small and neat, with a brushed metal finish and a little video screen that folded out from the body of the camera. There were seven automatic programmes, a wide-screen option, plus a light that warned you when the battery was low.

'How does it work then?' Winter passed it to Sullivan.

Sullivan examined it for a moment or two, turning it over in his hand, and then switched it on. He knew enough about gear like this to recognise the latest model.

'Seven hundred quid? Are you kidding?'

'There or thereabouts. Bloke next door to my mum and dad's just got one similar. Bought it to video his missus' amateur dramatics. Here.'

The serial number was underneath the camera, a line of tiny digits that Winter's eyes failed to resolve.

'9264570982/23.' Sullivan read them out for him.

Winter fired up the computer on his desk and typed in his password. Another couple of keystrokes took him into the Automatic Crime Recording system, the file that tallied reported crimes all over the county. Under 'Make' he entered 'Sony' followed – at Sullivan's prompting – by the camera's model designation. Seconds later, he found himself scrolling through a list of missing Sony TRVs. If Sullivan was right about this gear being brand new on the market, Hampshire burglars had been remarkably busy.

'Serial number?'

Winter typed it in. The list shrank to a single entry. On 14 January, the camera on the desk had been stolen during a break-in at a house near Compton. The house belonged to a Captain and Mrs Wreke, and they'd also reported the theft of hi-fi equipment, two televisions, a video recorder, an answering machine, cash, cheque books and credit cards plus – more worryingly – a brand new Purdy shotgun. The house had been done while they were away skiing in Val d'Isère, and the break-in had been phoned in by the woman who came in daily to feed the cats. SOC had found nothing in the way of forensics and the incident had been added to the ever-growing list of inquiries awaiting further developments.

Winter was impressed. On occasions like this, even he could admit that computers had their uses.

'Where's Compton?'

He glanced round to find Sullivan staring at the camera's tiny screen. He'd hit the play button and now he was going backwards through the most recent of the recorded sequences. He squatted beside Winter. On the screen was an old woman sitting in a wing-backed armchair. She was wearing a pink shawl and there were squirly yellow patterns on the brown carpet. She was shielding her face, the way you might ward off driving rain, but when the hand came down there was no mistaking the bewilderment in her eyes.

'Finch's nan.' Winter poked a finger at the little screen. 'You'd recognise that carpet anywhere.'

Sullivan froze the picture.

'She was going on about the telly, remember? Kept telling us she'd been on the screen?' Sullivan tapped the camera. 'That's because he'd plugged it in to show her. First he took the shots, then he played them back through the set.'

'Definitely puts Finch with the camera, then.'

'No question. Has to.'

He pressed the play button again and then reverse. The picture went to black then flickered into motion. They were looking at a man's face in extreme close-up. His left eye was purpled with bruising and the swelling had closed it completely. There was fresh blood seeping from a gash over the other eye and more blood trickling from the wreckage of his mouth. He appeared to be unconscious and when the shot widened, pulling away from the face, he turned out to be flat on his back on the floor.

Winter looked harder. No way was this Bradley Finch. The man was wearing a pair of jeans but he was naked from the waist up. There was more bruising around his ribs, angry scarlet welts, and the blood had splashed down over his chest. The camera lingered on the body for a while, a trophy shot, then panned slowly right. The room was small and bare. A couple of chairs had been pushed against the wall and the curtains were drawn across the single window. It must have been daytime outside because a strip of bright light showed where the curtains didn't quite meet in the middle. The camera moved on round, past a mantelpiece with a clock. The clock said twenty past two. Then, beyond the mantelpiece, the camera finally settled on another figure, vertical this time.

Sullivan froze the camera again, shaking his head in disbelief. The ponytail with its twist of scarlet ribbon. The awesome neck. The glimpse of tattoos beneath the blood-splattered singlet. His arms hung down beside his body, the huge hands still bunched, the knuckles crimson with blood. Sullivan unfroze the picture and the shot began to wobble in towards the head and shoulders. The man's face was barely marked and there was something in the eyes that spoke of a deep satisfaction. He'd enjoyed however long it had taken to pulp the body on the carpet. It had given him immense pleasure.

He looked at the camera and nodded, then the shot eased out again and he peeled off the singlet and tossed it across the room. The gesture had a slightly ritualistic feel and Sullivan watched as the camera tracked left, discovering the inert body of Foster's opponent, his battered face half covered by the singlet.

Sullivan at last tore himself away. Winter had produced a bag of Werther's.

'Kenny Foster,' he said mildly. 'What a surprise.'

Jane Bassam was out when Faraday knocked on her door. A woman in her sixties explained she did the cleaning. Mrs Bassam had gone for a walk. Faraday might find her out on the beach by the Square Tower if it was urgent.

The Square Tower formed part of the fortifications around Old

Portsmouth. After Langstone Shore, this was Faraday's favourite part of the city and he took his time, strolling the quarter mile down past the cathedral to where the High Street bumped up against the curtain of grey stone that walled off the heart of the old town from the sea. Back in the sixteenth century, the Square Tower had been home to Portsmouth's governor, and the pebble beach that lay beside it had seen countless generations of seamen row out to the men-of-war lying off Spithead.

The beach was empty, and Faraday picked his way past a tangle of construction Portakabins before mounting the long flight of steps that led to the top of the nearby Round Tower. For once it was a beautiful day, brilliant sunshine and clear blue skies with a tiny cap of cloud over the Isle of Wight, and he stood at the rail overlooking the harbour entrance, feeling the sharpness of the air in his lungs, trying to imagine what it would take to throw a ten-year-old clear of the rocks beneath.

He wasn't at all sure that he believed Anghared's explanation for the nickname Doodie, and one swift glance down at the foreshore was enough to confirm how reckless you'd need to be to even attempt such a stunt. But then recklessness was the currency of this city. Recklessness had sent men to war after war. Recklessness had kept the French at bay, and the Germans and the Spanish. And that same virus, that same appetite for defiance and a bit of a laugh, still bubbled in the city's lifeblood.

Faraday was watching a tiny fishing smack butting in against the tide. The harbour mouth was narrow, barely a couple of hundred yards, another rite of passage for Pompey kids. Centuries ago a heavy iron chain had been laid across to the Gosport shore, resting on the seabed. In times of war the chain could be raised, barring entrance to the harbour, and the remains of this primitive barrier were still visible, brown and rusting, at low tide. These days, of course, there were other ways of keeping the enemy at bay, but the longer Faraday spent in the city and the deeper he plumbed its depths, the more certain he became about what made the place tick.

Portsmouth owed its very existence to aggression. Without the vigorous push to expand British influence overseas, there would never have been a navy, and without a navy Portsmouth would still be a slightly larger version of Hayling Island, a flat, spiritless chequerboard of bungalows, smallholdings and poorly stocked corner shops, the perfect retirement location if you'd pretty much given up on real life. As it was, though, successive wars had been the making of Pompey, giving it pride and purpose, and the only problem with the enduring post-war peace had been the vacuum it left in its wake. Hence, perhaps, the city's current reputation as a great place for a fight. Robbed of an enemy of the state, the locals had to make do by battering each other.

True? Faraday didn't know. It was a neat enough theory and would serve to keep a conversation going, but just now he knew he was talking to himself. One of the blessings Marta had brought with her was the constant assurance of a listening ear. She'd always claimed she was at her happiest hearing him bang on, and after a while he'd believed her. Now though, his loyal audience had gone, and as the implications began to sink in he realised that the real loss would be her company. Not sex. Not the dancing fingertips and the scalding tongue. But laughter and friendship. She'd warmed the bits of him that were fed up with the solitary life, and he'd made the terrible mistake of assuming that somehow she'd be there forever.

He pulled his coat around him, watching the long, rippling V of the fishing smack's wake break on the ramparts across the harbour mouth. The next few weeks would be tough going. He missed her already. The knowledge that she wouldn't even be available at the end of a phone was hard to take. In some respects, he thought, it was better to pretend she'd died. Just like Janna.

He turned back, towards the steps, then caught a flash of red on the beach below. It was Jane Bassam. Even the bulky scarlet fleece couldn't disguise the tall, erect figure as she made her way towards the water's edge. He watched her for a moment or two as she bent for a pebble, wondering whether he wasn't using this woman as an excuse to get out of the office. Then he remembered the sight of her daughter, skew-limbed on the wet pavement beneath the flats, and he knew that he owed her, at the very least, a proper establishing of the facts.

She wasn't pleased to see him.

'What is it now?'

He explained about Niamat Tabibi. The man had been outraged at the suggestion that the baby might have been his. Which left Faraday with one or two problems.

'You believed him?'

'Yes. I can't be sure, of course, not until we get the results back from the labs.'

'You tested him?'

'He volunteered a swab.'

She shrugged and turned away. Another of life's little surprises, unspeakably cruel.

'Then it must have been someone else,' she said stonily.

'Exactly. Do you have any idea who?'

'None at all. But I don't suppose it really matters any more, does it?'

Faraday didn't reply. Had Niamat admitted it, or should the match yet prove positive, he was certain this woman would be baying for justice. That was one of the puzzles about committed Christians. In situations like these, they could be truly implacable.

'There's something else . . .' he began.

'About Niamat?'

'No, Mrs Bassam. About you.'

'Me?' She raised an eyebrow. 'What?'

Faraday took his time. Over towards the Isle of Wight, one of the huge Japanese container ships was inbound for Southampton.

'There's a man called Phillimore, a cleric of some kind connected with the cathedral. Do you know him at all?'

'Of course. His name's Nigel.' She thrust her hands deep into the pockets of the anorak, a gesture – thought Faraday – of defiance.

'Do you know him well?'

'Yes, as a matter of fact I do. We both sing in the cathedral choir. May I ask what any of this has got to do with you?'

Faraday hesitated. Strictly speaking, there were limits here, lines you shouldn't cross without a very good reason, but something in her manner made him dispense with the small courtesies of criminal investigation.

'I'm thinking about Helen,' he said slowly. 'Were there any grounds for her believing that you and Phillimore might have been . . .' he shrugged '. . . close?'

Faraday watched the effect of his question. Amazement first. Then anger.

'Helen?' she said hotly. 'You really think she'd spare two seconds to think about me? Highly unlikely, Mr Faraday. And no, we weren't having an affair.'

'Did you see a lot of him?' This time she faltered.

'There have been times, yes.'

'You were friends?'

'Yes.'

'Good friends?'

'I'd like to think so.'

'And you spent a lot of time with him?'

'Socially, you mean? Yes. He has a house around the corner from me. It belongs to the diocese, of course, but he has the run of the place.'

'And you used to pop round there?'

'Certainly. Divorce can be an awkward time, Mr Faraday. And Nigel has pastoral responsibilities.'

'He was counselling you?'

'I didn't say that. I counted him as a friend. We have similar tastes in theatre and music. Mahler. The Beethoven string quartets. Certain bits of Haydn. Excuse me, but is this any of your business?'

'I don't know, Mrs Bassam. I'm simply trying to get inside Helen's head. It may be that she thought you were up to something. I imagine that having another man around could be very disturbing if you'd just lost your father.'

'But that's why we always met at Nigel's place. That was the whole point. She didn't have another man around.'

'You're telling me you were trying to hide something?'

'I'm telling you I had her best interests at heart. She was fine. She had more friends than she could cope with. Me? I had Nigel.'

'A friend.'

'Yes, and a very good friend. For whom I was immensely grateful.'

She nodded, emphasising the point, and Faraday had a sudden vision of this woman on her knees in that chilly front room, giving thanks for the gift of Nigel Phillimore. He'd been a blessing, a little surprise parcel, wrapped and ribboned by the good Lord.

'And now?'

'Now's different.'

'Why?' Faraday frowned, making a little gesture with his hands. 'Surely now's the time you need support more than ever?'

Winter and Sullivan paid a visit to Dave Michaels. The DS was busy on the phone. They waited in his office. The moment he was free, Sullivan handed him the camera. He fired it up and put it to his eye, playing with the zoom control while Winter explained about the visit to Oddz 'n' Sodz. In a statement, Troy Smith had confirmed that he'd bought the Sony from Bradley Finch. As the video sequence in his nan's flat so amply confirmed.

By now, Michaels was engrossed in the material recorded on the mini-tape. There was yards of it, at least three separate fights. Given that the camera hadn't been nicked until 14 January, that made Kenny Foster a very busy man. None of the fights had lasted more than ten minutes or so but there'd been no guarantee of that at the start. No wonder he kept so fit.

Michaels glanced up at Winter.

'So who's the guy holding the camera?'

'Finch, presumably.'

'But how come Finch's in with a hard nut like Foster? He's not in Foster's league.'

'Pass. He might be a second of some kind, or the stakeholder. Brian Imber might know.'

'Stakeholder? Finch? You wouldn't trust him to hold your sweater. The boy was a pillock.'

Winter shrugged.

'Maybe it was just the fact that he had the camera then. Maybe Foster wanted a permanent record. Something to keep himself amused. Nights when there's nothing on the telly.'

'Sure.' Michaels shot him a look. 'But it's odd though, isn't it? Foster's a class apart.'

He reached for the phone and dialled a number. When it answered he asked for Brian Imber. Seconds later, the conversation was over.

'He's in London all day. Back tonight.' He picked up the camera again and weighed it in his hand. 'So where do we think this takes us?'

'We traced it to a break-in,' Sullivan said at once. He gave Michaels the details.

'You're saying Finch screwed the place?'

'Must have done. He's tooled up for it. We found the kit in his nan's place.'

'You think he did it alone?'

'Might have done. Hard to say.'

'What kind of job was it?'

'Quality. Alarm disabled. No prints. Nothing silly left behind. Quick in and out, according to the file. Plus they nicked a shotgun.'

'So you're telling me he was a serious burglar? An inbred like that?'

'Looks like it.'

'So why wasn't he rolling in money? Why was he skint all the time?'

Sullivan shook his head. He couldn't say.

'We only know that from the girl,' Winter pointed out.

'Fucking right.' Dave Michaels nodded, rueful. Surveillance had lost Louise Abeka en route back from the café. She'd been walking towards the centre of the city when a battered old Metro had hooted and pulled in. There'd been a young girl at the wheel. Louise had got in and the car had driven away.

'Registration?'

'Birmingham address. We're still trying to get someone round there.'

Louise had now been missing for nearly a day. She hadn't turned up at Margate Road and there were no other obvious places to start looking within the city. The students she shared with were clueless about her movements and, after them, the leads ran out.

'Does she have relatives here?'

'In London. Her uncle's a diplomat at the Nigerian Embassy. Says he hasn't heard a peep for weeks.'

'So what's happened to her?'

'Fuck knows. My money's on a mate giving her a lift in the Metro.

After that, it's anyone's guess. She sat an exam yesterday; we checked with the university. If she's got any sense, she'll have left town by now.'

Dave Michaels sounded genuinely concerned. He'd been through her statement a number of times and he agreed with Winter that the girl was completely out of her depth. Something had happened, something she didn't want to talk about, and Portsmouth was now the last place she wanted to be.

Winter nodded.

'What about Willard?' he asked. 'What's his take on her?'

'He's still kicking the furniture about the surveillance. Thank God he's out for the morning.'

He began to explain about the vehicle fire in the chalk pit. Sullivan stirred again. He'd lived up in Petersfield all his life. As a kid, he used to ride his bike in the woods round Butser Hill.

'Where did you say it was, this chalk pit?'

'Up past Rowland's Castle. Way out in the country.'

'Off Huckswood Lane?'

'Haven't a clue, son. Help yourself. Here.'

Michaels turned to his computer and called up a map of the area from the central database. The map was Ordnance Survey standard and Sullivan peered at it over Michaels's shoulder. At length he reached forward, tracing the line of a track running east from a small country road.

'Here? This one?'

Michaels nodded. 'That's it.'

'Brilliant.' Sullivan's finger crept along the track beyond the chalk pit. Within a couple of miles it came to a cluster of houses built around a junction. 'That's Compton,' he announced. 'Where the house got screwed.'

Chapter seventeen

Faraday sat at the long polished table, waiting for Hartigan to return from the loo. The uniformed Superintendent had chosen this afternoon to insist on a meeting on Faraday's turf and – as ever – he'd expressed a preference to confer in the panelled grandeur of the first-floor boardroom.

Highland Road police station had once been the headquarters of the local bus company, and the architects doing the conversion had suggested keeping as many of the building's original features as possible. The work had cost a fortune, emptying the force's refurb budget for the best part of an entire year, but Highland Road nick had become the gem in Hampshire Constabulary's crown, conclusive proof that policemen could be trusted with the best in urban heritage. Faraday had always loathed the room. It spoke of self-importance and hot air. But Hartigan, to no one's surprise, thought it was wonderful.

On this occasion, as on many others, he'd brought his management assistant along. Annabelle was a pleasant, good-looking divorcee in her early forties. You had to be bright to keep on top of a job like that but the rumour that she was screwing Hartigan after hours put a big fat question mark against her judgement, if not her taste. Given Hartigan's mania for paperwork and audit trails, she was probably required to keep minutes on their little trysts.

Annabelle wanted to know about Joyce, Faraday's own management assistant. She'd been off for nearly a week now, undergoing a series of medical tests. There were suspicions of a bowel tumour but she'd sworn Faraday to silence, telling him to blame it on something else.

'She's down with flu,' he said. 'Lots of it around.'

'You've got a temp in?'

'Yeah. Clueless.'

Hartigan appeared at the door, as neatly brisk as ever. He treated these excursions like a state visit, adopting a slightly imperial air, and Faraday often wondered when he'd start asking about the welfare of the natives. The troops on duty, though, largely ignored him. People like Hartigan were ships in the night, sweeping through to grander jobs.

'Now then.' Hartigan settled himself at the head of the table. '"Investigating Burglary". How's the PID coming along?'

Faraday looked down at the notes he'd scribbled half an hour earlier. None of it made very much sense and he'd got as far as a particularly persistent break-in artist honing his skills on student bedsits in Southsea when Hartigan interrupted. He didn't, after all, want to talk about MO patterns or the constant possibility of insurance fraud. Instead, he had another agenda.

'Listen.' He slid his leather-bound folder to one side. 'I suspect I may have some good news for you.'

'Sir?'

'The Crime and Disorder Partnership have just got themselves a hefty whack of Treasury money. The scheme's rolling out nationwide but you know how much we're talking about in this city? £130,000.' He nodded. 'Big bucks.'

Faraday glanced at Annabelle. She'd made a point of abandoning her shorthand.

Hartigan beckoned Faraday closer. Elsewhere in the county, he said, divisions were bidding for thirty per cent of cash from their own partnerships but Hartigan had more ambitious plans. In his view, the lion's share of the £130,000 should properly be at his disposal, ninety-five per cent at least. It would buy a couple of cars for the pro-active drugs unit and pay the kind of overtime necessary to get a handle on the bigger dealers. With careful budgeting, the small change might even cover a decent buy-and-bust operation from the Covert Ops unit. In principle, the chair of the local partnership was in total agreement with his plans. All Hartigan needed now was support from the Co-ordinator of the Drugs Action Team. In other divisions, the Treasury money was going to half-arsed warden schemes, fannying around with confirmed junkies. Only in Portsmouth were the likes of Hartigan prepared to tackle the drugs menace head-on.

'So . . . what do you think?'

Faraday smiled. The money would buy a great deal more than a couple of Astras and some serious undercover work. Grab the thick end of £130,000 and, in the cash-strapped world of policing, Hartigan would earn himself serious brownie points.

'I think it's very interesting,' Faraday said. 'And I wish you luck.'

'Luck doesn't come into it, Joe. Talk to the funding people the way I have to and you realise that luck is the last thing you should rely on. No.' He shook his head. 'It's all about changing perceptions, about appealing to hearts and minds. There's an important case to be put in front of the public and I'm determined that we shall be the ones to make it.'

The 'we' sounded ominous.

'What exactly do you mean, sir?'

'I'm talking about the kind of anarchy that comes with drugs, Joe. Everyone knows the city is awash with narcotics. It's been happening for years. In fact it's been happening for so long that it takes something pretty special to make people stop and think. We have to find that special story, that focus. And then we have to beat the drum.'

'Beat the drum how?'

'By compelling attention. By making friends that matter. By throwing down the gauntlet to one or two of our political colleagues.'

'Political colleagues' was code for the small army of local councillors that Hartigan liked to marshal behind his constant stream of policing initiatives. Of all the senior officers Faraday had ever met, this one had the keenest nose for political advantage.

'You agree, Joe?'

Faraday was beginning to lose the plot. Of course he acknowledged the social consequences of drug abuse but he was a policeman, a detective. Didn't evidence play a role here?

'I'm not sure—'

Hartigan dismissed his hesitations.

'I've been talking to the CIMU,' he said.

'About what, sir?'

'That young lass, Helen Bassam. The girl who went off the flats last week.'

Faraday stiffened. This, at last, was what Hartigan really wanted to discuss. Merry Devlin had been right. In the shape of Helen Bassam's young body, Hartigan had found the headline of his dreams.

'She was probably using. Isn't that what we hear?'

'It's possible. The tox should be back by the end of the week.'

'But you're making enquiries? Regardless?'

'Of course, sir.'

'And?'

It was a direct challenge. Faraday was thinking about Misty Gallagher and her daughter Trudy. In these situations, the last thing you did was part with hard information.

'It's ongoing, sir. We're developing leads, some of them quite promising.'

'And what do these leads tell you, Joe?'

'They suggest the girl might well have had contact with drugs.'

'You mean using?'

'I mean contact.'

'What kind of drugs?'

'That's yet to be determined, sir.'

He paused, alarmed by the short cuts Hartigan seemed determined to take. If his uniformed boss was prepared to risk his reputation, so be it, but Faraday wanted nothing to do with this dangerous blurring of fact and supposition.

He looked Hartigan in the eye.

'I understand you had a conversation with the girl's father, Derek Bassam.'

Hartigan stared at him for a moment, then nodded.

'That's right.'

'And he talked about drugs? In connection with Helen?'

'He did. Hence my interest.'

'But you didn't think to let me know? Pass the intelligence on down the line?'

'The conversation was in confidence, Joe. I had to respect that. What I also said, of course, was that Bassam should talk to you, as SIO. I take it he did.'

Faraday nodded, struck by another thought.

'You didn't give him my phone number by any chance? And my address?'

'Good Lord, no. Why on earth would I do that?'

The denial wasn't altogether convincing, and Hartigan knew it too. He leaned forward across the table, keen to return to this new crusade of his.

'It's a question of linkage, Joe. If the girl was up to mischief on Friday night, if we can put her on the top of those flats with a head full of God knows what, then so much the better. It's a wretched, wretched thing to happen. Frankly, it's a tragedy. But out of disaster, Joe, steps triumph. We have to turn a death like that to some kind of account. You agree?'

Faraday shook his head.

'No, sir. I'm not sure I do.'

'Why on earth not?'

'Because it's not evidenced. Not as far as the girl's concerned.'

'Of course it's not. But supposing it *was* evidenced? What then?'

'I still think it stinks.'

'*Stinks?*' He rocked back into his chair, affronted.

'Yes, sir. You're suggesting we publicise it? Issue some kind of public statement?'

'I'm suggesting we give the girl's story the currency it deserves; assuming she was on drugs.'

'And Mrs Bassam? The girl's mother?'

'She'd have a point of view, naturally. In fact I imagine she might well be onside. Remember Leah Betts? How positive her parents have been ever since?'

Faraday remembered only too well. Whether or not Jane Bassam was prepared to spend the next decade reliving her own failure as a mother was, at the very least, debatable.

'We have a duty of care here, sir.'

'Indeed.'

'And I'm not sure we discharge it by putting Jane Bassam through the mill.'

'Mill? What mill?'

'Publicity? Press? Television? Isn't that the way you spread bad news?'

For the first time, Hartigan hesitated. In situations like these, sniffing the wind, he had an almost animal instinct for trouble.

'You're suggesting I might have been in touch with our media friends?'

'I'm suggesting that's the shortest cut to the kind of audience you want.'

'Without proper evidence?'

'I've no idea, sir.'

'Of course you don't.' He glared at Faraday and then leaned across and tapped Annabelle's notebook. 'DI Faraday and Superintendent Hartigan discussed strategies for developing the new city-wide drugs initiative. They agreed to suspend discussion pending fresh information.' He watched Annabelle minuting the point, then reopened his folder and shook out the headquarters correspondence on 'Investigating Burglary'. 'Now then, Joe,' he muttered, 'where were we?'

Sullivan knew the way to the garage by heart. Winter sat beside him, relishing the prospect of the next half-hour. Purged by his penance with the CCTV tapes, Winter was back at the inquiry's leading edge, actioned to further develop Sullivan's initial encounter with Kenny Foster. Not only was Winter beginning to enjoy Operation *Bisley* but he'd twice made the point of telling Sullivan so. 'Classic' was the word he'd used, a gem of a job that the boy should take care to treasure. Just imagining himself missing even a day of this kind of fun caused Winter real grief. Never had a fortnight in Albufeira seemed a worse idea.

Frogmore Motors lay on waste ground in the shadow of the new stand at Fratton Park, home to the city's football team. Three lock-ups had been knocked into a unit big enough to work on a couple of cars. According to Sullivan, it was rare to find any vehicle later than an M-reg in there, and rarer still to catch Kenny Foster with a smile on his face.

Today was no exception As they bumped to a halt outside the garage, Foster was standing in the thin sunshine kneading Swarfega between his calloused fingers. Under the circumstances, Winter didn't bother with a handshake.

'Mr Foster?'

Foster was looking at Sullivan. His least favourite occupation was meeting detectives for the second time.

'Not in the gym then, pal?'

'Too busy.'

'You want to be careful.' Foster nodded at the unmarked Escort. 'Riding around in a motor all day, you'll be fat as a house.'

'You think so?'

'Know so. That ab machine sorts you out just fine.'

'So we noticed.'

'Yeah?' His face at last creased into a grin. 'All right, wasn't it?'

The Scots accent took Winter by surprise. He'd had Foster down as a local. He stepped into the garage, leaving Sullivan to it. Chains hung from a steel beam set beneath the corrugated metal roof and the concrete floor felt uneven and greasy underfoot. Buttoning his coat against the sudden chill, he took a closer look.

Two cars sat side by side, same-model Datsuns. One was missing a back door and the other had been in a sizeable shunt. Cut both in half, stick the good halves together with a welding torch, sort yourself out a bent MOT, and you were looking at a respectable profit.

Winter squeezed between the two cars, kicking aside debris on the floor. In the semi-darkness at the very back of the unit, squeezed into a corner, was an ancient wooden table piled high with bits and pieces from an engine. One of the legs was chocked with an oil-stained copy of *Yellow Pages*, and a small, squat pit bull was roped to another. It sat on its haunches, staring up at Winter, straining against the spiked leather collar.

'Name's Eddi. With an "i".'

Winter spun round. Foster moved like a panther, balls of his feet. He hadn't heard a thing.

'Yours, is he?'

'She. Treat them right, they're more vicious than the males. Careful, or she'll have you.'

'Why Eddi?'

'Eddi Reader, pal. Voice of an angel. Tell me something, will you? How would a voice like that come out of a dump like Glasgow?'

Winter shrugged. He hadn't a clue. He was here on a murder inquiry. As Foster might have gathered.

'My pleasure, pal. Your friend out there, he told me the very same thing. So how can I help you?'

Foster's smile revealed three missing teeth. Maybe the bare-knuckle game wasn't as risk-free as it seemed, Winter thought. Maybe there were moments when the other guy landed a punch or two of his own before Foster beat him senseless.

'We've seized a camera . . .' Winter began.

He described the video sequences on the Sony's mini-tape. Maybe Foster could help them with a bit of post-fight analysis.

'Not my style, pal.' He bunched an enormous fist and shook it at the dog. 'These do the talking.'

'Do you perform for money, as a matter of interest?'

'Pleasure.' The dog was cowering under the table. 'How was I? On a scale of ten?'

'Eight. The second bloke caught you a couple of times.'

'Paid though, didn't he? Taking the piss like that?' He glanced up at Winter, checking he had the right opponent. 'Big guy? Bit of a gut. Scummer tat up here?' He touched the outside of his upper arm.

Winter nodded. 'Scummer' was Pompey-speak for anyone unlucky enough to come from neighbouring Southampton. Twenty miles, in Portsmouth terms, was all that separated decent people from the Antichrist.

'I battered him good, din I?'

'You did.'

'Din come round for quite a while.'

'If at all.'

'Och, you're joking. He was out of there and in the pub within the hour. I should know. I was fucking buying.'

'These are friends of yours?'

'Fuck, no. But you beat the shit out of a man, the least you owe him is a wee drink.'

Winter turned away. It was hard not to think of the lolling head in the first of the Scenes of Crime photographs, Bradley Finch's skinny body dangling on the end of a rope. Had the beating started here? In this garage? Or had Kenny Foster taken his time and his pleasure elsewhere? Back at the MIR, he'd recommend full forensic on the garage – maybe a strand or two of matching nylon rope, maybe a hit on the dirt under Finch's fingernails – but for now he was still interested in the contents of the mini-tape.

'Those video pictures. Who took them?'

'Pal o' mine.'

'Has he got a name?'

'Sure.' He nodded. 'Everyone's got a name.'

'It wouldn't be Bradley Finch, would it?'

'Finch? Are you fucking deaf? I said pal o' mine.'

'You knew Finch?'

'Everyone knew him. Guy was in your face all the time. Never sussed when he wasn't wanted. Thought he was everyone's best mate. You'd tell him and it would still make fuck all difference. Back he'd come with that stupid grin of his.'

'You're not surprised he's dead, then?'

'Surprised? I'm only surprised he didn't cop sooner.'

'So who'd want to kill him? Any ideas?'

'Sure, pal. You got a day or two?' He shook his head, bending to the dog and stroking it softly behind the ears when it began to whine.

Winter changed the subject.

'So tell me about this friend with the camera.'

'Why, pal?'

'Because we'd like to talk to him.'

'About what? Me? The way I fight? What goes down in those little rooms? It's all there on the tape. You've got the whole story. Listen, let me tell you something . . .' He got to his feet again and beckoned Winter closer. 'It's here, pal. Just here.' He unbuttoned Winter's coat and tapped the swell of his belly below the rib cage. 'That's where the liver is. Hit it right, hit it hard enough, and the guy's history. Man did it to me once. Fairground boxer. My own fault. I had a few drinks and thought I was King Kong. He went for my head first, head and face, the way most fighters do, and just as I was settling down, nice and easy, he slipped a big one underneath. I never saw it coming. All I felt was a pain you wouldn't believe. Like I'd swallowed boiling water. After that, he could take his time, finish me any way he liked.'

'And?'

'Another one to the liver. Exact same place. The man was a sadist. He taught me a lot. You believe that, pal?'

Winter held his stony gaze. The palest blue eyes, emptied of everything.

'You still haven't given me a name.'

'Can't, pal. No point. Guy left for a holiday end of last week.'

'Where did he go?'

'Would nae say.' The smile again, evil, and the face very close. 'And giving you his name wouldn't be right, would it? A man shouldn't be bothered, not on holiday.'

Back out in the sunshine, Winter rejoined Sullivan. Winter had got nowhere with Foster. The man had stuck to his alibi for Friday night and challenged him to disprove it. He'd no idea how the camera had ended up with Bradley Finch, and fuck all interest in how his mate had laid hands on it. The world was a wicked, wicked place and, if Winter was telling him that the Sony had come from a break-in, then he supposed it must be true. If the camera was now going back to its rightful owner, he had only one wee favour to ask. If he bought a replacement mini-tape, might he keep the original?

The question, with its sweet innocence, was a wind-up and Winter knew it. Breaking this man wouldn't be easy and he'd need to have a great deal more on him to justify formal arrest. Kenny Foster, in short, had already justified his street reputation: clever, ruthless and almost impossible to pin down.

'What about him and Finch?'

Winter and Sullivan were back in the Escort, en route to Fratton nick. Winter, who was suffering more than he'd let on from last night, was trying to have a doze.

'Foster hated him,' he muttered. 'Loathed him. "Piece of shit" was the phrase.'

'He said that?'

'Absolutely.'

'And you really believe it wasn't Finch behind the camera?'

'Yeah, I do.' Winter opened one eye. 'But where does that take us?'

The Escort ground to a halt in traffic. Winter had noticed a café across the road. Just now, there might be worse things in the world than the all-day breakfast at £2.95.

He tapped Sullivan on the arm and told him to pull over.

'You know who we should be talking to? About the camera?' He reached for the door handle. 'One of those blokes Foster beat the shit out of.'

Misty Gallagher said they were lucky when Bev Yates and Dawn Ellis appeared at her door. She was thinking about wandering over to a fashion freebie on the retail side of Gunwharf but given such a nice surprise she thought she'd skip it. She gave Bev a kiss on the lips. It was good to see him again.

She invited them in and took them straight through to the sunny little lounge. The penthouse apartment was brand new, part of an elegant court at the back of the Gunwharf Quays development, and Yates – who'd fantasised about buying something similar – could even put a price on it. £340,000 bought you three en suite bedrooms, a fitted kitchen with granite worktops, a marble bathroom suite with telephone mixer taps, and the assurance of video security at the main entrance. Already, in nine brief months, sellers in for a quick profit were asking ten grand on top of the price they'd paid.

Misty had reappeared from the kitchen with a bottle of vodka and a carton of cranberry juice.

'We're camping here,' she announced. 'The harbourside blocks come up for release soon. We're having one of the ones on the front, for definite. You should see the plans. Makes this place look like a cupboard.'

Ellis, who'd never met Misty before, already disliked her intensely. Only spoiled kids or successful criminals were this brash.

'Who's "we", Mrs Gallagher?'

'Me and Trude.' Misty reached up and ruffled Yates's hair. 'You should see Trude these days, my love. Even you're not too old.'

Yates pushed her hand away and sank onto the sofa. Ellis joined him, producing a pocketbook from her bag. She began to ask about Trudy again but Yates reached across, folding the pocketbook shut.

'Where's all this come from then, Mist?' He gestured around. The widescreen Panasonic TV. The Bang and Olufsen speakers. The over-the-top framed photograph of huge green seas breaking around some Breton lighthouse.

'Fate.' Misty was beaming at him. 'The good Lord. My guardian angel. You know me, Bev. Lucky's my middle name.'

'Last time we met, you were skint.'

'Yeah, and pissed as a rat. Couldn't understand why you never came across. Not like the old days at all, eh, Bev? How's life, anyway?'

'Great, thanks.'

'Shacked up, are you? Spoken for?'

'Yeah.'

'Who's the lucky girl, then? Anyone I know?'

'I doubt it.'

'Kids?'

'One. Twelve months.'

'You should get married, then. Make the little bastard legal.'

'I did, three years ago.' He paused. 'Bazza popped the question yet? Or are you off the list?'

Bazza McKenzie, to Bev Yates's certain knowledge, had paid for all this. The kind of money the cocaine biz pulled in would buy half of Gunwharf. Misty settled herself in the leather recliner and splashed a great deal of vodka over ice cubes before topping it up with cranberry juice.

'Drink, dear?' She was looking at Ellis.

'No, thanks.'

'Suit yourself.' She nodded towards Yates. 'He used to be a knockout once, you know. I know women in this town who've shagged him twice and still wanted more. How many men could you say that about, eh? Hand on heart?' She laughed, tilting her head back, letting the mane of black hair fall halfway down her back, and Ellis knew that she'd been right from the start. Look in the waste bin in the kitchen and you'd find another vodka bottle, empty. This woman had probably been drinking since dawn.

'We need to ask you about Trudy,' she said again.

'Ask away.'

'She was mates with Helen Bassam. Right?'

'Yeah, big mates too. It'll be the funeral next, won't it? And I expect that dried-up old bag of bones will try and keep the bloody date a secret. Shame really, nice girl like that.'

'You're talking about her mother?'

'Of course I am. People get the wrong idea in this town. It's women like me get all the grief but you know something? At least I have a relationship with my kid. Me and Trude?' She crossed two fingers. 'Like that, we are. Really tight.'

'I understand she lives with an older man.'

'That's right. Lucky thing.'

'And she's sixteen.'

'Just.'

'You don't mind?'

'Mind? Nice bloke like that? Business of his own? Rich as well as tasty? *Mind?*'

'So how much do you see of Trudy?'

'Lots. I told you, dear, we're like mates. She's a gobby little thing, just like her mum. Comes over most days.'

'She's not at school?'

'Hates it. Bores her stiff.'

'Doesn't work at all?'

'No need. Money's not a problem, not being with Mikey. Miller's Motors ring any bells?'

Ellis glanced sideways at Yates. Misty had let her skirt ride way up her thigh but his eyes had glazed as if he couldn't quite connect the dots in this bizarre conversation. Sixteen years old. Should be at school. Shacked up instead with some poxy car dealer.

'Tell us about Helen.' He struggled upright on the sofa and planted his elbows on his knees. 'The kid's dead, Mist. This stuff's for real.'

'What do you want to know, love?'

'I want to know whether or not she was doing drugs.'

'Everyone does drugs. It's like the rain. You can't avoid it.'

'Including Helen?'

'Of course.'

'You know that for sure?'

'Yeah.'

'How?'

'Trude told me. Not real drugs. Not your serious gear. But tablets. Es at weekends, speed to stay awake, other stuff I've never heard of. It's not that they've got a habit or anything. It's recreational, isn't it? Sometimes I wonder, I really do.'

'Wonder what?'

'How we ever got by at weekends. Without drugs.'

Yates was looking hard at his hands. Ellis took up the running.

'Where does all this gear come from then?'

'All over, dear. I could give you phone numbers. Depends what you're after, of course, but you'd be unlucky not to score within half an hour, especially round here. It's like pizza delivery. Except pizza takes longer.' She nodded, then took a long pull at the vodka.

None of this was news to Ellis. Like every other detective in the city, she was resigned to kids getting off on anything they could stuff down their throats. What was truly shocking, though, was this woman's candour. It was her own daughter, her own daughter's mate. And she truly didn't care.

'Did Helen stay here ever?'

'Sometimes, yeah.'

'What was she like?'

'Like? As a person, you mean? She was nice, screwed up but nice. And a looker, too. She and Trude made a real pair. Walk into Tiger-Tiger with them and you wouldn't never put your hand in your purse.'

'But the drugs? You've seen them using?'

For the first time, Misty's foot found the brake pedal. She shook her head, emphatic. Neither kid ever did drugs under her roof. Not Trude. And certainly not Helen.

'How do you know?'

'Because I told them. I explained about it. House rules, I called it. And that's the point, dear. Get yourself a relationship with your kid and they listen. Lay down the law like that cow of a mother did to Helen and you just drive them away. No decent parent wants that, now do they?'

The question was addressed to Yates. He lifted his head and looked her in the eye, and Ellis knew at once that he'd had enough of all this bullshit. His life had moved on and he wanted Misty Gallagher to know it.

'So tell us, Mist. Tell us why you don't let these kids – Helen, Trudy – do their drugs when you're around. How does all that work? Just for the record?'

Misty reached for her glass again but this time she didn't drink. Instead, she tipped the rim towards him, the most intimate of toasts.

'Because I know that tossers like you will come onto me one day' – she smiled – 'asking fucking silly questions like that.'

Two calls to the Major Incident Room at Fratton failed to raise Brian Imber. At the first try, there was no reply. On the second occasion, the clerk on the other end didn't have a clue where he might be. Only when Faraday went back to the Crime Squad at Havant did one of the DSs tell him that Imber had gone to the Yard for a conference.

'Back tonight,' he said. 'Round seven.'

He gave Faraday Imber's mobile number and rang off. The mobe was on call divert but he left a message asking for an urgent meet. Whatever Yates and Ellis came up with at Misty Gallagher's wouldn't be enough. As far as drugs went, he needed the kind of in-depth, up-to-the-minute brief that only Imber could supply.

He glanced at his watch, thankful that Hartigan had at last departed. Angered by Faraday's lack of enthusiasm for exploiting Helen Bassam's death, the Superintendent had conducted the rest of the meeting like a masterclass in management theory, tearing Faraday's thoughts on domestic burglary to shreds. The deadline for draft submissions was barely a week away and he'd given Faraday four days to come up with a decently thought-out analysis.

Now Faraday reached for the phone again and dialled Anghared Davies's number. Wearied by Hartigan's little games, he wanted to know how J-J was getting on. Gordon Franks had been due at the house shortly after Faraday left this morning. He was taking the boy over to Somerstown for something he called induction. As far as delinquent kids were concerned, there was definitely a deep end and J-J was in for total immersion.

Anghared at last answered. Faraday could hear shouts and screaming in the background.

'J-J?' he asked mildly.

There was a pause, then the shriek of Anghared telling someone to shut it. Everything went briefly quiet. Seconds later, she was back on the phone, chuckling.

'Just went off, I'm afraid. Occupational hazard. What can I do for you?'

'J-J,' Faraday said again. 'How's he getting on?'

'Haven't a clue, Joe. He and Gordon went off with a bunch of them this morning and I haven't heard a thing since. Good sign that, in our line of business.'

The Portsmouth Arts Centre was housed in a disused school in the south-east corner of the city. The classrooms served as venues for writing circles, music sessions and classes in everything from calligraphy to watercolours, while a performance space large enough to accommodate modest drama presentations had been hacked out in an adjacent annexe. Gordon Franks had the ear of the caretaker, and when no one else was using this tiny theatre, he shipped in his own kids.

Today, there were half a dozen, aged thirteen upwards, all of them newcomers to drama. The theatre was small and claustrophobic – black-painted walls, lighting gantries, an audience ramp, no windows – and Franks considered it ideal for concentrating minds and compelling attention. This dark, slightly spooky space was the perfect backdrop for whatever stories he cared to spin, and experience told him that even the most damaged kids found it difficult to resist the spell that drama – pretending to be someone else – could cast.

They'd started off with a series of exercises and he'd signed instructions for J-J to join in. The exercises were largely mime – escaping from a burning aircraft, holding up a bank – and the kids had been fascinated by this lanky, poorly coordinated creature who could do nothing with his body except his hands. At first they'd laughed at him, at his awkwardness, but he'd plunged head first into the spirit of the thing, totally unembarrassed, and the way he could converse with Franks in a flurry of hand movements at first puzzled then excited them. Here was something truly exotic. How cool was a guy who could talk without using his mouth?

At lunch time, they had cheese rolls and played football in the playground. J-J, in goal, was truly hopeless. Then, with the score in double figures, Franks blew the whistle and laid out the plot for the afternoon. They were seamen aboard a frigate under Admiral Lord Nelson's command. They'd crossed the Atlantic with the trade winds up their arse and now they were cruising the Caribbean. There were rumours of a Spanish treasure ship and the prospect of untold plunder. And then, from the top of the tallest mast, came the cry: Ship ahoy!

Each of the kids was given a role. J-J was captain. The wind shifted to the starboard bow. They had to close the Spaniard and board her. The rest was down to J-J.

The kids set to with enormous vigour, thundering round the tiny stage while J-J signalled them to haul on the ropes, run out the guns, sharpen the cutlasses, prime the muskets, say their prayers and prepare for battle. Each of these stage commands J-J embellished with extravagant mime, whipping the kids to a frenzy, and they were seconds away from letting fly with the grappling irons when there came a noise at the door beside the stage.

Someone was trying to get in. J-J, oblivious, was still rallying the boarding party. Then, with a crash, the door flew open. J-J, alerted by the sudden influx of light, turned to see what had happened. Standing motionless in the open doorway, silhouetted against the light, was a tiny figure. J-J looked towards Gordon Franks. Should he carry on? Was it really all over when the Spaniard was there for the taking?

Franks stepped towards the door, but the moment he moved, the little figure turned and darted away. A couple of the boarding party began to snigger. One of them mouthed something to Franks. Franks nodded and turned back to J-J.

'Kid called Doodie.' He nodded at the imaginary galleon. 'Let battle commence.'

Chapter eighteen

Faraday was up to his eyes with a welfare crisis when Cathy Lamb appeared at his open office door.

'That nice PC from Operational Support has been on. Willard's hassling for more bodies and they're looking to us. Local knowledge is the line they're taking.' She nodded at the phone. 'I said you might like a little input before we strip the cupboard bare.'

'Who would we lose?'

'Yates and Ellis. They're off duty in an hour. You need to make a decision.'

Cathy waited for Faraday to make the call before sending them through but the brief conversation with Ops Support got him nowhere. The Assistant Chief Constable in charge of Special Operations was in the business of properly resourcing major inquiries and that was that. The good news was the time limit that he'd imposed. Willard had originally acquired ten extra bodies for just two days. That deadline had nearly expired but Ops Support were about to extend it to the end of the week, giving Willard additional help on top. Yates and Ellis would be part of those reinforcements but they'd be back in the Southsea CID office by Monday, guaranteed.

The moment Faraday broke this news, he could read the disappointment in their faces. On Major Crimes you worked around the clock. A posting to Operation *Bisley*, in terms of overtime, was a blank cheque. The last thing Yates and Ellis wanted was a speedy return to division.

Faraday asked about Misty Gallagher.

'The woman's a nightmare.' It was Dawn Ellis. 'Mothers like that, no wonder we've got a problem in this country.'

'But what about the girl? Helen Bassam? Are we talking drugs here?'

'Gallagher says yes but it's an assumption. She says she can't evidence it. There's no way she's going to give us a statement. And naturally none of it's got anything to do with her.'

'You think she's supplying?'

'Has to be.' Yates this time. 'She's tucked up with Bazza McKenzie and that guy scores charlie by the ton. Bloke told me the other day he owns half of Colombia. Wouldn't surprise me in the least.'

'You're telling me the girl was doing cocaine?'

'I doubt it. Misty seemed to think tabs, Es mostly. That sounds about right. Her age.'

Faraday scribbled himself a note. Yates and Ellis had also been back to Chuzzlewit House, chasing up the old boy who'd returned from holiday.

Ellis leaned forward. 'He said he'd seen the kid Doodie around a lot before last week.'

'Doing what, exactly?'

'All sorts. Up and down in the lift. Racing around the corridors. And out on the roof.'

'By himself?'

'Always. Apparently, he had a little game he played. He used to chuck pebbles off the roof. He had plastic bags of them, from the beach.'

'How does the old boy know?'

'People started finding dents in their car roofs. From the west side you can hit the car park. There was a cat found dead, as well, little black and white thing. There was no direct evidence but it was a real mess.'

'He threw a cat off the roof? This Doodie?'

'It's possible.'

Faraday looked at them both. Yates, no cat lover, was trying to hide a smile.

'What about recently? Has the kid come back?'

Ellis shook her head.

'We asked him that and we talked to the warden, too. No one's seen him since last week. That tells me he was definitely implicated. He used the place as a playground. Now he's gone elsewhere.'

Faraday got up and went to the window. If it was true about the cat, you had to wonder what else this child might be capable of. He made a mental note to talk to Anghared again, then paused.

'We still haven't got a decent picture,' he said.

'That's right, boss.'

'But if he was a regular visitor, there'd be video, lots of it. Right?'

'Absolutely.'

'So why don't you go back to the control room and ask for tapes before Friday. He's bound to be on there somewhere. Then we can take hard copy and push a decent mugshot around. No?'

'You're right.' Yates nodded. 'Except you're telling us we're off to Major Crimes.'

There was a long silence while Faraday considered the options. The Helen Bassam inquiry was already five days old. A lot of other crime had happened since then, none of it especially dramatic but all of it demanding attention, and he didn't need Cathy Lamb to tell him that an odds-on Death by Misadventure verdict was already way down the list of priorities. Week after week, he found himself in exactly this same situation, totally shafted.

Something inside him snapped.

'This is bloody silly,' he raged. 'We've got a girl who chucks herself off a block of flats, a woman who says she was doing drugs, and a ten-year-old we can't find. On top of that, there's bugger all we can do about it. We're supposed to be on top of this job. We're supposed to be the people in the know. We're supposed to be way, way ahead of the bad guys. So what's gone wrong? Anyone like to tell me?'

'They're not the bad guys,' Ellis muttered. 'They're kids.'

'I know, I know, but you think that makes it any easier? Kids today, criminals tomorrow. Either that or fucking dead. Great prospect, eh?'

He turned to the window and stared out, his hands thrust deep in his pockets. In the CID office, Faraday had a reputation for maintaining an almost Buddhist calm in situations where others would have gone ballistic. He rarely let himself get wound up. He coped with almost everything the job could throw at him. Now, Yates and Ellis exchanged glances. Maybe Paul Winter had been right. Maybe Faraday really was losing it.

Finding one of Kenny Foster's luckless opponents was a great deal easier than Winter had anticipated. Back at Fratton, they toured the incident room with the seized Sony, showing freeze-frames of Foster's handiwork. They were after a positive ID on one of the battered faces, and it was Paul Ingham, the DS in charge of outside inquiries, who poked a finger at victim number two.

'His name's Billy,' he said. 'Billy Carter. He's got previous for nicking stuff off building sites. Always gets caught. Never fails. And I'll tell you where to find him, too. You know that place in Fratton Road that does all the disabled gear? In there.'

Winter nodded. He knew exactly where he meant.

'What's he like, then?'

'Thick.' Ingham took another look at the video. 'Wouldn't have felt a thing.'

The shop was a five-minute walk from Fratton nick. The front of the building looked newly painted and there was a row of electric wheelchairs displayed on the pavement outside. Winter and Sullivan crossed the road. The shop window was full of retirement aids, items to smooth the journey to the grave, and Sullivan had time to count four kinds of potty before Winter steered him towards the door.

Inside, the shop appeared to be empty. There were more goodies stacked on the shelves, and Winter paused to examine a rubberised undersheet which promised to take the misery out of night sweats. When Sullivan made a joke about the job Foster must have done on Billy Carter to warrant all this gear, Winter remained stony-faced. Those last weeks nursing Joannie had made him a world expert on night sweats. Some mornings, it was like waking someone up in a swimming pool.

There was a movement at the rear of the shop and a big man appeared, lumbering towards them. As soon as the light from the shop window settled on his face, Winter knew they'd found their target. The swelling had settled down by now but his face was still a mess, the purple bruises beginning to turn yellow. He loomed over them, wiping his mouth with the back of his hand, a figure from a child's cartoon.

Winter snapped open his warrant card. Sullivan did the same. They were here to talk to him about Kenny Foster.

'Yeah? What of him?' He had a deep voice, Pompey-gruff.

'We understand you fought him.'

'How d'you know?'

'We've got some pictures, video pictures. You remember the camera?'

'Yeah.' He nodded. 'Little git.'

'Who?'

Carter shook his head. He'd said enough already. Did they want to buy anything or could he go back to his tea?

Winter didn't move.

'Foster thinks you were crap,' he said softly. 'He wonders why he even bothered to get out of bed that day.'

'Kenny? He said that?'

'Yeah. He's got a little nephew. Kid of six. He told us he should have sent the boy along to do the business. Saved himself the trouble.'

'You kidding?' Carter looked genuinely hurt. 'Kenny?'

Winter nodded, saucing the insult with one or two extra bits of fiction. The longer he watched this man, the more he wondered about Ingham's description. Thick was one thing, thick he understood, but there was something about Carter's eyes, a hint of derangement that suggested a more serious condition. Had Foster added brain damage to his usual list of injuries?

'About this camera.' Sullivan had taken up the running. 'Little git, you said.'

'He was, too.'

'Did you know him?'

'Yeah, I knows him.'

'Wasn't Bradley Finch, was it?'

'No.' He shook his massive head. 'I knows Bradley. It wasn't Bradley.'

'But you know Bradley's dead?'

'What?'

'Someone killed him. Friday night.'

'*What?*'

This wasn't fake surprise, and both men knew it. Billy didn't stretch to pretending. Just getting the basics in the right order was quite enough for one day.

'Kenny?' he queried.

'Why do you say that?'

''Cos Kenny can be rough. Me? I can handle myself. If you seen them pictures you know that. Kenny's the only guy ever got near me.' He offered them a grave nod. 'That's how good he is, Kenny.'

'You think Kenny might have fought Finch?'

'Yeah.' Carter nodded. 'That's what you said, ain't it? Fucking mismatch, that. Says me, anyway.'

Winter was studying the rubber undersheet again. Portsmouth never ceased to amaze him. Here was a man who thought Kenny Foster had killed Bradley Finch in a stand-up fight. With seconds present and a guy with a camera. And all that without anyone being any the wiser.

'How does it work then, this fight game?'

'Ain't nothing illegal.'

'I know that. I'm just curious.'

'Well . . .' he shrugged, lost for words '. . . we just fights. There's a bit of betting of course, but it's really the fighting. Hardest man in Pompey. That's what it's about.'

'And Kenny?'

'Hardest man in Pompey. For definite.'

'So he took money off you?'

'Yeah. Couple of quid. But that ain't all, since you're asking.'

'What else then?'

'He didn't tell you?'

'Remind me.'

Billy looked from one face to the other, trying to work out whether they were winding him up, then shrugged again.

'He must have told you about shagging my bird after. He told every other fucker in the world.'

'Oh, right . . .' Winter began to laugh '. . . that. I thought you meant something serious. She shags for England, apparently, your good lady. Didn't even have to be asked. Isn't that right?'

'Is that what he said?' Billy's face had darkened.

'That's what he told us. Could be fantasy, mind. He wouldn't be every woman's wet dream.'

'No, they definitely shagged. Trace told me. He wasn't any good, either. She said it was like being at the dentist, my Trace. Never felt a thing. He tell you that, did he?'

'No, he didn't. He said they were at it like rabbits. Both times.'

'*Both* times?'

'Yeah.' Winter frowned, checking with Sullivan. 'Just the twice, wasn't it?'

'So far.'

'There, then.' Winter turned back to Carter. 'Just the twice.'

Carter was brooding. That hurt look was back on his face. He was seeing Trace tonight. They were going to the movies. She was mad about Sean Penn. He'd have it out with her then.

'And what if it's true?' Winter asked gently.

'I'll hammer the bastard.' Carter nodded, telling himself it was possible. 'He'll fucking regret it. And that's a promise.'

Winter didn't say anything. It had begun to rain outside, and the silence was broken by the steady drip of water somewhere close at hand. At length, Carter stirred. He'd been thinking. He'd come to a decision.

'The bloke with the camera.' He stole a look at Winter. 'You know Tosh Harris?'

'Course I do.'

'It was him.'

Dave Michaels knew Tosh Harris.

'Double glazer from Stamshaw,' he said briefly. 'Real name's Terry. Got a twin brother, Mick. Bent as ten-bob notes, both of them.'

Winter and Sullivan were sitting in the DS's office. Winter had been racking his brain about Tosh Harris, dredging his memory for the name, but had drawn a big fat blank. Sullivan was amused, for once, that Michaels had to come to the rescue.

'Well known, is he? This Terry Harris?'

'Depends who you talk to. I happen to know him because I pulled him on a couple of jobs. The double glazing is a hobby. He buddied up with a guy years ago who'd been made foreman in a factory up in Hilsea. They made plastic extrusions for the trade. This bloke sorted out offcuts for Harris, just for a drink, and he started doing cut-price double glazing, mainly outside the city. It's the simplest thing in the world. You get a half-decent van and some letterheads and you're off. It's the moneyed people you're after, big spreads in the country or decent gaffs in places like Chichester and Arundel. Those kind of people always love a bargain and while you're there you can case the joint for later. That's where the real money comes from.'

'He goes back?'

'Yeah. And he was a smarmy little bastard, too. Used to chat up all the housewives, find out when they were off on their hols, then . . . bingo! In he went. Access wasn't a problem because he'd put the bloody windows in in the first place and most times he'd sorted the alarm, too. Clever little bastard, Harris.'

'And Mick? His brother?'

'Not really in the same league. Not smart enough to make a decent housebreaker. Last time I heard he was into contraband booze and fags. Used to take a van across to Cherbourg and load up for the week. Suited him down to the ground, They were close, mind, Terry and Mick. Both Stamshaw boys, obviously.'

'Did Terry Harris go down on those jobs you mentioned?'

'No. We fucked up big time on the forensic.' He pulled a face but didn't go into details.

Winter was still thinking about the video camera. In these situations you moved very carefully, one step at a time. Say Billy Carter was right. Say Terry Harris was the guy with the Sony at the bare-knuckle fights. Where did he get it?

Dave Michaels turned to his computer. He went into the ACR program and scrolled through the list of stolen Sonys until he found the camera seized at Fawcett Road. With the Compton address went a phone number. He dialled the number and then handed the phone to Winter.

Winter's eyes were glued to the screen. A woman's voice, oldish, refined.

'Mrs Wreke?'

'Speaking. Who is this?'

Winter introduced himself. He was investigating a major crime and there were indications that links might exist to a series of local burglaries. She and her husband had returned from holiday last month and reported a break-in.

'That's true, Mr Winter. Though we've heard nothing since.'

'Then I may have some good news.'

He described the camera. It was definitely theirs. There might even be a possibility of recovering more of the items. Someone would be out to check through the list they had supplied. In the meantime, he had another question.

'By all means.' The voice sounded warmer. 'Go ahead.'

'Have you had any work done on your property recently?'

'No, I'm afraid not.' There was a pause. 'Wait, we did have a little job done before Christmas. We have an outhouse in the garden, wooden windows, absolutely terrible state.'

'And?'

'Charles found a little man in Portsmouth. Extremely reasonable. Plastic, of course, but they do the job.'

'Can you remember his name at all?'

'I'm afraid I can't. Do you mind hanging on a moment?' Winter heard her calling her husband's name. There was a mumble of conversation, then she was back on the phone. 'Harris, we think.' She sounded slightly breathless. 'Is that what you wanted to know?'

Willard had just returned from a crime strategy meeting at headquarters. He cleared the conference table and asked Sullivan to sort out some coffees. In every major investigation, there comes a moment when the dominoes start to fall and the slightly tight smiles around the table told their own story. This, in all probability, was it.

It was Willard, naturally, who took command. He wanted to be sure, first of all, that they knew where to find Terry Harris. Dave Michaels read out an address in Stamshaw. It was two years old.

'Have someone check it out,' Willard grunted. 'Quietly.'

'Done.'

Willard nodded. Next, he wanted to be sure of the link between Foster and Harris. All they had to go on so far was Billy Carter's word.

'Carter's done a statement,' Winter volunteered. 'Harris had the camera for all three fights.'

'What else does he say about Foster and Harris?'

'He says they're mates.'

'They screw houses together?'

'He doesn't say that. He's not daft, sir. Just mates. Harris acts as Foster's second in all these fights. I'm reading between the lines but I think Harris gets off on the violence. That would certainly explain the videos.'

'Understood. So how did the camera get into Finch's hands?'

'I've no idea, sir. But Billy Carter gives me the impression that Finch might hang out with Harris. We found the full kit at Finch's nan's place, don't forget. That might put Finch with Harris on some of these jobs.'

'Like Compton?'

'Absolutely. That would explain how Finch knew about the camera.'

'You think he borrowed it off Harris?'

'It's possible. Though you'd be asking why he sold it on the side. To the bloke in Fawcett Road.'

'You're suggesting he nicked it off Harris?'

'I'm suggesting guys like him would nick anything. Off anyone.'

'He's right, sir.' Sammy Rollins had joined them late. 'It's all up for grabs as far as blokes like Finch are concerned. That's something that comes back in the intelligence. That's why he wasn't Mr Popular.'

'We need Brian Imber, don't we?'

'He's in London. Back at seven.'

'OK.' Willard glanced at his watch, then leaned back to let Sullivan distribute the coffees. 'Let's say that Paul Winter's got it right. Let's say that Harris and Finch screwed the place out at Compton. They nicked a load of stuff, including the camera. Finch took a fancy to it, nicked it off Harris, fucked around with putting his nan on the telly, then sold it. Where does that take us?'

Winter needed no prompting.

'Harris is pissed off, number one. And number two, Foster is pissed off big time.'

'Why?'

'Because Finch's already wound him up over the stop-check, giving the traffic blokes his name and address. That's major lack of respect. And then Harris comes on to him and says the camera's gone walkabout. With all Foster's precious fights on it. Situation like that, Foster and Harris would put their heads together.'

'But how do they know Finch's nicked the camera?'

'Maybe they don't. But the guy's got form as far as they're concerned – and there's another thing, too.'

'What's that?'

'The call I got on my mobile about the job at Brennan's. The one that turned out to come from Finch. Let's assume that Harris had set the job up and that Finch was along for the ride. And let's assume that there'd been some kind of falling-out. Setting Harris up would be exactly the kind of twat move a bloke like Finch would have made.'

'Why?'

'Because he'd think it would teach Harris a lesson. Plus take him out for a while. A job like that, Harris would go down, wouldn't he?'

'And you're suggesting Harris got to find out about the call?'

'I haven't a clue, sir. But even if he didn't, you still get the whispers, don't you? Blokes like Harris and Foster listen to stuff like that. Finch fucks them over with the stop-check and the camera and here he is doing it again, grassing them up. That's big time aggro. The least they'd do is ask the boy a question or two.'

'Are you saying that's what happened?'

'No, sir. I'm saying that's what might have happened. They might have slapped him about. It might have got out of hand. You know the way these blokes live. Nothing happens at all until they're half a dozen lagers down and coked out of their heads.'

'Foster doesn't drink,' Sullivan said quietly. 'He told me that first time round at the garage.'

'OK.' Winter shrugged. 'Let's say that's true. Let's say he doesn't drink. Let's say he's the only criminal in this city not to like a bevvy or two. That doesn't make him any the less violent, does it? Or pissed off?'

Willard held up a hand, stilling the argument. He'd just got a first read of the full post-mortem report on Bradley Finch. It confirmed that he'd been assaulted before he died, and that some of the injuries suggested earlier beatings.

'A couple of rib fractures, at least,' Willard said. 'And he'd lost teeth, too. So tell me, was this lad some kind of punchbag? Did everyone take a swing at him?'

'Happens.' Sammy Rollins again. 'It's a bit like school. Once you're a target, everyone has a pop.'

'But what about Terry Harris? Supposing it's true he likes violence? How might all that work? Does he do the business himself on Finch? Or does he just watch?'

'Same difference, isn't it? Either way, Finch didn't seem the kind of bloke to put up any kind of fight.'

'So why would he stick around with Harris? Assuming Harris was the one giving him a hard time?'

Sammy Rollins shrugged and said he didn't know. Winter pushed his chair back from the table. The longer this debate went on, the more he was convinced that there was someone else who would probably have at least some of the answers.

'Where are we with the girl, Louise?' He asked.

Willard was sipping his coffee. He'd circulated her details on an all-forces bulletin and put another call through to her uncle at the Nigerian embassy. So far, with absolutely no result.

'She'll be able to help us with Finch.' Winter tapped his notes. 'I guarantee it.'

'How come?'

'They were close. I don't know whether it was a sexual thing and in a way it doesn't matter. The point is, he saw a lot of her. He didn't have a mum and dad, not really, and his nan's off the planet. Everyone needs someone to talk to and my money's on the girl. She's the type. She'd have listened. And I tell you something else, too. Her looks, she'd have blokes like Foster and maybe this Harris sniffing all over her. How come a tosser like Finch is screwing class crumpet like that? No wonder he ended up in her knickers.'

'But they might not have been screwing,' Willard pointed out. 'You said so yourself.'

'I meant hanging under the tree.'

'Ah.' Willard was impressed. 'I see.'

He returned to the post-mortem report. What especially interested him was the puncture wound in the foot. According to the pathologist, it was very recent, barely hours old. He'd recovered microscopic particles from the wound, suggesting a rusty nail of some kind.

'Maybe they tried to crucify him first?' Dave Michaels reached for the biscuits. 'It's amazing what Stella can do.'

Even Willard laughed.

'Unlikely,' he said. 'One of his trainers had a hole in the sole. Matched the wound perfectly.'

'You think he trod on something?'

'Yeah.' Willard looked at Winter again. 'Tell me about that garage of Foster's. What kind of state's it in?'

'Chaos. Stuff everywhere.'

'Underfoot? Nails? Something sharp?'

'Could easily have been.'

'So that would put Finch at the garage, wouldn't it? Some point before he died? Assuming we could evidence it forensically?'

'Of course, sir.'

'Then we'll do it.' He turned to Sammy Rollins.

'Do what, sir?'

'Full forensic on the garage. Where are we? Scene of crime four?'

Rollins totted up the running score. The patch of muddy earth under the tree on Hilsea Lines was SOC one, Finch's body two, the house in Margate Road three, the burned-out Fiat four.

'SOC five, sir. I'll talk to Jerry Proctor, get it organised.'

'Do that. Have him standing by for tomorrow morning.' He looked around the table. 'Now then, time to take a few prisoners . . .'

Half an hour later, Winter and Sullivan were back in the Escort. Stamshaw was an area on the western side of the city, a little enclave of terraced housing adjacent to the firing ranges on the harbour shore and the scrapyard under the motorway that had become a graveyard for various bits of clapped-out naval hardware. Families tended to stay in Stamshaw for generations, as beached as the rusting hulks down the road, and Winter was curious to know whether Harris was one of them. Willard wanted a preliminary interview before making a decision about formal arrest but it was odds-on they'd be back at Harris's door at first light tomorrow morning. Unless, of course, he had a cast-iron alibi.

They were still looking for the street when Sullivan asked Winter about the puncture wound in Bradley Finch's foot. Finch, according to Eddie Galea, had appeared at the café on Friday afternoon, limping. Didn't that suggest he'd copped the injury earlier?

'Of course it does.'

'Then why didn't you bring it up?'

'Because Willard's hot to do the garage. He thinks Finch might have been slapped around in there before they drove him up to Hilsea Lines and he might be right. At the moment, it's a question of getting the time line right. No point complicating things when it's looking so sweet.'

Sullivan was peering ahead through the windscreen. It was dark now and under the orange lamps some of the streets appeared not to have names.

'There,' he said suddenly, pulling left.

Winter counted the houses. Number 62 Aboukir Road was near the end. Sullivan nudged the Escort into the kerb and killed the engine. This was the lower end of Pompey's housing stock – flat-fronted terraces with doors straight onto the street – but 62 looked smarter than the rest. Flowers in a vase in the front window and fresh-looking paint on the door. Winter knocked twice, hearing an answering bark from the back of the house. Footsteps pattered down the hall, and then came the sound of someone wrestling with the lock. Finally, a child's face peered up at them through a tiny crack as the door opened.

'Yeah?'

'Your dad in, is he?'

'No.'

'Your mum?'

A woman pulled the door fully open. She was in her thirties, blonde hair in a topknot, no make-up. She looked exhausted but managed the beginnings of a smile.

'What is it?'

Winter had his warrant card out.

'Mrs Harris?'

'That's me.'

'Your husband in?'

'Afraid not.' She glanced at her watch. 'He's working in Guildford today. Should be back any time now.'

Chapter nineteen

Faraday made it to Fratton shortly after half past six. Trying to unknot his day hadn't been made easier by a long email from headquarters containing an inspection report by a neighbouring force. There were important invasion-of-privacy implications for various levels of surveillance but Faraday had lost the drift within seconds. It was late in the day for an in-depth exploration of RIPA authorisations. What he wanted now was a drink.

Brian Imber, on the train back from London, had agreed a meet. His day sounded even worse than Faraday's and he'd be up in the bar at Kingston Crescent around seven. Faraday climbed the stairs to the top floor. There were half a dozen people up there already and, to his surprise, they included the bulky figure of Geoff Willard. Spotting Faraday at the door, he broke off his conversation and insisted on buying a drink. There were a couple of things he wanted to discuss. Stella OK?

Faraday took the top off his pint and joined Willard at a table over by the window. There was something different about the Detective Superintendent and it took him a second or two to realise what it was. The man was smiling.

'How's it going?' Willard nodded at the empty seat.

Faraday made himself comfortable, wondering whether he should take the question at face value. Was Willard really interested in duty rosters and the implications for Easter overtime? In the traffic jam of e-mails that threatened to clag up his computer forever?

'Fine,' he murmured, tipping his glass towards Willard in a toast. 'You?'

'Never better, Joe. You won't be up to speed with *Bisley* but I think we're getting there. Winter's playing a blinder. Have to watch him like a hawk but we knew that already, didn't we?' He chuckled to himself, then told Faraday about the call Winter had found on his mobile way back before Finch had met his end. Winter had thought it was some routine grass warning him about Brennan's.

'I know, sir. He was working for me then.'

'Of course he was, Joe.'

'And we staked the place out. Remember? Made Hartigan's day when no one turned up.'

'Sure.' Willard beckoned him closer. 'But it turns out the call came from Finch himself. He had a contact inside Brennan's and it's odds-on that Finch and another person of interest to us were planning a job that night, and that Finch had decided to grass him up. Only the bloke never turned up. And you know why? Because Finch was getting himself slapped around. Maybe by this very same bloke. Amazing, isn't it?'

Faraday managed to raise a smile. 'Person of interest' was Willard's code for prime suspect, a linguistic sleight of hand that saved him piling all his chips on a single square before he had a ton and a half of evidence. He sat back nursing his glass while Willard offered one or two other little gems from the treasure chest that was Operation *Bisley*. How the Pompey underworld had clammed up. How Kenny Foster had frightened them all shitless. And how the MIT now had every chance of securing a couple of worthwhile arrests.

Most of it Faraday managed to follow but the more expansive Willard became, the more he found himself thinking about Marta. Early evenings was the time she'd normally phone. She'd still be at the office or en route home and, like Pavlov's dog, Faraday had become conditioned to these calls. The last half-hour, every time his mobile had rung, his hand had plunged into his breast pocket, praying to find her number on the readout. And every time it turned out to be work – Cathy after a decision on a CPS file, Hartigan's management assistant wanting to check his diary – his heart had sunk. Less than twenty-four hours had gone by since he'd left her in that hideous kitchen and already he was a head case. So much for his new-found freedom.

'Something up, Joe?'

Willard, no fool, had cocked an eyebrow. Faraday shook his head.

'Nothing that can't be sorted.'

'The job? Or private?'

'Both, if you want the truth.'

'Can I help at all?'

It was the last question Faraday expected, not least because Willard plainly meant it.

'The job's impossible,' he admitted. 'But then we've all known that for years. Everything else?' He shrugged. 'You tell me.'

'A woman?'

'Yep.'

'Crashed and burned?'

'Something like that.'

Willard nodded. He kept his own social arrangements to himself, refusing to mix real life with the job, but Faraday had heard enough to suspect that he had a longstanding liaison with a psychologist in Bristol. Willard's marriage was dead and buried and he had no kids to worry about so a nice tidy relationship with a fellow professional probably served him pretty well.

Now he leaned across the table and touched Faraday lightly on the arm, a gesture that reminded Faraday of a sympathetic GP. There were things that might be done here, a course of treatment that might help.

'We had a conversation the other day, Joe. Up at Hilsea Lines.'

'We did?'

'You bloody know we did. The job coming up on the MIR.' He sat back, glancing at his watch. 'Definitely worth a thought, eh?'

Winter and Sullivan sat in the Escort outside Harris's house for the best part of half an hour. When he didn't turn up, Winter decided it was time for a serious chat with his wife. When she answered the door, Winter invited himself and Sullivan in. Was there somewhere they could talk before her husband came back?

With some reluctance, she led them down the hall and into the long lounge-diner that stretched the length of the house. The place was immaculate and the furniture looked brand new. A line of photographs on the mantelpiece recorded her daughter's progress through primary school and there was a framed watercolour of Bosham, a little village up the coast, on the opposite wall. A bookcase in the corner was piled with old copies of the *National Geographic* and there was even a small electronic piano with the score of 'Clair de Lune' propped against the music stand. Try and imagine a burglar's gaff and the last thing you'd come up with was this neat, cosy little nest.

Mrs Harris gestured at the sofa and settled herself in an armchair. She looked tense and physically wiped out, but behind the obvious exhaustion there lurked a sense of bewilderment. This was a woman who'd got on the wrong train, Winter thought, and hadn't a clue how to get off.

Sullivan already had his pocketbook open. Mrs Harris's first name was Jill. The child was called Maisie. She was the apple of Mum's eye.

The child sat on the floor, her head back against her mother's knees, while Sullivan briefly explained about the enquiries they were pursuing.

It was important to establish where Mrs Harris and her husband had been on Friday night. She could start, if she liked, around six o'clock.

'But you still haven't told me what all this is about.'

Winter took up the running.

'It's a murder inquiry, Mrs Harris. Like DC Sullivan said.'

'But who? Who got murdered?'

'A man called Bradley Finch.' He paused. 'Know him at all, did you?'

Mrs Harris looked pole-axed. Finally, she managed a nod.

'Yeah,' she said. 'He came round here sometimes, thin boy, silly laugh.' Her hand found her daughter's shoulder. '*Murdered?*'

'I'm afraid so.'

She shook her head and pulled her cardigan more tightly around her. Sullivan went back to Friday night.

'So where were you, Mrs Harris?'

'Here.'

'All evening? All of you?'

Mrs Harris just stared at him. She was frightened now, and it showed in her eyes.

'We stayed in, didn't we, Mum?' It was her daughter.

'That's right.' Mrs Harris nodded. 'We had pancakes with maple syrup, your favourite.' She reached down and stroked her daughter's hair. A thin little hand reached up for hers.

'You all stayed in?' Sullivan offered Maisie an encouraging smile. 'Dad, too?'

'He went out.'

'Mrs Harris?'

'That's right. I remember now. Maisie's right. Terry went out.'

'What kind of time?'

'Don't ask me. I have enough trouble getting my name right some days.'

'Early,' Maisie said. 'Dad went out early.'

'How early?'

'Seven o'clock?' She looked up at her mother.

'And what time did he come back?'

Maisie shrugged. She'd been in bed. She hadn't a clue. Sullivan turned his attention back to Mrs Harris. By now, she was acutely uncomfortable. Whatever loyalty she owed Terry Harris was stretched to the absolute limit.

'I really don't want to talk about this any more,' she said finally. 'Don't get me wrong but it's just not . . .' She frowned, lost for the right word.

'Fair?' Winter suggested.

She began to colour, shaking her head, and then came the clatter of a diesel engine in the road outside and Maisie was on her feet and across to the window, peeping round the curtain.

'Dad,' she announced.

Tosh Harris was still in his working gear. He stood in the open doorway in stained jeans and an old sweatshirt, a bulging tool bag in his right hand. His wife was on her feet as well, explaining about their surprise visitors. Detectives, she said quickly, wanting to ask about Friday night. I explained you were out early, round seven, back late. You remember?

'Yeah . . .' Harris nodded slowly. 'Yeah, that's right.'

He was medium height, mid-thirties. The cropped hair was rapidly receding and he hadn't shaved for at least a day. A small silver cross dangled from one ear and there were serpent's head tattoos on the backs of both hands. His nails, Winter noted, were bitten to the quick. Wherever else this man belonged, it wasn't here.

'Do you mind, Mr Harris?' Winter nodded at the chair his wife had vacated. 'This needn't take long.'

Harris didn't sit down. His daughter had vanished. He looked from one face to the other, totally unflustered, and Winter realised he'd been expecting this for days.

'It's about Bradley Finch,' Winter began. 'You'll know he's been murdered?'

'I read about it, yeah.'

'And he was a friend of yours? Is that right?'

'We knocked about a bit, yeah.'

'Work, was it? Or more a social thing?'

'Both. He helped me with jobs sometimes, not that he was very clever with his hands. Then we'd have the odd drink, you know, like you do.'

'And he'd come to the house?'

'Yeah.'

'So your wife knew him?'

'Yeah, she met him a couple of times, yeah.'

'So why didn't she know he was dead?'

'Dunno, mate. Ask her.'

'That's not my question, Mr Harris. I'm asking you why you never told her. The boy was a mate of yours. He'd been round here a bit. Then suddenly he's dead. Not just dead but murdered. At twenty-one. That's the kind of thing you'd mention to your wife, isn't it?'

'Slipped my mind, mate. Been busy.' Winter gazed at him.

'So what was he like? This Bradley?'

'*Like?*'

'Yes, as a person.'

'He was . . .' Harris frowned '. . . Bradley. That's all you could say, really.'

'You don't sound very upset.'

'About what?'

'The boy getting killed like that.'

For the first time, the question struck a spark. Harris took a step towards Winter.

'Listen, you blokes barge into my house, and here I am, eight hours straight and not even time for a wash. It's me should be asking the questions, not you. It's my bloody house, in case you'd forgotten.'

'Of course it is. And your wife was kind enough to invite us in. So here's the deal. Either we talk here or we go down to Central. Up to you, Mr Harris. Your call.'

Harris shrugged, back in control of himself, feigning indifference.

'Why don't you just get on with it?' He yawned. 'Then I can have my tea.'

Winter returned to Friday night. His wife had already established that Harris had gone out. Now Winter wanted to know exactly where he'd been. Harris screwed his face into a frown. More play-acting. Finally he nodded.

'Up Petersfield way. We went to a pub called the Plough.'

'Who's we?'

'Me and Mick. My brother.'

'What time did you get there?'

'Half seven? Eight? I wasn't counting.'

'Busy was it? The pub?'

'Yeah.' He nodded. 'We were upstairs, though, me and Mick, up in Steve's flat there. Steve's the landlord. You know Steve Pallister? Used to have a pub in Portsea?'

Winter ignored the question.

'Why the flat?' He enquired. 'Why not the pub itself?'

'Gets very crowded, Friday nights. We play cards – cribbage mostly – me, Mick and a couple of local lads. Steve comes up after closing time.'

'These lads. You've got names?'

'Course.'

He offered two names. Sullivan wrote them both down. When Winter asked for phone numbers, Harris told him to give Steve Pallister a bell. He'd know for sure.

'And your brother? Mick?'

Harris said the number was in the book but Mick hadn't paid his last two bills so the phone was still probably cut off.

'Does he have a mobile?'

'Yeah.'

'You've got the number?'

Harris produced his own mobile and keyed his brother's number. Sullivan wrote it down.

'Address?' he queried.

'Windrush Road. Can't remember the number. He's away today.'

'Anywhere nice?'

'France. He goes over to Cherbourg with a few mates on them cheap trips. Always the same bars. Off their faces by five o'clock.'

Mrs Harris appeared with a mug of tea. Harris reached for it, avoiding her gaze. She didn't ask whether Winter and Sullivan fancied a drink, returning at once to the kitchen.

'So what time did you get back here? Friday night?'

'We didn't. Amount we'd put away, you wouldn't. Couldn't, more like.' He frowned, then called through to his wife. 'Eight o'clock, was it, love? Saturday morning?' He looked at Winter again, giving him a conspiratorial wink. They'd stayed over at Steve's place, kipping on the floor, and set off early Saturday morning because Mick had to be back.

'And Steve was there?'

'Course he was.'

'And the other two lads?'

'Went home. Both local.'

Winter nodded, checked with Sullivan that he had it all, then stood up. Harris, holding his tea, looked astonished.

'That it then?'

'Yes, thanks. We'll give you a ring if anything comes up on Bradley. What's your number?'

Harris hesitated a moment before giving him a mobile number, and then watched them leave. Winter called goodbye to his wife along the little hall but she didn't reply. Back in the car he looked up at the house, catching the child's face at an upstairs window. He gave her a little wave, then told Sullivan to get going.

'Guilty as fuck,' he said.

'What about the alibi?'

'Phoney.' He glanced across at Sullivan. 'You're a Petersfield lad. Know this pub, do you? The Plough?'

'Not personally, but I can make some enquiries.'

'Do that. I'll get Brian Imber to sort out the mobes. It's always the billing that shafts scum like Harris.' Winter grinned in the darkness of the car. 'What a twat.'

Willard called a squad meeting for eight o'clock. He'd listened to Winter's account of the interview with Harris and he agreed that the alibi sounded dodgy. The video camera put Harris alongside Bradley

Finch, and the sequences on the tape argued that the double glazer was into violence as well as burglary. Willard would have preferred more time to prepare for the custody interviews but events had forced his hand. Unless he moved fast, precious forensic evidence might be lost.

He'd already told Sammy Rollins to sort out overnight surveillance on Harris's Stamshaw house. Now they had to plan the next stage.

'Early doors,' he grunted. 'Harris, his brother and Kenny Foster.'

Heads nodded round the incident room. 'Early doors' was CID-speak for dawn arrests. Under the PACE rules, Willard could hold a suspect for twenty-four hours. Application to a uniformed Superintendent would extend the custody period to thirty-six hours. An arrest at, say, seven o'clock in the morning would therefore give him two full days in the interview rooms. If push came to shove, he could go to the magistrates and ask for yet another extension, and experience told him that might well be necessary. So far, they had precious little to throw at any of the three men. Only by getting bodies out on the ground and giving the alibis a good shake while the suspects were still in custody would they start to make progress.

Dave Michaels would be organising the arrests. Willard wanted each of the three men taken to different police stations elsewhere in the county. At least a couple of hours would be occupied by the police surgeon taking DNA samples and the lawyers getting their acts together, and Willard didn't anticipate the interview teams sitting down to business until late morning. That gave him a fighting chance to get the TIAs up to speed. He'd already asked Sammy Rollins to appoint three Tactical Interview Advisers, all DCs, and these would be charged with sorting out intelligence briefs from Brian Imber's cell. They'd monitor the interviews from adjoining rooms, offering a touch on the tiller during the compulsory comfort breaks.

'Forensic, sir?'

It was the DI responsible for the SOCO teams. Willard nodded. He wanted full forensic on all three addresses, special attention to Harris's address and Kenny Foster's garage. They were looking for signs of a struggle, mopped-up bloodstains, hidden weapons, discarded clothing – anything that could connect the properties with events on Friday night. Washing machines were to be seized, drain traps taken apart, surfaces dusted for prints, carpets and furniture taped, floorboards lifted, gardens turned over and motor vehicles given a thorough seeing-to. People like the Harris brothers often had lock-up garages. These, if they existed, were to be located and searched.

'What about Mrs Harris and the kid?'

Willard acknowledged Winter's query. In situations like this, you had to find somewhere for Harris's wife and daughter to go. No way would they be permitted to stay, not with the property sanitised for the SOCO team.

'Travel Inn, Sammy?'

Rollins nodded. The Travel Inn was a new hotel on the seafront and the MIR had opened an account to lodge potential witnesses. With Harris under arrest, mother and child would be swifted off for an early breakfast.

'But I want her interviewed,' Willard added. 'Not the child, just the mum.'

Rollins made a note while Willard returned to Dave Michaels. The next two days might well be make or break for *Bisley*. There were never enough bodies on the ground to satisfy Willard but it was up to himself and the management team to squeeze the available resource as hard as they could.

Willard had propped himself against a desk. Now he eyeballed the faces around the room, and Winter prepared himself for the pre-match team talk. This was the moment when guvnors like Willard let themselves go, and if they were any good, then the message was always broadly the same. Get out there amongst the bad guys. Work your fucking socks off. But whatever you do, whoever you're talking to, make sure you can prove it, and make sure it stays proved. Every inquiry's a chess game. Every move you have to anticipate and counter. So think elegant. Think alternatives. And above all think *court*. We're not here to fanny around with hunches; we're here to lock the bad guys up. And the way we do that is by being miles ahead, light years ahead, of any smart fucker who wants to stand in our way.

The latter phrase brought a smile to Winter's face. Willard had a knack for sending messages in the plainest possible terms. His massive body was hunched, classic prop forward, and his voice was low but you had to be deaf as well as blind not to get the gist. If justice was a game of rugby then Willard was only interested in a thrashing. He wanted big points on the board. He'd enjoy the major piss-up afterwards. But at this point in time, if anyone dropped the ball, they were history.

'OK?' He dared anyone to say a word. No one did. 'Go to it then. And good luck tomorrow.'

Two hours later, Faraday managed to drag Brian Imber out for a curry. The Intelligence Cell were still hard at work preparing briefs for the interview teams but Imber himself was exhausted. Just now a change of subject would be more than welcome, and if Faraday wanted to talk about an infant tearaway called Doodie, then so be it.

As it happened, Imber had actually met Doodie only six months before. He'd gone looking for his mother's current partner on a smack inquiry and ended up in the flat at Raglan House. Doodie, for once, had been at home.

'So what was he like?'

They were sitting in a Bengali restaurant barely five minutes' walk from Kingston Crescent. They'd known each other for years, ever since J-J had made an unsuccessful bid to turn out for the colts rugby team Imber used to run, and the friendship had survived.

'Small, thin, shaven-headed, pale, stud in one ear.' Imber picked at the remains of his chicken bhuna. 'He's one of those kids who comes at you at a thousand miles an hour. You ever meet his mother?'

'I did.'

'Then you've got the whole story. Kid never stood a chance. Not that he isn't bright.'

'So where do I find him?'

'Find him?' Imber smiled wearily, pushing the plate away. He hadn't gone into details about his day at the Yard but Faraday could tell that he wasn't the only one battling against the current. 'The problem with these kids is they have a city of their own. You and me think we know Pompey. We think we've got the place sussed. But we're wrong. You want to find someone like this Doodie and you've got to get inside his little head. He knows all the short cuts, all the safe places, all the properties empty and up for sale, all the offices with dodgy windows and knackered locks, all the buildings with scaffolding round them, all those little corners where he can get his head down without being rolled. They're cluey, these kids, they really are, and they have to be, otherwise they wouldn't make it.'

'How do they eat?' It seemed, to Faraday, a reasonable enough question.

'Some of it's nicked. Some of it they buy. You see them in pub gardens in the summer. They go round asking for sweet money. It's begging really but if you've had a few pints you don't begrudge the odd fifty pence. Then there's the nastier side of it. You and me know life's a market, and so do the kids. You've got a nice arse, you don't mind helping out with a bit of wrist shandy, you're on an earner. There are blokes in this city will pay good money for personal services.'

'You're telling me Doodie's on the game?'

'I'm telling you it happens.'

'Of course it does, but at *ten*?'

'Ten would make him unusual, sure, but . . .' Imber shrugged '. . . fuck knows.'

For the first time it occurred to Faraday that he owed Doodie a duty of arrest. Not for society's sake, but for his own.

Imber wasn't having it.

'So what? Say you're right? Say you catch a kid like Doodie? Say you nick him for shoplifting, or vandalism, or whatever else he's up to? What happens then? If these kids are old enough they're marched off to court but in the end they're going to be in the hands of the social workers. They're going to be listened to, and interviewed, and assessed to death. Don't get me wrong, Joe. Frankly, I don't know what the fuck else you do. But the fact is most of these social workers are clueless. They're straight out of university. They've talked the talk, they've read the books, and they're falling over backwards to be these kids' *friends*. That's great but you've got to know who you're dealing with. These are kids from the tower blocks, fifth generation unemployed, multiple stepfathers, mothers on the piss, the full Monty. They take one look at these new buddies of theirs and they know they're on Easy Street. These kids are practically feral, Joe. They're animals, tough as fuck, and what's more they don't care any more. This Doodie's not alone. There are dozens of them out there. We give them all the guff about society and citizenship and taking responsibility for yourself but they're just not interested. They've sussed us. They know society's all bollocks. They're out there on their own and that's the way they want to stay. Can you blame them?'

Faraday, for a moment or two, was robbed of an answer. Over the years he'd never heard anything like this from Brian Imber. He could be passionate, like a number of other CID specialists charged with keeping their ears to the ground, but there was something extra here, something that must have happened over the last couple of years since their last conversation. The man wasn't just angry. He was swamped.

Faraday watched him swallow the remains of his lager.

'You think we've lost the plot?'

'I fucking know it. And so do you. And so does anyone with half a brain in this city. Blaming the kids is the easy bit. Try working out where it all went wrong. And then try sleeping at night.'

'That bad?'

'Absolutely. Don't get me wrong, Joe. I love my kids. But I tell you something else. If I was starting all over again, I'd have the chop.'

Imber nodded, then made a graphic downward gesture with his open hand towards his lap, scissoring two fingers. He gestured Faraday closer. A decade of Margaret Thatcher might have seemed a good idea at the time but read the kind of street intelligence that went over his desk daily, and you'd start wondering what the Brits had signed up to. Thatcherism had long survived the Iron Lady. Indeed, in many respects life had become even more brutal.

Faraday gazed at him. Exhaustion could do this to you, he thought, and so could clinical depression. Yet he'd never had Imber down as a depressive. On the contrary, he'd rarely come across anyone with such a ready appetite for life. Maybe that was it. Maybe, if you pushed your body hard, if you ran all those miles, you knew what was possible for anyone willing to make the effort.

'So what's made the difference? Are we talking drugs?'

'That's part of it, certainly.'

Imber signalled the waiter for more lager and then bent towards the table again. The mention of drugs had lit another fuse. The narco biz, in Imber's view, was capitalism in the raw. The mark-ups were huge, the client base was ever expanding, and you didn't have to invest one penny in advertising because word of mouth and the chemicals themselves would do the selling for you.

'Now isn't that neat?' He was smiling. 'Isn't that just the most beautiful thing in the world? No wonder criminals don't bother with bank jobs any more. Why should they give themselves all that grief when there's a million tons of cocaine out there?'

'Bazza McKenzie?'

'Perfect example. Guy starts as a painter and decorator. Seven years later, with Harrison off the plot, he owns half of Southsea. Café-bars. Estate agents. Student lodgings. Condemned hotels to house asylum seekers. Big chunk of the taxi business. Are you seriously telling me all that comes out of a van and a couple of litres of white emulsion? Of course it doesn't. But there's the rub, you see, Joe. Kids watch people like Bazza. Some of them work for him, run drugs for him, do legit jobs in Café Blanc. He's become a kind of folk hero. He's become a role model. He's become Robin fucking Hood. And you know why? Number one because he's got more dosh than he knows what to do with. And number two because he couldn't care a fuck. He flaunts it all. In our faces. The kids see that and they make a note or two. No wonder they give us such a hard time.'

This time Faraday could only agree. After Marty Harrison's exit to Spain, MacKenzie had the cocaine business to himself.

'So what's the answer?'

'As far as Bazza is concerned?' Faraday nodded. 'We screw him. We invest lots of money, lots of time, lots of resources, and we nail him to the ground by taking every last penny off him. The legislation's there. All we need is the balls to use it.'

'And the wider problem?'

'Legalise the lot. Destroy the market.'

'And you think any of that will ever happen?'

'Absolutely no fucking chance. Anything to do with money laundering, anything to do with taking on the professionals, all that goes straight in the too-difficult basket. As Bazza knows only too well.'

Faraday ducked his head, then told Imber about the Helen Bassam inquiry and about his team's exchanges with Misty Gallagher. Just the name was enough to light Imber's fuse again.

'She's another one. Bev's right. She's shagging McKenzie and she doesn't much care who knows it. These people are the new aristocracy, the new rich. With the kind of money McKenzie's making, there's no one you can't buy. You've got a problem, right, because you've got to start washing all that cash? You need professional help for that, you'll need the guys in the white collars, but it's amazing what people will do if the price is right. I could name you solicitors in this city who've saved their careers on the back of MacKenzie. Legal practices going down the tubes rescued by some tosser from the wrong side of the tracks. He stitches these people up. He puts them in his pocket and from that point on they're doomed. Believe me, Joe, Mackenzie's got it taped. Until we decide otherwise.'

'And Misty?'

'She'll be lucky to last a year.' He shrugged. 'Though she might get to keep the Gunwharf place.'

More lager arrived and Faraday tried to change the subject. He'd learned quite enough about the drugs scene for one evening and he thought that he and Imber owed themselves a laugh or two. But Imber wasn't having it. Whatever family tragedy had taken him to drugs intelligence in the first place had left a deep scar, and he was determined – above all – to mark Faraday's card.

'I've been thinking about this kid Doodie,' he said. 'Given the weather and the time of year, there are a couple of places you might look, one in particular. You know the old ABC cinema? Mile End?'

Faraday nodded. Before the arrival of the big multiplexes – Port Solent, Gunwharf – cinemas like the ABC were the only option if you were a film buff. A big brick-built structure with steel framed windows and an imposing entrance, the ABC had recently been closed and was now awaiting demolition. Faraday often passed it on his way out of the city. Every window was smashed now, and at street level the boarded-up swing doors were plastered with fly posters, but ten years ago he and J-J had been there several times a month to catch a decent movie.

Imber was explaining about the kids. Word on the street suggested they'd spent most of the winter colonising the place. Some used it as the ultimate drop-in centre. Others seemed to live there.

'What's it like inside?'

'Wrecked, as far as I know.'

'Access?'

'Supposed to be impossible. The agents say the place is secured. They're obviously wrong.'

'Have you been inside?'

'You're joking. Even the fire brigade are cagey. They're saying it's structurally unsound.'

'So where does Doodie fit in all this?'

'I've no idea, Joe.' He folded his napkin and reached for his glass. 'I suppose it depends how badly you want to find him.'

J-J was in the bath when Faraday finally made it home. Four pints of Kingfisher had done nothing for his judgement and he'd crawled home at the kind of speed that would have made him a sitting target for any traffic patrol. Luckily the streets had been empty, and now he was standing at the bathroom door, eager to know how J-J's day had gone. There was no point knocking or trying to conduct any kind of conversation through an inch of wood, so he walked straight in.

J'J's long body was largely invisible under a duvet of bubbles. His eyes widened as his father appeared.

'How was it?' Faraday signed.

'Brilliant.'

'Even better than Caen?'

'Much. Gordon's a star.'

The way J-J signed 'star' a big firework burst, both hands, brought a smile to Faraday's face. He hadn't seen J-J like this for years.

He perched himself on the side of the bath.

'What were the kids like?'

'Crazy. Crazy but OK. Gordon gets them doing stuff. They love it.'

'And you?'

'I love it too.'

He was going in next day, for sure, and if Gordon thought it was a good idea he'd try to join the place full time. He didn't care about money. That wasn't important. What mattered was what he could do for the kids. If the feedback and stuff was all OK, then he was certain he could help them. One or two of the kids were already really friendly. Tomorrow he might hang out with them after hours.

Faraday felt the first tiny prickles of anxiety. J-J's raw enthusiasm was often his downfall. He took people on trust and that wasn't always such a great idea. He'd seen it happen dozens of times.

'You be careful, eh?' he signed.

J-J grinned at him and a pink thumb emerged from the bubbles. Of course he'd take care. He knew what his dad meant but these were kids, and kids were different.

'By the way,' he signed, 'there's a message downstairs on the answerphone. Might be Gordon.'

Faraday nodded and stepped back onto the landing. Marta, he thought. She's as miserable as I am and she's got back in touch. Her husband's returned, and absolutely nothing has changed, and she's realised that the last twelve months can't simply be buried.

He clattered down the stairs, catching his balance at the bottom, and picked up the phone. His finger found the replay button on the message panel and he waited for the familiar voice. It was Cathy Lamb.

'Me, boss,' she said. 'Bloke called Phillimore's been in touch. Says he wants to talk to you. It sounded urgent so I thought I'd call.' A local number followed, then Cathy rang off.

Faraday stood by the phone, staring blankly out at the harbour. Then he caught a movement reflected in the big glass doors and he looked round to find J-J wrapped in a towel, halfway down the stairs.

'Anything important?' he signed, nodding at the telephone.

Faraday shook his head.

'Afraid not,' he murmured.

Chapter twenty

The arrests took place at dawn. Given the theft of the shotgun from the house at Compton, Willard had decided to request support from the Tactical Firearms Unit at Netley, and calls at all three addresses were spearheaded by armed police. Whether or not this level of precaution was justified was, in Willard's view, immaterial. Bradley Finch's dangling body had signalled a jokey contempt for both human life and law and order. Now he wanted to send a message of his own: up the game to homicide and expect the business end of a Heckler and Koch on your doorstep.

To Dave Michaels, three hours later, it was the individual reaction of each of the three suspects that was interesting. Terry Harris, at half six in the morning, had seemed less than surprised. He'd asked the arresting DC to keep his voice down in case the noise woke his daughter up and had walked out of the house without a backward glance. In the car, when the DC had explained about the impending Scenes of Crime search, he'd simply shrugged. His wife could deal with all that hassle. Just as long as Maisie got to school.

'What about Foster?'

Paul Winter had dropped into Michaels's office before driving out to the Plough, the pub near Petersfield. There, he was to meet Gary Sullivan before testing Terry Harris's alibi on the landlord.

'Kenny?' Michaels pulled a face. 'Apparently he was amused. Asked one of the blokes whether he'd take an offer on the shooter.'

'No grief, then?'

'None. Sweet as a lamb.'

'Shit.'

'Exactly.'

'And Harris's twin? Mick?'

'Pissed off big time. He was back from his jolly in Cherbourg and the gaff was up to here with booze and fags. He was so hung-over he thought the blokes were from Customs and Excise and he kept telling the guys with the guns it was his birthday. How much Stella do you need to celebrate your thirty-fifth?'

Winter chuckled. He'd lost count of the number of early doors he'd attended, hauling villains out of bed at God knows what hour, but he'd always found the ritual deeply rewarding. At that time in the morning, just for a moment or two, you could truly play God.

Terry Harris and his twin brother had been driven to Waterlooville police station and were now in adjoining cells awaiting the arrival of their respective solicitors. Kenny Foster, meanwhile, was banged up in Fareham nick, doubtless arguing the toss with the police surgeon over blood samples and nail scrapings.

Winter glanced at his watch. It would take a couple of hours for the briefs to sort themselves out. In the meantime, he had an alibi to destroy. He looked up at Michaels.

'How do I find this bloody pub, then?'

For once, Faraday couldn't blame his blinding headache on the Macallan. He'd drunk barely anything last night, too depressed to have the slightest faith in malt whisky. Now, manacled once again to his computer, he could barely read the dancing lines of text on his thirteenth email. Abandoning a must-read circular on the latest Home Office priorities – 'Civic interaction and neighbourhood partnerships are the weapons of choice in the fight against volume crime' – he picked up the phone. The number Cathy had given him last night answered on the second ring, and he found himself listening to a recorded message. The voice was cultured but warm. Nigel Phillimore would be away until tomorrow night but callers were more than welcome to leave their names and numbers. So much for the urgent need for a chat.

Faraday put the phone down, wondering about the accent. In this job, he thought, most of your working life was sandpapered with a hundred versions of working-class Pompey. Lay aside all the PC nonsense about class-free policing, and that's where the bulk of divisional CID work belonged. The city's council estates were far from affluent, and with poverty went crime. It wasn't a justification. It wasn't even an excuse. It was simply a fact. Add crap education and the grab-it-while-you-can culture, and no wonder you ended up with nicely packaged mission statements about neighbourhood partnerships and civic interaction.

He gazed at the screen, trying to still the thunder in his head, and for the first time he began to give serious thought to Willard's suggestion that the time might be ripe for a move to Major Crime. Divisional CID work was the career equivalent of nailing water to the wall. The longer you persevered, the wetter your feet got. And the wetter your feet got, the less prepared you were to take another plunge into the swamp. What he needed was the chance, just for once, to pursue a single investigation, more for the sake of his own sanity than any fanciful notions about justice.

His hand found the phone again. Anghared Davies was at her desk in the Brook Centre.

'Doodie?' he said briefly. 'Still no joy?'

'Can't help, I'm afraid. We're as clueless as you are.'

'What about this cinema?'

Faraday recounted last night's conversation with Brian Imber. Word on the street suggested that the old ABC had become an adolescent squat. Was that something Anghared's kids ever mentioned?

'Can't really say, Joe. It's Buckland, remember. Bit out of Doodie's territory.'

The comment at last brought a smile to Faraday's face. The distance from Raglan House to the boarded-up cinema couldn't be more than a mile, but in a city as tribal as Portsmouth geographical distance was meaningless. To kids from Somerstown, the badlands of Buckland might as well be on the moon.

'So what do you reckon? Worth a scout?'

'Depends how brave you are. Apparently the place is a wreck.'

'How do you know?'

The question caught Anghared off guard. Faraday heard her laughing.

'You're right,' she said at last. 'The kids do talk about it.'

'And?'

'Definitely worth a visit.'

The Plough Inn lay on a picturesque country lane ten minutes' drive south-east of Petersfield. A couple of hundred years ago, the place would have been no more than a cottage – soft red brickwork, slate roof, curl of woodsmoke from the single chimney – but successive generations had added outhouses and an extension at the back. The adjoining car park had recently been resurfaced and a brimming builder's skip beside the brand-new Shogun told Winter that this small corner of rural Hampshire was doing very nicely out of cask-conditioned real ale and £6.99 Sunday lunches.

At ten o'clock in the morning, the front door was still locked. The clink of bottles led Winter and Sullivan round the back. A tall, lean figure in jeans and a hooded top was bent over a plastic tub of empties. The clientele evidently drank gallons of Bacardi.

'Steve Pallister?'

The work stopped. Pallister was in his early forties. His big square face was scarred around one eye, and too much booze had reddened the rest of it, but he moved with the ease of someone who still worked out.

'Who are you then?'

'CID.'

Winter snapped open his warrant card. Sullivan did the same. Pallister inspected them both then looked up, grinning. His handshake was wet and slightly sticky.

'Business, is it?' He nodded towards the open door. 'Or do you fancy a drink?'

The saloon was dark and still smelt of last night's beer. Pallister gestured at the row of optics behind the bar but Winter and Sullivan settled for coffee. Pallister yelled through to a kitchen at the back and a woman appeared. She was wearing a T-shirt and jeans and didn't bother to peel off the rubber gloves when Pallister did the introductions. Gina, he explained, was his partner.

Sullivan was looking at the framed photos that hung in a line above the bar. They featured buddy shots of heavily armed soldiers, the same faces recurring in print after print. The story began aboard some ship or other and ended against a flat, treeless landscape dotted with sheep. The final photo had caught a younger Pallister necking the remains of a bottle of Bells. There was a church in the background with a corrugated iron roof and pink walls. Pallister's face was still daubed with camouflage cream but the combat smock hung open and he was winking at the camera.

'Goose Green,' he explained briefly. 'Two Para. My moment of glory.'

Gina reappeared with a tray of coffees. She ignored Sullivan's smile and told Pallister she was off to sort out the goats. Back later.

'Goats?' Winter was watching her tight little backside as she made for a side door.

'Yeah. It's a woman thing. Gina fancied a mountain top in Wales so we settled for a couple of fields round here with a bar attached. I couldn't cope with all that fucking rain. Not after the Falklands.'

'You've been here twenty years?'

'Ten. We had a trial run up near Aldershot.'

'And?'

'Disaster. Squaddies and booze don't mix.' He touched the scarring round his eye. 'Thought I'd have learned, wouldn't you?'

Winter explained briefly about the Bradley Finch inquiry. A young lad had been killed down in Pompey. They needed to sort out one or two details about a couple of blokes called Harris.

'Terry and Mick?'

'That's right.'

'Up for it, are they?'

'Is that a serious question?'

'No, mate. It's a joke. What do you want to know?'

Winter asked how well he knew them.

'Pretty well.'

'They come up here a lot?'

'Yeah.'

'Regulars?'

'Definitely.'

'Like a drink, do they?'

'Just a bit.'

'What about getting home, then? Taxi, is it?'

The hesitation brought a smile to Winter's lips. Pump up the conversation like this – repartee, ping-pong – and it was child's play to insert the simplest of traps. Fifteen miles was a long way to come for a serious drink, especially with a big fat cab fare at the end of it.

'One of them drinks, one of them doesn't.'

'They toss for it?'

'Yeah. And the loser gets to win at cards. Never fails.'

'You always play cards?'

'They do, yeah. There's a regular school. Two other blokes, locals.'

'What do they play?'

'Cribbage.'

Pallister yawned and looked at his watch. Winter hadn't touched his coffee.

'So when did you see them last, then?'

Pallister mugged a frown, pretending to dredge his memory, and a sideways glance at Sullivan's face told Winter they were on a hiding to nothing. Pallister must have rehearsed this conversation a thousand times. Not that it made his performance any the more convincing.

'Friday,' he said at last. 'Friday night. Both pissed as rats. Stayed over upstairs.'

'Anyone corroborate that?'

'Yeah, Gina. And the other two lads.'

Winter glanced at Sullivan again. Sullivan wrote down their names. They both lived in Petersfield and Pallister had a mobile number for one of them.

'What about the punters?' Winter gestured round at the bar. 'Who else might have clocked them?'

'No one. They play upstairs. Friday nights, you can't hear yourself think down here. Madness, it is. Our fault, really. Shouldn't be so popular.' He leaned back against the bar, looking Winter in the eye, then tilted his head upwards towards the line of Falklands photos. 'You know the funny thing about war? After shit like that, nothing fucking gets to you.' The grin again. 'More coffee?'

It fell to Dawn Ellis and Bev Yates to interview Terry Harris's wife. By mid-morning, the Scenes of Crime team had completed their initial trawl through 62 Aboukir Road.

So far, amongst the stack of suspiciously new consumer goods, they'd found nothing in the way of bloodstained clothing or potential weapons, and there was no sign of items which might conceivably have belonged to Bradley Finch, but a cardboard box in a spare room upstairs had yielded a rich haul of videos. In with the usual helping of Scandinavian porn was a collection of nastier material: poorly shot sequences featuring extreme violence. Whether or not this stuff was faked wasn't the issue. As the DC charged with viewing the videos put it, what kind of human being spent his leisure hours watching a black stripper first gang-raped then beaten unconscious by three white guys?

'Do you have a view on that, Mrs Harris?'

Harris's wife occupied a bare, overheated bedroom on the second floor of the seafront Travel Inn. Her daughter, Maisie, had gone off to school in a taxi and now Mrs Harris sat in the only armchair, the tea and biscuits at her elbow untouched. Willard had decided not to interview her under caution, sensing an advantage in getting her onside. This woman had put up with Harris for a considerable time. Maybe now was the moment to sort out her real priorities.

'I'd no idea he even had the videos,' she said. 'What he does with stuff like that is his own business.'

Ellis was sitting on the edge of the bed, Yates leaning against the wall behind her. She put her notebook to one side.

'You don't watch television together?'

'Sometimes we do but mostly' – Mrs Harris shrugged – 'he's not around.'

'So where is he?'

'Out.'

'You know where?'

'No, not usually.'

'Out late?'

'Yes.' She nodded. 'Quite late.'

Yates took up the running. They'd already been through the events of Friday night and she'd confirmed the version passed on by Paul

Winter. Terry had left early, spent the night up near Petersfield, and come back next day with a terrible hangover. She couldn't go into details because she simply didn't know.

'There's a lot you don't know, isn't there?'

'That's true.'

'What about the boy, Bradley Finch?' Ellis had a photo. She passed it across. 'Is the face familiar at all? Did you ever meet him?'

Mrs Harris gave the photo the briefest glance. She seemed to have been preparing herself for this moment but it took a while before she nodded.

'He came to the house a couple of times.'

'What was he like?'

'I don't really know. Thin. Cocky. I think he used to help Terry out with jobs.'

'Are we talking double glazing?'

'Of course.'

'Nothing else?'

'Not that I know about.'

'What if we were to tell you that Terry was a burglar?'

'I wouldn't have a clue about that.'

'But would it surprise you?'

'I don't know. I just don't know.'

'But it's reasonable, isn't it? All those late nights? Not knowing where he is? New stuff appearing round the house? Didn't you ever ask where it all came from? Or was it Christmas every day?'

'It wasn't every day. Nothing like.'

'But didn't you ask? I would. Your husband comes home with a brand new set of tools, say, or a television, or a CD player. This stuff doesn't fall off trees, does it? Not where I live, it doesn't.'

She gazed at him a moment, then shook her head. Terry had funny ways, she muttered. She'd like to help them but she just couldn't.

'You mean won't. Let's just get this thing straight. You mean won't.'

She shook her head again, staring up at him. She'd come to the hotel with a single hastily packed carrier bag and now the contents lay spilled across the bed. A change of knickers. A Littlewoods sweatshirt. Two toothbrushes and a flannel in a polythene bag. A battered copy of a Danielle Steele paperback. Spare clothes for Maisie. A hairbrush. Not much to show for nine years of married life.

Ellis reached for a biscuit.

'We'll be listing all that gear at your house,' she said quietly. 'We use computers now. It's easy to check if it's stolen.'

'Really?'

'I'm afraid so. And if that becomes an issue, then so does Maisie.'

'Maisie?' She looked suddenly startled. 'What do you mean?'

'If the gear's stolen, and we can prove it, that puts your husband inside.'

'And me?'

'Some juries might think you'd known about it.'

'But I didn't.' She frowned. 'I mean I wouldn't have done.'

'So you say.' Ellis made a tiny regretful movement with her hand. 'But juries can be funny that way. Two people sharing the same house. Man and wife. Just how many secrets can you keep?'

'And Maisie?'

'Well . . .' That same gesture. 'The care arrangements these days are quite good but it's never really the same, is it?'

'Same as what?'

'Having a proper mum.'

Paler than ever, Mrs Harris stared at Ellis. She wanted help. She wanted a way out of all this.

Ellis offered her a smile and then stood up, brushing the biscuit crumbs off her skirt. It was a couple of steps to the window. She stared out at the rain for a moment and then beckoned Yates over. The hotel abutted onto the funfair at Clarence Pier. During the winter, the place was empty, the cars on the Waltzer shrouded with tarpaulins. Etched against the grey skyline stood the gaunt steel tracery of a ride called Skyways. Out of season, still and abandoned, scenes like these never failed to move her.

She fogged the cold glass with her breath and then drew a little butterfly.

'You ever come here as a kid?' she murmured.

'All the time. Mad for it when I could con the money.'

'I meant in winter. Like now.'

'*Winter?*' Bev stared down at her. 'Why would you ever want to do that?'

Ellis smiled, then returned to the bed. Mrs Harris hadn't moved. Ellis took the conversation back to Friday night, back to the moment when Terry Harris had stepped out of the house en route for Petersfield, and asked Mrs Harris to go through it all again. She wanted every last detail. Above all, she wanted times. The woman stared up at her, then shook her head.

'I can't,' she whispered. 'I've told you already.'

'But I don't believe you, Mrs Harris.'

'You have to. It's true.'

'I don't think Terry went to Petersfield at all. I think he stayed in Portsmouth and at some point that night I think he came back home. You'd have known about that. He'd have woken you up. He'd have had things to say. He might have been in a bit of a mess. You'd have talked. I know you would. And that would have been the kind of conversation you'd never forget.' Ellis's fingers found the photo of Maisie again. Mrs Harris wouldn't look at it.

'No,' she said. 'It was the way I told you before. He was out all night.'

'In Petersfield?'

'That's what he said.'

'But do you believe him?'

This time she didn't have an answer. There was a long silence, broken by the trilling of Yates's phone. Only days ago he'd downloaded the opening notes of the theme from *Mission Impossible*.

He turned to the window again, shielding the phone. There was a mumble of conversation. Then he snapped the mobile shut and threw a look to Ellis over his shoulder.

'You know the video camera that was blagged from the Compton place?' Ellis nodded. 'They've found a mini-tape at Aboukir Road. Two lots of pictures on it. One of the couple from Compton. The other of a little girl playing a piano.'

'Wouldn't be Maisie by any chance?' Dawn turned back to Mrs Harris. 'Would it?'

Driving back to Portsmouth, Winter was sunk in gloom. After an hour with Steve Pallister, he'd well and truly hit the buffers. Getting a statement off the bloke hadn't been a problem. He'd simply repeated his little fantasy about the Friday night cribbage school and happily added his signature at the end. Back in Petersfield, attempts to trace the two local lads he'd mentioned had come to nothing. The mobile phone wasn't responding and when they'd finally got an address for the other name, neighbours said he'd gone away on holiday.

Now Sullivan was on his mobile to a mate of his in the Petersfield CID office. He'd heard a whisper about Steve Pallister and he'd been trying to check it out since last night. The conversation over, he pocketed the mobile and stared glumly out at the driving rain. On the motorway, beyond a couple of hundred yards, everything was a blur.

'He's flogging dodgy booze and fags,' he said at length, 'but they can't evidence it.'

'Contraband? Through the pub?'

'Yeah. Apparently it's a free house. He's making a fortune.'

'I bet.' Winter nodded. 'And guess who supplies him? Bloody Mick Harris.'

It made perfect sense. The reason Mick Harris paid all those visits to Cherbourg was to stock up on cheapo supermarket booze. Add ten

thousand fags a run and the van loads he'd deliver to Steve Pallister
would make them both very happy. Pallister would flog the stuff over
the bar to selected locals while Mick Harris would pocket a modest
percentage of the profits. What better reason would Pallister need to lie
his socks off about Friday night?

Sullivan wasn't convinced.

'You really think he'd take the risk? Perverting the course of justice?
Conspiracy to murder?'

'Good question, son, but the answer's yes. All that stuff about the
Falklands wasn't bollocks. I've met these guys before. They went out
there for Maggie, and Queen and Country, and by the time they came
back they felt well and truly shafted. Don't ask me why or how but
that's the way it was.'

'But we won, didn't we?'

'Yeah, and that's the puzzle.' Winter glanced across. 'It wouldn't
matter tuppence except in situations like these it's impossible to get at
them. Older bloke I was trying to pull in Pompey once summed it up.
"Paul," he said, "I've been to places you can't even fucking dream
about, so put your little pad away." That was Korea, mind.'

'Korea?' Sullivan was looking blank.

'Different war, son.' Winter frowned at the windscreen and then
turned on the demister. 'Bit before our time.'

It was nearly two'o'clock before Faraday found the time to drive down
to the old ABC cinema. It stood between Portsmouth's main commercial precinct and the big dual carriageway which sluiced traffic in and
out of the city. There was a car park across the road, in the shadow of a
pair of giant council blocks, and he sat in his Mondeo for a couple of
minutes wondering whether or not he really wanted to put Brian
Imber's theory to the test. The worst of the headache had gone now but
it had left behind a thick, silty residue. He felt uneasy and vaguely
troubled. He'd like nothing more than a plate of something warm and
comforting, and after that a longish kip.

The cinema was the usual post-war confection, the sheer brick walls
and turreted corners punctuated by metal-framed windows. The
entrance doors along the front had been boarded up, attracting layer
after layer of peeling fly-posters, and the spray-can kids had gone wild
on every available surface. Above the ground floor, not a single pane of
glass had survived, and one of the window frames above the big display
panel had been pushed out completely, leaving a gaping hole that
offered a glimpse of what Faraday might expect inside. Smashed light
bulbs, he thought, and yellowing walls daubed with yet more graffiti.
Whatever had become of the temple of dreams?

254

He laced on a pair of the boots he normally wore for birding and tested the big torch he'd borrowed from one of the uniformed sergeants at Highland Road. According to Imber, there was an unsecured window round the side, the favoured entry for local kids. He crossed the road and skirted the front of the building. The window Imber had mentioned was masked by a line of bushes. Someone had been at the security boards with a jemmy and the splintered remains lay in the deep concrete gully that separated the path from the window.

Feeling slightly ridiculous, Faraday checked behind him before straddling the gully. With one leg on the sill, he was committed. There were still tiny shards of glass in the window frame and he briefly regretted leaving his gloves in the car before taking the weight of his body on his arms and swinging his other leg across the gully. Seconds later, out of breath, he was catching his balance on the flight of concrete steps inside.

The stairs led downwards into darkness. Underfoot, in the light from the window, he could see more broken glass. Dimly, where the light gave out, a radiator had been ripped from the wall and now hung drunkenly outwards, secured by pipework alone. He flicked on the torch, tracking the beam to the right until it settled on some kind of door. The place smelled of damp and neglect. Stand absolutely still, ignore the low rumble of traffic from the road outside, and for a moment he thought he heard movement.

Faraday stepped carefully downwards, the 'crunch-crunch' of glass echoing back from the stairwell. He pushed at the door and it began to open. Inside, he felt a sudden chill, and the soft clunk as the door closed behind him brought the torch beam whirling round. Take it easy, he thought. Ten metres away from the pavement and already this place has got you spooked.

He edged towards the wall and swept the torch beam across the yawning space ahead. This had once been one of the smaller cinemas, Screen Two or Three. He could remember sitting here, in this same darkness, J-J beside him, settling into a Steve Martin comedy or one of the Oliver Stone movies. *Platoon* had been a favourite of J-J's. The dialogue was beyond him but he could sit and watch the action sequences for hours on end. Faraday's torch at last found the long curve of the back wall which had once served as the screen. This was where Charlie Sheen had confronted the realities of Vietnam. And this was where J-J had upset an entire bucket of popcorn when the Viet Cong sprang their major ambush.

The noise again. Footsteps this time. Definitely. Faraday felt his pulse begin to quicken as he followed the strip of carpet up the ramp towards the back of the cinema. The carpet was wet underfoot and twice he detoured to avoid little curls of turd. Another door took him into some kind of vestibule. He paused, listening for movement, then called out, mapping the wreckage around him with the torch. There was more glass, abandoned bottles, crushed cans of Castlemaine and Special Brew, and a pile of charred wood that must once had been a door frame. There was a smell too, more distinctive this time. It was a bitter, acrid stench that tugged at his throat, and he tried to visualise living amongst this chaos. Would people really try and make a home for themselves here? Was life that bad that you'd trade sunshine and fresh air for this sour darkness?

He stood absolutely still for minutes on end, listening. Faintly, he could hear the wail of a car alarm. It went on for thirty seconds or so, then stopped. When nothing else happened – no footsteps, no sign of movement – he picked his way across the vestibule and down a shallow flight of steps at the end. It was lighter here, and as he rounded the corner he could hear traffic again. Then he stopped. Before him lay the cinema's foyer. The ticket booths and popcorn bar were in ruins, everything smashed. A false wall had been wrenched away and kicked to pieces. Tiles, broken glass and lengths of splintered wood spiked with rusting nails littered the floor, and the area near the boarded-up doors was ankle deep in more empty cans, Stella this time.

Faraday was trying to remember the layout of the old cinema. He'd been right about Screens Two and Three, he was sure he had, but the biggest screen was upstairs. Maybe that was where the kids hung out. Waiting, as ever, for the main attraction.

Not bothering to hide his presence, he pulled a length of timber aside and cleared a path for himself up the stairs. At the top, through the sagging remains of the big double doors, he found himself in another vestibule. The floor was covered with cladding ripped away from cable runs and there were bare wires hanging from the ceiling. Off to the right, exactly where his memory suggested, was another door and another flight of steps. It was dark again, pitch-black this time, and he took the stairs one at a time, only too aware of Anghared's warning. Structurally unsound, she'd said, closing their last conversation with a sigh.

At the top of the stairs, he knew he'd found Screen One. The long black curve of the ramp stretched away into the darkness. Stripped of seats, it seemed to go on forever. He edged slowly forward, one step at a time down the long emptiness of the ramp, the light from the torch pooling at his feet. Then, without warning, the light from the torch abruptly diffused, dropping into nowhere. Faraday stopped, chilled to the bone, rocking back on his heels. Before him was a void, a drop so sudden and so deep that the torch beam couldn't locate the floor below. Anghared had been right. This place was a death trap.

Faraday closed his eyes, trying to still his racing pulse, telling himself that he was OK, that he'd got away with it, then he began to step sideways, easing back from the void. He tracked the torch to the left, looking for the door that would take him back to the vestibule, and as he did so, he spotted a shape in the darkness. The torch was shaking in his hand. He couldn't hold it steady. He was looking at a tent. It was a ridge tent, green, sagging, not big, and it was about a dozen paces away. He swallowed hard. Who, in his right mind, would camp out in a place like this?

He crept towards it, pinning the tent with his torch, oblivious of the obstacles in between. More glass. More crunching. At last, clammy with sweat, he was there. The entrance lay at the upper end of the ramp, the two triangles of nylon loosely laced together. He squatted in front of it, pulling the flaps apart, shining the torch inside. There were two sleeping bags, both unrolled. An open biscuit tin contained three candles, a bag of sugar, two Snickers bars, three packets of cheese and onion crisps, and a two-litre bottle of something that looked like water. For a moment, taking in this strange tableau, he was reminded of scenes from the Antarctic. He'd happened across a tent in the middle of nowhere, a perfect time capsule, long abandoned, and it struck him that the questions it raised were just the same. What had happened to the people who'd lived here? Perched on the edge of the world? What had driven them to this appalling place?

Clothes were bundled at the farther end and Faraday caught sight of an envelope propped against the tent pole. On his hands and knees, he crawled into the tent. The envelope was pink with a big 'N' scrawled across the front. Someone had already opened it and he could feel the card inside. Holding the torch under his chin, he slipped it out.

It was a greeting card, embossed with a huge heart. 'My darling,' it read, 'by the time you read this I'll be waiting for you in that special place. Yours always. Helen.'

Helen?

Faraday read the message again and then checked the envelope. Helen Bassam. Niamat Tabibi. Couldn't be. Had to be.

His mind began to race, checking back, day by day, to that grey, chill, rain-lashed morning when he'd stood on top of Chuzzlewit House, peering down at the splay-limbed shape of Helen Bassam. Was this really her writing? Her card? Was this why she'd tipped herself into oblivion? Was there some pact here? Some bizarre agreement to step into another world, a better world, with a man she couldn't have? Had the Afghan mused aloud about Islam, given her a taste for the afterlife?

Another footfall, up towards the top of the ramp, unmistakable this time. Faraday froze, flicking off the torch. The sudden darkness crowded in on him, thick, oppressive, laden with menace. The footsteps were getting closer. They were deliberate. They knew exactly where they were heading. Someone heavy. Someone big. Faraday began to inch himself round in the tent, holding the torch ready, and as shapes slowly materialised from the blackness around him he saw a movement beyond the open flap. Someone was crouching down. A disc of white appeared.

Faraday snapped on the torch, staring at the revealed face. For a second or two he refused to believe it. Then, as the long slender hands began to reach out for him, he knew it was true.

He brought the torch up to his own face. The hands stopped. Then, in the spill of light from the torch, they signalled the old greeting.

'Dad?'

Faraday said nothing, and as the beam settled once again on J-J's face at the open flap he heard another set of footsteps, much lighter, scuttling away.

Chapter twenty-one

'It's Valentine's Day, boss. It means someone loves you.'

Willard took the unsigned card and propped it on the window sill above his desk. The envelope had come in with a tray of coffees and the ripple of applause around the big conference table was a rare glimmer of light on an otherwise gloomy day.

The arrest and interview stage of *Bisley* wasn't going well. At Waterlooville and Fareham all three suspects had been invited to describe their movements on the Friday night of Bradley Finch's death. This first stage of the interview process, dubbed 'open account', was designed to pin a suspect down to a sequence of events which could later be probed and challenged. Interviewed under caution, with everything tape-recorded, this initial version of events often flagged the path to a later confession, chiefly because it gave the two-man interview teams something to go on. If chummy was lying through his teeth, then a small army of DCs were out there waiting to tear his story to pieces.

Yet it wasn't happening. Both the Harris twins and Kenny Foster had stuck to their previous alibis. Terry had driven Mick up to the Plough around half seven in the evening. They'd played cards all night and got pissed. Next morning, they'd come home again. End of story. As for Foster, he'd been working out at Captain Beefy, and had a helpful little video to prove it. Afterwards, he'd gone back to Simone's place and picked up where they'd left off.

Open account had occupied the first session. After the comfort break, the interview teams had moved into the probe stage, looking for loopholes in the open account, but in all three cases they were hitting the same brick wall.

'They've gone no comment?' Willard was looking at Dave Michaels.

'All three, boss. I'm not saying it's a surprise but it's certainly a

259

problem. We've got nothing to hit them with. The blokes are running out of questions.'

Willard turned to Brian Imber.

'What about the phone billings?'

Imber glanced down at his pad. The bids on the Harris brothers' mobiles had only just gone in but the TIU in Winchester had faxed through the last two weeks on Kenny Foster's mobe, and while the results were amusing, they didn't shed much light on Bradley Finch.

'Amusing?'

'There's one number crops up all the time, boss. The girl, Louise Abeka. He's been phoning her virtually every hour. When she bothers to answer, the calls never last more than ten seconds so she's obviously blowing him out. Wise move, too. Have you seen the video?'

'But why is that amusing? If we can evidence some kind of obsession, we're starting to talk motive.' He glared down the table at Imber. 'No?'

'Maybe you're right, sir.' Imber shrugged, acutely uncomfortable. 'My reading says he was trying to get into her knickers.'

'Which ended up on Finch's dead body.'

'Of course, but . . .' He shrugged. 'OK, let's say I'm right. Let's say he really fancied her. What's that got to do with Finch?'

'Finch was shagging her. According to Paul Winter.'

'Can he evidence that?'

'No, of course he can't. But that's not the point, is it? If Foster thought the same, then Finch's in the shit. Especially if he's already pissed Foster off on a number of other issues.' Willard paused, then softened slightly. 'What about calls to Finch? On Foster's phone?'

'There aren't any.'

'*None?*'

'None at all, sir. He talks to Terry Harris from time to time.'

'Friday night?'

'Yeah.' Imber checked his pad again. 'Two calls late afternoon.'

'Duration?'

'One long, eleven minutes. At 19.04. One short.'

'Was the last one the short one?'

'Yes, sir. 22.21. They talked for less than a minute.'

'So where would that put Finch?'

'Margate Road, with the girl. Pissed out of his head.'

'With no one else in the house?'

'Exactly. All three students were out.'

'OK.' Willard was warming up now. 'Derek. Give me that forensic brief again.'

The DI in charge of the SOCO teams went through the analysis on the first batch of forensic submissions. The news that the blood in Louise Abeka's bathroom had tested positive for Bradley Finch raised a murmur around the table. Willard held his hands up, stilling the conversation.

'Early days,' he said at once. 'But it's worth running this thing through. Kenny Foster wants to shag the girl Louise. He thinks Finch's screwing it up for him and he's pissed off with the boy anyway. Terry Harris feels the same. They decide to sort Finch out, give him a slapping. Something happens Friday afternoon to trigger all this. Maybe it's Finch flogging the video camera. Fuck knows. They talk on the phone at . . . Brian?'

Imber studied his pad again.

'19.04, sir.'

'Fine. They make some plans. Agree to meet.' He paused, struck by a sudden thought.

'What about Finch's phone? We've got billings for that?'

'Until the beginning of the previous week, sir. After that, the phone's dead.'

'You mean he's not using it?'

'Not that phone. They cut him off because he never paid the account. There were others before but they got cut off, too. He could have bought a pay-as-you-go and binned it but I think that's unlikely.'

'Why?'

'He had fuck all money. Until he sold the camera and bought the champagne.'

'So there's ten days when he had no phone at all?'

'That's right, sir.'

'So assuming I'm there or thereabouts with Friday night, how did they know where to find Finch?'

This time, Imber was smiling. He'd anticipated the question and had one finger anchored on the billing from the TIU.

'Foster phoned the girl at 21.20. And again at 22.18.'

'Did she answer?'

'Both times.' He ducked his head. 'Just under a minute on the first call. Fifteen seconds on the second.'

'Which was just before he phoned Harris for the second time?'

'That's right, sir.'

'And after that?'

'Nothing.'

'No calls at all?'

'None.'

'Not Saturday or Sunday?'

'No, boss. Nor Monday, nor yesterday.'

'Shit.' Willard was baffled. 'If Finch's off the plot, he'd be all over her.' He frowned. 'Wouldn't he?'

Faraday stood in the pouring rain beside the cinema. It had taken ten minutes or so to pick his way out of the inky darkness, chiefly because he'd tripped over a length of cable and twisted his ankle. Only J-J's supporting arm had brought him out intact.

Now he leaned against the railings beside the yawning window, guarding the cinema's only exit. What he needed, fast, was informa-tion. He gestured J-J closer.

'Who else is in there?' he signed.

J-J was looking at the pub across the road. He'd quite like a coffee. Faraday asked the question again.

'Kids,' J-J signed back at last.

'Which kids?'

'The ones on the project. Anghared's kids. Gordon's kids.'

'But which ones in particular?'

J-J threw both hands up, an all-encompassing gesture. Could be any of them. Depends.

Faraday shifted his weight against the railings and came at the conversation a different way.

'That tent.' He shaped it in the air. 'Who lives there?' J-J smiled at him. A different shape this time, tiny.

'Little kid?' Faraday queried. J-J nodded.

'Name?'

The smile faded, replaced by something closer to suspicion. Maybe there were confidentiality issues here. Should he really be having this kind of conversation with a policeman?

Faraday was still waiting. He wanted a name. He put the question a second time and leaned very slowly forward when J-J shook his head.

'Listen to me, son.' Faraday tugged his own ear. 'I don't put you through this without a very good reason. A girl is dead. I need to know why.' He reached inside his jacket and produced the pink envelope. 'This card may have come from her. Again, I need to know why. The little fella in the tent may know. That's why I need his name. You follow me?'

J-J was thinking fast. Faraday recognised the symptoms – the refusal to make eye contact, the faintest hint of a frown. Finally, Faraday's patience gave out.

He reached across and gripped the top of J-J's denim jacket. Then he shook the boy hard, before releasing him and signing the name, letter by letter.

'D-o-o-d-i-e?'

J-J was staring at his father. In twenty-three years, there'd never been anything like this, not once.

'Well?'

J-J blinked, then nodded, watching in bewilderment as Faraday turned away, fumbling inside his jacket for his mobile.

'Cath?' He wiped the rain from his face. 'I need five bodies. Now.'

It was nearly dark when Dawn Ellis gave Bev Yates a nudge. They were sitting in an unmarked Astra in a car park on the seafront with line of sight to the Travel Inn's front entrance, waiting for Steve Pallister. So far, they'd phoned half a dozen registration plates back to Dave Michaels at the MIR but none had belonged to the landlord of the Plough. Until now.

'Say again?'

'Blue Shogun. W 365 DKG.'

There was a brief pause. The Shogun had parked on a double yellow outside the hotel.

'Who's driving?' Dave again.

Bev squinted through the gloom.

'Big bloke. Leather jacket. He's just gone into the hotel.'

'OK. His name's Steve Pallister. Take him on the way out and bring him down to Central. Arrest him if you have to.'

'On what charge?'

'Interfering with a potential witness.'

Dave Michaels rang off and Yates turned to Ellis. Headroom on the Astra didn't allow him to punch the air.

'Result.' He beamed. 'Get your kickers on.'

Outside the cinema, after fifteen minutes in the pouring rain, reinforcements finally arrived: two DCs toting heavy Dragonlite torches, quickly followed by Cathy Lamb. She appeared round the corner of the building, still zipping up her anorak. She must have been running because she was out of breath.

Faraday, anchored with J-J beside the gaping window, wanted to know where the rest were. The cinema was a warren. Even five bodies probably wouldn't be enough.

'There's a problem.' Cathy fumbled with her hood. 'The other two guys were with Hartigan. I phoned them on the mobe. He wanted to know what was going on and they told him.'

'What were they doing with Hartigan?'

'The run-in last week. Remember?'

Faraday nodded. Two DCs on their way home had been stopped by a traffic car. They'd taken exception to hassle from the uniforms and had been hauled out and breathylised. They were both under the limit but the embarrassment of a public row on the kerbside had been quite enough for Hartigan.

'So what's he saying?'

'Dunno, boss. But he wants a word before we get stuck in.'

'At Fratton?' Faraday couldn't believe it.

'No, boss. Here.'

They waited in the rain. Faraday muttered his way through a rudimentary brief. There was a kid in there, Doodie, the ten-year-old. He was a registered Misper and intelligence put him on the roof of Chuzzlewit House the night the girl died. The two DCs, as wet as everyone else, registered polite interest, cupping their cigarettes against the swirling rain. Cathy made a series of calls on her mobile to sort out other crises. Finally, a small neat figure emerged from the gathering darkness. Under the striped golfing umbrella, Hartigan seemed to be unusually cheerful.

'Joe,' he said, 'what on earth's all this about?'

Wearily, Faraday went through it all again. Hartigan's eyes kept straying to the spintered boards in the gully beneath the window.

'You went in *there*?' he said.

'Yes, sir.'

'Without a hard hat? Or protective gear?'

'Yes, sir.'

'Do you know the state of this place? It's a condemned building, Joe. It's structurally unsound.'

'There are kids in there, sir. And they don't have hard hats, either.'

'So you tell me.'

'It's true. This is J-J, my son. He works with them.'

Hartigan eyed J-J for a second or two, then turned back to Faraday.

'There are Health and Safety implications here, Joe. I don't have to spell it out, do I? Duty of care? Say our guys go in. Say one of them, two of them, get hurt. Where does that leave us when the shit hits the fan? We have a responsibility here, Joe, and it's my job to exercise it.' He paused for a moment. 'Have you done a risk assessment, by any chance?'

Risk assessment? Faraday closed his eyes a moment, fighting to control his temper. After six days, he'd finally cornered Doodie. After six days, he was finally minutes away from laying hands on a ten-year-old that no one else in the city could find. Not his mother. Not the welfare agencies. Not a couple of hundred policeman. The kid had vital information. Plus the kid needed a bit of care and attention. And here was Hartigan, neatly uniformed, warm and dry, talking about risk assessments.

Faraday glanced at Cathy. She was staring staight ahead, refusing to meet his eyes. The two DCs were transfixed. This conversation would be all over the city within hours.

'So what do you suggest we do, sir?' Faraday said at last.

'Do, Joe? I suggest we take a deep breath and consider our options. Maybe the Fire Brigade. Maybe that's the answer.'

'They've just condemned the building. They're hardly going to go back in.'

'But we could ask them.'

'Sure. Or maybe we could start a fire. Smoke the kid out.'

One of the DCs tried to suppress a snort of laughter. Cathy silenced him with a look.

'I'll ignore that, Joe,' Hartigan said. 'Unless you'd like to apologise.'

Faraday could feel the rain inside his collar. He shook his head, said nothing. Finally, Hartigan stepped forward and peered into the black hole beyond the gaping window frame.

'There's no way, Joe, absolutely no way. If this child is that important, I suggest we wait.'

'Wait?'

'Absolutely.' He was upright again under the umbrella. 'Is this the only exit?'

Faraday glanced at J-J and signed the question. J-J shook his head.

'There's another place you can get in.' He gestured into the darkness. 'Round the back.'

Faraday's heart sank. Leaving the DCs outside the window, the four of them trudged round the building, Faraday grateful for J-J's supporting arm. J-J led them to a hole at ground level that must have been a heating duct. The protective grille had been ripped off and lay beside it. The hole was big enough for a body. Just.

Hartigan inspected it. The mud around the hole looked freshly churned. He glanced up at Faraday.

'Do we know if the child's still inside?'

'Obviously not, sir.'

'Then we have a problem, do we not?'

The two men stared at each other. The rain, if anything, had got harder. Finally, Faraday gave up. He offered a nod to Cathy, another to J-J, and turned on his heel, hobbling away into the wet darkness.

Willard wanted Winter and Sullivan to sort out Pallister, and left it to Dave Michaels to make the arrangements. Winter and Sullivan found

Michaels in the bar at Fratton nick staring glumly at the remains of a cheese roll.

The interviews at Waterlooville and Fareham had now stalled completely. All three suspects were refusing to answer any further questions and their solicitors were pushing for early release. Custody could be extended beyond the seven o'clock deadline on application to a uniformed Superintendent but even Willard was beginning to wonder what purpose another twelve hours of 'no comment' responses would serve. What they needed was a breakthrough on one of the alibis, and it wasn't happening.

Winter was wondering about a pint before tackling Pallister again.

'What about the premises?'

Michaels shook his head.

'We got lucky at Terry Harris's gaff. The people out at Compton have ID'd the mini-tape so it definitely came from the nicked camera.'

'What's Harris's line?'

'He says he bought it off a bloke in a pub. Can't remember the bloke. Can't remember the pub. Pathetic, isn't it?'

'What about the rest of the stuff?'

'Even that's a maybe. Turns out he's got receipts for most of the new gear we had down as nicked. Made a bundle on a couple of horses and bought it as a late Christmas present for the missus. This guy was born lucky.'

'What's he saying about Finch?'

'Not a lot. Says the boy came along on double glazing jobs just to help out. They had the odd drink or two in the evening and that was about it.'

'The girl? Louise?'

'Never heard of her.'

'Kenny Foster?'

'Mates, definitely. He's coughed to being second at the fights but we can hardly do him for that, can we?'

Winter decided against the pint. Sullivan wanted to know about Kenny Foster.

'Dead end.' Dave Michaels drew a finger across his throat. 'He's stuck to what he told you about Friday night and isn't about to add any more. He's a cocky bastard, too. Says he's got another fight on tomorrow morning and says he'll do us for loss of earnings if we don't let him go.'

'And the garage?'

'The blokes are still there but they're not hopeful. What they really wanted was a hit on the rope used on Finch but there's nothing remotely like it. They've taken all kinds of grease samples for a match on the boy's runners but it's going to be a couple of days at least before they get anything back. If we go for an extension beyond thirty-six hours, I can't see the magistrates wearing it.' He paused. 'The only thing we could do him on is storing petrol. He's got gallons of the stuff there.'

'Mick Harris?'

'Yeah.' Michaels brightened for a moment. 'The blokes are telling me he's all over the place, you know, body language-wise. At least we've got him fucking worried.'

'Has he said anything?'

'You're joking. His brief's given him the script and "no comment" isn't a lot to learn, is it?'

Winter glanced at his watch. If Michaels was serious about an early release, they had barely an hour to squeeze something out of Pallister. It hadn't been necessary for Bev Yates to arrest him. He'd driven down to Central voluntarily and was now waiting in one of the interview suites.

'Yeah?' Michaels finished the roll and pushed the plate away. 'Bad fucking sign.'

The last thing Faraday expected was sympathy.

'You're soaking wet.' Mrs Bassam peered at him under the porch light. 'Come in.'

Faraday stepped into the neat little hall. There was a small suitcase on the floor beside the occasional table and a coat spotted with rain draped over the banisters.

'I've just come in myself,' she said. 'Filthy weather.'

She disappeared upstairs and returned with a towel. Faraday mopped his face and hair. The towel smelled of air freshener.

'Tea?'

Without waiting for an answer, Mrs Bassam disappeared into the kitchen. Faraday, mystified, limped after her. His ankle was swollen now. He'd checked it in the car, switching on the vanity light and rolling up his trouser leg, and the throbbing made him wonder about a visit to the QA hospital at the top of the city. A couple of hours waiting in the A & E department was normally the last thing he could afford but just now he'd do anything to avoid going back to his claustrophobic little office.

'What's the matter with your leg?'

Mrs Bassam was busy with the teapot. Faraday began to explain about the cinema, then stopped.

'Did Helen ever say anything about the ABC?' he asked instead. 'The place up at Mile End? The one they've boarded up?'

Mrs Bassam said yes. Helen had never gone into detail because conversation wasn't her thing but she'd mentioned it a couple of times.

'Was she ever in there?'

'Not to my knowledge. It's some kind of squat, isn't it?'

Faraday nodded. He wasn't sure what kind of word he'd use to describe the squalor inside those towering brick walls but squat would do for starters.

'It's like somewhere you can't imagine,' he said softly. 'I've been around this city twenty-five years but I've never seen anything like that.'

Something in his voice brought Mrs Bassam to a halt. Abandoning the tea, she waved Faraday onto one of the stools at the tiny breakfast bar.

'What do you mean exactly?'

'I'm not sure.'

He gazed at her. It was the truth. He simply didn't know. What he'd seen had spoken of disintegration and chaos, of lives spinning out of control, but the worst of all was the sheer physical state of the place. Turn on the torch and you were looking at pictures from some undeclared war. The bombs had gone off. The smoke had drifted away. And everything was in the process of falling apart.

'Does that make sense? To you?'

'Yes.' Mrs Bassam had followed his every word. 'I'm afraid it does.'

'There are kids living in there. Young kids.'

'As young as Helen?'

'Younger. Ten years old.' He lifted his hands, a gesture – he later realised – of resignation. 'One of the richest nations on earth and we've got kids living like animals.'

He at last put the towel to one side and fumbled in his jacket pocket. The envelope, like everything else, was damp to the touch. The big 'N' on the front had smudged but the card itself seemed to have survived. He opened it and passed it across. He needed to know about the writing. Was this a hand Mrs Bassam might recognise?

She took the card and studied it. Then she nodded.

'Helen wrote that,' she muttered. 'I can even show you the receipt upstairs.'

Pallister was on his second cup of coffee by the time Winter and Sullivan made it to Central police station. The Custody Sergeant had done his best to advise the presence of a solicitor but Pallister was adamant. He had nothing to hide. The blokes who'd been up to his pub earlier had been nice enough. He was only too happy to help in whatever way he could.

Winter stepped into the interview room and shut the door behind him. The interview suites had just been refurbished but there wasn't a paint job on earth that could soften the starkness of these four walls. Two chairs on either side of a table. A cassette machine with four tape decks and a clock. And that was that.

Pallister greeted them like old friends. You didn't have to be a traffic cop to know that he'd been drinking.

'My pleasure, boys.' He offered them a big, cheesy grin. 'What can I do for you?'

Winter formally cautioned him. Anything he said would be recorded and might be used in evidence against him. He wanted Pallister to know that they weren't discussing a parking offence. A man had died and it was Winter's job to find out who had killed him.

'What about your mate there?' Sullivan was sitting beside Winter. 'Does he get a speaking part in all this?'

Winter ignored the dig. He wanted to know why Pallister had driven all the way down to Southsea to see Harris's wife.

'She phoned me.'

'Why?'

'Because she was fucking upset, that's why. You blokes barge into her house at God knows what hour, all tooled up, drag her husband away, upset her nipper, tell her to pack a bag, start tearing her kitchen apart, what the fuck else is she supposed to feel?'

'And she phoned you for comfort?'

'She phoned me for advice.'

'Like what?'

'Like what to say to her daughter. The kid's gone to a friend's for tea. She's not used to sleeping in hotels in her own fucking city.'

'But why you? Why ask you all these questions?'

'Because we're mates, that's why.'

'Mates?' Winter raised an eyebrow.

'Think what you like.' Pallister shrugged. 'It's possible to be friends with a woman and not shag her. At least in my world it is.'

Winter let the point ride. Bev Yates had told him about the interview at the Travel Inn. The woman was scared shitless that a burglary charge would take her from her daughter. So far she'd stuck by her husband's alibi but – in Yates's judgement – she wasn't far off cracking. Everything in life boiled down to the balance of advantage. Just now, Maisie weighed heavy in the scales.

Sullivan stirred. So far, he'd done little but pick at his nails. Now, he looked Pallister in the eye.

'Say we think different,' he began. 'Say we hear a whisper that you're knocking out fags and booze on the black. Say we get curious about just how much money you're turning over in that pub of yours. You with me?'

Pallister's smile had vanished.

'Go on, son.'

'OK.' Sullivan nodded, the soul of reason. 'And say, just say, we get evidence that Mick Harris is your buyer, that Mick Harris is the one who's making all those heavy trips across the Channel and bunging you contraband by the vanful.' He paused, inviting Pallister to join him on this speculative little journey. 'Wouldn't that give you every reason to keep Mick sweet? And wouldn't keeping Mick sweet extend to his brother?'

'But why, son? Why would I be interested in doing that?'

'Because Terry Harris is in trouble. Friday night, we think he murdered someone. That's deep shit. He needs an alibi. He needs to have been somewhere else. So guess what? He has a word with Mick, and Mick thinks of you.'

'That's a fairy tale, son. You should be onto the bigger books by now.'

Winter took over. The exchange had brought a smile to his face and now he leaned forward.

'He's got a point though, hasn't he? Our Gary? You're telling us that Mick and Terry came up on Friday night. Didn't leave until Saturday morning. No one else clocked them. No one else except your good lady and the two blokes in the cribbage school. Your good lady naturally sees it your way and the two other blokes we can't trace. Not yet, anyway. So, my friend, that leaves you in exactly the same boat as poor Mrs Harris. She stands to lose her daughter. And you?' Winter leaned back, his hands held wide. 'It's a good business, Steve. Be a shame to fuck it up.'

There was a long silence. Down the corridor, a banged-up junkie was shouting for more tea. Sullivan drew a pad towards him.

'Maybe we should start all over again,' he murmured. 'Let's pretend you haven't told us anything about the Harris twins and the cribbage school. Let's imagine we've only just met. So . . . what really happened Friday night?'

Pallister looked from one face to the other. For a moment, just a second or two, Winter thought they had him. Then he leaned back in the chair and clasped his hands behind his head.

'You guys make me laugh,' he said. 'You must think I'm off my fucking head.'

By half past seven, Faraday was parked outside Marta's house. He'd phoned her four times in the last hour, dialling her mobile number, but had got no further than the messaging service. On each occasion he'd muttered his name and asked her to call back, but so far she hadn't bothered. The pain in his ankle he could cope with. Even the scene outside the cinema had its lighter side. But this – the blank indifference – had become unbearable. They'd shared thirteen unforgettable months. And now she wouldn't even lift the phone.

The rain had stopped by now and it was much colder. The wind had backed round to the north-west and shadows from the trees danced on the wet road. From the car, Faraday had perfect line of sight to Marta's house and it was impossible not to wonder what was going on inside. Her own Alfa was parked on the hardstanding outside the garage. Was her husband's motor locked away behind that big metal door? Had he come back? Had they kissed and made up? Had they promised each other a new start? No more affairs? No more dumping their surplus baggage on passing strangers?

He shook his head, trying to rid himself of the wilder fantasies. There was a light behind the front door, another in one of the bay windows upstairs. Was this their bedroom? Had they somehow got rid of the kids for the evening? Might this be the moment Marta broke out the body oils and the scented candles, paying her debts for a year of betrayal? Until Marta came along, Faraday had never believed in physical abandon, never truly let himself go. But once it had happened, once he knew that total surrender was possible, then everything changed. A relationship like that could lead to a thousand mystery destinations. And one of them was here.

He sank deeper behind the wheel, trying to ease the pain in his ankle. For once in his life he hadn't the faintest idea what would happen next. Should he phone her again? Tell her he was parked across the road, as pathetic and helpless as some desperate adolescent? Should he hobble across and knock on her door? Throw stones at the window? Smash his way in? Did he have any rights here? Apart from the need to simply see her? Smell her? Touch her? Sit her down and tell her exactly what was happening to him? Should he apologise for walking out last time? Offer to start all over again?

He looked away a moment, distracted by a cat prowling in the shadows beneath a nearby hedge, then he heard the noise of a door opening and he looked back towards her house in time to see Marta's silhouette in the light from the hall. She was talking to someone who'd just stepped out. Faraday wound down the window, catching a snatch of Spanish. Then a laugh and a wave from Marta, and a flurry of movement as the other person, a woman, ran to Marta's Alfa. She bent to the door and got in. The rear lights came on and the car backed onto the road. Seconds later, it had gone.

Upstairs, briefly, Marta appeared in the window. Then she pulled the curtains and the light went out. Faraday sat motionless. She was definitely there. Her car had gone. She probably had kids to look after. Was now the moment?

He got out of the car, his good foot first. Thirty metres to her front door seemed to take an age. He rang once, then again. He heard footsteps coming down the stairs, and the sound of a woman humming. He recognised the tune, something from *Carmen*. He felt about fifteen.

The door opened. Marta was standing there. Her feet were bare and she was wearing a dressing gown Faraday had never seen before. It was a man's dressing gown, far too big for her. Her husband must have come back, he thought. What happens now?

'Joe.' Her voice was cold. She wasn't pleased to see him.

'Yeah.' He nodded. 'Me.'

'What do you want?'

'I'm . . .' he frowned '. . . not sure.'

She was looking beyond him, out into the darkness.

'That's your car, isn't it?'

'Yes.'

'Have you been watching me?'

'Yes.'

She pulled the dressing gown more tightly around her. Faraday wanted to ask a thousand questions. Instead, he could only manage one.

'Who was the girl?'

'My au pair.'

'*Au pair?*'

'Claudia, Joe. She's been with me eighteen months.'

Faraday did his best to hide his confusion. Not once had Marta ever mentioned an au pair.

'Why do you need her?' he asked.

Marta studied him a moment. Upstairs, a bath was filling.

'My husband left me two years ago.' She began to close the door. 'If you really want to know.'

Chapter twenty-two

Faraday knew he had to start all over again, assuming nothing.

The colour of the night sky? Black. The first pale hint of dawn? A cold, metallic grey. The first angry flare of sunrise? A deep, crimson red. Red was the colour she'd loved most of all. Red was the colour she flaunted with those beautifully cut summer dresses. If you packed up her life in a box, red would be the colour you'd choose for the wrapping.

Faraday sat in his study, gazing east across the harbour. He'd been here all night, brooding. J-J had brought him tea before he'd gone to bed, asking him again what was wrong, but the last thing he wanted to do was compare emotional traumas. When the boy had persevered, signing his concern with hands spread wide, Faraday had blamed it on the weather. Touch of flu, he'd said. Given the trembling deep inside and the waves of choking nausea, it seemed a close enough description. Were there drugs for this kind of betrayal? Should he make an appointment with the doctor?

He was a detective, for Christ's sake. Every working day, he dealt in the currency of deceit. He'd spent half a lifetime learning to recognise the difference between right and wrong, between a lie and the truth, between fiction and reality, and he had a long tally of successful clear-ups to suggest he knew his trade. Yet a year in this glorious woman's company and he'd never once suspected the depth of her deception.

The signs, he now realised, had been there all the time. It had taken her several months to reveal the fact that she was married and he remembered the circumstances only too well. He'd had a breakthrough on the Gunwharf job. He was excited. He'd phoned her from the car to share the news, catching her at home. She'd sounded nervy, breathless. There were other voices in the background and she'd whispered an apology for having to call him back later. My bloody husband, she'd muttered. He's back home early.

My bloody husband?

Faraday had been astonished. Husband and kids – a whole ménage – had never formed part of the Marta he knew. But the next time they'd met she'd glossed it all over, the way she always did, burying the awkwardness of real life beneath another brilliant evening. Because it was easier and because he loved her, Faraday had done his best to put it all to one side, to accept that he occupied only one compartment in her busy, busy life, and in a way he'd made a kind of peace with his guilt. Making love to Marta had seemed less and less like theft. Until now, when – with a single phrase – she turned this strange, dizzying relationship on its head. Not the robber any more. But the robbed.

Maybe he'd deserved it. Maybe the fact that he'd happily gone on screwing her, believing that she really was married, had piled up this savage retribution. Maybe he'd been set a test and failed it. Maybe there really was a God, a keeper of accounts, and it was Faraday's turn for a slapping. But this, he knew, was nonsense.

Why had she taken over his life and filled it with such sweet laughter? What had she really been thinking, the nights they'd lain next door in his bedroom? What kind of woman, what kind of human being, played games this elaborate, this cruel? Was it a control thing? A need to keep him a door or two away from the very middle of her? Or was it something infinitely simpler, a device to enable her to terminate the relationship at a time and place of her own choosing?

He suddenly thought of the message she'd shown him, the one her husband had allegedly left. No wonder it had been typed. By using a laptop, she'd sidestepped the problem of having to fake his handwriting. Clever.

The image of her in the dressing gown returned yet again. It was far too big. It belonged to a man. Had he been upstairs, waiting for her to step out of the bath? Was it his turn next for the beautifully lit showroom that was Marta's love life? Had he, in short, been swopped for a newer model?

As the study began to fill with light, Faraday rubbed his face and peered down at his watch. The more the questions piled up, the less real the whole experience seemed, and in some dimly understood way he realised that this very process, this relentless picking at the scab, might offer a kind of deliverance. The best year of his life had turned out to be a fantasy. From now on, like the half-arsed detective he saw in the shaving mirror every morning, it might be wise to take a harder look at the rules of evidence.

You'll have to start all over again, he thought. Assuming nothing.

Willard convened a squad meeting for nine o'clock. He'd known from the off that circumstances had forced his hand with Foster and the Harris twins but he hadn't expected the cupboard to be quite so bare when it came to arrest and interview.

Kenny Foster had been released at seven the previous evening, blowing the Custody Sergeant a farewell kiss, and the Harris twins – in all probability – would be out by lunch time. Possession of the video camera had been enough to have Terry Harris formally charged with handling, while Mick faced a separate Customs and Excise action over the illegal importation of tobacco and alcohol, but on neither count were there grounds for refusing police bail. For the time being, as far as Operation *Bisley* was concerned, they were free men.

Willard surveyed the faces around the incident room. He wanted to make it plain that this wasn't about blame, because blame would indicate some kind of failure. No, this was about consolidation, about analysis, about pausing to review and regroup. Resources, sadly, weren't unlimited. Some of the squad would be returning to division. But Willard wanted to say here and now that they'd found the bit of the jungle that mattered and they'd given the right trees a good shake. Speaking personally, he had absolutely no doubt that the Harris twins and Kenny Foster were implicated one way or another in Finch's death. Their alibis, in his view, were plainly rehearsed, and over the coming weeks he and the rest of the reduced squad would be making it their business to screw down every particle of evidence.

Forensically, it was still early days. They were still awaiting full analysis on the burned-out Fiat. He had every faith that items from Foster's garage – stuff off the floor – would prove a match for the wound in Finch's foot. Likewise, there were indications of bloodstained fibres in the filter from Mrs Harris's washing machine. Brian Imber and the Intelligence Cell were beginning to build an interesting story from the first tranche of telephone billings, and cell-site analysis might well drive a horse and cart through the Friday night alibis.

Without any question, all was far from lost – unless, unthinkably, the men and women in this room had lost their appetite for putting away the kind of animals responsible for a crime like this. The full post-mortem report had made it clear that Bradley Finch had taken a savage beating before being dragged up Hilsea Lines. When the noose was slipped around his neck, he was very probably still conscious and it was only too likely that they'd taunted him further before kicking away the plastic crate. No one was trying to pretend that the boy had been an angel but as far as Willard was concerned, episodes like this were unacceptable. *Bisley*, in short, had only just begun.

Winter nodded in approval. Willard, he'd concluded, talked a good war, and if you found yourself working for the robber barons on Major Crime then it was comforting to have someone that stubborn and that single-minded in charge. The stuff about cell-site analysis was especially interesting. These days, given enough time to access the records, technology allowed you to identify precise locations for individual calls. Had the Harris twins been using their mobiles on Friday night, Imber's boys could plot their movements with amazing accuracy.

The squad meeting over, Dave Michaels beckoned Winter and Sullivan into his office. Willard, he said, was going back to first base. That meant developing the Thursday night phone call on Winter's mobile, the one from Bradley Finch that had warned of a break-in at Brennan's. Ray Brennan had now supplied a list of current staff. None of them had previous but a CIMU clerk with a memory for names had checked the database and discovered that one lad – Lee Marchant – had been stop-checked a couple of weeks before by a traffic crew on the M27. There'd been another bloke in the passenger seat, who'd given his name as Claridge, but the patrol officer had been contacted and after a good look at the mugshot, thought it possible that he might have been Bradley Finch. He was certainly wearing black. And he was certainly extremely extremely pissed.

Winter wrote down the name.

'He's still at Brennan's?'

'Yeah, and expecting a call.'

Winter handed the name to Sullivan.

'Does this mean we're still on the squad?'

'Depends whether you fucking behave yourself.' Michaels reached for the phone, waving them out of the office.

Out in the corridor Winter ran into Phil Paget, a DC from Cosham who'd been part of the team tasked with interviewing Mick Harris. Unlike Winter, Paget was en route back to division.

'What's with this Mick Harris then?' Winter was steering him down the corridor towards the kitchenette.

'Guilty as fuck.'

'Who says?'

'Me, mate. The bloke's as thick as bricks. Take the brief away and we'd have been through by lunch time.'

The kitchenette, for once, was empty. Sullivan seemed to have disappeared. Winter began to sort out two Gold Blends. He'd known Phil Paget since his days as a probationer. They'd hunted together on a number of famous occasions and had the scalps to prove it. Lately, Phil had remarried and his new wife seemed to have squeezed the juice out of him.

'Are they close? Mick and his brother?'

'Listen to Mick and you'd say yes. I don't know about the other one, Terry. The blokes interviewing him up at Waterlooville said he was a horrible bastard, but clever. Mick's not like that at all. Big bloke, fat, couple of sandwiches short of a picnic, know what I mean? Loyal as you like though. Do anything for Mr Nasty.'

'Mr Nasty?'

'Terry. Tosh. Whatever the fuck his name is.'

Sullivan had appeared at the door. Watching Winter spoon sugar into his coffee, he tapped his watch. Michaels had set the Brennan's meet up for 9.45. It was already half past.

Phil Paget was looking amused. He nodded towards Sullivan.

'Got you on a lead, has he? About time some fucker did.'

Faraday had been in his office since eight. Ravenously hungry, he'd made himself a double bacon sandwich in the staff restroom and stirred two spoons of instant into a mug of boiling water. J-J had been asleep when he'd slipped out of the house, and he'd left a note telling him they needed to talk more about Doodie. The five-pound note beside his alarm clock would buy him a cab to Southsea police station.

Back in his office, amongst the usual overnight screenful of emails, Faraday had found a note from the pathologist who'd done the post-mortem on Helen Bassam. He'd had a conversation with the toxocologist over at Southampton and had some interesting news about the blood sample.

Faraday lifted the phone and dialled the pathologist's home number. When he finally answered, it was obvious he had his mouth full. The fact that these guys could sink a cooked breakfast before carving up the morning's quota of corpses had always amazed Faraday.

'Helen Bassam,' he said. 'You've obviously got the results.'

'I have. It seems we're talking morphine. Does that sound right to you?'

'Morphine?' Faraday was no chemist but he'd investigated enough junkie deaths to know that heroin, after four days in the bloodstream, showed up as morphine on tox analysis. Normally, though, street heroin was cut with other substances. Glucose and baking powder were favourites.

'Anything else?'

'Yes, alcohol.'

'How much?'

'About three hundred mgs.'

That was a lot. Faraday tried doing the sums.

'Three Bacardi Breezers?'

'More. Say four. Or the thick end of a bottle of wine. Or half a dozen Martinis.'

'Martini? What fourteen-year-old drinks Martini?'

'You'd be amazed.' The pathologist laughed before ringing off. 'Try doing my job for a week.'

Now, Faraday looked up to find Cathy Lamb at his door. She had a wish-list of problems that needed sorting and number one was Hartigan.

'He's demanding an update on the ABC,' she said. 'He's shitting himself in case we still go in there.'

'Fat chance.' He reached for the phone and punched in the Superintendent's number. 'The kid's long gone.'

Hartigan sounded unconvinced about Doodie. Once again, he wanted to make it absolutely clear that he wasn't in the business of hazarding any of his officers in a condemned building. As it happened, he'd won himself a bit of time this morning – a cancelled meeting with the Chairman of the Police Authority – and Faraday was only too welcome to pop over to Fratton and read the relevant guidance himself. Like every other Superintendent on the force, he'd recently had to attend a Health and Safety seminar and he'd come away with a big fat action pack. If Faraday wanted to borrow it, he only had to ask.

Faraday declined the invitation.

'I've had the pathologist on,' he said. 'About Helen Bassam.' He began to describe the findings. At the first mention of morphine, Hartigan leapt in.

'He means heroin,' he said at once.

'He said morphine, sir.'

'Of course he did, but what he means is heroin. Heroin shows as morphine. It's exactly what we feared.'

Faraday was groping his way back through the fog of the last twenty-four hours, trying to remember the previous conversation. They'd had a ruck about the drugs issue, certainly, but he didn't recall nailing Helen Bassam to an armful of smack.

'There were no reported track marks,' he pointed out.

'Immaterial, Joe. They smoke it these days.'

'Her mother says she hated cigarettes. Wouldn't touch them.'

'Makes no difference. Mums are the last people to know what their kids get up to. What about that allowance of hers? Forty pounds a week, wasn't it? No, we're talking heroin, Joe, and I must say that puts a totally different slant on the affair.' He paused. 'What about the ten-year-old?'

'We lost him,' Faraday said stonily. 'Last night.'

'I know that. I'm asking you what's happened since. You told me he was up there on the roof with her. Now you're telling me she was out of her head on booze and heroin.'

'With respect, sir, the pathologist said—'

'No, Joe, just listen to me for a change. I'm sick of playing catch-up in this job. There's an agenda out there and it's about time we seized it. Two Ss, is it?'

'What, sir?'

'In Bassam?'

Without waiting for an answer, Hartigan hung up. Cathy was at the door again, a scrap of paper in her hand.

'Our nice Mr Phillimore,' she said. 'The one I mentioned the other night. He's just phoned up again. Wonders whether you might spare the time to call him.'

Lee Marchant turned out to be an affable twenty-one-year-old with a silver nose ring and a big Pompey grin. Ray Brennan had told him to take an early tea break and he was reading a copy of yesterday's *Sun* when Winter and Sullivan pushed in through the door. The staff restroom was one half of a big, windowless container behind Fitted Bathrooms with a Coke machine, an electric kettle and a cardboard box full of tea bags. The calender on the wall was still showing December 2000 and someone had drawn a moustache on a curling photo of Jennifer Lopez Sellotaped to the wall.

Marchant wanted to know what all this was about. Sullivan briefly explained.

'Yeah.' Marchant nodded. 'I knows Brad.'

'Knew. I just told you. He's dead.'

'That's what I meant. Me and him knocked around a bit, more in the early days like, when we was still at school.'

'School' was the big comprehensive in West Leigh. They'd regularly bunked off together, hiding in nearby woods for a decent smoke.

'What about lately?' Winter hadn't come here for a chat about Bradley Finch's schooldays.

'Like I said, just now and again.'

'But the other week you were with him? No?'

'Oh, yeah, yeah.' Marchant grinned again. 'You mean me and the Old Bill? Out of order, that was. Just cos the motor's a wreck, ain't no reason to pull me. I wasn't pissed or nothing.'

'No, but Finch was.'

'Brad's always pissed. Brad's been pissed since he left school.'

'Why's that then?'

Marchant hesitated for a moment, looking from one face to the other. Only now did it seem to occur to him that trouble might lie at the end of this conversation.

'What's this about then? It ain't just Brad, is it?'

'Not entirely, no.' Winter paused. 'I asked you a question, son. Why was he always pissed?'

Marchant shrugged, reluctant to carry on. Winter glanced sideways at Sullivan. Sullivan shut his pocketbook.

'Off the record?' Winter nodded. 'Well, Brad . . . see . . . he always gets himself in trouble. Always. Never fails. He just winds people up. Don't ask me how he does it. I don't know whether he even tries. Maybe he doesn't know he's doing it. Maybe it just happens. He's got that kind of way with him . . . Know what I mean, like?'

'What kind of people?'

'Everyone. Even the people here.'

'He worked *here*? Finch?'

'Yeah. Only three days, mind, but that's the point, see? People weren't nasty to him, nor nothing. No one shouted at him, not to begin with. It's just the way he is – gets on yer nerves, gets on everyone's nerves.'

'When was this?' Sullivan's pocketbook was open again.

'A month ago? I dunno, can't remember. But like I said, he just came and went. I hadn't seen him for a while, that's why we had them couple of beers a couple of weeks back, the night the Old Bill stopped me.'

Winter was juggling dates. The early spring sale had started on Saturday. When was the stuff ordered?

'A month back.'

'Was Finch involved?'

'Yeah, me and him was working in the warehouse, we both were. We had to draw up the stock lists, like, but Brad couldn't handle it.'

'Why not?'

'He can't write. Not proper. Never learned how. No problem blagging his way into the job cos he's got a real mouth on him but he was out of the door by Wednesday.'

Sullivan wanted to know more about Brad's mates.

'He never had no mates, that was half his problem. Plenty of cunts ready to take a drink off of him, nights when he was carrying, but no one you'd call a mate.'

'No names? No blokes he mentioned at all?'

'No.'

'Did you get the impression he was keeping heavy company?'

'Haven't a clue, mate.'

'You're sure about that?'

'Definitely.' Winter paused. Sullivan took up the running.

'Girlfriends?'

'Only one he talked about. Black chick. Never had the pleasure, me, but he was crazy about her.'

'Had they got it on?'

'He said yes. Non-stop.'

'Did you believe him?'

Marchant paused again, weighing the question. A staff break had begun now and a succession of girls in matching blue Brennan's smocks were queueing for the Coke machine.

'No,' Marchant said at last. 'If you want it straight, I don't think he stood a prayer with anyone.'

Faraday parked his Mondeo beside the Square Tower and limped slowly up the High Street. The rain had cleared overnight and thin sunlight bathed the soft grey stones of the cathedral. Leaving the office, given Cathy Lamb's current mood, was an act of some bravery but Faraday was beyond bitter asides about impossible workloads and part-time bosses. He didn't even care that J-J had failed to show up at Highland Road. Just to feel the sun on his face was enough.

He paused on the pavement, looking up. He'd always liked this cathedral. A recent appeal had extended the nave towards the west but the building itself and the surrounding close still had a scale altogether in keeping with Portsmouth's standing in the world. While it might lack the grand Gothic gestures of the calendar cathedrals – towering spires, flying buttresses – it had a certain down-home charm Faraday always found immensely attractive. It didn't keep you at arm's length. It wasn't stately and slightly intimidating, the way Salisbury and Lincoln could be. On the contrary, it seemed to beckon you in, offering the most domestic of welcomes. The cathedral, like the city itself, was a mongrel, growing like Topsy as the years drifted by. In the grander order of things, it always knew its place.

Phillimore's house lay further up the High Street, between the cathedral and the neat little cul-de-sac where Jane Bassam lived. There was a poster for an anti-mines charity in one window and a big glass crystal suspended in the other. Beside the crystal, enjoying the sunshine, was a slender Siamese cat.

Phillimore opened the door to Faraday's knock. He looked early middle-aged, forty at the most. He was wearing a T-shirt and a pair of baggy jeans. He had a runner's build, slight, but it was the face that drew you in. He had a face made for laughter and the sparkle in his eyes offered immediate, unconditional friendship. This was a man who'd show you the brighter side of everything. No wonder Jane Bassam had sought the Lord within these walls.

Faraday introduced himself. Phillimore's handshake was warm. He was grateful that Faraday had found the time to pop down and he hoped his journey wouldn't be wasted.

The house smelled of joss sticks. The framed colour shots in the hall looked African, and there were more as the stairs wound upwards. Hundreds of families camped out on an abandoned railway station. Old men bent under bundles of firewood. A legless child peering up from a hospital bed.

'Angola,' Phillimore murmured. ''Ninety-eight.'

The sitting room was up on the first floor, a small, warm, intimate space with a threadbare oriental carpet and postcards pinned to the cluttered bookshelves. A piano had somehow found space for itself against the back wall and a cushioned seat in the tiny bay window was littered with copies of the *New Statesman* and *Private Eye*. Two more cats sprawled in front of the hissing gas fire and Faraday was reminded irresistibly of a weekend course he'd once attended at one of the older Oxford colleges. If you needed a glimpse of a peace the world had left behind then this was surely it.

'There's coffee if you'd like one.'

Faraday said yes, scanning the bookshelves while Phillimore disappeared downstairs again. Albert Camus and J.D. Salinger. The *Rough Guide to Venice*. A handful of African poets. Phillimore returned with two Oxfam mugs. The coffee was a freshly brewed bitter roast, a world away from the swill at Southsea nick. It came, said Phillimore, from a cooperative in Brighton, imported straight from a people's plantation in Jamaica. He had a leaflet with the details and insisted Faraday take it.

'Spread the word,' he said. 'Please.'

Faraday folded the leaflet into his jacket. What, exactly, did Phillimore want to discuss?

'Good point.' He cleared a space amongst the magazines and settled himself in the window. 'It's about Jane Bassam.'

He wanted to be frank with Faraday because there was no point wasting his time. He'd first met Jane through the parish choir. He sang with the tenors. She was an alto. They'd shared the odd conversation after choir practice on Friday nights and bumped into each other at various social functions. Then, to her very evident distress, her marriage had begun to collapse.

Faraday stirred. He didn't feel altogether comfortable with this kind of candour.

'Does Mrs Bassam know—?'

Phillimore held up his hands, anticipating the question.

'We've discussed it at length, Mr Faraday. In fact it's Jane's idea that

I talk to you. I'm an outsider. That's the beauty of the church. It's easier for people like me.'

Outsider? Faraday wanted to ask.

'Go on,' he said instead.

One of the cats stretched, yawned and stalked across the carpet towards the window. Curled up on Phillimore's lap, it began to wash itself.

'Jane was going through a very tough time. We talked, of course, and I did what I could to comfort her.'

Faraday nodded. Duty of care, he thought. He ought to throw a little party of his own and introduce this man to Hartigan.

'What about her daughter? Helen?'

'I'm afraid that's the point.'

'Afraid?'

'Yes. Helen was in the choir, too. In fact she'd been in the choir for some time, way before I joined the chapter. Good voice, nice kid.'

'And?'

'She . . .' he frowned, treading carefully now. '. . . got the wrong idea. She thought – assumed – we were having some kind of affair. And I must say she wasn't the only one. Cathedrals are strange institutions, Mr Faraday. I don't know how familiar you are with church politics but it can sometimes be just a touch claustrophobic. We watch each other like hawks. And we don't always draw the right conclusions.'

Faraday knew absolutely nothing about church politics but experience had taught him that one organisation was very much like another. Gossip came with the territory, whether you were a policeman or a cleric.

'There were rumours?'

'Yes, and Helen picked them up.'

'Were they true?'

'No.' The smile again, total candour. 'They weren't. Jane and I were very good friends. We're still close. We even went away together; took a little trip up to Bath only yesterday.'

Faraday remembered the suitcase in Jane Bassam's hall and the sudden transformation in her attitude. Was comfort and conversation really enough to put a smile like that on her face?

'Friends?' Faraday queried.

'You sound disappointed.'

'Not at all. Adultery isn't a crime, by the way, and I'm not in the business of passing judgement. But I'm still not sure where all this leads. You're a priest. You offer comfort. But why phone me about it?'

'Because Helen Bassam was an extremely disturbed young woman.'

'She came to you too?'

'Yes. At first she was angry. With me. It was way before Christmas. She sat here in this room and wanted to know exactly what was going on. No, that's not quite true. She'd already made up her mind what was going on and she wanted to know why, what right I'd got to smash her parents' marriage up.'

'She said that?'

'Oh, yes. Her father had gone by then and I was the one who'd driven him out. Ironic, really, given the circumstances.'

'What did you say to her?'

'I told her the truth. I told her that marriages are seldom made in heaven and that her father had found a new partner. She knew that, of course, but she was having problems with the . . . ah . . . chronology. She was putting the cart before the horse, and in this instance I was the cart. The whole sad episode was down to me, my fault.'

Faraday was thinking of the Afghan, Niamat Tabibi. Helen must have unloaded on him, too. No wonder he'd pointed Faraday in Phillimore's direction.

'She believed you?'

'In the end she did, yes. But you have to be careful in these situations, Mr Faraday. Girls like Helen can be very unpredictable. Fourteen's a very tricky age.'

'What are you telling me?'

'Anger, hate . . . Emotions like that can turn to something else. It can happen very quickly.'

Faraday stared at him, suddenly realising where this conversation was going. N for Niamat. N for Nigel.

'She got a crush on you?'

'Yes, I'm afraid she did.'

'A serious crush?'

'Yes, oh yes.'

She'd been round at the house all hours. Her mother had a key and she'd taken a copy, letting herself in, preparing little treats in the kitchen, having the kettle on for when Phillimore got home.

'Playing the wife?'

'More the mistress. She began to turn up in clothes that were . . .' he frowned '. . . inappropriate to say the least.'

'How do you mean?'

'I mean revealing. She was sending me a message. I'd have been blind not to have received it.'

'And how did that make you feel?'

'Concerned, if you want the truth. Helen wanted to be part of my life and she only knew one way to make that happen. The Church of England has become very cautious, Mr Faraday. Helen was still a child and when I tell you that there are rules that govern our behaviour, I mean just that. Take the choir. If I'm alone with a choirboy – or girl – I have to keep the door open. If I want to pat them on the back, encourage them, congratulate them, it has to be between here and here.' He touched his shoulder blade and the top of his arm. 'I know it sounds absurd but that's the way it is.'

'To protect the kids?'

'No, to protect us. We've allowed ourselves to become caged, Mr Faraday, and it's a very great shame. Physical contact is where comfort begins. Believe me, it's difficult to reach out when you're not allowed to touch.'

Faraday was still thinking about Helen.

'So how hard did she push all this?'

'Very hard. And when I said no, it simply added insult to all her other problems.'

'No to what?'

'No to going to bed. No to making love. No to giving her what she thought she wanted.'

'And what was that?'

'A baby.'

Faraday reached down for his cup. *Pour vous*, he thought. The coffee was cold.

'You knew she was pregnant?' he asked at last.

'Yes. Her mother told me a couple of days ago. That's why I thought it important we meet.'

'And what did Mrs Bassam make of all this?'

'All what?'

'You and Helen. Her daughter behaving like this.'

'It was extremely difficult. As I explained, Jane and I were close but the truth is that Helen came between us.'

'She thought you were . . .?' Faraday didn't know how to end the sentence.

'Screwing her daughter? Yes, she did. Which made life in that little house even more hellish. In fact Jane even went to the Dean about it.'

'The Dean?'

'My boss. He'd heard the rumours of course but there's a natural reluctance to believe something like that until the need becomes truly pressing. We had an exchange of views.'

'And?'

'He believed me but thought I was being foolish. Reckless is the word he used. He thought I should put the Church before Helen, and indeed before Jane. I disagreed. In my view, God comes first.'

'They're the same, aren't they? God and the Church?'

'Not necessarily, Mr Faraday.' The smile had returned. 'Sadly, there can sometimes be a difference.'

He lifted the cat from his lap and offered it to Faraday. There was more coffee in the pot downstairs. Faraday took the cat and let it settle, wondering what else was to come. He wasn't altogether convinced by Phillimore's account but if the bit about the Dean was true, the man certainly had a mind of his own. To take Jane Bassam away for the night after a scandal like this was an act of some courage.

From the kitchen there was the trill of a phone, then the mutter of conversation as Phillimore answered it. Moments later, he was back upstairs again, empty-handed.

'That was Jane, I'm afraid. In a bit of a state.'

Chapter twenty-three

Winter thought nothing of the envelope waiting for him at Fratton nick. It was A4, manila, with something hard and oblong inside, a book maybe. It had been hand-delivered after lunch and one of the counter clerks had brought it up to the MIR.

It turned out to be a VHS cassette. There was a play machine in the big office at the far end of the corridor and Winter made himself a tea before slipping the tape in. At once he recognised the setting: the damp stains on the wallpaper beside the door, the pulled curtains that didn't quite meet in the middle, the thin strip of daylight in between. Kenny Foster, he thought. Another mauling.

He checked the envelope again. Blue biro. Clumsy capitals. 'MR DETECTIVE WINTER'. Like he was trying to take the piss. He turned back to the video. Foster had appeared on screen in his trademark jeans and singlet. He must have a whole drawer of singlets, Winter thought. He must buy them by the dozen, one per fight. The camera edged the other man into view. He was huge – six two, six three. The cropped bullet-shaped head was too small for his shoulders and he stood absolutely still, staring Kenny Foster out. He wore black, paint-stained tracksuit bottoms and an enormous pair of scuffed trainers, and his arms hung down beside his body, his fists already bunched

Foster was kneeling on the carpet, massaging his heel. His feet were bare and Winter caught sight of a blue dagger tattoo stabbing at his ankle. For once he'd abandoned the twist of red that tidied his ponytail in favour of green. He got to his feet, did a couple of lazy stretches, and then winked at the camera. Winter watched, fascinated. The last person you'd want to be just now was the big man with the tiny head.

The fight began. Foster circled his opponent the way a plasterer might check out a dodgy wall, wondering which bit to start on first, but the other guy wasn't going to be so easily psyched out. Instead he simply adjusted his balance, lumbering sideways on those huge feet, watching Foster's every move. Foster stopped. Abruptly, his fists went down. He started to laugh. Then he extended a hand. Confused, the huge man went to shake it, assuming this formed part of the opening ritual, but the moment he relaxed Foster was inside – short, vicious jabs to the body, then a neat uppercut that was only inches wide. The other man gasped with pain. Already you could see the panic in his eyes. Foster took half a step backwards, then drove his head into the man's face. His hands went up, then down again as Foster slammed punch after punch into the soft flesh beneath his ribcage. The liver, thought Winter. Always the liver.

The big guy was on his knees now, blood pouring from his broken nose. Foster took another step backwards, giving himself space, then half turned his body and karate-kicked the crimson face with his heel. The blow jerked the tiny head back and Winter watched the blood splatter on the wallpaper behind. The scream from the video brought a couple of DCs in from the office across the corridor, then a couple more. They gathered round the set, kids watching a fight in the playground, enthralled as Foster hauled his opponent back up onto his knees before driving another flurry of punches into the wreckage that had once been his face. By now, the big man looked like something out of an abattoir – raw meat – and seconds later he was sprawled across the carpet, plainly unconscious.

Foster studied his knuckles a moment, stirred the inert body with his foot, then peeled off his singlet. Down on one knee, he used the singlet to mop the blood from his victim's face. Then he was on his feet again, four-square in front of the camera. He held up the singlet, then pointed a finger at the lens. The gesture was all too obvious and Winter felt the stir of bodies around him. You, Foster was saying. You next.

Sullivan had joined the group. Winter stopped the video and put the machine into rewind. Everyone else was waiting for a reaction. Winter ejected the cassette and slipped it back into the envelope. Then he caught Sullivan's eye.

'Foster give you his home address?' Sullivan was staring at him.

'No,' he said, 'but Dave Michaels has got it.'

Faraday didn't wait for Hartigan's management assistant to ring through to the inner office. Twenty-three years in the job, and he'd seldom felt so angry. He stepped through the half-open door and pushed it shut behind him. Hartigan was behind his desk, signing a pile of letters.

'Jane Bassam's got *News* journalists crawling all over her,' Faraday said. 'They've phoned three times so far and now they're threatening to send a photographer.'

'I'm pleased to hear it.' Hartigan barely spared Faraday a glance.

'Did you have a hand in this, sir? Was it your idea?'

'Of course it wasn't. As I understand it, they're already taking an interest in Mrs Bassam. Something to do with her teaching days. I've simply added a note to the file. Informally, of course. Editor level.'

Faraday gazed at him, astonished at his recklessness. The Coroner had yet to hold an inquest. Leaking any information before the official verdict on the girl's death was courting prosecution.

Hartigan, carefully laying his pen to one side, wouldn't have it. He insisted he held no candle for the press, far from it, but there were important public issues at stake and he wasn't about to ignore them.

'I don't know about you, Joe, but I refuse to sit on my hands while all this stuff is going on. We have responsibilities here. We have to draw a line. I simply will not tolerate fourteen-year-olds getting off their heads on heroin. Not on my patch.'

'Can you prove that? About the heroin?'

'As a matter of fact I can.'

'How?'

'By talking to the pathologist.'

'And have you done that?'

'Of course I have. Do you seriously think we'd be having this conversation otherwise?'

'And what did he say? The pathologist?'

'He agreed with me that there was nothing to rule out heroin.'

'He agreed with you? What does that mean? I talked to the man this morning. What he said was that it *could* be heroin. Not a definite. Not for certain. Not one hundred per cent. A maybe. You've turned it round. Not only that but you've made him party to this pantomime.'

'Joe, I—'

'No, sir. Listen to me. The girl's mother is quite adamant that she wasn't doing hard drugs. She'd have noticed. She'd have seen the symptoms. And I agree with her.'

'Joe, that's a supposition, nothing more. These things are notoriously tricky.'

'Are they?' Faraday paused for a second, then took a deep breath. 'OK, let's say it was heroin. Let's say it was smack off the street, stuff she scored from some two-bit dealer. Where were the traces of all the other rubbish they cut it with? Or are we talking pure here?'

Hartigan hadn't moved. His mouth had tightened into the thinnest of lines.

'I happen to have been back to one of the drugs DCs in the CIMU, and since you've asked the question, let me share their intelligence with you. Number one, heroin's never been so cheap in this city. Number two, it's never been so pure. If those aren't good reasons to run the flag up the pole, perhaps you'd be good enough to tell me why. This is never an easy job, Joe, far from it. But I must say life would be a great deal simpler if I felt you had our collective interests at heart.'

This was tosh and Faraday knew it. 'Collective interests' was one of those management phrases that Hartigan put so much trust in. He had dozens of them stored away, bits of glue to stick all those self-important memos together.

'We still can't be certain the girl was doing smack,' Faraday insisted. 'And it's irresponsible to think otherwise.'

'Is it?' Hartigan offered him a cold smile. 'You'll know that Jane Bassam's ex-husband has a different opinion.'

'Bassam's got a serious guilt problem, as well he might.'

'That's another supposition. I don't think it helps progress this debate a single inch.'

Progress this debate?

'There are lives on the line here, sir.'

'I couldn't agree more, Joe. And there might be lots more Helen Bassams.'

'I'm talking about her mother.'

'I know you are, and for the record I want you to know that I find this whole business deeply, deeply repugnant. I hate the bloody press as much as you do but under the circumstances I think you'll agree they do have their uses. Of course the mother is going to be upset. What mum wouldn't be? But it's means and ends, Joe. And in my judgement, the greater good is served by addressing the largest possible audience.'

'And that's that?'

'I'm afraid so.'

Faraday nodded. He'd taken this exchange as far as he could and there was no point in pressing it any further. The greater good, in Faraday's opinion, had more to do with Hartigan's career prospects than ridding the streets of heroin but the drugs and public awareness issue was increasingly the currency of advancement.

Faraday thought of Brian Imber that night in the restaurant when a couple of pints of Kingfisher had swamped his inhibitions. The day that Hartigan stood up for legalisation and lobbied for a major push against the big dealers was the day Faraday would believe he had a real commitment. For now, he was simply playing to the gallery.

Hartigan was watching him carefully. Whatever his other failings, the man had an acute appreciation of body language.

'Are you with me, Joe? Or must we go through this whole tiresome business again?'

Faraday shrugged. The last thing he was going to give Hartigan was the satisfaction of an apology.

'I have to say I think you're wrong, sir,' he said stiffly. 'Our enquiries are still ongoing. As the Coroner's Officer well knows.'

'And what does that mean?'

'It means I'll keep you briefed.' He pushed back the chair and stood up. 'Depend on it.'

Kenny Foster lived in a basement flat in St Andrew's Road, a stretch of tall Victorian villas that ran north from the bars and one-stop convenience stores of Southsea's Elm Grove. Sullivan parked the Escort and shot Winter a look.

'I'm coming in with you.'

Winter shook his head.

'No chance,' he said.

He got out of the car without another word, then paused at the kerbside, extracting the video cassette from the envelope.

'Hang on to this, son,' he said. 'Might come in handy.'

Sullivan took the envelope and said again that Winter was potty to confront Foster single-handed.

'Confront?' Winter said mildly. 'This is about manners, son, not all that macho crap.'

Foster must have seen him coming. The moment Winter started picking his way down the mildewed steps towards the basement, the front door opened. Foster was wearing a purple dressing gown and not much else. He held the door open and gestured Winter to step inside. The flat was freezing. Someone had just burned the toast and there was an overpowering smell of damp. Nothing in the dark little front room matched the pictures on the videos.

'Where do you fight then?'

'Somewhere else, pal. You'd know it if you saw it.'

Winter became aware of a woman's voice calling from the room next door. She wanted to know who'd just come in.

'Friend o'mine,' Foster yelled. 'Called round for a wee chat.' Winter was studying a poster of Robert de Niro taped to the wall over the mantelpiece.

'Doesn't sound like Simone,' he said.

'That's because it isn't.'

'Not the bird the fat guy you just flattened was shafting, surely?' He turned to face Foster. 'Guys like you kill me. You're like dogs, aren't you? Got to leave your smell everywhere. Can't pass a lamp post without pissing on it.' Winter produced the video from his coat pocket. 'So what's all this bollocks got to do with me?'

'Just thought you might fancy it, pal. Change from *Antiques Roadshow*.'

'Not trying to send another message, were you?'

'Another message?' Foster scratched his head. 'Now why would I want to do that?'

'Fuck knows. Here. Have it back.'

He tossed it across the room, chest height. When Foster caught it, Winter smiled.

'Left-handed, are we? Southpaw?'

'Aye.'

'And you write left-handed? The envelope that crap came in?' Winter stepped closer. 'You want to be fucking careful, my son, and you know why? Because my guvnor hates leaving jobs unfinished. Me? I'm old school, too. Which means I'm only too happy to agree with him.'

For a moment, watching Foster's face, Winter thought he'd pushed it too far. There was madness in this man, an unpredictability that expressed itself in a thousand little ways. He needed to be top dog, every waking second of the day, and he wasn't interested in compromise. He eyed Winter for a moment or two, baleful, malevolent, then stepped past him and left the room without a word. Seconds later he was back. He was carrying something in his hand, a garment of some kind, and as he shook it out and held it up, Winter recognised the bloodstained singlet from the video.

'Dried out nicely, pal. Thought you might like it.'

He tossed the singlet across. Winter let it fall to the floor, not taking his eyes off Foster's face.

'In my business,' he smiled, 'we call that standard MO. You want to be careful, Kenny, and you know why? You're doing what all crap villains do in this city. You're beginning to repeat yourself.'

Faraday stood outside Chuzzlewit House, peering up. Sunshine made all the difference. The last time he'd paced this little square of pavement, the rain had been swirling around the gaunt, twenty-three-storey block. Now the low February sunlight lanced off the windows, a line of dazzling reflections climbing into the blueness of the afternoon sky.

Start all over again. Assume nothing.

He rang the caretaker's button on the entryphone at the main door and asked her to let him in. When he stepped through, she was waiting for him outside the lifts. He wanted to know whether Grace Randall was up to receiving visitors, and had to be reminded of the number of her flat.

'131. Afternoons, she normally takes a little nap. I've got a key if you need to get in.'

She fetched a Yale from the office and offered to accompany him up to Mrs Randall's. Faraday thanked her but said no.

He took the lift to the twenty-third floor. When the old lady didn't respond to his second knock, he used the key to let himself into the flat. The smell hit him at once, the same sickly mix of almonds and bleach. He stood in the hall for a moment, looking into her bedroom. She was propped up against the pillows in the little single bed, one thin hand cupping the clear plastic mask that fed oxygen to her bubbling lungs. Discarded magazines lapped against her chest and she appeared to be asleep. Faraday crept on down the hall and into the living room. The flat faced south and the view from the window, sunlit this time, took his breath away.

He lingered a moment, watching one of the big Brittany ferries pushing out through the deep water channel. The white of the hull against the blue of the sea belonged on a postcard. He stayed by the window a minute or two longer, waiting for the perfect V of the ferry's wake to curl against the beach, then retreated to the kitchen.

Assume nothing. Start all over again.

He opened the fridge, not knowing quite what he was looking for. A carton of milk and an open packet of Cheddar. Six eggs and a curling slice of corned beef lying on a plate. Apart from that, nothing. The cupboards above were full of crockery and there was a glass jar stuffed with tea bags beside the electric kettle. Only when he was standing by the sink did he think to sort through the rubbish.

There was a small swing bin in the corner near the door. An empty tin of mackerel was dripping oil on a twist of newspaper, and when he unwrapped the newspaper it was full of potato peelings. He took his jacket off and dug deeper. Eggshells and the stalky bits from a cauliflower. Then, at the very bottom, he found a small white box. There was a pharmacy label on the side and he pulled the box out for a closer look. Beneath Grace Randall's name, a neat line of type described the tablets inside. 'Morphine Sulphate' it read. 'One tablet every 12 hours, as required.'

Assume nothing.

Faraday used kitchen roll to wipe the oil from the box, then carried it through to the bedroom. Asleep or otherwise, there was a conversation to be had here. At the open bedroom door, he paused. Grace Randall was awake by now and didn't seem the least surprised to find a stranger in her flat.

'DI Faraday. We met last week.'

'We did?' One thin hand shadowed her eyes, as if she were peering into a bright light. 'How pleasant. Have you been here long?'

Faraday explained about the caretaker's key. He was a policeman, a detective. He'd come up last week about Helen Bassam and he was back to ask more questions.

'It's the kids,' she murmured.

'What is, Mrs Randall?'

'They play with the phone thing. From outside.' She gestured limply towards the door.

'I'll see what I can do.' Faraday made a mental note. 'Tell me about young Helen. Tell me what you remember.'

'Helen? Lovely girl.' The voice had sunk to a whisper. 'She would have made someone very happy.'

'You wouldn't know who, by any chance?'

'What, dear?'

'You wouldn't know who she was keen on? Who she was seeing? Did you ever talk about these things?'

Grace put a hand to her mouth and smothered a cough. The slightest movement seemed to exhaust her. She pulled the bed sheet up around her chest, composing herself.

'It's so difficult, isn't it?' she said. 'We were all that age once. Me, I was a scallywag. I suppose that's why we got on so well.'

'You and Helen?'

'Of course. I had so much to tell her.' She nodded, closing her eyes.

For a moment Faraday thought she'd gone to sleep again. Then she sighed.

'I told her once about a love affair I had. Older men can be good for a girl. I honestly believe that.'

'She was having a love affair?'

'So she said.'

'With an older man?'

'I imagine so.' She smiled up at Faraday. 'It's names, isn't it? Always the first to go at my age.'

'She gave you a name?'

'I can't remember. Might it be important?'

It was a good question. Faraday said he didn't know. He showed her the box of tablets.

'Are these yours by any chance?' He read out the label. Morphine sulphate.

Grace fumbled for her glasses.

'Yes,' she said at last. 'MST.'

'And you take them regularly?'

'I'm afraid I have to.' She patted her chest and took a couple of deep breaths. 'They're painkillers. The best. The pain just goes.' She waved her hand. 'Just like that.'

The pain just goes.

Faraday was thinking about the Thursday night: Helen up here in the flat, another crisis, another rejection, yet another brick wall on the road leading nowhere. Last time Grace Randall had offered him a sherry. Maybe it was just a formality, a social reflex she'd never quite thrown off.

He settled himself on the end of her bed. *Assume nothing.*

'Do you keep alcohol here, by any chance?'

'You want a drink, dear?'

'Yes, please.'

'In the lounge. Next to the television.'

It looked like the kind of cabinet you might keep glasses in. Faraday opened it. Two bottles of sherry, one half empty. Another of Martini. And a quarter bottle of Scotch. Quite enough to take you up the stairs to the roof. Add twenty mgs of morphine sulphate, scale the retaining wall, have another think about that shitty, shitty life of yours, and gravity would do the rest.

Faraday heard a wheezing noise in the hall, then a 'clack-clack' he couldn't quite explain. He closed the cupboard and turned round. Grace Randall was standing by the open door anchored to a Zimmer frame.

It took her a while to catch her breath. Finally she gestured towards the cabinet. 'You found what you wanted?'

Faraday nodded. He'd sorted out a card with his direct line at Southsea police station, and now he laid it carefully on the cabinet.

'My number,' he said, 'in case the kids come back.'

Winter shared his news with Dave Michaels. Willard was up in Winchester attending a lecture from a DI on the anti-terrorist squad.

'Foster's left-handed,' he repeated, 'just like the bloke who tied the knot.'

'What knot?'

'The knot on the rope. Finch's knot.'

'Gotcha.' Dave Michaels nodded. 'And?'

'Has to be him. Has to be.'

'Because he's left-handed?'

'Yeah, and because he's a vicious, sadistic bastard who gets off on hurting other people. We're talking serious head case here, skip. I'm telling you, the guy's a psychopath. Not only that, he's got a fucking God complex. He's the man and he wants the whole world to know it.

That's why Finch looked the way he did, poor little bugger. That's why he was strung up the way he was. Foster might as well have written us a letter. It's that fucking obvious.'

'Evidence?' Michaels asked drily.

'It'll come. He'll make a mistake because he's not as bright as he thinks he is. I just hope it happens in time. Before he does it again.'

'Yeah?' Michaels grinned, pulling a sheet of paper towards him. 'Well, I might have some good news for you.'

'What's that?'

'You know the girl? The black girl? Louise?' Winter nodded. 'She's been in touch with one of the students in the house. She wants him to bring some gear up, clothes mainly.'

'Up where?'

'Waterloo. Tomorrow morning, eleven-thirty by the Burger King. She's sending him fifty quid for the trip. He's over the moon.'

Winter thought hard for a moment. The fact that the girl seemed to be in one piece was good news. But why the elaborate arrangements?

'Apparently she's not keen to come back down here. Ever.' Dave Michaels grinned. 'Hard to believe, eh?'

Faraday treated himself to two pints in the pub across from the cathedral before walking the hundred yards to Nigel Phillimore's house. His ankle, like his head, felt infinitely better and he was gladdened by the sight of a light in Phillimore's upstairs window.

Phillimore opened the door. This morning he'd been wearing a T-shirt and jeans. Now he was clad in a cassock.

'Detective Inspector,' he murmured. 'What a surprise.'

Faraday followed him upstairs. Phillimore said he was lucky to catch him in. Evensong had only just finished and he'd normally be at his desk in Cathedral House, catching up with paperwork.

'You've got a moment?' Faraday found himself looking at the photographs again.

'I've got all evening. Sit down. Make yourself at home.'

Phillimore went downstairs again and returned with a bottle of wine and two glasses.

'Red OK? It's only Sainsbury's, I'm afraid.'

Faraday smiled. Whatever else Angola taught you, this man certainly knew how to put visitors at their ease.

He sat down in the window seat while Phillimore uncorked the wine. The last couple of hours, he'd been haunted by something Grace Randall had said. *Older men can be good for a girl.* Was this an old woman's fantasy? A phrase plucked from her own life? Or had Helen Bassam sat down and poured her young heart out?

'There are aspects of Helen's death we still find . . . ah . . . troubling,' Faraday began.

'I'm sure.' Phillimore passed him a glass of wine.

'One of them has to do with drugs.'

'You mean heavy drugs?'

'I mean heroin.'

Phillimore raised an eyebrow.

'Not much surprises me about Helen,' he said at length, 'but that does. I'm sure she dabbled; most kids seem to these days. But heroin?' He shook his head. 'Frankly, that would be a bit out of her league.'

'How can you be sure?'

'I can't. Of course I can't. Kids keep secrets like everyone else. But heroin's something she would have mentioned, I'm sure of it. She shared every other trauma in her life.'

'Maybe she'd have been ashamed?'

'You might be right. But it would have showed. I was in São Paulo for a while. I saw a lot of heroin in the *favelas*. If you've got a serious habit, it's not something you can keep to yourself.'

'Then maybe she was experimenting.'

Faraday explained about the tox results from the post-mortem. The presence of morphine in her bloodstream had opened up another line of enquiry. Somehow or other, it had to be explained.

'I'm sure.' Phillimore was smiling at him. 'It must be strange, putting together someone's life after they've gone.'

Faraday thought about the proposition. 'But don't you do that?' he said at last. 'Officiating at funerals? Talking about someone you've never met?'

'We do, you're right. But we're looking to celebrate, not to blame. I suspect there's a difference.'

Faraday acknowledged the point with a wry nod. The sunshine, he thought. Not the shadows.

'Did Helen ever mention a Mrs Randall at all?'

'An old lady? Up in one of those tower blocks?'

'That's it.'

'Yes, she did. She had a friend called Trudy. Mrs Randall was a relative of some kind. As far as I could make out, they used her flat as a kind of den.'

'They went there a lot?'

'Yes. Helen thought the world of her. Home from home was the phrase she used.'

'Rather like here?'

'Hardly. Helen came here because she was looking for something that didn't – couldn't – exist. She went to Mrs Randall's because it was warm and comfy. Both of us answered a need, I suppose. But in Mrs Randall's case it was rather less complex.'

Older men can be good for a girl.

'Helen talked to Mrs Randall a lot . . .' Faraday began.

'Indeed.'

'About all kinds of things. Including her love life. Mrs Randall got the impression that she was seeing an older man.'

'She was. She was seeing me.'

'But more than that.'

The smile again, but fainter this time.

'What exactly are you suggesting, Mr Faraday?'

'I'm not suggesting anything. We have a set of events here. A young girl is found dead at the bottom of a block of flats. She has a history of disturbance. Her family has fallen apart, her relationship with her mother is in tatters. She has traces of morphine in her bloodstream, and alcohol too. She's extremely upset. She's extremely vulnerable. And then we discover she's pregnant. Like I say, a set of events.'

'You think there's an issue of blame here?'

'I think there may be an issue of culpability, yes.'

'Whose? Her father for leaving her? Her mother for having her in the first place? Mrs Randall for happening to have the key to the roof?'

The phrase stopped Faraday in his tracks.

'You know about the key?'

'Of course. She told me.'

'Why? Why did she tell you?'

'Because she'd threatened to do this before.'

'Throw herself off the roof?'

'Indeed. You could accuse Helen of a multitude of sins, Mr Faraday, but holding back wouldn't be one of them. That's why I don't think she was using heroin. She'd have told me.'

'So what did you do? When she threatened to kill herself?'

'I told her that we all have a responsibility, for ourselves and for each other. I also told her that life is a gift, something precious, not to be thrown away.'

'Did she understand?'

'Yes, I think she did. Did it make any difference? No, it plainly didn't.'

'And did you share this . . . knowledge . . . with anyone else? Her mother, for instance?'

'Jane was in a worse state than Helen. One of the few positive ways I could help was by *not* telling her.'

'Social Services? Some kind of counsellor?'

The suggestion brought the smile back.

'I'm a priest, Mr Faraday. I'm a counsellor in a black frock and a funny collar. That's my mission, my calling. That's what I do.'

'But in this case you're involved, heavily involved. Doesn't that make it awkward?'

'Extremely. As the Dean was kind enough to point out.'

Faraday nodded. In the ongoing grind of criminal investigation, it was rare to have a conversation like this. So many tracks to pursue. So many unanswered questions.

He put the wine to one side for a moment.

'Were you the father of her child?'

'No.'

'Do you know who was?'

'I could give you a list of names but I won't.'

'Was one of them an Afghan? A man called Niamat Tabibi?'

'No. They were all Helen's age.'

'And she told you about them?'

'In great and glorious detail, Mr Faraday. It was part of the game she was playing. She wanted me to know there were others. She wanted me to know she was wanted. Whether or not all of it was true I have no idea, but if you're serious about looking for a father then one of those names would be the lad you were after. She was truly desperate. She'd do anything to send a message.'

'To you?'

'To me. To Niamat. To her father. To whoever would spare the time to listen. The message got through, of course. But I expect all the pathologist had was a form.'

Faraday gazed at him, then folded his pocketbook and put it to one side. He believed every word this man was saying.

'There's another child we're trying to find. Younger.'

Phillimore nodded.

'Doodie. Jane said you'd mentioned him.'

'You know Doodie?'

'Very well. Helen brought him round.'

'Here?'

'Indeed. He's been staying, off and on. I have a couple of spare rooms upstairs. Under the circumstances, it's the least I can do.'

Faraday gazed at him, and then began to laugh. Six days of looking high and low, six days of phone calls and Misper registers, circulating the name and description to every beat car in the city. And here was young Doodie, tucked up with a priest.

'*Staying* here? Was that wise? Given you and the . . .' he shrugged '. . . Dean?'

'Wise is an interesting word, Mr Faraday. And so is sanctuary.'

'Is that what you were offering?'

'Indeed. Plus food and shelter. Or maybe they're the same thing.'

'So where is he? Doodie?'

'I've no idea. He was here a couple of nights back. He comes and goes. It's an informal arrangement.'

'He has a key?'

'Of course.'

'And you talk to him?'

'As much as I can.'

'Has he mentioned Helen at all? Thursday night? The night she died?'

'Not really. I asked him about it, of course I did, but he just changes the subject.'

'Were they together that night?'

'He says not.'

'Do you believe him?'

'I don't know. He's a funny lad. He'll talk all the time, tell you anything you think you want to know, but most of it's a smokescreen. If you think Helen was damaged, you ought to meet Doodie.'

'I'd love to,' Faraday said drily. 'Maybe you could arrange it.'

Winter was asleep when the phone beside his bed rang. He rolled over and fumbled for it in the dark. It was Dave Michaels.

'You're gonna love this,' Michaels began. 'We've got a problem with Terry Harris.'

'What's that, then?'

'He's dead.'

Chapter twenty-four

When Dave Michaels made the obvious point – that someone had saved them all a great deal of time and money – Willard finally lost it. It was ten past eight in the morning. Three members of the management team had already soured the atmosphere at the Major Crimes suite by turning up late. Now they all paid the price.

'That is totally out of order,' Willard said softly. 'We're here to put the lid on serious crime. We do that by sorting out decent investigations. What happened to Finch was unacceptable, and so is this. Either we understand that and start behaving like grown-ups or some of us pack it in. Understood?'

Heads nodded around the table. The fire at 62, Aboukir Road had clearly been deliberately set. The neighbours on both sides of the property reported a strong smell of petrol as they evacuated their own properties and a preliminary investigation by the Fire Brigade believed the seat of the blaze lay just inside the front door. Terry Harris, sleeping alone in the upstairs bedroom, had made it as far as the landing before being overcome by smoke. By the time the rescue crew fought their way through the blaze, he was dead.

'What about his wife and the nipper?'

It was the DI in charge of forensics. Willard looked to Dave Michaels for an answer.

'They never went back after the hotel, sir. She's moved in with her mum-in-law in Paulsgrove.'

'You mean Harris's mum?'

'Yes, sir. Apparently they're very close. It's her husband she can't stand.'

'Who told you that?'

'Dawn Ellis. It's not statemented but she talked to the woman at the Travel Inn and she's put two and two together.'

Willard nodded and scribbled himself a note. Then he looked up again.

'So what time did all this happen?'

'The treble nine was logged at 01.13.' It was Sammy Rollins, the Deputy SIO. 'The bloke at number sixty raised the alarm.'

'Anyone see anything before?'

'Not so far. Uniforms are still doing the house-to-house.'

Willard was looking at Brian Imber. He wanted to know about word on the street.

'We've heard nothing, sir. Nothing to suggest anything like this.'

'What about the association chart on Harris? What does that tell us?'

'Not a lot. The obvious suspects would be friends of Finch's but there's a problem there because he hadn't got any friends.'

'What about the lad from Brennan's? The one Winter interviewed?'

'Highly unlikely. He's got no previous and from what Paul's saying, they weren't that close anyway. They had a drink a week or two back but you don't burn someone's house down on the strength of a couple of lagers.'

'The girl? Louise Abeka?'

'I suppose it's possible if they really were an item but it doesn't feel right to me. For starters, she's in London.'

Dave Michaels reminded them that the girl was due down after lunch. He was sending Winter and Sullivan to arrest her at Waterloo.

'I'm with Brian. I just don't think she'd come back down here. Not unless she absolutely had to.'

Willard drew a line through a name on his pad, then looked up.

'So where does that leave us? If we're not talking revenge where do we go next?'

'Pre-emption, boss.' Michaels again. 'Someone who wanted to shut Harris's mouth. I've been talking to Winter about Kenny Foster. He's saying the bloke's off his head. If he wouldn't think twice about putting a rope round Finch's neck, setting fire to Harris would be a stroll in the park.'

'So why would he do it?'

'Dunno. Maybe he's worried about Harris grassing him up. He knows the bloke's nicked for burglary and maybe he thinks he's going to cop a plea. He knows Harris much better than we do and even we think he's a greasy little shithead.'

Willard nodded and scribbled himself a note.

'Anyone talked to Foster yet?'

'First on the list this morning, boss. Yates and Ellis are down at the garage now.'

*

Faraday was reluctant to declare his own son a Misper but by nine o'clock, setting off for work, he was seriously worried. Not only had J-J failed to show at Highland Road yesterday morning but there'd been no sign of him since.

Faraday had got back from Phillimore's at around ten last night. There was still half a slice of cold toast on the kitchen table and J-J's bedroom was the usual shambles but there was no sign of the boy himself. Neither was there a note of any kind. J-J was as disorganised and chaotic as he'd ever been but he was normally careful to let his father know what he was up to. For obvious reasons, Faraday had always kept him on a tight leash, insisting that J-J keep him briefed on his movements, and old habits died hard.

From his desk at Highland Road, he called Anghared Davies. Gordon Franks picked up the phone.

'I'm looking for my son,' Faraday said.

'Join the gang. Where is he?'

Franks had last seen him yesterday afternoon. He had been offered the use of a minibus all day today and J-J had offered to help him out on an expedition to the New Forest. They'd agreed to meet at eight. It was now 9.25.

'I thought he must have overslept. I'd have rung but there's no point, is there? He'd never hear the phone.'

Faraday was thinking about Phillimore, last night.

'This Doodie . . .' he began. 'Is he around at all?'

'Haven't seen him for days.'

'You know J-J was with him in the cinema?'

'The ABC?' Franks's voice quickened. 'When?'

Faraday explained about breaking in on Wednesday. Doodie seemed to have some kind of doss in there, not that he'd be silly enough to use it again.

'You're right. The kid's really cluey. Never makes the same mistake twice.'

'So where is he now? And where's my bloody son?'

'Pass. If I had some ideas you'd be the first to know.' It didn't help that Franks sounded worried.

'You think we've got a problem?'

'I think J-J might have. If he's with Doodie.'

J-J had never been inside a house in Old Portsmouth before. Two decades in the city had given him a working knowledge of Southsea and the eastern suburbs but never this little enclave of cobbled streets and swinging tavern signs, of mullioned windows and thick oak doors.

He settled himself in a chair beside the bookcase, gazing out at the cathedral, wondering vaguely where Doodie had got to. They'd taken a cab from near the ABC where they'd stayed overnight and Doodie had let himself in with his own key. Did this fabulous place, with its shadowed nooks and crannies, belong to a relative? A friend? Some grand species of social worker? J-J simply didn't know.

He sat back, leafing through an old copy of the *National Geographic*. Seconds later, Doodie was at his elbow. He'd found a bottle of wine from somewhere and a corkscrew but he didn't have the strength to pull the cork. J-J gazed at the bottle. It was half past ten in the morning. Did the Persistent Young Offender project stretch to getting pissed this early?

He gave Doodie a look and shook his head, using his fingers to signal the letter 'T'. There was an electric kettle downstairs in the kitchen, he'd seen it, and there'd be milk in the fridge. They could have a cuppa instead. Doodie ignored him, taking his hand and wrapping it round the neck of the bottle. His other hand, at Doodie's insistence, found the corkscrew. Then, suddenly, the boy was gone – only to reappear seconds later with two glasses.

They were crystal, truly beautiful, and J-J watched the boy place them on the small occasional table with infinite care. The gesture, with its elaborate delicacy, made J-J laugh. He knew from Gordon Franks that Doodie couldn't care less about other people's possessions. He'd trash a car, or someone's front garden, as casually as other kids would kick a ball. Yet here he was, auditioning for the part of a waiter in the drama of his dreams.

J-J beamed at him for a moment, then put the bottle between his knees, tightened his grip on the corkscrew and began to pull.

Bev Yates and Dawn Ellis waited nearly an hour before Kenny Foster turned up at his garage. An Aqua cab bumped down the rough path from the main road and Foster stepped out of the back. He was carrying a Jaguar sports bag and stood watching them for the best part of a minute until Yates and Ellis got out of their car.

'You people make me laugh,' he said. 'Deep cover, is it?' Yates looked him up and down. He and Foster had met a couple of times before and on neither occasion had Yates paid the slightest attention to Foster's attempts at intimidation.

'We're cutting to the chase here,' he said briskly, 'because it's fucking cold. Where were you last night?'

'Who wants to know?'

'Who do you think, dickhead? Me.'

'You, pal? And why would that be?'

'I'll tell you in a minute. Just do yourself a favour. Where were you?'

304

'Isle of Wight. Ventnor. Pier Approach Hotel. Room 209. Give them a ring, pal, and ask for a barmaid called Nathalie. Nice French lady. Sweetest fuck imaginable.'

Yates was writing down the details. Then he glanced at his watch. 'You've got a phone number?'

'On the receipt.' Foster put his holdall down and dug in the pocket of his denim jacket. 'Here.'

Yates glanced at the receipt, then nodded at the garage.

'Stick around. I'll be a couple of minutes.'

He returned to the car and phoned the hotel on his mobile. The receptionist had been on first thing this morning and confirmed that Foster had checked out around seven. Asked whether she knew for certain that he'd stayed the night, she started to laugh.

'How's your French?' she said. Yates pocketed the mobile. Foster emerged from the garage.

'You haven't answered my question, pal. Why the questions?'

'Bloke died last night in a house fire.' He looked at Foster. 'Terry Harris?'

'Wee Terry?' Foster whistled softly. 'My, my.'

Waterloo station was busy when Winter and Sullivan stepped off the Portsmouth train. They'd briefed the student to invent a story that kept Louise on the concourse for a couple of minutes. Maybe he should get her to check through the bag, make sure he'd remembered everything. Anything to give them a chance to approach her from the blind side. The last thing they wanted was the aggravation of a chase.

Louise was already waiting outside the Burger King. Sullivan spotted her first. She was wearing the same black puffa jacket but she had a yellow scarf wound round her neck and she'd dug her chin deep into the folds. She looked cold and apprehensive, her hands thrust into the pockets of the jacket, and she stamped her feet from time to time as she searched the crowd for the student's face.

Winter and Sullivan disappeared behind the W. H. Smith bookshop, leaving the student to approach her from the other direction. By the time they arrested her on suspicion of conspiracy to murder, the student was on his hands and knees, the contents of the bag strewn across the concourse.

'Twat,' Winter said.

The student sensibly disappeared. Winter allowed Louise to put a call through to her uncle at the embassy. When she discovered that he'd already left for lunch, she began to cry. The last thing in the world she wanted to do was go back to Portsmouth. Couldn't they talk here?

'Trust us, love.' Winter took the mobile and gave her arm a little squeeze. 'We're detectives.' They took the next train back to Portsmouth.

Mick Harris turned up at Kingston Crescent police station just after one o'clock. Dave Michaels came down to talk to him. Harris demanded to know what they were doing about his twin brother. It was fucking obvious that someone had been round with a couple of gallons of unleaded and he wanted to know who. Michaels assured him the matter was under investigation. As a matter of interest, where had he been last night?

Harris took the question personally.

'You're putting me in the frame? My own fucking brother?'

'No, my friend. I'm asking you where you were.'

'At home. In bed.'

'Alone?'

'Yeah. You gonna do me for that? Only you guys are starting to get me seriously pissed off.'

Michaels reached for a pen and pad.

'How do you spell pissed off?' he asked.

By mid-afternoon Faraday was convinced that something serious had happened to J-J. At lunch time he'd driven home, searched the house room by room and even checked the garage. Finding no sign of him, Faraday had gone through his bedroom, turning everything upside down, looking for his cheque book and credit cards. They, too, had gone. His passport was still in the side pocket of his rucksack – some small consolation – but the little cache of French francs he'd been saving for emergencies had also disappeared. That and whatever credit he had on the cards wouldn't get him very far but that wasn't the point. By now the image of Doodie had begun to preoccupy Faraday, not least because of Phillimore's input when they'd settled down and talked last night.

At first the priest had been guarded about the boy. It really wasn't his business to do Faraday's work for him and there were confidences that he, Phillimore, was obliged to respect. Nonetheless, it was incontestable that Doodie had severed the mooring rope that ties the individual to society. His father had become a stranger. His mother had given up. His teachers had begged for his exclusion. And so there was no one – no agency, no individual, not even the saintly Anghared – whom Doodie regarded as anything but a traitor. The child was on the run behind enemy lines. He trusted nobody. Five years earlier, in Phillimore's opinion, he might have been diagnosed autistic. In five years' time he would in all probability be behind bars. But for now he was one of those rare creatures who simply didn't know the meaning of either restraint or fear.

Faraday had pressed him to explain further. Fear of what, he'd asked, and Phillimore had stepped across with the bottle, emptying the last of the Médoc into Faraday's glass. Fear of consequences, he'd said. Fear of authority. Fear even of gravity. Doodie's tale of going off the Round Tower was probably true, not simply because he had courage and lots of it, but because he just didn't care any more. Kids like Doodie were shown the game of life and there were a million people more than eager to spell out the rules. But then it dawned on Doodie that he didn't have to play this game, didn't want to play it, and at that point he stepped into a different world, utterly removed, utterly surreal.

Some nights, when Doodie had stayed over, Phillimore had found himself talking to the boy about his mother. Deep down, if you pressed hard enough, he'd admit he missed her, even loved her. Deep down, God knows, it might even be true. Once, a week or so back, he'd confided to Phillimore that he wanted to buy her a really good present. Invited to explain what that present might be, Doodie had said a destroyer, a big destroyer like the ones you saw in the harbour, lots of guns and missiles and a helicoptor on the back. Something she could do whatever she wanted with. Take across the sea. Take somewhere where she could get brown and be happy. On her destroyer.

'And you know what I asked him after that?' Phillimore had said. 'I asked him what *he* wanted to do. And you know what the answer was? He wanted to get big and really strong. He wanted to eat loads and go to a gym. And then, when it had all worked, he wanted to find the bloke and break his legs.'

'Who? Break whose legs?'

Phillimore hadn't a clue. In his view, Doodie had lost his grip completely, swapping some childhood fantasy for real life. That's why the boy needed help. That's why he'd been happy – no, *obliged* – to offer him sanctuary.

Faraday wasn't convinced. There was another interpretation here, infinitely more cynical, and the more Faraday thought about it, the more likely it became. Doodie wasn't stuck in some childhood time warp at all. On the contrary, he'd discovered the kind of freedom that can only be recognised by someone who has made a clean getaway, by someone who has stepped out of society and found himself in a world ungoverned by any constraints. Not loyalty. Not respect. Not compassion. And certainly not – as Phillimore had rightly concluded – fear. Clinically, there was a word for people like Doodie. They were psychopathic, and that made Faraday very nervous indeed.

Phillimore, inevitably, had disagreed. If they were talking psychology, he'd said, then Doodie was addicted to extremes: to shoplifting, to vandalism, to housebreaking, to the spray can, to the kind of wild public adventure that had taken him to the top of the Round Tower. Anything to attract attention. Anything to get himself noticed. There was potential in that kind of behaviour, the possibility of goodness, of redemption, and it was wholly wrong to stuff him away in a box and label it 'psychopathic'. There were too many boxes in the world and too many labels, and if the experience of Angola had taught Phillimore anything, then it had to do with the infinite potential of the human spirit. Drag a child out of a minefield, bandage up what remained of his legs, and he was still a human being, still capable of the most incredible achievements. Doodie, he'd insisted, was like one of these kids. Maimed, yes. But not beyond salvation.

The evening had ended in stalemate, a polite agreement to disagree, but half a day later the policeman in Faraday, and the parent, was only too aware of what someone like Doodie was capable of. He'd seen these kids on countless occasions with their pale, dead eyes. They looked like figures from some black and white newsreel, refugees from a long-forgotten war. Damaged, yes. But terrifying, too.

Louise Abeka was only too happy to accept the Custody Sergeant's offer of the Duty Solicitor. Hartley Crewdson was duty that day, an experienced defence lawyer with a substantial reputation in front of the magistrates. He'd built a successful criminal practice in the north of the city, hoovering up offenders from the Paulsgrove and Leigh Park estates, and brought a sharp dress sense and a flamboyant personal style to the dowdy world of the bench. Winter had known him for years and had always sensed an unspoken kinship. Both men had a talent for interpreting the rules to their own advantage. And both men understood the distinction between means and ends.

'She's in the shit, Hartley.' Winter had cornered Crewdson outside the interview room. 'Maybe not from our point of view but certainly from hers.'

He outlined events to date. There was strong circumstantial evidence to suggest that she'd been pressured by Kenny Foster. An affair with Foster wasn't a proposition that any woman would take lightly. If you were silly, naive, or strong-minded enough to blow him out, then you risked certain consequences. And those consequences, in Winter's opinion, had flagged the path to Hilsea Lines.

'She needs to be frank with us,' he concluded. 'You'd be amazed how nice we can be sometimes.'

The interview started twenty minutes later. Winter hadn't a clue what Crewdson had said to his new client but the transformation was remarkable. The defensiveness, the glint of panic in the eyes, had gone. Instead, if anything, she looked relieved. Stuff to get off that magnificent chest. A chance to sort out the last chaotic month or two.

'You want to start when you met Finch?' Winter gave her an encouraging smile.

Louise thought about the question. She was under caution, the tape decks were running and the clock was on.

'It was like I told you the first time,' she said at last. 'It was the summer. He kept coming into the café. We met there.'

'And?'

'We talked a lot. He got to know when we weren't too busy. When Mr Galea wasn't there, we'd have tea.'

'Who was buying?'

'Me, always me. I didn't care.'

'You liked him?'

'I felt sorry for him.'

Winter glanced at Sullivan and grinned. Sympathy for this stray who'd wandered in from the cold. Exactly the way Winter had called it.

Louise went on. She and Bradley had started going to the beach together on her days off, and on one occasion they'd taken the hovercraft to the Isle of Wight. Then, round October time, Bradley had suggested a trip to London. She'd said yes because she didn't go to London very often and she'd just got a cheque through from her father in Lagos. They'd seen a favourite band of Bradley's in Shepherd's Bush and it had gone on longer than they'd expected. The last train back was at a quarter to midnight and they hadn't bothered.

Winter stirred.

'So what did you do?'

'We found a place, a cheap place.'

'And stayed?'

'Yes.' She nodded.

'Together? One bed?'

'Yes.'

'And that was the first time?'

'Yes.'

There was a long silence. Sullivan was praying that Winter wouldn't push it any further. Louise Abeka was class. You didn't ask a girl like this how it had been.

'So how was it?'

'It was fine. Like I said, not too expensive.'

'I didn't mean that.'

'No?'

309

Crewdson shot Winter a look. Winter put the question a different way.

'Regular boyfriend? After that?'

'Yes.' She looked down at her hands.

'At his place?'

'He didn't have a place.'

'He moved in with you?'

'Not really. He often stayed over but he had other places too.'

'Like where?'

'He'd never tell me. Apart from his nan's place.'

'You think he went with other women?'

'I don't know. He said not. He . . .' She frowned. 'It was so hard with Bradley because he was like a little boy sometimes. So obvious.'

'Obvious how?'

'His lies. He lied all the time.'

'And you didn't mind that?'

'Not really. I knew when he was doing it. I knew every time. Like he'd tell me sometimes he had a son, a little boy, but I knew that wasn't true. He had no one.'

'He had a mum,' Sullivan pointed out. 'We met her.'

'No one who loved him, though.'

'You loved him?' Winter again.

Louise was still looking at Sullivan. Then she ducked her head, refusing to answer the question.

Winter pushed the story onwards. Christmas came. Louise and Finch swapped presents. She gave him a ring and he gave her a necklace of shells he'd picked up from a beach in Dorset. Nicked, thought Winter, as she described the Christmas dinner she'd tried to conjure from a microwave and a couple of battered saucepans. Then, in the New Year, the phone calls started.

'From?'

'His friend. Foster.'

'What did he want?'

'Me.' She glanced at Crewdson and whispered something in his ear. He nodded and patted her arm, telling her to carry on. 'Bradley had some pictures of me. I thought he'd been fooling with the camera. I didn't realise there was film inside.'

'What sort of pictures?'

'Photos. Of me.' She shrugged. 'Naked.'

'And he showed them to Foster?'

'He must have. He said he hadn't but he must have done. Some of the things Foster said on the phone he could only have known . . .' Her voice trailed off. 'I was really angry with Bradley. I shouted. He could be so stupid.'

Winter scribbled a note to himself. She was right. Bradley Finch had been a very silly boy. Sharing those pictures with Kenny Foster had probably cost him his life.

'So Foster kept phoning you?'

'Yes, until I changed phones.'

Sullivan leaned forward. He wanted the numbers of her mobiles and Winter nodded in approval, remembering the crossed-out mobes in Louise's address book.

Louise said she couldn't remember them. By now it was late January, barely a fortnight ago, and Foster was beginning to pay her occasional visits.

'I just wouldn't answer the door,' she said hopelessly. 'I hid from him upstairs.'

'What about the boys downstairs?'

'They were never in. They never met him.'

'Did he threaten you at all? Foster?'

'No, not me. Bradley. He'd give me messages and tell me to pass them on.'

'What kind of messages?'

'He'd say how he wanted me for himself and if that happened he said I'd never go with Bradley again, and Bradley would know it. He scared me, that man. He really did.'

'And Bradley? How did he react to all this?'

'He kept saying it was just a joke. Everything was a joke to Bradley. He could be really childish. He just didn't understand.'

'A *joke*? Are you kidding?'

Winter was back in Foster's basement flat hearing the woman's voice next door; back in Captain Beefy watching Foster servicing Simone. He hadn't been wrong. Foster really was a dog. Show him a woman like Louise Abeka and you'd start a war.

'So what happened on Friday night?'

This time Louise shook her head. Even now, even after all this, there was something holding her back. Given what he knew of Foster, Winter wasn't surprised. Self-preservation was a very good reason for suddenly going no comment.

'You need to talk this through with your lawyer, love,' Winter murmured. 'I suggest a little break.'

He reached for the tape deck, announced the time and switched it off. Minutes later he found Hartley Crewdson down the corridor beside the coffee machine.

'I suspect we're talking witness protection,' the lawyer said. 'Is there somewhere quiet we can discuss this?'

Winter found an empty interview room. He shut the door. Louise was prepared to go on but only on the absolute assurance that she'd never set eyes on Foster again.

'No can do,' Winter said. 'She'll have to give evidence.'

'Of course she will. That's what I told her.'

'We can talk to the judge about a screen. She need never actually see the guy.'

Crewdson shook his head.

'She won't do it.'

'Are you sure?'

'Positive. She's terrified of him.'

'So how much does she know?'

Crewdson looked at him and then smiled and shook his head again. Even if he knew himself, there was no way he was letting on. There were lines in the sand here that even Winter shouldn't ignore.

Winter glanced at his watch and then frowned.

'Give me ten minutes,' he said.

Outside, in the car park, Winter used his mobile to contact Dave Michaels. He outlined the problem and asked how Willard would view an undertaking not to produce her as a witness in court.

'He won't do it,' he said at once. 'I know he won't. Witness protection, yes. Screens, by all means as long as the judge agrees. But if she's got something to say then she definitely appears in court.'

'That's what I told Crewdson.'

'And?'

'She definitely won't do it.'

'So what happens next?'

'I don't know.' Winter glanced at his watch. 'The PACE clock's still ticking. I'll bell you later.'

Winter returned to the interview room. Louise was looking glumly at her coffee while Sullivan chatted to Crewdson about a recent Nicholas Cage movie. The moment Winter sat down, he started the tape machines again and announced the time.

Crewdson stared at him.

'You've talked to someone?' Winter nodded. 'And?'

'Witness protection, no problem. Screens, no problem. But she has to stand up in court. Assuming, of course . . .' he gestured at the space between them '. . . your client has something material to say.' He paused, looking from one face to the other. 'You want us to leave you to it for a bit?'

Winter stopped the tape machines again and ushered Sullivan into the corridor. Moments later, they were back. Hartley Crewdson, for once, was looking apologetic.

'No can do, I'm afraid.'

'Your client's told you what she knows?'

'Broadly speaking, yes. In Miss Abeka's own interests, I'm afraid it's no comment from here on in.'

'And that's final?'

It was Louise who nodded.

'Yes,' she whispered. 'It is.'

There was a long silence. Winter looked at his watch, started the tape again and then announced the interview suspended.

'Suspended?' Crewdson was frowning.

'We arrested your client at 12.04,' Winter said. 'I'm afraid she'll be with us for a while yet.'

Back out in the car park, Sullivan unlocked the Escort and got in. As they were nosing out into the rush hour traffic, Winter turned to him.

'Mick Harris has a mobe, yes?'

'Yes.'

'You've got the number?'

Sullivan stared across at him.

'No,' he said. 'Why?'

Chapter twenty-five

Faraday sat in Hartigan's office, wondering what exactly lay behind the peremptory summons. The moment the door opened and Hartigan stepped in, he understood.

'Simon Pannell,' Hartigan waved at his guest, 'from the *News*.'

Pannell was a youngish man, tall and bulky with a slight squint. He produced a biro and a small ring-binder pad and accepted a chair at the conference table opposite Faraday.

'Simon's masterminding a series of drug-related features.' Hartigan slipped his jacket off and sat down, glancing at Faraday. 'I thought it might be helpful if we were both here.'

'Of course, sir.'

Hartigan turned to Pannell.

'Joe's been heading the Helen Bassam inquiry. If anyone can give you what you're after, then Joe's the man. He's also been looking for a rather remarkable ten-year-old. Right, Joe?'

Faraday nodded, saying nothing. Pannell was consulting his notes.

'Gavin Prentice?' He looked up. 'AKA Doodie? Lives rough? Doesn't go to school?'

Faraday was staring at Hartigan. Where had all this stuff come from?

'Joe's drawn a blank on Doodie so far,' Hartigan said smoothly, 'which I think speaks volumes about life on the street. You're right, Simon. This child is feral. And he may well be into serious drug abuse.'

'What kind of drugs?'

'Off the record? Heroin. Almost certainly.' Faraday raised an eyebrow.

'We can't evidence that, sir.'

'No, we can't Joe, but the girl Helen was using heroin and it's a reasonable inference that the boy might have been into it too. They were certainly together the night she died.'

'A ten-year-old on smack?' The reporter was looking at Faraday.

'I doubt it.' Faraday shook his head.

'But if this girl Helen was using heroin, then surely—'

'But she wasn't, Mr Pannell.'

'I'm sorry?'

'I said she wasn't using heroin.'

Pannell looked to Hartigan to clear up this sudden confusion. Hartigan had edged himself forward on the chair, his face a picture. First astonishment. Then alarm.

'I beg your pardon?'

'I said she wasn't using heroin.' Faraday offered a regretful smile. 'Sir.'

'Then what did the tox give us?'

'The night she died she'd stolen some tablets from a woman called Grace Randall. They were morphine sulphate. It's a painkiller. It's easy to confuse it with heroin on tox analysis but she wasn't using smack.'

The biro was motionless. The reporter was looking at Hartigan.

'Superintendent?'

Hartigan hesitated for a long moment, weighing the balance of advantage. Then he forced a smile.

'Joe's right,' he said silkily. 'Although in these cases it's important that we explore every avenue. The outcome, of course, is the same. Heroin is diamorphine. The girl was off her head.'

'But my editor mentioned smack before. In connection with the girl.'

'Then I'm afraid he was wrong. It was morphine sulphate. Like Joe says, it's a tricky judgement call, even for a forensic analyst, but a case like this is where we come in. The law hates ambiguity, Simon, and it's our job to present the clearest possible evidence. Right Joe?'

Before Faraday could reply, there was a knock on the door and Hartigan's management assistant appeared.

Hartigan waved her away.

'No interruptions, Annabelle.'

'But Mr Hartigan—'

'I said no interruptions.'

Annabelle retreated, closing the door behind her. The reporter wanted to know how many of these tablets the girl had swallowed before making it onto the roof.

'The tox gives us thirty micrograms,' Faraday said. 'And she'd been drinking as well.'

'Drinking what?'

'Impossible to say. Alcohol, certainly, and lots of it.'

Pannell made a note, then looked up again.

'So what makes a girl like that end up on a tower block, smashed out of her head?'

'It's an indictment, Simon,' Hartigan said at once, 'of the gravest possible kind.'

'An indictment of what?'

'Of society. Of the mess we've made for ourselves. And that's the point, really. Unless we can get on top of all this, unless we can nip these problems in the bud, then there'll be more Helen Bassams. And that, of course, carries certain cost implications.' He paused, waiting for Pannell to write it all down. Instead, the reporter glanced across at Faraday.

'You agree?'

'Up to a point, yes. Mr Hartigan's right. Society's all over the place. Families are falling apart. But we're policemen, not sociologists. It's our business to deal in the small print, in individual cases. We're there to connect particular sets of dots. Whether they form a larger pattern is down to someone else.'

'And Helen Bassam?'

'We simply don't know. We have suspicions, of course. We know a certain amount about her background, about the people she mixed with, but this is pretty personal stuff.'

'My editor gave me the impression this was going to be the full brief.' Pannell was looking at Hartigan.

'It is, Simon, it is. What Joe's saying is that it's tough being an attractive fourteen-year-old these days. Someone like Helen, the situation she was in, I'm not sure what anyone would do. Eh, Joe?'

Faraday felt the trap closing around him. On the one hand, a professional journalist paid to ferret out certain kinds of truth; on the other, a publicity-obsessed senior policeman with one eye on the next interview board.

'Helen Bassam certainly had problems,' Faraday conceded, 'but in my view that's not what this is about. Mr Hartigan's right. Society's a mess. In our job, we sweep up afterwards; in yours, there's money to be made. If bad news sells newspapers, you're all going to be very rich.'

Pannell put his biro down. Hartigan was looking visibly angry. Another knock at the door.

'Come,' Hartigan barked.

It was Annabelle again. This time, she was looking at Faraday.

'It's Cathy Lamb,' she said breathlessly. 'I think it's really urgent.'

'What do you think she could tell us?' Willard was back at his desk in his office.

Michaels and Winter sat at the conference table, Winter consulting notes he'd made during the first interview with Louise Abeka.

'I think she knows most of what happened on the Friday night, sir.'

'And that would be enough to put Foster away?'

'Definitely.'

'How can you be so sure?'

'Because he's holding the full deck. Number one, he's got loads of motive. He fancies the girl. Plus Finch's pissed him off big time. We can evidence that on both counts. Number two, he's got the track record. This is a bloke who settles every debt in blood. And number three, he's got the opportunity.'

'Except he wasn't there.'

'The alibi's bollocks. They could have knocked the video up any time. A child can fiddle around with dates and times.'

'Yeah, but can we prove it?' Willard was tapping the end of his pencil on the desk. Tap-tap. Tap-tap.

'The girl can,' Michaels pointed out. 'If she'd only bloody talk to us.'

'And you're saying she won't?'

'That's right, sir.' Winter gestured at his pad. 'She'll take it up to last week. Then it's the big no-no. I don't know what he said to her but there's no way she'll go anywhere near him. We can buy her a new life, a new name, whatever, but it won't solve the problem if we need her in court.'

'Of course we need her in court. That's where this thing begins and ends.' He paused. 'How much do we know about her background? She's a student, isn't she?'

'That's right, sir. Third year at the university. That's why she stayed here after what happened. She had a big exam on Monday, then she went off to London. Now I gather she's trying to negotiate some kind of deal on the rest of the course. She wants to go back to Nigeria and teach.'

'Hmm.' The pencil again, tap-tap. 'OK, here's what we do. Re-interview her. Give her an opportunity to talk about last week and suggest that she might be up on a Perverting the Course of Justice charge if she doesn't. That might shift the logjam.'

Winter glanced at Michaels. Perverting the Course of Justice could carry life imprisonment. Nigeria might be further away than Louise Abeka thought.

There was the patter of running feet in the yard outside, and then the sound of car doors slamming. Willard was on his feet, peering into the gathering dusk. The first of the sirens began to wail as a squad car accelerated towards the road, then another.

'Fucking cavalry,' he muttered, sinking into his chair again.

Faraday was in the third car, wedged in the back between two uniforms. In his bleakest moments, he'd never once thought it would come to this. Cathy Lamb had taken a call from Mrs Randall at Chuzzlewit House. The little boy was back, the one who'd come with Helen. This time he had someone else with him – a tall man, very quiet, no hair. They'd taken her key and a bottle or two from her cupboard. And she thought they'd gone up to the roof.

It was barely a mile from Fratton police station to the flats. The squad cars squealed to a halt in the parking lot outside the main entrance and Faraday fought the temptation to lean over the lap of the man next to him, craning his neck upwards to steal a glimpse of the roof. There'd be plenty of time for that. He knew there would.

The uniforms pushed out of the squad car. To Faraday's alarm, there were already two fire engines parked round the corner, their engines running. If it's true that Doodie's up there on the roof, he thought, then this circus will give him exactly the audience he's always craved. Little tiny men in uniforms. Fire engines. Squad cars. And soon, presumably, ambulances. All because of Gavin Prentice. If you were looking for a rationale for years and years of vile behaviour, for breaking every rule and making umpteen lives a misery, then this was surely it. Add a couple of TV crews, and the tiny figure up there on the roof would be soon be looking for an agent.

He peered upwards, feeling the first spots of rain on his face. It was nearly dark by now and it was difficult to be certain but he thought he detected movement against the blackness of the sky. Let it not be J-J, he prayed. Please God let, it not be J-J.

There was a touch on his arm and he turned to find himself looking at Cathy Lamb.

'What happened?' he muttered.

She went through it again. Grace Randall, number 131, had put a call through Faraday's private line. Intercepted by the switchboard, it had come to Cathy's desk. The old lady had explained about the little boy, the wicked one, and Cathy had begun to put two and two together.

'You're saying she mentioned someone else,' Faraday said quickly.

'She did. Some deaf guy.'

'How did she know?'

'She said he kept using his hands. She called it cat's cradle.'

Cat's cradle. J-J. Faraday made for the main entrance, Cathy calling after him. The incident was already in the hands of a uniformed Inspector. More senior officers were on their way. Access to the roof was tightly controlled. Faraday fumbled in his pocket for his warrant card.

The main entrance was chocked open, two PCs standing guard. One of them recognised Faraday and waved him through. Both lifts were way up the building so Faraday made for the stairs, taking them two at a time until his legs began to jelly. By the tenth floor, he was gasping for breath. He slowed, checked the lift again, then headed upwards. There were little knots of residents standing in the corridors, peering down at the activity below. Forcing himself up yet another flight of stairs, he felt his breath rasping in his chest. Floor 20. Floor 21. The numbers began to blur. At last, dizzy with the effort, he made it to the twenty-third floor, sweat pouring from his face. One day, he promised himself he'd get fit. One day, he'd be in the kind of shape to deal with a crisis like this. One day.

As Cathy had warned, access to the roof was controlled. There was a Sergeant and another PC on the stairs. The Sergeant peered at Faraday's ID, uncertain what to do.

'Who's out there?' Faraday sucked air into his burning lungs.

'A kid and someone older, sir.'

'How much older?'

'It's dark. I'm guessing. Twenty?'

'Tall?'

'Yeah?'

'Have you tried to talk to him? Has anyone?'

The sergeant nodded. Both he and the PC had done their best to get them down but neither would play ball. He was now awaiting instructions from his Inspector.

'Down?' Faraday felt a deep, deep chill.

'They're up on the parapet on the retaining wall, sir.' He glanced at the PC and motioned him aside. 'Take a look for yourself.'

Faraday climbed the last flight of stairs to the roof. The door was open, the night air suddenly cold on his face. Lines of washing criss-crossed the roof space, flapping in the wind. Absurdly, he wondered why no one was getting all this stuff in. The rain was getting heavier by the minute.

He began to circle the roof, peering upwards. The retaining wall was eight, maybe nine feet tall. He'd scaled it before, exactly a week ago, using the metal grille that permitted a view of the city on all four sides. It hadn't been easy for him. How come a ten-year-old had managed it?

He didn't know, didn't care. All that mattered was J-J. He'd covered two sides of the square now, finding nothing, then suddenly he saw the figures outlined against the pale remains of the dusk. J-J was unmistakable – tall, thin, gawky. He had both arms stretched wide, the way you'd walk a tightrope, and every time the wind blew and the washing flapped he'd sway from side to side, fighting for his balance. Beside him, running up and down the parapet, was another figure, infinitely smaller. Doodie, Faraday thought. He'd turned real life into the drama he craved and now he was the superstar of his dreams.

Faraday closed the distance between them, moving slowly. He was aware of figures behind him, of bursts of conversation from police radios, but his world had narrowed to the figures on the parapet above. There was no way he could reach Doodie without climbing the walls. If he was to get between the kid and J-J, between Doodie and this unfolding disaster, then he had to be up there on the parapet with them.

Doodie was off on another little excursion. He ran like the child he was, skipping through the rain, oblivious of danger. He ran to the end of the parapet, coming to a halt at the right-angled turn, then disappeared behind the tower that overlooked the roof space. For the first time Faraday caught sight of J-J's face. He was terrified. It was there in his eyes, in the slight bend of his knees, in the way he was trying to will his feet to glue themselves onto the concrete. He'd never liked heights, and now his worst nightmare had come true. Jumping the nine feet back to the roof was clearly unthinkable. A step the other way would send him tumbling into the void. He was paralysed with fear.

Faraday shook his coat off and reached up, securing a handhold on the metal grille. He levered his body up and sideways, using a brick abutment to brace his feet. Handhold by handhold, he inched upwards, praying for Doodie not to return. Slowly, sweating again, he clawed his way up the wall. Then, suddenly, he felt the wind on his face. He was half lying on the parapet now, one wet leg bent beneath him. He eased the other leg up, then, very slowly, got to his feet, bracing himself against sudden gusts of wind. Of Doodie he could see no sign. Looking down, he knew, would be sudden death. He inched his body round, keeping his head up, searching for his son.

A face swam into view. It was J-J. His eyes were wide and his face looked chalk white against the darkness. Faraday began to talk to him – hand language, the old conversation. It's me, he signed. I'm here. Everything's going to be fine. We'll sort this out. Just don't do anything rash. J-J nodded. Slowly, his hands began to move. Behind you, he signed. Look out behind you.

Faraday heard a wild yelp of laughter and turned in time to see Doodie running along the parapet towards him. He was right about the skipping, right about the child's absolute disregard for the rules. Even the terrifying suck of gravity didn't seem to give him pause for thought. Even the prospect of a 200-foot fall didn't, for a single moment, slow him down. This was now a party for three. What a laugh.

Doodie came to a halt a pace away and for one heart-stopping moment Faraday thought he was going to push his way by. There simply wasn't the space, Faraday wanted to explain. Try and get by me and one or other of us will end up on the pavement. Just like Helen Bassam.

'Awright, mister?' The old Pompey greeting. Faraday nodded.

'Yeah. You?'

'Yeah. Brilliant, ain't it?' He nodded down. 'All them fire engines. You lives here, do you?'

Faraday wanted to laugh. Did he live here? On the edge? One permanent step from disaster? The answer, he thought, was probably yes.

Who's your friend?' Faraday gestured back towards J-J.

'Deaf bloke. Complete nutter. Cool, though.'

'Mate, is he?'

'Yeah.'

'What's the game, then? Up here?'

'Dunno really. We just fancies it. Here.' He made a sudden lunge at Faraday, catching him at waist level, and for an instant Faraday imagined himself in mid-air. Then the boy had gone again, screaming with laughter, back towards the corner of the building, and Faraday realised he was still on the parapet. Just.

Faraday could taste the fear. Another moment like that and he'd be over. He knew it. For a single, dizzying moment he looked down and his racing brain took a snapshot of the scene below. A tiny Lego ambulance had arrived. The back doors were open and two stick figures were pulling out a stretcher. There were knots of people gazing up, little blobby faces, and off to the left, on the main road, another squad car was carving a path through the rush hour traffic. Faraday swallowed hard, turning to J-J again, and as he did so he caught sight of Cathy Lamb on the roof immediately below him. There were two uniforms with her and she was cupping her mouth with both hands.

'Grab him,' she yelled, pointing to J-J, 'and jump this way.' Grab him? Faraday measured the distance between himself and J-J, and then nodded, bracing himself against another gust of wind and stretching his hand out towards his son. J-J didn't move. He was looking beyond Faraday, along the parapet, his eyes wide with fear. Then his hands came up again.

'Behind you,' he signed. 'He's coming back.'

Winter sat in the interview room with Sullivan, waiting for Louise Abeka and Crewdson to reappear. He'd explained the legal consequences if Louise maintained her silence over the events of last week, and left them to make a decision. Shortly, he hoped they would be back with a smile on the girl's face. If her evidence was as damning as Winter imagined, then Foster would be spending the pre-trial period in a remand cell. A case like this seldom made it to Crown Court in less than six months. Louise could complete her degree, present her evidence and be on a plane to Lagos without the slightest danger of any contact with Foster. Apart, that is, from an hour or so in court.

Sullivan wanted to know why Winter was interested in Mick Harris's mobile number. He knew he'd got it from Brian Imber because he'd been there when Winter took the call and, as ever, he'd been the one with the paper and pen.

'Why Harris?' he asked again.

Winter ignored the question. He could hear the murmur of voices outside. He got to his feet and stepped out into the corridor, thinking it was Crewdson and Louise. Instead, he found himself looking at the Custody Sergeant and a uniformed Inspector.

'What's going on?'

The Inspector mentioned an incident at the flats across the road. There was talk of jumpers on the roof. And one of them was apparently a CID officer.

'Chuzzlewit House?'

'That's right.'

'Shit.'

Chuzzlewit House was the tallest block in the city. Even if you were truly desperate, there were kinder ways of bringing it all to an end. Some kid had gone off only last week but you'd be seriously deranged to even think of a drop like that.

'Who's the CID, then?'

'Faraday.'

'*Faraday?* As in DI Faraday?'

'You got it.'

Winter rolled his eyes. He'd long had his doubts about Faraday and this was as much proof as any reasonable human being would need to confirm that the bloke had finally lost it, Some guvnors rode with the punches. Others, like Faraday, took it far too personally. But Chuzzlewit House? Was the job really that bad?

The Inspector was looking at him, a smile on his face.

'He's not a jumper,' he murmured. 'He's trying to sort the bloody thing out.'

Crewdson and Louise appeared in the corridor behind him. The Inspector moved to let them through and Winter knew at once that the girl hadn't shifted one inch. Crewdson confirmed it with a tiny shake of his head.

'She won't do it,' he said.

'You explained the consequences?'

'Makes no difference. It's her decision. I have to respect it.'

'OK.' Winter nodded, then poked his head round the door of the interview room. Sullivan was picking at his nails. 'I want you to sort out Louise with the Custody Sergeant,' he said briskly. 'Get her in a cell for the night.'

Faraday stepped in from the rain, his arm round J-J. He could feel the deep trembling in his son's thin frame. A bird, he thought, injured and scared half to death. He gave the boy a squeeze and brushed the rough stubble on his face with the back of his hand. Then he put his lips to his ear, wondering whether – by some miracle – his hearing might have been restored.

'Love you,' he whispered.

J-J looked at him blankly. A paramedic was waiting at the top of the steps, a blanket folded over his arm. Faraday took the blanket without a word and draped it round J-J. Then he borrowed a handkerchief from Cathy Lamb and wiped the rain from his son's face. The boy was limping badly from the impact when Faraday had pulled him down off the wall but he didn't appear to have broken anything.

'The kid?' Faraday gestured back, towards the wet darkness. 'Doodie?'

Cathy told him to forget it.

'We'll get him down,' she said.

'Yeah?'

For a second they looked at each other, sharing the unvoiced thought. Maybe it was best to leave the kid there. Maybe it was better to hope against hope that he'd make a mistake, lose his balance, fall to his death on the pavement below. But that wouldn't happen and in his heart Faraday knew that it shouldn't happen. There were arrangements to be made. Calls to be put through. Social Services to be alerted. Doodie taken into emergency care. Tomorrow, first thing, the Child Protection Unit would step into the case. An interview strategy would be agreed. And the long struggle to tease some sense from the child in the rain would begin. Whether, at the end of it, they'd be any the wiser about Helen Bassam was anybody's guess but, just now, Faraday didn't care.

'Favour, Cath?'

'No problem.'

'Give us a lift home?'

Cathy Lamb stayed for drinks, and then more drinks, and then cooked supper. J-J wedged himself in the bath for an hour – endless changes of scalding hot water – while Faraday perched on the side of the tub, unspeakably thankful that the boy was still in one piece. At first he wasn't keen to explain what had happened, but slowly and with infinite care Faraday managed to piece the story together.

A couple of the other lads at the PYO project had taken J-J to the derelict cinema. None of them understood sign language but they all agreed that J-J was a pretty amazing bloke, cool in a mad kind of way, and deserved an invite to the place they'd made their own, to the place they called home, to the ultimate den. In the cinema, blessed with a pocketful of cash, J-J had found himself the guest of honour. He'd gone to the off-licence and bought a stack of lager. He'd toured Aldi, the cheapo supermarket, and come away with a bag of goodies. More money had gone to a twelve-year-old called Shannon, who'd disappeared into Buckland and scored enough draw to make the rest of Thursday night a blur.

'You went back to the cinema? After we'd been in there?'

'Yeah. The kids know every inch of it.'

'But what if we'd sealed the place off? Put loads of men in?'

'They had petrol.'

'Petrol? How?'

'In lemonade bottles.' He shaped them with his hands. 'They suck it out of cars and fill the bottles up.'

'And what would they do with it?'

'Do with it?' The question brought a grin to J-J's face. 'They'd have burned the place down.'

Faraday stared at him.

'And you? You'd have let them?'

'Of course not.'

Friday morning, J-J left the cinema with Doodie and walked the mile to Old Portsmouth, where his new friend had the key to a house in the High Street. The house had been empty. They'd drunk some wine and then gone back to the cinema after J-J had spent the last of his money on chicken and chips from the KFC in Commercial Road. Later, Doodie had insisted on taking him to Chuzzlewit House. The roof at Chuzzlewit was where he got his kicks. A drop that awesome really turned him on.

'But you hate heights.'

'I know. I was brave, wasn't I?'

'*Brave?*' Faraday shut his eyes a moment, feeling the room begin to spin. Maybe it was the heat, he thought. Maybe I'm a glass or two over the top. Or maybe, just maybe, there's a limit to what the human brain can take. He'd been right all along about J-J, right to be fearful, right to worry the night away, trying not to imagine the worst. Like Doodie, this boy of his had no fear. Not where other people were concerned. Not when it came to plunging head first into other people's lives.

'You could have died,' he signed.

J-J gazed up at him, briefly troubled by the thought, then nodded. 'I know.' His hand fluttered briefly over his heart. 'I was terrified.'

Downstairs, Cathy had cooked a huge panful of spaghetti with Bolognese made with mince from the fridge and a fierce top-dressing of raw chillis. Faraday broke out a third bottle of Chianti to wash it down. The talk was of good times – of a sailing holiday Cathy was planning with Pete, of how great it was to have a man back in her life – and afterwards, for the first time in a decade, Faraday put on one of his old Beatles albums, vinyl for God's sake, and they pushed back the sofa, rolled up the rug and danced. J-J was the world's worst dancer, all arms and legs, but long after Cathy and Faraday had collapsed against the big glass doors at the front he was still whirling around, imagining the tunes in his head. Faraday, hopelessly drunk, couldn't stop watching him. Deliverance, he thought. Or maybe – for reasons he couldn't fathom – a kind of redemption.

An hour or so later Cathy crawled to the phone and ordered herself a cab. Peering at the answerphone display, she gestured Faraday across.

'Message,' she muttered. 'For you.'

Faraday, up on one knee, did his best to focus on the line of digits. Finally it dawned on him where the call had come from.

'Marta.' He was gazing at his son again. 'Marta?'

Chapter twenty-six

Nobody phones me at half past seven in the morning, Dawn Ellis thought. Not on a Saturday. Not without good reason.

She struggled out of bed, dispensing for once with the pot of tea and the wake-up burst of Five Live. She'd left her card with Jill Harris the afternoon she'd been tucked up with her sponge bag and her *OK* magazines at the Travel Inn. Now the woman wanted an urgent word or two, something really serious. She was staying with her mum-in-law in Paulsgrove. Could Ellis come over? Right away?

The roads were empty this time in the morning and Portchester to Paulsgrove was ten minutes. Gilkicker Drive was on the edge of the huge estate, a long street of one-time council houses bought for a song and proudly badged with new porches. Number 35's already needed a coat of paint.

Jill Harris was wearing a green towelling dressing gown and not much else. She hugged herself, shivering in the freezing wind.

'Come in.'

The gas fire was on in the front room and it took Ellis several seconds to spot the object propped against the battered two-seat sofa.

'Where did this come from?'

It was a shotgun, double-barrelled, and it looked shiny enough to be new. Jill Harris was keeping her distance. She stood by the window, tousle-haired, hugging herself. She couldn't take her eyes off the gun.

'I've had about enough,' she muttered at last. 'Honest.'

'The gun, love. Where did the gun come from?'

'Mick brought it.'

'Mick who?'

'Mick Harris. Terry's brother. He brought it round last night. Two in the morning. Scared his mum half to death.'

'Why? Why would he do that?'

'He wouldn't say. He just said to hang onto it. He'd never been there. That's what he said. He'd never been there. He was in a right state.'

'Never been where?'

'I dunno and I don't care but I just want all this to stop. I'm telling you, I've had enough. Maisie's off her head about her dad, won't sleep a wink, and now this. What kind of a thing is it to get a woman of sixty out of bed at two in the morning? And then hand over a gun?'

'Is he coming back for it? Mick?'

'I haven't a clue. I just thought . . .' On the edge of tears, she sniffed. 'You gave me that card. Remember?'

Ellis stepped across and gave her a hug. Skin and grief, she thought, under the thin dressing gown.

'You did right, love. I'll sort it.' She held her a moment or two longer, then turned to make a phone call on her mobile. Maisie's tiny face was peering round the door, staring at the shotgun.

Willard had been at his desk in the MIR since seven. Losing one suspect to an arsonist was bad enough. Losing the other to a firearms incident was even worse. For a detective who prided himself on the rallying of troops and assembly of evidence, on the baiting of traps and slow tightening of the investigative noose, *Bisley* was turning into a nightmare. Two more sudden deaths, each of them warranting a separate major inquiry. Already, in twenty-four brief hours, he'd practically run out of detectives.

Willard ran a hand over his face. He'd boxed off the weekend for a visit to Bristol. He'd booked to take Sheila to a show at the Colston Hall, and then a meal at a new restaurant in Clifton. Now this.

'OK, Sammy.' Rollins was perched on the corner of the conference table. 'The guy's in bed. He gets a knock at the door.'

'That's a supposition. But probably, yes.'

'He was in his bloody jim-jams, wasn't he? And it's half one in the morning?'

'Sure.'

'So he hears a knock at the door. He goes to answer it. And bam . . . Goodnight Vienna. Elegant, eh?'

A terrified neighbour, hearing gunfire, had dialled treble nine. Picking their way cautiously down the basement steps, the uniformed patrol had found a body slumped inside the open front door. He'd been shot in the chest, probably twice, and reports from Jerry Proctor's Scenes of Crime team had made a special point of mentioning the tattoos. Amazing what a mess lead shot can make, Proctor had grunted on the phone. Nothing left of Kenny Foster's precious cobra except the tail.

'So where do we start, then? Are we still interested in motivation or do we just let these bastards sort it out for themselves?'

Rollins thought that might not be such a bad idea. Dave Michaels had taken a call from Paul Winter this morning. Winter had heard about the shooting on the radio. The victim hadn't been identified but mention of St Andrew's Road and a basement flat had been enough for Winter to draw his own conclusions.

'He's thinking Mick Harris,' Rollins said. 'Keeps it in the family.'

'Why?'

'Winter's got Foster down for the fire at Terry's place. That's the way these guys sort things out. If Mick had the same thought then Foster should have been expecting a visit.'

'But Foster was on the Isle of Wight that night. I've seen the statement he gave to Yates. It all checks out. Yates said so.'

'But Mick Harris didn't know that, did he?' Rollins paused. 'Say he suspected Foster anyway? And say he heard a whisper? Mick's the kind of bloke who doesn't have much time for thinking things through. If his twin brother had gone up in smoke and he thought Kenny Foster did it, he'd be round there smartish.'

Willard wasn't convinced.

'What about a gun? Where did he get his hands on that?'

'SOCO have it down as a shotgun. A new Purdy was listed missing on the job out at Compton, the Wrekes. Dave Michaels went through their file this morning. It all checks out.'

Willard shook his head. Too simple, he thought. Too neat. According to Brian Imber, half this city had one reason or another to want Foster off the plot. Compile a suspect list, do the job properly, and *Bisley* might stretch to next Christmas. He eyed the phone, wondering whether it was too early to call Sheila in Bristol. Saturdays, she normally slept in.

'Sir?' It was Dave Michaels at the door. He'd just taken a call from Dawn Ellis.

Willard gestured him in.

'And?'

'She's up in Paulsgrove, with Terry Harris's missus. She and Harris's mum got an early morning visit from Terry's twin, Mick. And guess what he left?'

Willard stared at him for a moment.

'A shotgun,' he said slowly. 'Go on, surprise me.'

'You're right, sir. A brand new Purdy. Prints all over it, bet your life. Plus forensic from the discharge. Sweet, eh?'

'You kidding?' Willard shook his head, abandoning the phone in disgust. 'City like this, who needs fucking detectives?'

Faraday was on his fourth coffee by the time the DS at the Child Protection Unit confirmed a meet time at Havant. The Child Interview Suite occupied the upper floor in a converted police house near the fire station and the pre-interview briefing was now scheduled for 10.30.

'You found the little bugger, then?'

The question was innocent enough but Faraday's head was far too fragile to risk a serious answer. The feeling of vertigo, of toppling irresistibly forward, had stayed with him all night and just the memory of the washing flip-flapping across the roof space made his stomach heave.

'The lad's with Social Services,' he growled. 'They'll be bringing him up to Havant.'

'What about his mum?'

'She doesn't want to know. The only adult the lad's mentioned is a priest from the cathedral.'

The DS wanted details. Faraday explained about Phillimore.

'He's been close to the boy for a while.' Faraday was choosing his words carefully. 'He kept an eye on him.'

'How?'

With some reluctance, Faraday explained.

'This guy's married? Single?'

'Single.'

'And he's been sharing a house with a vulnerable ten-year-old who's run away from home? How appropriate is that, sir?'

It was a direct challenge. The Paedophile Unit operated from the same suite of offices as the CPU at Netley. These guys were tuned into the slightest nuance as far as kids were concerned and the key word here was 'vulnerable'.

'This boy is a force of nature.' Faraday felt his head beginning to thump again. 'If anyone needs protecting, it's probably the rest of us.'

'They all say that, sir.'

'Who's "they"?'

'People in these kinds of situations. Don't get me wrong, sir. You're telling me that the child has been kipping under the same roof as a virtual stranger. I'm just asking whether that's the kind of situation we should have been tolerating.'

'I think he's ideal,' Faraday grunted. 'More than that, I think we're lucky to have him.'

'We? You mean the child, surely.'

'No. I mean we.'

Faraday glanced at his watch. The DS at Netley would be bringing a specialist PC up to Havant to handle the interview with Doodie. He wanted at least half an hour for a proper brief.

'Better make that ten'o clock then,' Faraday said.

It took Winter several seconds to realise that no one had told Louise Abeka about Kenny Foster. They were back in the interview room at Central, Sullivan nursing a hangover after a piss-up following rugby training. Louise sat across the table, visibly anxious, her solicitor at her elbow. She must have spent her night banged up in the cells wondering how long she'd get for Perverting the Course of Justice, thought Winter. And here's little me, Mr Sunshine, about to change her life. Again.

He started the cassettes rolling and announced the time. He tallied the names around the table and then bent forward.

'I'm going to have to ask you again,' he began, 'about last week.'

Louise flinched, then shook her head. There was no way she was going to change her mind. Not now. Not ever.

'There's nothing we can say to you?'

'No.'

'You're sure about that?'

She closed her eyes, swallowed hard, then nodded.

'I am,' she said. 'I don't care what happens, but I am.'

'Then he must have done something terrible, mustn't he, this Kenny Foster? Isn't that a reasonable assumption?'

Hartley Crewdson leaned forward to intervene. Winter reached out, putting a hand on his arm. He was still looking at Louise.

'Suppose I was to tell you that Foster's dead?' he said softly. 'Suppose someone came along last night and killed him?'

Something happened in her eyes, a tiny spark. Winter could see it. Just the thought of Foster gone had lit a fire in Louise Abeka.

'What do you mean?' Her voice was so low he could barely hear it.

Winter told her what had happened, nodding in confirmation when Crewdson raised an eyebrow. There was a long silence. Then Louise beckoned her solicitor closer and whispered in his ear. Crewdson nodded and got to his feet.

'May I suggest we suspend the interview?' He nodded down at the cassette decks. 'My client would appreciate a word in private.'

Doodie and the social worker were already at the Child Interview Suite when Faraday arrived. There was a waiting room downstairs with a couple of armchairs and a low table, and the social worker had sensibly planted herself between Doodie and the front door.

Doodie had been found a change of clothes overnight. The jeans and sweatshirt were at least two sizes too big and made him look like a badly wrapped parcel. He sat sideways across the armchair, kicking his legs, and the moment he spotted Faraday he was up on his feet. An old friend. A familiar face.

'Mister! What you doing here?'

Faraday explained he was a policeman, a detective.

'Why's that, then?'

In spite of the state of his head, Faraday couldn't resist a smile. It was the sanest question he'd heard in weeks.

Upstairs, he found the DS and the PC from the Child Protection Unit. The PC looked about eighteen – open unlined face, ready smile – and Faraday sensed at once that Doodie would eat him alive.

'Right.' Faraday unpacked his briefcase. 'First things first.'

He went through the events of the last week, adding to the CPU file. Every indication suggested that Doodie had been living rough for large parts of the last couple of years. He was tough and he was streetwise, but above all he seemed totally oblivious of the linkage between cause and effect, between his own impetuous charge at life and the trail of damage he left behind him. His file record could never do justice to what he'd really been up to. Undoubtedly there'd been dozens of other occasions when he'd broken the law but the only incident that really mattered just now was the death of the young girl, Helen Bassam. According to one witness, Doodie had been with her before she fell. A video camera had caught his departure from the flats. This morning's task was to shed light on the half-hour or so in between.

'You say she fell, sir.' It was the PC. 'Is there a suggestion the lad was involved?'

'I don't know.'

'But you think it might be possible?'

It was a good question and Faraday hesitated before answering it, remembering the little figure skipping along the parapet last night. Say the boy had tried to push past him and Faraday had lost his balance and fallen? Say he'd given him a playful push just for a joke? Did that qualify as murder? Or a kid's game with some terrifying photographic evidence at the end of it?

'I don't know,' he said at last. 'I just want to establish the facts.'

The DS leaned forward. DI Faraday ought to be aware that there were rules here, procedures that would constrain the interview. Everything would be videotaped for subsequent use in court. Leading questions were strictly off-limits. The child would be encouraged to explain exactly what had happened, and there was scope for clarification if it wasn't clear what he really meant, but beyond that the interviewing PC's hands were tied by the Rules of Evidence. In these matters, the judge would have ultimate discretion. Not the CPU. Not the DS. Not Faraday.

Faraday nodded. It was the standard health warning. The interview itself would take place in the room in which they were sitting. There was a sofa against one wall and a couple of sturdy armchairs. A trio of teddy bears occupied one corner of the window sill and soft-focus pictures of country life hung in a line above the sofa. Looking at them, Faraday wondered what Doodie would make of this adult bid to put him at his ease. The two wall-mounted video cameras would be much more his style, he thought. Another chance to perform. Another opportunity to put his tiny hands around the world's throat.

'OK, then?' He glanced at his watch. 'We go for it?'

Convinced by her solicitor that Winter hadn't been lying about Kenny Foster, Louise Abeka at last opened up.

Last week had begun badly. Stopped by the police, Bradley had given them Foster's name and address.

'Were you in the car?'

'No. Bradley told me later when he came to the café. He said he'd done it as a joke. Foster' – she shivered – 'he went mad.'

'Mad how?'

'He kept phoning Bradley up, lots and lots, day and night, about what he was going to do to him.'

'But Bradley didn't have a phone. His mobile had been cut off.'

'I'd given him mine. I didn't want it any more because Foster had the number and kept phoning me.'

Winter glanced at Sullivan and nodded down at his pad. All those calls to Louise's mobile. Not for her at all but Bradley Finch.

'What was he saying? Foster?'

'He was telling Bradley he was in for trouble. There was stuff about a camera, too. Bradley had borrowed it from another friend.'

'Who?'

'I don't know his real name. He called him Tosh. He used to work with him sometimes but something bad had happened. Bradley hated him. He wanted to get back at him. I don't know why.'

'And when was this?'

'Last week. Just before it happened.'

Winter was thinking about the phone call he'd taken on his mobile, the tip that had sent them all scuttling round to Brennan's. He'd known it had been Finch since he'd heard the boy's voice on his nan's answerphone but now he had a name for the guy who'd never turned up the night they'd staked out the Superstore. Tosh Harris. Had to be.

Realising he'd been grassed up, he'd called the job off. Yet another reason for Bradley Finch to end up on Hilsea Lines.

'What about this camera, then?'

'Foster wanted it back. So did this Tosh man. Bradley wouldn't let them have it.'

'Why not?'

'I don't know.' She paused, biting her lip. 'Sometimes I think it was for me, to impress me, you know, that he didn't care about Foster but that wasn't true. He kept telling me it was all a joke but I knew he was frightened.'

Friday came and Finch appeared at the café just after lunch.

'He'd hurt himself,' Louise said. 'He'd hurt his foot. He had a really bad limp.'

'How did that happen?'

'He'd been in some cinema, a place that was all boarded up. He said it was dark in there and really spooky.'

'What was he doing in there?'

'He didn't say but he'd trodden on a nail or something, a piece of wood with a nail maybe, and the nail had gone right into his foot.'

'He was bleeding?'

'Still a little bit, yes. He took the shoe off and showed me. There was blood on his sock, everywhere.'

'So what did you do?'

'I told him to go home to my place and wash it properly. Maybe go to the hospital for a jab. Those things can be dangerous.'

'He went back to your place to sort out his foot? In the bathroom? Is that what you're saying?'

'Yes.' She nodded. 'That's what he did.'

Winter was grinning. Better and better, he thought. Of course the blood in Louise's bathroom was Finch's. Because he'd washed his injured foot in her sink and hadn't bothered with the stains round the splashback. Hence the traces of blood for the Scenes of Crime boys.

'So where are we time-wise?' Winter queried. 'Friday afternoon?'

Louise nodded.

'Bradley came back to the café afterwards and I made him some toast. Then he said there was something he had to do. He wanted to meet me when I'd finished work. He said he'd come and pick me up.'

'And he did?'

'About six o'clock.' She nodded. 'I'd almost given up but he did come. We went for a drink and I was really surprised.'

'Why?'

'He had so much money. He showed it to me. So much money.'

'Where did he get it from?'

'He wouldn't say. It was just a job he'd done.'

'Did he mention the camera at all?'

'No.' She hesitated. 'You think . . .?'

Winter nodded.

'He sold it,' he said. 'To a bloke down Fawcett Road. That would have been the same camera Foster was on about. Not a clever thing to do.'

Louise was studying her hands. Sullivan reached across to comfort her and it took a moment for Winter to realise that she was crying.

'You want to stop this? Take a break?' It was Sullivan. She looked up and shook her head. Her eyes were shiny with tears.

'No,' she said. 'You need to know the rest.'

Faraday was monitoring the interview with Doodie from the tiny windowless control room at the back of the upper floor. Pictures from the two cameras appeared on monitor screens and the DS would cut them into a single sequence for presentation in court. On one screen, in a wide shot, Doodie sat in the armchair, his feet dangling above the carpet. On the other, a close-up jerked left and right as the DS struggled to keep his head in the frame. The kid never stopped moving. Not in real life. And certainly not here.

The PC was doing his best to coax some kind of story from the chaos of Doodie's memory. Yes, he remembered Helen Bassam. Yes, he'd knocked about with her and some of her mates. Yes, she'd been inside the cinema. And yes, that Thursday night they'd both gone up to the old lady's flat in Chuzzlewit House.

'Tell me what time that was.'

'Dunno. Late.'

'Very late?'

'Dunno.'

Faraday was watching the wide shot, fascinated by Doodie's body language. Every question, every answer, produced a little kick. He wriggled too, the way Faraday remembered J-J wriggling as a baby: always looking for the comfiest spot, never content with what he found.

'Tell me about Helen.'

'What you want to know?'

'Was she happy? Sad?'

'Sad, yeah, sad.'

'Why was that?'

'I dunno. She was always sad except when she had the drink and stuff.'

'What drink?'

'Drink we'd nick off the old lady. All sorts. Vodka. Gin. That Martini stuff. All sorts.'

'You went up there a lot?'

'Yeah. I hid most of the time. The old lady was in bed.'

'And you drank, too?'

'Not much.' He pulled a face. 'Didn't fancy it. She put sugar in for me once but it was still horrible.'

'Who did?'

'Helen.'

There was a pause and Faraday wondered whether the PC was looking at his notes. Then he cleared his throat and began again, as patient as ever. He wanted to know about medicine. Had Doodie ever seen tablets in the old lady's flat?

'Them tablets, yeah.' He was grinning again. 'That night she had loads.'

'Helen?'

'Yeah. She was pissed too, know what I mean? I sees her take them. Then she said about the roof.'

'She said what about the roof?'

'She said she wanted me to take her up there. I'd told her, like. I used to go up there loads. She wanted to come with me.'

'Why?'

'Dunno.' He shrugged, arms wide, the picture of innocence. They'd left the flat and taken the stairs up to the roof. Doodie had the old lady's key. It was terrible weather, raining, and they'd got really soaked.

'What happened then?'

'She said she wanted to do what I did.'

'What was that?'

'Get up, like. Up on the top of the wall thing.'

'And you helped her?'

Faraday felt the DS beginning to twitch. There was a very fine line between inviting an open account and leading a witness, and the PC was beginning to stray across it. Given the circumstances, Faraday didn't blame him.

Doodie was on his feet now, dancing around in front of the chair, mugging for the camera. When the PC asked him to sit down he just laughed.

'She got up, like this and this, up the wall.' He started to mime the girl's climb. 'It was really hard for her.'

'Did you help her?'

'I did at first. But then I couldn't reach no more. She was just hanging on, like this.' His little hands grabbed at an imaginary grille. 'And then she started climbing up again.'

'Was she saying anything?'

'Dunno.'

'What happened then?'

'She got to the top, yeah, down flat . . . like this.' Doodie threw himself full length onto the back of the sofa. This time the PC didn't try and coax him into the armchair. Far more important was where this story was leading.

'And?' he said.

Doodie peered up at the camera, peekaboo, the same cartoon grin. Then, very slowly, he rolled off the back of the sofa and disappeared.

Faraday watched him, knowing that this was the truth, sickened by the evidence in front of his eyes. He'd been wrong all the time – wrong to imagine the girl standing there in the windy darkness, wrong to put thoughts in her head, wrong to visualise her arms spread wide – trying to garnish those final moments with a little grace, a little dignity. No, the boy Doodie had seen it all and this was the way it had really been. Helen Bassam, pissed out of her head, numbed with morphine, sick of life, had simply rolled into oblivion. End of story.

Faraday touched the DS lightly on the arm.

'We need a break,' he said softly.

There was no need any longer to prompt Louise Abeka. She and Bradley had driven to the off-licence with Bradley's money. He'd bought champagne and a bottle of something else for his nan. They'd dropped it off on the way back to Margate Road. And then they'd gone home to celebrate.

'Yeah?'

To Winter, this was like hearing someone describe a movie he'd seen. The thin figure in black limping across the road. And the missing minutes on the video coverage when he thought he'd lost them.

'You drank all the champagne?'

'Yes. Bradley had most of it.'

'How long did all that take?'

'I don't know. We were in bed.'

Winter paused. He had the billing from Foster's phone on the pad at his elbow. Two calls, one at 21.20, another – briefer – at 22.12.

'Did the phone go at all?'

'Yes. Twice.'

'Who was it?'

'Foster. Bradley spoke to him. He was really silly, really rude. He called Foster all kinds of horrible names but he said it didn't matter because Foster didn't know where he was. The second time I took the phone away from him. Switched it off.'

'And later?'

'He was just standing there.'

'Who?'

'Foster. He was standing by the bed. I must have been asleep. We both were. It was . . .' She shook her head, her eyes beginning to glisten.

Crewdson produced a handkerchief and did his best to comfort her. Even Sullivan extended a sympathetic hand. At length Winter began again. He wanted to know how Foster had got in.

Louise blew her nose.

'I don't know,' she whispered. 'It all went mad.'

'What happened?'

'Foster just ripped off all the blankets, the sheets, everything.'

'You were naked?'

'We both were.'

'He raped you?'

Sullivan glanced across at Winter. Crewdson stiffened. Then Louise shook her head.

'No. But he said he would. He said he'd come back and rape me and then . . .' she shrugged '. . . kill me if I ever told anyone about this.'

'About what?'

'About what happened next.'

She looked towards the door for a moment, as if checking that Foster wasn't out there listening, then ducked her head, her voice fainter.

Foster had lifted Bradley out of bed and tied him with rope to the back of a chair, bent over like a naughty boy. Then he'd picked up her thong from the floor and stuffed it in Bradley's mouth. He'd had tape, a big thick roll, and he wound it across Bradley's face. Then he'd taken one of the empty champagne bottles and told her what he was going to do with it. He was inches from her face, spelling out his next move. Bradley needed a lesson, he kept saying. Bradley had it coming to him. Louise had begged him to stop but he'd ignored her. When she tried to get out of bed, tried to get between them, he'd told her again he'd rape her and kill her. And she'd believed him.

Winter nodded.

'And then he took the bottle to Bradley?'

'No.' Louise shook her head. 'He didn't.'

'Why not?'

'His mobile went off.'

The phone call had been brief, she said. Foster had gone to the front window and looked down into the street, and then he'd untied Bradley and made him get dressed again.

'You're telling me there was someone down there?'

'I don't know. There might have been.'

Winter eased himself back in the chair.

'This rope . . .' he began. 'What colour was it?'

'Blue.'

'You're absolutely sure about that?'

'Definitely. It was an old rope, dirty but still blue.'

'And what happened once Bradley had got dressed?'

'They both just left. Foster had the keys to Bradley's car.'

'And did you go to the window after they'd gone? Check the street at all?'

'No. Foster pulled the curtain before they left and told me not to look. If I looked he said he'd definitely see me and then . . .' She shook her head again and stared down at her hands.

Winter gave her a moment or two to compose herself, then he leaned forward over the desk.

'What about the rope?' he said softly.

There was a long silence. Then Louise stirred, looking Winter in the eye.

'Foster made Bradley carry it.'

'And the thong?'

'That, too.' Her eyes were moist again. 'And the bottle.'

The interview with Doodie recommenced at 11.17. The break had given Faraday the chance to take the PC aside and ask him to explore what had happened to Doodie after the girl had tumbled to her death. He was happy with the boy's account of events on the roof. Now he wanted to know why Doodie hadn't gone for help.

'Scared,' Doodie said at once. 'Everyone blames me for everything.'

'You thought they'd blame you for Helen?'

'Yeah. Bound to. Everyone thinks I'm shit.'

The PC let the phrase register. Then he moved gently on.

'So what did you do? Where did you go?'

'I went to find my dad.'

'Your *dad*?'

The DS glanced back at Faraday. Faraday couldn't take his eyes off the screen. Doodie didn't have a dad. That was half his problem.

'Where was he? Your dad?'

'All kinds of places but sometimes he'd come to the cinema.'

'The ABC?'

'Yeah, where we was living, me and them others.'

The ABC cinema had formed part of Faraday's brief. The PC was back on terra firma.

'Tell me about your dad, then. At the cinema.'

'I knows him a couple of months. I knows him in the summer.'

'You didn't know him before that?'

'No.'

'How did he find you?'

'He asked my mum. My mum said about the cinema. He knows my name, too, my nickname. That's how. That's how he found me.'

'And he really was your dad?'

'Yeah, he really was.' The grin nearly split his face in two. Then, abruptly, it vanished.

His dad had got into trouble. He knew he had. Bad trouble.

'How? How did you know?'

'I sees his picture in the paper.'

'Why?'

'Because he was dead. Someone killed him. Yeah.' He nodded. 'Someone killed my dad.'

'And did that make you sad?'

'Fucking right, mister.' He nodded, this tiny figure in the armchair. 'And we had petrol. Lots of it. Big bottles of it. In case.'

'In case what?'

'People came after us in the cinema.'

There'd been arrests. Men had been nicked for killing his dad. There were blokes selling drugs used to come into the cinema and these blokes knew who'd done his dad. Except the geezers who got nicked got away with it. Got set free.

'You had names?'

'Yeah.'

'And addresses?'

'One of them, yeah. Stamshaw geezer.'

'So what happened?'

'I burns his house down.' The grin was back again, and the legs were kicking. 'Bit of guttering like that.' He held his tiny hands out wide. 'I stuffs it in the letter box and then pours the petrol down it.'

'Did you think there was anyone inside the house?'

'Yeah. The bloke who killed my dad. They puts his name in the paper next day. Mush called Terry.' He nodded, proud as well as happy. 'Went up lovely, he did.'

When Faraday put a call through to the MIR, a couple of hours later, Willard had gone to Bristol. The voice at the other end belonged to Dave Michaels.

'Urgent, is it? Only he keeps the mobile on.'

Faraday wondered whether or not to call him. Up at Havant, he'd brought the interview to a halt and arrested Gavin Prentice on suspicion of murder. The DS had driven them both down to Central. There, Faraday had handed Doodie over to the Custody Sergeant. Later, the boy would be interviewed again, this time by a DC. If he repeated his story under caution, and Faraday saw no reason why he wouldn't, then he'd be standing trial on a charge of murder. Whether or not Gavin Prentice understood the gravity of all this was no longer the issue. From here on in, the boy was well and truly nicked.

'You want Willard's mobile?' It was Dave Michaels.

'Please.' Faraday reached for a pen.

Willard was on the outskirts of Bath when Faraday got through. He explained what had happened. The length of the silence suggested that Willard had trouble believing him.

'The kid's making it up,' he said at last. 'It's attention-seeking. Comes with the territory. They all do it.'

'Really, sir? So what happens if it all checks out? I've got a POLSA team into the cinema. According to the kid, some of Finch's stuff is in there. I've also had someone round to see the mother.'

'Why?'

'To check out Finch, sir. Confirm he really was the father.'

'And?'

'She says she doesn't know. Might have been, might not. But when Finch asked her recently she said yes, for definite, just to get him out of the flat.'

'So why didn't she tell you all this to begin with?'

'Because she hates us, sir. Just like they all hate us.'

Another silence. Faraday could hear a police siren. Bath or Southsea? He didn't know.

'That still doesn't put the kid at Harris's place,' Willard said slowly. 'It may stand up, the paternity thing, but we can't do the boy for arson just because he happens to fancy it.'

'I'm afraid we can, sir.'

'How?' Willard still refused to believe it.

'He's telling us he left his signature round the back at Harris's place. There's a rear entrance. The kid's a real artist with the spray can. We're looking for a praying mantis with a big "D" underneath. Probably in pink.'

'And?'

'It's there. On the brickwork under the kitchen window.'

'Scenes of Crime never mentioned it.'

'No?'

Another silence. Willard must have stopped the car because there were no more gear shifts in the background.

'So let's get this straight, Joe. You're telling me this kid, a ten-year-old, burned someone else's house down? No guarantee there weren't kids asleep in there? Or Harris's wife? You're saying he just went ahead and did it?'

'Yeah. That's exactly what I'm saying.'

'Shit.' This time Willard sounded shocked. 'What the fuck have we done?'

Epilogue

Faraday, at Willard's insistence, took the next week off. Relations with Hartigan were at an all-time low but Willard despatched a long memo to the Assistant Chief Constable in charge of Special Operations. Headquarters, he said, owed Faraday a substantial debt. Only by persisting with the Helen Bassam inquiry had he made the key linkage between Bradley Finch and his ten-year-old son. In manpower hours alone, he'd saved the MIR budget a small fortune. Some viewed this as a bid to flag Faraday's path to the Major Crimes team. Others, Faraday included, were just grateful he'd survived in one piece.

Bisley, in investigative terms, was dead and buried. Mick Harris was remanded on suspicion of killing Kenny Foster, the kid Doodie was only too happy to tell any passer-by how he'd poured petrol through the letter box of 62 Aboukir Road, and the weight of circumstantial evidence from Louise Abeka was enough to convince Willard that Foster had been responsible for the Hilsea Lines killing. Whether or not he'd ever set out to murder Bradley Finch was beside the point. Games like this could get out of hand, as young Doodie had demonstrated only too well.

Terry Harris's involvement in Finch's murder was less clear-cut. Louise hadn't actually seen him in the street outside her flat when Foster took Bradley Finch away but Willard was convinced that Harris was implicated throughout. There was no direct evidence to put him on Hilsea Lines, and in front of a jury Harris might well have been acquitted. Either way though, it no longer made any difference.

The *News*, meanwhile, published a thoughtful double-page feature about teenage suicides in the city. While the article was clearly pegged to Helen Bassam's death, there was no attempt to peer behind the curtains at 27, Little Normandy. Even Jane Bassam found Simon Pannell's treatment sympathetic and Hartigan fired off a long memo to HQ, pointing out the linkage between adolescent turmoil, teenage deaths and the city's exploding drug scene. Two days later, stirred into

Although she had eaten far too much breakfast, she could
not help but search for the source of the marvelous smell.

When Valentina spotted Monster, surrounded by sugary
pink clouds, perhaps she should have felt fear.

But instead, she hugged him.

Monster was touched.

He taught her how to create buoyant cotton-candy clouds—delicate, round ones as well as others, elongated and slim.

Then he gave her a special cloud, the lightest of them all.

"Better for your teeth," he said.

Every time the clouds dyed themselves gray,
Valentina would visit Monster in the forest.

His fur grew brighter.
And she stopped having nightmares.

Strolling through the forest, they imagined they were
skywalking. Valentina would jump on the clouds,
trying to reach the moon.

One night, she scratched herself on a tree branch.

"Nothing a bandage can't cure," Monster said.
"Or a kiss. A gentle kiss can cure anything."

Although Monster never asked her, he
knew Valentina was happy when they
were together. He knew he was loved.

And so spring, summer, and fall passed
among sweet, soft cotton-candy clouds.

Until winter came . . .

. . . and darkness covered everything.

Valentina went to visit Monster.

But he wasn't there.

"Where are you, my friend?" she cried out.

Nobody answered.

The unbearable silence was soon broken by the
sound of small footsteps crunching on dried leaves.

The animals came from every corner of the forest
to hug and hold Valentina.

The rabbit elder approached her with great tenderness.

"Life is a beautiful journey that we share with all that surrounds us. But at some point, when the body grows old, it stops feeling, stops breathing. It fades away. We leave this world to start a new journey. It was Monster's time to journey on."

Valentina was furious with Monster for leaving her. She cried hot, angry tears, terrified that her nightmares would come back.

But then she remembered how much Monster loved her, and how much she loved him.

So she put all her love in a box, along
with a picture and some cotton candy,
to accompany Monster on his new journey.

Her nightmares never came back, but Valentina still missed Monster terribly. Her grief was something a kiss couldn't cure. She was sure she would never be happy again.

But life went on. Valentina grew up.

She knew she could be happy. And indeed she
was, far from the forest, among the clouds.

Now, each year, the forest animals eagerly await Valentina's visit. She comes with her beautiful child.

"Do you think if we jump on the clouds we will reach the moon?" she whispers to her daughter, as pink cotton candy melts in their mouths.

Meanwhile, in the night sky, the biggest star of all shines down ever so brightly . . .